THE FERRY WOMAN

A Novel of John D. Lee and the
Mountain Meadows Massacre
by
Gerald Grimmett

Limberlost Press 2001

Limberlost Press
17 Canyon Trail
Boise, Idaho 83716
(208)344-2120
limlost@micron.net
www.limberlostpress.com

This book is for my daughter, Pilar

And for my son, Gerard,
Who never got to ride
And who reached the end
Of the trail before me
With all of God's speed.

Foreword

This is a work of fiction cut from the tattered cloth of history. The history of the Mormon Church and its people is one of persecution wherever they tried to settle. Time and again in the mid-19th century they were driven from their prosperous settlements in Illinois and Missouri by violent, extra-legal mob action. After the Mormon prophet Joseph Smith was martyred in Illinois in 1844, Brigham Young—called rightly an American Moses—led the Saints across the frozen Mississippi and on into Utah Territory seeking isolation and religious freedom.

Once in the Salt Lake Valley, or Zion, Brigham Young established and presided over a vast and efficient theocracy. The Utah Territory was governed by the Mormon Church, which did not kindly bend to what was considered to be unrighteous federal authority. The courts, the polls, and the collection of taxes were all controlled by Brigham Young and his counselors. If this were not enough, the practice of polygamy caused a national outrage.

In 1857, a U.S. Army expeditionary force was sent to Utah under the command of General Albert Sidney Johnston after President

Buchanan declared the Utah territory to be in a state of rebellion. The imminent arrival of Johnston's army caused Brigham Young to declare martial law and to issue a call to arms against the "invasion." In the grip of war hysteria and understandable historical paranoia, the Mormons prepared to resist and defend their refuge against all outsiders.

It was in this context that high church officials in Southern Utah, along with Indian allies, took part in the wholesale massacre of an emigrant wagon train at the Mountain Meadows in September, 1857. In an act of the utmost treachery, John D. Lee saw to the disarmament of the Fancher train, and lured it into a column, where 127 utterly defenseless men, women, and children were slaughtered in cold blood.

I have taken many liberties to tell the story of Emeline Buxton Lee, the fictional sixteenth wife of John D. Lee, who ran Lee's Ferry between the banks of the Colorado River in the 1870s. Some names, chronologies, and settings have been altered in this story not to revise history, but to explore its intricacies

For those who wish a thorough historical account of the life and times of my fictional Emeline and John D. Lee, there is no finer source than the books of Juanita Brooks, on which I have relied, and to whom I acknowledge a debt. I much admire her work for its unflinching scholarship. I have used some few fragments of dialogue and fleshed out historical scenes as Miss Brooks describes in her definitive biography, *John D. Lee: Zealot, Pioneer Builder, Scapegoat.*

The Mountain Meadows Massacre is her other brilliant work, which, as an historical resource, I have also relied. The shocking confession and graveside oration of John D. Lee is in his own words, and some of the trial scenes and dialogue are taken directly from that historical record. History being sometimes the fiction of the tellers, I wrote the story the way I imagine Emeline would have told it to me, and to you.

Gerald Grimmett
Red Cliffs, Utah

CHAPTER ONE

The heart must have many rooms. How else may it contain love and hate and all of the other things that color our reason? I think there are strong doors between the rooms that have each a different lock. Sometimes the keys are accessible, so one might slip from room to room with ease, but the doors between love and hate must remain forever locked; this is to forestall madness.

From the window desk where I sit each morning, I can see the tops of white buildings through a blue gauze of summer heat. It is a sticky heat that smells of brackish water and tar and the mulch of animals in the street—a fog of odors. But when I lift my pen I smell the clean dry heat of the desert whose fragrances are subtle as French scents, and whose colors are earthen and pastel against the rich green vista of city. As I dip the silver nib into the black ink, I stir the changeling waters of the Colorado, and see clearly the wagons of the travelers coming down to the ferry from a far mesa across the river; savage or missionary—they were all the same to me.

If I had been present the day Brigham Young advised John to

"take along a woman who has faith enough to go with you, take her along & some cows . . ." I'd have crowned the Prophet with the butt of my whip. I still resent Brigham Young's comparison after all these years. In the end, John followed Brigham Young's advice. What choice, really, did he have? John was one of the few men on earth who knew the whole truth of the horror that took place that day in a meadow in Zion. Brigham Young had to get him out of the way, and make sure he never fell into the hands of a vengeful United States government.

In these pages I need to quit the secret house of the heart so a new home might rise out of the blue-clay dust and ashes of John's past. I must enter the chamber of my willful blindness, that place where I hid in the lie that my husband was not party to wholesale, cold-blooded murder of untold women and children. I must look within to banish the fear, else how shall I live, or ever love again?

It was in the spring when we left the beautiful fields and orchards of our home at Harmony in southern Utah. Some would say the roofless pile of rocks on the Colorado to which we fled was all the family of John D. Lee ever deserved. A lonely dell. Even then I would not admit to myself why we were sent—or fled—into exile on the river.

It was a body-wearing, 130-mile high-summer ride and walk from the Rio Virgin across the red, slick-rock desert to Kanab, and then down into the sinuous slot canyon of the Paria to the place we were sent for John's safety. Or, rather, I should say John was driven to that god-forsaken outpost by Brigham Young, one of the most powerful men between the Mississippi and California.

If John had known of the dark room wherein I held my feelings for President Brigham Young and his all-powerful priesthood, he would have divorced me and thrown me in the river, or turned me loose to be taken by the Navajos to do with as they pleased. That is how innocent John was to the counsel of that evil man. He obeyed him and his deputies without question. His was the kind of faith more blind than love, and in the end, more cruel than love can sometimes be.

There were eight of us, three wagons, five cows with calves, a small Remuda of John's best horses, and a rummage of the useless oddments that one always takes on an uncertain journey. There were John and I and our three children—Elizabeth, David and Porter and there was Rachel Andorra—one of John's senior wives-and her two children Amos and Nephi. Her other five children were by now grown and scattered along with the rest of John's family.

On the journey, Rachel refused to unwrap the crocheted shawl from around her shoulders despite the heat. She became more withdrawn with the passage of each mile-a fearful brown face in the canvas shade of her following wagon. But I had known Rachel for many years, and a tougher woman never lived. Faith in John, and faith in God made her eyes burn.

At last we arrived at a place called Jacob's Pools on the middle Paria river, or the *Pahrea* as the Paiute called it; Bad Water. I could see the turmoil it cause John to have to leave Rachel alone at that wild place with but a few pools of water to sustain their lives. We toiled another week under a brassy sun trying to make some kind of tolerable living arrangements for Rachel. The result was a pitiful hovel of sticks and mud and canvas. I had lived better in Liverpool. But without Rachel on lookout upriver, we were defenseless against the federal marshals. Rachel and her two boys were John's only means of early warning. John was torn apart by having to leave her thus.

Soon we were ready to leave down the Paria for the Colorado. Rachel came to the wagon. Amos and Nephi hid behind her skirts, wide-eyed at the knowledge that they were being left alone in a wilderness empty as God's hand. Rachel reached up and took my hand and kissed it. Her eyes were dry. Then she walked around the wagon and rested her hand on John's knee. It was an intimate gesture, a touching gesture.

"Don't you fear for a moment, John," she said. "We'll be all right." Her voice was steady as she gazed upwards at her husband. She said it because John had tears in his eyes, and she wished to comfort him and me, not once demanding sympathy from either one of us. My heart hurt for her as deeply as anything I'd ever felt for one of my sister-wives. Rachel looked utterly forlorn standing in the bitter blue dust waving us on our way. If it had been me that

John left standing on that dry tongue of river I think I should have abandoned him like most of his other wives eventually abandoned him. Down the right hand bank of the Paria, it was only a large handful of dry miles to where it emptied—when there was water to empty—into the mysterious Colorado.

As we made our slow way south I remembered the night young Anna Winthrop came to me in my small new brick house in Harmony, tears in her eyes. Her heart-shaped face had a blush of the chill winter's eve. Outside I could see snow on the red earth through the glazed windows of which I was so inordinately proud. Anna was quite the youngest of John D.'s wives. She came to me for comfort when the burdens of polygamy threatened to break both her back and her will. I played elder sister to a sister-wife.

"Has John told you the terrible news, Emeline?" she asked. I temporized by pouring tea and wrapping her legs in a shawl before seating her at the hearth.

"Yes, he explained it to me this afternoon, dear," I said.

"Why?" she wailed.

"I could say it is God's will, but I won't," I said. Anna must have been only twenty. I had the unnerving sensation of looking into a mirror. I saw therein a motherless and fatherless English girl living upon the kindness of strangers, or, rather, indentured to strangers whose kindness was conditional. I saw myself swept up into an inextinguishable passion for a man twice my age which I can not fairly explain to this day. When you are twenty and handed hope by earnest young men with a golden book, and are told that your soul's salvation depends upon a polygamous marriage, you do not ask many questions about the temporal arrangements. In this matter I was more than blessed, because the man who chose me was also the man I loved.

"I don't understand God or the Devil, governments or fishes," Anna said with youth's petulance. "But I do love Mr. Lee," she insisted. "He is a kind man."

"The people in the United States think our polygamous lives to be abominations," I said. When I was Anna's age I was taken up by strangers with the promise of food, land, and salvation—gratitude will stretch many scruples. When God tells one to do something, it isn't a request. Living within the damp, soot-covered walls of a tenement in Liverpool, the notion of Paradise is not lost on an impressionable young woman. If plural marriage meant the highest degree of Celestial Glory—and I believed this fervently for many years—then strike up the wedding march, said I.

I knew that Anna had a hard adjustment living with the Lees, although John D. Lee never took a wife without his having a great affection. The Church taught that love had nothing to do with the union of a man and a woman. In time that would come, they said. What was love on earth compared to the eternal love of God? Count yourself lucky, the church instructed. The making and bearing of children are your duty and your honor, though you may weep out your eyes.

"Perhaps the people of the United States are right," Anna flared. "The other wives hate me just because I am young."

"Nonsense," I said with feeble conviction. I too had felt the occasional barb of sharp tongues of the elder wives jealous of my beauty. How I loathe those twin relics of barbarism—slavery and polygamy—but back then hell's fire was more of a concern than the consequences of sharing a husband with fifteen other wives.

"It has to do with our freedom," I said to her, thinking that to be the whole truth.

"It's not fair," Anna said. She might have stamped her feet, had they not been bound in the shawl. "The marshals never come south just to chase polygamists," she insisted. "And when they do the men are always warned. There must be another reason. How can we leave all this?" She spread her arms expansively, indicating my own small privileged and comfortable home. As Anna's own house was not yet built, I knew how difficult it was for her to have a sense of attachment to the Lee family.

"Brigham Young thinks it wise for John to disappear. As I understand it, the federal government wants to try him for murder, of which he is quite innocent," I said innocently.

"What murder? Why?" I could not tell her, for I myself did not really know, or wish to know. The tenements in my heart were quite comfortable and well furnished, thank you.

"Hush, child, with your whys. Brigham Young and John D. Lee

have been friends—like a father and son—since the days of our Prophet. They were together in the early days of the church. They were near the Prophet when he was slain. They led the way to the valley of the Salt Lake and established Zion in the wilderness. John will do Brigham's bidding not only because he is asked, but to save his family from having to suffer the loss of his husbandry if he were to go to prison. That is all you need to know."

"Well, I won't be going to an awful desert with him," Anna declared, the first open shot in the rebellion. I knew then that John D. Lee's family was in dissolution. His past had come to haunt us all. But even as I scorned the treachery of the other sister-wives I was secretly questioning my own faith and love for John D. Lee. Remembering young Anna's defiance, I looked at the man beside me on the wagon seat as if at a stranger.

"What do you think, Em?" he asked, turning his sun-dark face away from the heart-breaking sight of Rachel left standing bereft in the dust. My two sons, the tow-head David and Irish-dark Porter (saplings in the gritty trail behind the wagon) were driving the little herd of livestock behind us.

"I think it's a glimpse of hell, John," I said. He ruefully shook his head. John always held my outspoken disposition to be one of the reasons he loved me. I sometimes think he regretted my forthrightness. I know I did—at times.

"If this is Brigham Young's notion of a land of opportunity, I'd hate to think how he must envision a poor place. I miss Harmony terribly, John," I added in wistful voice, something not of my character. He did not reply for a long time. We rode in heat-creaking silence for the better part of an hour.

I was changing. My questions were becoming sharper. To be disastrously uprooted from a verdant Paradise on Zion's south shoulder demanded a better explanation than the one's I'd been given. Of course I knew John D. Lee was wanted for murder. But the comfort I always had was that I truly believed my husband had not shed innocent blood. Which led to the question of innocence. Which led to deeper questions of his culpability until it all became hair-splitting sophistry to me. But my husband had vowed to me he had shed no blood that day in the meadows. As I was to discover, he may as well have shot them all—the result was the same. One of the Prophet Joseph Smith's articles of faith is that Man will be punished for his own sins, and not for Adam's transgressions. That notion was an abomination to my poor dead Catholic mother. And I was to learn that she was right; Adam's sin taints us all to the very depth of the womb.

"Of course you'll miss Harmony," John said finally, picking up an hour's pause in which I had forgotten my wistful complaint. "As will I always miss it. But I've left better for worse prospects than these," he said, indicating the looming Sinai ahead of us down the trail.

I heard Elizabeth begin to whimper in the back of the wagon. I hefted her from her bed of quilts and put her on the breast, leaning back in the bouncing shade. "I'm going to choose to look upon this move as an adventure," I said, gazing at the fractured red stone cliffs on either side of the river. "Although my growing impression is this is a poor place for Brigham Young to send anyone with a family."

"There is no choice in the matter," John said grimly. "We'll make do in this place, Em. The Lord leads."

Leads us and leaves us, I thought. I am not one to carp or complain, and the prospect of life away from the settlements and the huge family did have its appeal. Privacy and polygamy are strangers.

"That makes it no less difficult, Mr. Lee," I said. "The leaving of it, I mean." His reply to me was contained in the utterly freezing look in his grey eyes which quickly dissolved to sadness. I returned his gaze forthrightly. I was not at all satisfied with John's vague explanations and evasions, nor the full reason for Brigham Young's edict that for safety John should remove himself from the reach of the federal marshals.

I pinned back my hair, trying to discover the good things about this stony place. It took some searching. We road for miles in a hot silence. John acted as if taking off into the wilderness was an everyday thing. And then I reflected upon the history of the Mormons with whom I had joined in faith as fervently as I'd given my heart and my body to John D. Lee. Perhaps, I thought, I should get used to the notion that I had joined a rag-a-tag bunch of Israelites doomed to forever seek the promised land. God knows, we had enough practice. Utah was supposed to be a place where we could worship as we pleased without the interference of worldly governments. A place called freedom.

I stepped down from the slowly moving wagon and walked with the boys for a time. David and Porter were delighted with the new country, and their light-hearted driving of the cattle and throwing of stones at skinny rabbits made me smile. Every step for them was an adventure and a discovery. If I viewed our journey to the Colorado with wariness, the two boys were taking a journey to a place where their manhood would be forever molded by the challenges I expected them to have. The lessons, I feared, would be harsh. Let them explore and dream, I thought. I teased dark-haired Porter into replacing his hat. "Your hair will bleach to the color of your brother's hair," I said, knowing that would not do at all, and Porter clapped the hat back onto his head in a flash. I wondered where they had come from. They were as different as daylight and darkness.

After walking out the kinks, I got back up in the seat and placed my hip firmly against John's hard hip. I took up the canvas water bag and offered it to John. He took it and smiled—rather bleakly I thought—drank and handed it back to me. The water tasted slightly bitter, and was the same temperature as our blood. John surprised me by picking up the thread of our earlier conversation as if a half-hour had not intervened.

"You asked me about leaving. In 1844, when you were still a little girl in England, the mobs came and forced us across the frozen Mississippi and into the wilderness," he said quietly, "Hundreds died. I had a home as fine as at Harmony in the city of Nauvoo near the new temple, and a good farm outside the city. I watched them both burn to the ground, Em."

"Rachel said you had a fine place in the east," I said.

"Have you ever heard of Haun's Mill?" he asked quietly, concentrating on negotiating the stony track.

"Of course," I said. "A whisper here, a whisper there. It seems much of church history is but a whisper."

"Much of church history is a lie told by gentiles," he said firmly. "Haun's Mill is something that should never be whispered, but shouted from the very roof of Heaven."

"Well, then tell me," I insisted. "Why do you have to be so closed up? I've always wanted to know everything of your life before I met you. You never speak of . . . that place over on the other side of the Pine Valley Mountain either except by the most circumspect evasions."

By now the Mountain Meadows lay as heavily as a stone upon all of our lives, though, truthfully, I still thought it had nothing to do with me. I was but an emigrant fresh off the boat when it happened, albeit with worn shoes by the time I'd walked to Salt Lake City.

"I am not evading, I am protecting you," he said sternly. I bit my lip. He knew my mind. I'd lent him many pieces of it over the years. But I had also given him my heart's devotion, and my vows and my body. My place was beside him no matter the weathers of the present. And, God, it was hot.

"Will you tell me? I know it was a horror."

"Aggatha was there, did you know that? She barely escaped with her life."

"Where? At Haun's Mill?" He nodded.

"She was a witness," he said.

"That explains her abiding bitterness," I said. "When the men came and torched the barn that night at Harmony she was ready to fight. She loaded that old musket as if she'd practiced it."

"Poor, dear woman." John was not a man to sigh, but I heard one someplace out there in the barren, blue-clay gullies.

"God rest her," I said fervently.

"Did you know she was well past sixty when she was sealed to me? I was but twenty five or so at the time. Brigham Young came to me and said she was in a dire circumstance, her husband and children dead in Jacob Haun's blacksmith shop. I gladly assented to having her sealed to me, and have supported her all her life, although we never had relations. There were several others of that age who needed my protection," he said vaguely.

"Forgive me, but I always thought Aggatha was a little disturbed."

"Haun's Mill."

I waited, checked back in the wagon where little Elizabeth slept soundly despite the heat. Whenever we put her in a wagon she slept like she'd earned it. Sweet girl. David and Porter were skipping rocks in the still pools between which lay a dry, rocky river bottom. "You boys stay close," I said needlessly as they scampered up the bank and took a switch to the rump of a particularly obstreperous young black and white heifer.

"Were you there?"

"I came upon the scene. We were riding hard, first chasing the mobsters, and then running for our lives. We'd heard that two hundred of Governor Boggs' mobsters and bogus militia were heading for a little settlement in Gallatin County in Missouri, but we were otherwise occupied at Crooked River. You know, dear, in those days I thought I was bullet proof. Still do."

Those words reverberate like rifle fire in my mind even to this day.

"The Battle of the Crooked River wasn't really a battle, Em, but it was reported to Governor Boggs that we Mormons had massacred hundreds—slain whole hosts of men. The truth is, the Missouri Militia lost one man, and we Mormons lost three. In order to stop the bloodshed the Prophet surrendered himself up to the mob that called itself an army, and we laid down our arms. That is where I lost my sword, at Crooked River. The Prophet saved many lives that day."

"Were you hurt?"

"Only my pride. I wanted to fight. But Joseph Smith's cooler head prevailed, and we still held a hope they would leave us alone."

"I've always found it hard to understand their enmity, John. I suppose I've retained an emigrant's perspective. Or, perhaps, a willful ignorance. But we can amend that shortcoming." I laid my hand on his arm. "Since we were married I found there was too much living to be done to be concerned with the past. We are, after all, really alone for the first time since we've been married. Maybe it's time we got to know one another a little better." It was a weak jest, but I loved so to needle the man in a lightness of spirit.

"I think I'm going to enjoy that, Em. I've never been able to get enough of you, or your time."

"Life and living never precluded my susceptibility to your flattery, Mr. Lee," I laughed. And then more seriously, "Please tell me, John. They are my own people, you know. Aggatha and Rachel were not prone to giving history lessons, merely sharp rebukes for breaking crockery."

"In due time, perhaps," he said vaguely. "As to the whys of it, well, it's pretty plain. People who claim to have the only truth in the world, and who are not reluctant to point out the error of their neighbor's thinking, can be mighty unpopular. But mostly we just wished to be left alone. And of course we ran our own courts, and elected our own officials and collected our own taxes and did not properly render up unto Caesar all that Boggs thought was coming to him. It was the same way when we came to Utah. Many reasons—but not a single one of them good enough to justify the spilling of our blood, or theirs. But they would not desist in their attempts to get rid of us. There were written *extermination* orders, Em. God's truth."

"I would've wanted to move west too," I said, "under those circumstances."

"I think Joseph Smith always knew we'd someday settle out here."

"Perhaps not here, John," I chided, indicated the heat-seared valley into which we were descending. He smiled, and ignored my jibe.

"More and more knowledge was available of the western country. Brigham Young knew it too, I think. It was Brigham who saved the church by bringing us west. We could not withstand their hatred on their own ground. Our homes and the city of Nauvoo were beautiful, more beautiful than Harmony."

"That is hard to imagine."

"It is hard to imagine," he agreed.

"Haun's Mill? Crooked River?" I gently prompted him.

"We didn't know part of the Governor's militia had broken away and gone to Jacob Haun's Mill. Just a little settlement, some houses, the mill, a blacksmith shop. The terribly sooty blacksmith shop." I saw John had taken a sudden chill. Gooseflesh raised on inner side of his large arms, and this in a hundred degrees.

"There were about thirty-seven or so men, women and children when the alarm was taken up. Thinking the blacksmith shop to be as safe as anyplace, they locked themselves inside and tried to defend themselves. The Missourians stood behind trees and picked them off one by one through large, fatal cracks between the wall boards. Several of the women tried to flee from the shop with their children, and were shot down in the cold mud."

"Oh, no," I said.

"Worse. When they stormed inside the shop, they found some survivors. There was a little nine-year-old boy, Sardius I think his name was—No, that was his first name—Sardius Smith, no relation to the Prophet. Sardius was hiding under the bellows. His younger brother, who'd been shot in the hip, played dead, and heard the men as they came in and found Sardius. 'It's best to hive them when we can,' one man said 'Nits make lice,' and blew the boy's brains out."

"Oh, God," I exclaimed.

"After dark the women went back inside the shop. Of the thirty-eight who were at Haun's Mill, seventeen were slain, and fifteen wounded. It was a massacre beyond anything since . . . since . . ." and then my husband suddenly threw down the reins, leapt off the wagon and disappeared behind a creosote bush. I could hear him retching at first, and then came the sound of his sobbing until I thought my heart would break.

"What is wrong with father?" David asked, and I could not answer. Then did I know? In time, he returned, took up the reins, and we set out again. We rode the rest of the day in a numbing silence, and I had no notion in the world how to comfort him.

CHAPTER TWO

Hallo the ferry!" We were awakened by the call that I had come to dread. I feared the cross-river summons as much as the burring warning of the tail of the rattlesnake. One never knew who would be across the river, more often foe than friend. The call came just at first light. John scrambled from our bed of boards and dressed. He was a man who greeted every morning as if the world was of a newly struck mintage, and nothing of the old realms and tokens of Europe's sovereigns had ever been.

"Will you come across with me?" he asked, looking out the open door frame into the clear coming of the sun.

"I suppose I must," I said, unsuccessfully hiding resignation.

"You have to learn to steer, Em," he said firmly. "I will be leaving for Skatumpah in two days time. We must have lumber for the buildings and foodstuffs for the winter. Someone must learn to steer while the boys, or the passengers, pull the oars."

"Of course, John. Let me wash."

He left through the doorless opening and walked across the hundred yards of white sand beach to the river's edge and began to pull the canvas from the *Colorado*. Then he upturned the little skiff *Paria*, named after the river which emptied—when there was water to empty—into the Colorado at our Lonely Dell.

The ferry was John's Pride & Joy, months in the building. He had to sell the bountiful estate at Harmony for a dime on the dollar. John's faith—be honest Em—his past, had reduced us to near poverty. After John distributed most of the proceeds from the sale of Harmony among the wives and children who chose to leave him, he sunk—no pun meant—the remainder of his money into the building of the ferry. Brigham's cunning was apparent to me from the outset. He would have someone to build and man a ferry crossing for the Saints to populate Arizona, and at the same time keep John D. Lee out of the hands of the government.

The Colorado was a long-waisted, blunt-nosed thing with a shallow draft. It was an ugly craft with pitch leaking from the seams of warping pine above the waterline. John had to haul every board of lumber from the mill that we built up at Skatumpah a hundred miles north where sister-wives Polly and Levina said they would wait for us if we ever returned.

"Who is it?" I called as I left the house after pushing the heavy fall of my straw-colored hair into a twist at the base of my neck. John was standing near the ferry with the sun in his face, his hand up to shade his eyes.

"It appears to be Brother Hamblin and party returned from the Moenkoeppi," he called, his voice carefully neutral. Jacob Hamblin was nominally John's superior in matters of the Church. The irony had the taste of iron. Brigham Young excommunicates John from the bosom of the Church, and then calls him on a Mission to build a ferry to serve the church! The letter of excommunication which came before we left Harmony almost killed my husband. There was a shadow upon his soul which never thereafter lifted. The ferry gave John but a dubious refuge, and Brigham a means to spread the gospel. John still paid his tithes and gave his fealty to a church that officially shunned him, and branded him a murderer. My faith was stretched to the breaking. Confound men and their tiresome intrigues! John's trust in Brigham mystified and exasperated me to a distraction.

Jacob Hamblin was called by many a friend to all of the Indians. He had a way to make the Lamanites tractable—with fear, hunger, and empty promises. But he was just another one of Brigham's back-shooters, in my opinion. History, no doubt, will make a Saint of him. I should have killed him in the courtroom.

I found steering and crossing the ferry quite easy. The ungainly thing skimmed across the low river with John's strong pulling on the oars.

"See that point of rock with the two piñon?" John pointed far upriver. "You must steer for that point until mid-river." Dutifully I pulled the long steer sweep to the right—upstream—and John's rhythmic pulls soon had us headed in that direction as if we sailed upon wind. As we reached halfway, perhaps seventy-five yards, he pointed his head toward the group of waiting horsemen. "Now you can steer directly for the passengers."

I pulled over the sweep, and looked into the river, clear now in the late summer, a deep green roil of power that I have always feared, for I am not a strong swimmer. It reminded me of the mindless courage—call it dedication—of Major Powell and his men who'd come all the way down the Green River some years before without knowing what disaster could lie around every bend. This was an excursion, compared.

"Hello, Jacob," John called, as he gave a final, powerful pull on the oars and grounded the Colorado on the rocky beach. Hamblin still sat on his horse, Lord High Commissioner to the Natives, as if he expected John to hold his stirrup while he climbed down. It was a motley lot of half a dozen men, thick layers of dust on their shoulders, the horses tired and drooping. Hamblin's lank black hair hung under his round-topped hat that had a short ragged brim. He looked like a scarecrow, a grim frightener of children. I saw there was an Indian guide hanging at the back of the pack who looked as if he hadn't eaten in days which, I learned, he hadn't. Hamblin likes to keep his Indians hungry, so they'll lick the hand that feeds them.

"Hello, Mrs. Lee," he said to me coldly.

"Mr. Hamblin, gentlemen," I acknowledged him, returning chill with frost.

"I'll have to charge you for the crossing," John said to Hamblin.

"Charge be damned, we're on church business," Hamblin said. "By whose authority will you charge us for the crossing?"

"By the authority of Brother Brigham," John said lightly. I knew there was a secret glee in his voice, but one has to know him to hear it. It was only the past week a letter came from Salt Lake which stated clearly that there were no free rides for the Saints anymore than for the Indians. "You've got to make a living there," Brigham wrote. "Set the prices accordingly, but I would suggest $1.00 for horse and rider, 50 cents per grown man or woman; 10 cents for children in arms; 25 cents for horse or cow, calf or foal; $1.00 per wagon etc."

"Lee's Ferry, Brigham's prices," John added.

"I'll not pay," Hamblin scowled, still on his horse.

"Then you'll swim," John said, standing with arms akimbo, holding the bow rope.

"Hell, I ain't swimmin'," a man in the rear said, climbing down off a Pinto in a cloud of dust. "I can't swim."

"Nor I," another man said. "How much, Brother Lee?"

"$1.00 for horse and rider," John said. "I'll ferry across the dust you wear for free." Some of the men grinned.

"That's fair," another man said. Hamblin sat on his horse, his dark eyes fast on the far shore, his jaw muscles working beneath a beard that grew in ugly patches.

"That's highway robbery," he finally muttered, climbing down.

"No, that'd be piracy, as you're crossing water," John said, and the men laughed generally.

"I'll report this to President Young," Hamblin muttered.

"Report away," John said cheerfully. "Now, who's first? With strong arms to row and pole, Mrs. Lee will be free to fix us a breakfast that'll carry you clean to the settlements. Ten cents per man for the cooking. You supply the grub," he added sheepishly. The men pressed forward with an eager will while John put down the plank on the boat's blunt bow. The Colorado could carry four horses and riders, so we crossed them quickly with all those extra arms.

Corn meal mush—they had a handful of meal between them—

and coffee was the best they could supply, but I had milk from the cow. It was much appreciated, for these men were starved. John's generosity was a source of some irritation with me, for he shared equally with all men. If it were not for his uncanny capacity to turn a sack of meal into two sacks of meal, there was many a time we should have starved ourselves. He could leave our place at Harmony in the morning with empty pockets and an old wagon, and return by sunset with a fine coach and some jingle in his pockets to boot. And all save his enemies swore he was as fair a man as God ever made. With fifty mouths of his own family to feed at times, it was a handy talent.

After the meager meal, the men went to lazing and dozing in the skinny shade of the rock house while John and Hamblin held a long conference within. Hamblin and John did have an agreement that Hamblin would send us foodstuffs in exchange for John's selecting and making improvements on a piece of ranch land between Jacob's Pools and the Lonely Dell. Hamblin had been first in this country—thus Jacob's Pools, a series of potholes in the riverbed that lasted through the summer—and laid claim to both soil and souls without discrimination. I had no difficulty with that arrangement, for John's abilities far outstripped any horse-trading abilities Hamblin himself possessed, in my estimation.

I walked outside and saw the Indian guide who was sitting some distance away from the house in the shade of some rock overhang. I saw he still had nothing to eat, and flushed for their neglect. I went back into the house and spooned the last of the corn mush and milk into a bowl and carried it outside. Approaching the young man, I saw he had a cast in one eye, and was probably shunned from his tribe. All of his ribs—including the one Adam pilfered from women—showed through his dark brown skin. He was a sad figure. It was said Hamblin fed hundreds of Indians, but apparently he'd forgotten this one. I handed him the bowl and he looked up at me with a somber expression. His eyes remained flat as the river, and then he suddenly dipped his head in thanks and wolfed down the mush with his fingers.

I harbored a pity for the Indians we came across, a dispossessed people in their own land. But I also feared them. The Navajos were ever making war. According to the Book of Mormon, the Indians were descendants of one of the Lost Ten Tribes, an ancient people called Lamanites, and therefore blessed. Of course the state of their blessing depended upon how readily they received the Gospel. From my observation it never took, and was a dubious enterprise. Did they not have the rights to their own religion, I wondered. John would have upbraided me severely for having such thoughts.

When John and Hamblin came out of the house after their apparently satisfactory conference, John asked if any of the men would like to see the site he had selected to cut the Dugway to the canyon top, and several men averred they did. One man, Babbitt, elected to sleep in the shade while the others began to walk to the site perhaps a mile away. Hamblin, for some reason, also stayed behind.

When the men were out of sight, Hamblin ambled around the point of sand and rock we called our home, gazed at the river, gazed silently at me, and then made a beckoning motion. I come for no man without he speak with me. I do not obey hand signals as if I were a favorite hunting dog. He motioned me again to join him near his horse. I turned my back to him and walked into the half-roofed house. Already it was hot.

His shadow fell across the floor, and he came into the house, filling it with his bulk.

"I wish to speak with you," he said. "Didn't you see me beckon?"

"I'm accustomed to some politeness," I said, turning to meet his gaze, so that I might see his eyes. I like to see a man's eyes when I speak with him. The eyes of most men lack nuance. But the eyes of men who are blinded by God? They can look you in your eye and move their mouth in a lie that you'd swear was utter truthfulness. It is chilling.

"Women who consort with excommunicates are little better than curs, Jezebels," he hissed, his voice strangled with fury. I was quite stunned by the strength of the man's hatred.

"How dare you speak to me like that?" I said in a voice that matched his for tone. I had a knife to hand, which I slipped behind my back.

"That you should whore yourself, and bear him another child, is to your eternal damnation. He is cut off from the church, and you should cut yourself off from him as well!" He took a step toward me. I was terribly frightened. How could this man, whom I barely knew, have such hatred for John? They were business partners.

"You evil man," I said. "Get out of my house!"

"I'll see that Brigham annuls your marriage, cuts you off from the ordinances. You must leave him, and marry a man who is faithful." It was then I realized the man was looking at me with a thinly disguised lust. I was chilled and shaking with both fear and fury.

"Get out!" I shouted. "I've borne the man four sons and a daughter, and by God I'll bear him four more be he the Devil himself!"

"He shall be punished for the massacre at the Mountain Meadows! No good Mormon woman should have anything to do with that murderer of women and children. Evil woman, harlot . . ."

Hamblin saw the flash of the knife as I brought it from behind my skirt. As he ducked the blade caught him across the cheek, just a nick when I wished it had severed his head from his body. I made to lunge at him again when he caught my arm and twisted the knife away. I thought he had broken my arm. I made to kick him in his bollocks when he shoved me and retreated out of the house.

The fall knocked the breath from me, and I was just rising when the doorway shadowed again and I looked to where John kept his pistols. But it was a small shadow, and in the backlight I heard Babbitts' voice, "Are you all right, missus? Have you fallen?"

"No, Brother Babbitts, it is all right. Is John returned?"

"They are just in sight," he said, backing away.

"Say nothing of this," I said to him. My voice must have been terrible, for he backed away, stammering.

"If that's what you want, Miss. The man treads quicksand."

"It's none of your affair."

"Not from my mouth, Miss, but if John D. Lee learns that Hamblin has insulted you, he'll horsewhip him, and the consequences be damned."

"If Mr. Hamblin wishes to avail himself again of the opportunity to insult me, Mr. Babbitts, then Mr. Lee will find himself horsewhipping a tongueless man," I said, running my thumb along the kitchen blade.

CHAPTER THREE

One day, as I carried two buckets of water with a yoke across my shoulders, the brave river man, Major John Wesley Powell, whose second Colorado River expedition was camped nearby, took the burden from my shoulders and carried it to the parching garden. The boy and I were desperately trying to coax a green furrow of life from the clay delta where the Paria emptied into the crossing of the Colorado. John was working a mile away on the sieve of a dam he was building across the Paria. After the Major set the buckets down, he said, gesturing to the hot, white sky, "You know, Mrs. Lee, and no offense, but most Mormons I've met would've made good Jesuits. You've that singleness of purpose."

"The raising up of the Kingdom of God on earth takes blinders to prudence at times," I said. "That is the substance of miracles."

I recall John and I were alone one evening at the place we had named the Lonely Dell before Major Powell put it on the U. S. geological survey maps as Lee's Ferry. The shadows were a flowing black geometry on the vividly colored cockscombs and spires and parapets that crowned the far canyon walls. The place had grown on me despite the hard work. It was a place where beauty would not be compromised by our effort. We were sitting in the dooryard of the half-completed house of rocks we had mined from the banks of the Colorado. That wonderful river was green as jade against the red rock, the cool of the evening just beginning to breathe off the water.

David and Porter were helping Rachel Andorra at Jacob's Pools that week. My little Elizabeth lay in the cooling house, asleep. It had turned out that Rachel Andorra and I were the only two wives who followed John. The rest of them, those that did not openly break with him, were scattered with friends and relatives all over Utah. John didn't know if he would ever see some of them again. I was a young woman in love with a man twenty years her elder, and Rachel had been married to John for more years than I had lived.

I looked at his dear, craggy face, lined now in the dying light, and saw the care that his blind faith had heaped upon him until I thought we both should break.

"It's beautiful at this time of day," I said. I took his hand in mine and let it rest there, our calluses clashing like sandpaper.

"Looks more or less like the Holy Land, don't you think?" he said lightly. "Better for goats than for cattle," he observed.

"So, do you think of me as a cow?" I asked when John wryly told me of President Young's characteristic comment. "I follow you like livestock, is that it? Does the Prophet tend his wives like he tends his livestock?" I was teasing John, an activity of which I was fond.

"I'm glad to see you still retain your humor, Em," he said.

"So Rachel Andorra is the other cow?"

"We are all of us sheep," John laughed.

"Led far astray," I said, gesturing to the lonely canyon spires. "I'm sorry," I said, instantly regretting my sarcasm. God, that I could sometimes bite off the thought before it reaches the tongue. Had we more food I may have been carefree, for the evening shadows were falling with their promise of relief from the inferno of the day's sun.

"There is promise in this place, Em, you just have to look a little harder than you might otherwise," he grinned at me. "God will sustain us."

"Of course," I murmured. When camels replace horses, I thought, and was ashamed of myself again. Initially the Lonely Dell was a Golgotha to me, a habitation of skulls. And coming to think on it, the Navajos were the Bedouins of the country, and sometimes just as cruel. We're Zealots, not Jesuits, Major Powell.

"The ferry tolls will keep us in flour until the crops come in," he said, gazing across the river, a distance, to my eye, of an ocean.

"At least the garden is in, but I don't see how we can keep it alive if I have to carry water from the river by the bucket. I don't know how much longer me and the boys can keep it up, John."

"I'll have the dam across the Paria soon, days now with any luck. If it rains in the upcountry we'll get a trickle down here, enough to hold, and put out on the crops. We'll make something of this place yet, Em," he said to me, his voice strong with conviction, and I had to believe him, for there was nothing else to cling to. "And I do doubt the laws will be down in this direction any time soon. If there's six white men within a radius of a hundred miles I'd be surprised. Brigham will sort it all out. With the federals chasing the brethren in northern Utah they'll forget us down here. Perhaps we'll be left alone. The United States must have something better to do than chase polygamists."

And I listened to the tacit lie that we were in this exile because of polygamy. And believed it. To do otherwise would have collapsed the walls wherein I held my hope, and faith, and love.

What a fiction we all lived. The United States wanted nothing more than to destroy Brigham and the Church. Brigham had to publicly disavow John D. Lee to demonstrate he was not in league with the accused murderer. But it was all a charade. Brigham was expert at playing both ends against the middle. He would do anything to further his own ends. It is with a bitter taste of iron that John remained loyal to the Church and to Brigham almost to the end. John suffered to protect Brigham. He suffered to keep his solemn vow of secrecy, and in John's sacrifice I was witness and pawn, lover and willing participant. However would my exile end?

"But if Brigham ever does 'sort it out' as you say, we've no place to return, our home is gone." Stop your naggery Emeline, I told myself.

"We must see this as another mission calling."

"That's the first time I've ever heard of flight from prosecution as a mission," I returned wryly, trying to raise a smile again, living the lie. "You must admit we moved quite smartly along that wretched trail, considering my age and disposition."

"Oh, my dear Em," John said, folding both of his hands around mine. "You sustain me."

"And you me," I said, with all of my heart breaking until the walls of the rooms began to fall apart and I could not distinguish between love, or hate, good or evil, daylight or darkness.

"Major Powell has given me a thermometer!" John suddenly declared, raising from the burlap bag which I had filled with fragrant brush to use as a cushioned sofa. "I'd forgotten it." He strode into the house, his long white hair afly, for he had washed in the river after supper, and the salt stains from his shirt were rinsed clean. He came out of the rock house waving the little glass rod with glee.

"By heaven, it reads 100 degrees," he announced, holding it aloft as if he were proud of the fact.

"I'm not surprised," I said.

"Why, hell, that must mean, at the height of the sun, we had temperatures exceeding 115 degrees today, perhaps more."

"Hell indeed, old man," I said teasingly. "I never knew the earth could be so hot." I had unbuttoned the front of my shirt for the coolness, the tops of my breasts were milk blue-white against my brown arms. It was unconscious display; I was opened for the coolness. But God knew he was a handsome man, in this hell of sand and savages, and my body was ready for him, if that was his mood.

"Old man, am I?" he said, sitting down, jamming the thermometer in the sand as if to take the earth's temperature, and then he kissed me softly on the mouth, his hard hands holding up my breasts. I placed my arms around his shoulders, as if gathering in a large bulk of stone so strong was he, and stronger still as he lifted me and carried me into the coolness of the rock house.

He gently put me down on the pallet of skins and our one good quilt. The light of the dying sun glowed through the door, filling it with a rose-colored light. As I opened my dress front he lay beside me, and his hard hands slipped up and down my body like breaths of cool wind, my breast-tips singing. With ageless fervor we blessed one another, and he was a man forty years younger. And in that hard pinning his mouth went to my breasts, and we gyred in our flesh and I soared in the same incandescence I felt the night we were married. Never the same, always the same, our mood now savage, now sweet, and John made me know that he and I were one, always. I forgot the merciless sun, and the endless seas of ancient sand upon which we rocked. The sand had turned to stone, the air a whistling frost. Outside, only the river birds were there to hear my cries.

CHAPTER FOUR

Thus we toiled away the first spring and summer. In the fall, John left for Skatumpah for food and lumber. For thirty days I had heard nothing of his progress or his safety. The days shortened, and the leaves of the cottonwoods were turning to a bleached golden curl. There was no word from John, and no visitor, not even the Indians, which was a blessing. David and Porter were living in a lean-to up on the flat ground next to the Paria a half-mile from the rock house on the Colorado. There we hoped to build the ranch. My darling infant daughter slept nearby.

In John's absence, I invented little games with the boys, and spent hours with them in the slow of the evening. They would come down from the brush house at the ranch for supper, and then would sit at my feet in the dooryard as I read to them from Mr. William. Shakespeare and from the Holy Book of Mormon. I found they preferred the bard to Joseph Smith's translation of the Golden Plates that the angels of God revealed to the Prophet when he was David's age. The plates were hidden in a hill of dirt in upper New York State. David—the bookish one—said one night that the Book of Mormon sounded a whole lot to him as if it had been cribbed from the Holy Bible. If John had heard him say that he'd have been whipped until he couldn't sit down. I'd thought the same thing myself from time to time, but it wasn't a subject of discussion that any Mormon I ever knew would tolerate.

Lieutenant Dellenbaugh, one of Major Powell's river men, came to see me often in the afternoons until I told him it was not seemly for us to be seen together so often. A woman knows when a man is enamored. They shamble, and draw figures with their toes, and don't seem to know whether to leap in the air, or crawl into a hole in the ground. Lt. Dellenbaugh was a man of some education, and as sophisticated as Major Powell, and in my presence he turned it to his advantage. I welcomed his visits, but they made me feel both gay and guilty, innocent as they were. James was a man with a charming shyness. John was always intense, convicted even while he forked hay or mended harness. The Lieutenant left me with the feeling of a low, glowing fire more comforting for its warmth than its light.

"People will talk," I chided him.

"The way I see it," he said, his handsome face deeply brown, his teeth white, "there are about twenty men and one woman on this beach. I wouldn't wonder at the gossip. They're all jealous of me." Lt. Dellenbaugh was forever teasing me. I confess I delighted in his company. "I thought I'd finish that brush fence for you," he said.

"You've done enough work for us," I said.

"It's my pleasure," he smiled. "We'll be leaving soon," he said, looking at the river.

"Yes," I said, hiding my heart in a somber shadow. "I'll miss all of the activity."

"And I'll miss you," he said boldly.

"And I shall miss . . . all of the activity," I said, meaning him, but could not say it. He studied me, his eyes a hard quest, and then he walked away without another word. I felt like crying. I would miss Major Powell's comings and goings as he surveyed the country. But most of all I would miss the visits of Lieutenant Dellenbaugh. Night after night I lay alone, breathing darkness, waiting for the sun to light my work. I desperately fought resentment against John, and the church. But most of all I lingered upon the thought that Brigham Young had put me here to die. How had I come to this place?

With Elizabeth sleeping at my side I lay on the bed of skins and quilts and listened to the shushing of the river, the cry of the night owls, the whisper of the cold night wind. Oh, I knew, but did I KNOW? His words to me, before he made his proposal of marriage, were clear.

"I've done some terrible things, Miss Emeline, for which I'm ashamed, and for which I may be punished by the United States."

Oh, I had heard the dark rumors while on the long foot-trek across the frontier, but I chose not to believe them. I reasoned, in love's opacity, that John could never be a murderer. This was the man I loved. However can we delude ourselves that the past lives as much in the heart as the present despite our best efforts to banish it. On the hard bed that long night I saw myself fall in love all over again. The memory of the recognition ever thrills me.

I was a fresh-cheeked, but road-worn emigrant when John D. spotted me in the front row of the 14th ward in Salt Lake City in 1861. In my mind I was still living in England, remembering biscuit boxes made of red brick. Rooms narrow as the grave. I remember the tenement where we were forced to live after my father's farm failed in 1844. That was the same year the Prophet was shot down in cold blood in a hateful jail cell in Carthage in America. The tenement rooms were the size of casks for skeletal children, windows empty as death's gaze. I remember being lifted down from the drayman's cart, noticing my father's hands were already black with soot from the air around us, his face dark; only his red eyes showed him to be an Englishman.

I remember from our farm fresh milk, and sweet tea, and the lowing of cattle in the barn nearby the small cottage. My childhood was a happy childhood, for my father free-held a small plot of land in the Shire. Because he owned land, when I was twelve I was sent to a tutor up at the manor house along with two other young women whose families were free-holders.

In Lord Harrington's red brick house—manse—we were tutored

in the classics, and pampered shamefully by Lady Harrington who had always wished for daughters, but instead had a crop of surly sons. We spent long afternoons while a prim-faced tutor filled our heads with images of men with strong hearts and thighs like columns of marble. We learned of Persephone's flowing hair, of the orchards of the gods which bore only golden fruit. I learned my letters well, but that uncommon idyllic for a commoner abruptly ended one sad day.

Lord Harrington's son Cedric, who was my own age, had the languid brow and manner of the aristocracy, and an aristocratic taste—he tried to disrobe me one afternoon in the formal garden and I laid him out with a kick in the bollocks. Thereafter, the balance of my education took place at home. My sisters and I read to one another poetry, and we swooned in the moonlight at the wonder of our womanhood. Our becoming. Whoever could have imagined I would become a leather-faced woman of the American west?

I was fourteen when some sort of blight fell upon the crops, or was it a failure of the economy? This was at the time of the potato famine in Ireland, but I don't know if that was connected to the troubles we had in England. Our cottage, land and animals were sold at bankruptcy, and so we were dispossessed. No wonder the Mormon missionaries found such fertile ground, such willing women. I was so young, my head filled with books. My father never spoke of the cause that forced us into Liverpool to live in the cold, hateful squalor of the city. I had two elder brothers, two older sisters, my mother, and my father.

In the city they died before my eyes. Benjamin of the black consumption. Willard of alcohol. Jenny of the syphilitic pox and sweet Virginia just disappeared like a smudge of chimney smoke. My mother and father were bereft, but tried to keep us alive. It was when my father, sick now too with the consumption, that my mother had to go down into the streets to beg for offal from the butcher, for gin for my father's lungs, for a scrap of white bread that was black from the coal smoke.

My mother was the religious part of our family, and clung to the Hope of Christ tenaciously throughout our hardships. I remember clearly the sight of the two Mormon elders as they tramped grimly up and down the dark hallways of the tenements, seeking souls, desiring to convert anyone to the new church in America with the promise of land, freedom, and, above all, deliverance from hunger.

But she would have no part of it, she vowed, even unto seeing her last child die of hunger before her eyes. She was a Catholic, and the new Mormon faith was anathema to her ears and eyes. My father, from his sick bed, grasped at the proffered hope with the same tenacious grasp that my mother resisted their teachings. I remember their arguments into the night with the young Mormon elders siding with my father, pleading, promising, wheedling, praying—eyeing my blossoming body with sincere eyes—I remember the Mormon elders chasing prospective converts over the rooftops and from room to room in their zeal, waving their Book of Mormon and declaiming the truth of their Prophet.

One of my mother and father's greatest fears was the commandment of Polygamy which the Elders openly espoused—no pun meant. The missionaries addressed this most troubling question with open sincerity. Joseph Smith's imagined truth was every bit as powerful as verifiable truth. When it was explained that plural marriage was a necessary condition for women to attain the highest degree of Celestial Glory, I accepted it without question, Glory being preferable to hacking tuberculosis, filth, and hunger. By the time the missionaries ticked off the so-called advantages of plural marriage I, for one, became a true believer. I had never before had something to believe in after leaving our farm. A new truth in a new country is a powerful goad. Land and freedom and truth are why we walked across America without shoes.

It was thus, under pressure too great to bear, that my mother finally relented, surrendered would be more apt, and consented to having the whole family baptized into the church of Jesus Christ of Latter Day Saints. The American Prophet Joseph Smith had reaped another crop of English souls. It was with utter dismay that my mother succumbed, but it seemed to her the last hope for my father and my own future. She too was baptized at the Mouth of the Mersey. When she arose from the foul, freezing water her eyes were haunted, and remained so until the day she died. It was as if she had glimpsed Hell's antechamber.

We sailed on the good ship *Charley Buck*. There were two hundred of us, packed in our own juices and oils, odors and oddities like the silvery sardines from the sea. I was, by that time, a whole member of the faith, for the elders turned out to be kind, and helpful. My father's health was restored—he says by his faith—I say by the Hope alone that was offered. The Perpetual Emigration Fund paid for our passage to Utah. We were the second draft of the handcart pioneers, so called because we were our own draft animals. My father died in the traces near Laramie. My mother was another one of the fifty-seven who also died on that journey. She emptied her insides upon the endless snows, and died of thirst beside an icy stream. She died thinking she was going to Hell as a Mormon, without the benefit of a Priest's last unction, and there was terror in her eyes even as they closed . . .

My poor Catholic mother, dead on the trail these many years, fervently believed in the sin of the blood—that Adam's dalliance and disobedience was ever with us. A sinful state was our birthright, according to her. But Joseph Smith turned that doctrine on its head, which has its attraction. Joseph's message demanded personal responsibility for our own actions. We could not explain sin by laying it off on some dead and distant figure at the dawn of creation. On the other hand, from whence would Man have come had Adam not been tempted beyond all endurance? Woman is not a temptress. She is merely a whole creature to whom knowledge is a very valuable thing. The very nature of man as well as woman was revealed from the first day of creation. Today I know we carry Adam's sin in the deep of our own red liver and to the center of our soft white marrow. I am not a prescient soul, but my life's journey was nothing less than a learning and a relearning of that awful truth.

CHAPTER FIVE

It was December, and I had been in Zion but a few months. John was in Salt Lake City from the south—the Dixie Cotton Mission—as a member of the Legislature. The first time I saw him was at a prayer meeting. As he was a guest in the ward, he had been called upon to deliver the invocation. His blue-gray eyes looked at me directly before he bowed his handsome head, his hair shot with salt, and I felt something in my heart actually move, as if the rooms were being rearranged to accommodate finer furnishings.

At the time I was sealed to Brother Kippen, although I was nothing more than a maid servant, thinking the sealing was a kind of marriage, but it was not. There was never any suggestion of a carnal consummation. I was simply indentured. Brother Kippen invited John to the evening meal and, as I was the cook, I did my best Middleshire cooking, roast beef done just so with a perfectly browned Yorkshire pudding. John sat across the table from me and remarked that I cooked better than his sixth wife, Sophia. My blush could have lit rooms.

A week later John called on me out of the blue, although he had prearranged it with Brother Kippen. We went to the ward dance in his fine surrey with a matched pair of liver-colored geldings. The air was full of frost, and I sat close to him wrapped in a buffalo robe. O, the dance! We whirled the schottische and sedately paced the quadrille. Here was a man handsome as I've ever seen. I was twenty-two years of age, and John was forty-six, and I'd loved him from the moment he finished his prayer. I cannot to this day explain to myself his magnetism, the pull of his being to my being. I was drawn to him with a certainty that locks the heart and stops the breath.

"Are you cold?" he asked me as we drove through the snowy streets of Salt Lake. Stars flamed overhead. O, the fire . . .

"Not really," I said. "I'm still warm from the dancing."

"A pretty girl like you must have no trouble finding a husband," he ventured, looked over the steaming backs of the horses. Earthquakes in the rooms, pictures aslant, furniture tumbling, breathless.

"I am sealed to Brother Kippen," I said, "I'm not sure if I'm married or not." And with that he roared laughter into the night.

"I think you would know if you were," he finally said.

"Is sealing the same as marriage?"

"Technically. Have you ever . . . ?"

"Never in my life," I snapped before he finished his question.

"I meant to ask you if you had ever been south of Salt Lake," he laughed.

"Oh," I said, starlight and cold blueing my crimson face.

"Does Brother Kippen allow suitors then?"

"Yes, he does," I said. "But a girl doesn't take just any chance she gets. I've found none, though, who suit me. Remember that," I said, and looked at him.

"I will remember that," he said, almost shyly, which is a manner not native to the man. I knew he already had a dozen and more wives, but I didn't care. I was well instructed in the truthfulness of the Principle of Polygamy before my family converted in England and then sailed for America on the *Charley Buck*. Polygamy is a revealed truth, a duty, and a necessary ingredient to attain the highest degree of glory.

"With you, it's different though," I quickly amended. I don't know from where the courage came that so emboldened my tongue. "You know that night at meeting? I knew you were the one for me as soon as you started to pray."

Where did I find that conviction, that unbecoming forwardness, I wondered even as I rushed on. "You had such a good voice. Then I opened my eyes and watched you all the time. I wondered how long it would be before you saw me in the audience. I thought you would," I said. "I tried to make you."

"Yes, I saw you but you would never look up again. You knew I was smiling at you, and you wouldn't look up. And when it was over, you ran away."

"I was frightened. I thought you would find me if you really wanted to."

John was silent for a time. The tack jingled on the harness, frost plumed from the nostrils of his fine horses. Some said he had the finest eye for horseflesh in all of Zion. I began to be nervous in his silence, felt the solemnity of the world rest upon the moment.

"There is something you must know about me. I feel that I am a good man. I have stood by the Church in ways that I do not wish to recollect. I believe with all my heart in Joseph Smith and the Book of Mormon. It is an inspired revelation, and the Gospel has been restored to the earth. I will gladly die for the church and its leaders if I am so called upon to make that sacrifice. The suffering we have experienced, driven west, is something I hope the church never forgets, but we must continue to build up Zion. It is to that purpose I have dedicated my life.

"I have a fine family, flocks and fields in the south that've taken me years to build up. It's a hard life down there. The heat of summer turns men and women and beast alike into husks. Three drops of rain we call a deluge. I was sent south as a farmer to the Indians by Brigham himself. But in recent times, I and other members of the church who choose to practice the Principle have been harassed by the federals. In the time of which I speak, the United States and the 'Mericat mobs were gathering to try to destroy Zion. I am pledged even today to defend ourselves, tooth for tooth."

"Of course. I hear the words of the Elders," I said. "I have faith the Church will withstand all persecutions if the past record is of any account. With men like yourself, how can we not withstand any trial the Lord sends?"

"Good, good," he muttered. "There is something else, Miss Emeline Buxton," he said, thwacking reins on the horses' rumps. The streets of Salt Lake City were frozen, the houses dark. I made to move closer to him, and rearranged—like a wife—the buffalo robe over his legs. I was full of hope, holding myself to a still place within where I visit when I wish to hold hope untroubled. I'm not blessed with premonitions as I have learned John to be so endowed. To me, the future is ever a surprise. Dare I? Would he?

"I've a mind to tell you something else," he finally said. "So as you know all."

"Yes?" I asked, untroubled.

"I was at the Mountain Meadows," he said. I was stunned. There was no one in the United States who did not utter those words without a curse upon the perpetrators.

"I understand it was a terrible day," I said. "The blood thirsty savages," I said in ignorance.

"More terrible than you should know, but know you must," he said. "It was not the Indians, finally, who saw the massacre to its completion. Although for bloody work they are unsurpassed. They are refined in their cruelty in ways even I cannot comprehend. Be that as like we—I—had a hand in it from the first. It was to defend ourselves, I thought. It was a deed in which I participated thinking that I was doing the Lord's work. You see the soldiers who walk upon our streets? Well, that year they were here to invade us, to wipe us out. The people in the Fancher train were but harbinger of more to come." He paused again, and drew a deep breath full of the crisp air, and blew it out, as if he were realigning a weight. "There were women and children. It is for them that I suffer. The men be dammed."

"Yes, I know," I said quietly, fearful, bewildered. I grasped for the calm center of the thought of God and his righteousness. "But President Young negotiated us out of the troubles, did he not?"

"Oh, it will never be over," John said. "I mean to make a vow to you, Miss Emma. I shed no blood that day. It is important for you to know that."

"The past makes no difference to me, Mr. Lee," I said. "I long for the future." I was such an ignorant and foolish young woman caught up only in my own desires and dreams. Blood shed in any manner in defense of the truth, I thought at the time, was like a colored water, nothing more.

"As do I, but it may not be as bright as it ought to be. The hope is the government will forget that deed. But the relatives of the slain, the army, the 'Mericats will never forget it. And, were it my own family who lay there on that bloody field, I would thirst for revenge myself. Indeed, I could not rest without vengeance. Do you understand why I am telling you this?

"I hope I don't misunderstand," I said.

With that, John Doyle Lee proposed that I become his 16th wife.

And I accepted with a fullness of heart, and a sincerity of love in which a part of me abides to this day.

"Then we must speak with Brother Brigham," he said decisively.

The next day he called about noon. It was snowing.

"We have an appointment with Brigham Young in an hour," he announced. "Brother Kippen has been informed of my intentions, and he gives his glad consent. He says he will miss you."

Thus it was that I first met Brigham Young. John took me in the buggy to the Lion House near the foundations of the temple. We were escorted into a gloomy office by a fawning clerk. I stood in awe of the man. As he stood I noticed his bulk, sensed in him a power that was not physical, that was not of this earth. Curiously, I sensed no holiness. Just . . . power. He had a round face wreathed with a beard. His chin was bare. He had ox-like features, if I may venture, until one beheld his eyes. They were every bit as penetrating as John's eyes.

Brigham looked me over, and then searched my face for a long time. I saw in his large dark pupils a reflection of myself. I remember seeing in a flicker the image of a shadow passing briefly over his face before he smiled his approval. Whatever it was that caused his unease passed. But I knew he had seen something in me which caused him pain. Here was the man who preached that women were Saints, and treated them like chattel. Here I stood before my destiny.

I did not avert my eyes from his. He did not like that. Brother Brigham had adopted John as a son many years ago in the custom of the early church. Thus it was certain Brigham would accede to John's wishes.

"So, you came with the Martin company, Sister Buxton," he said after we were seated.

"Yes sir," I said, feeling my color rise. John sat with his hat on his knee, handsome in black broadcloth and high leather boots.

"Did you freeze your feet crossing the streams?" he asked. What an odd question, I thought.

"No, sir. I removed my shoes and stockings before I crossed. Then I dried my feet with my woolen neck cloth, and so stayed warm that way. I asked the Dear Lord to help me take care of myself since there was no one to look after me. Mother and Father died crossing the Sweetwater. I promised that if I came through whole I would never complain of my lot." That seemed to satisfy him.

"Your parents' death bestows upon them the glory of remembered martyrs," he said, trying, I suppose, to be comforting. "Their deaths will gain them Heaven. You are sealed to Brother Kippen, I understand," he said. "Have you not complained at that?"

"I was sent to his house to live, and I earned all I got by washing and cooking and ironing and scrubbing," I replied. "I was servant maid to his first wife. I thought that the sealing was as a protection to give me a home, and then I could choose my husband."

"And do you think that you have found the man you want now?" he asked.

"Oh, yes sir," I replied with the whole conviction of truth within me. John was the most handsome, the most gentle man I'd ever known. In our brief courtship I saw that he could be hard, and brusque, but under all lay a caring heart that I came to know was shared willingly with all who loved him. His fire was as young as my fire. I knew this with every chord of my being. In his presence

I felt I had passed from girl to woman. And when I crossed that threshold with him, it was as if our love flamed as brightly as the winter stars.

"You understand the order of this Kingdom," Brigham said. "You understand that John has other wives, and you are willing to take your place among them?"

"Yes sir."

"You fully appreciate that plural marriage is a sacred principle? Your soul is in the balance if you should ever fail John or your sister-wives," Brigham said in a rumbling voice.

"I do, sir," I replied, allowing my gaze to fall to the floor. Odious old man.

He rose and walked from behind his massive desk of dark wood. Then he took my hands in his and said, "Sister Emeline, I bless you in the name of the Lord. You are free from any bonds with any man previous to this hour. You will find Brother Lee a kind husband, who does not expect any one woman to be subservient to another, but each to have her own place as a wife by his side. Be faithful to him through all adversity, and you will find him a pillar of strength to you. Make your preparations, and meet us here at twelve o'clock tomorrow and we will perform the ceremony."

How could I not have initially loved the Prophet, whose blessing became a curse? This Lion of the Lord, emperor of a sagebrush kingdom. Brigham Young gave me my heart's desire with few words. He held the power of life and death among the Saints. He gave and took of both freely. May he still be alive in Hell so black ravens may roost on his eyes.

We left Salt Lake City the next day and drove south along the snowy road, the wagon piled high with goods for his farm and family at my new home in Harmony. John always brought his wives some notion or article or implement which they had their heart set on. I remember the wagon had an iron stove in it, and window glass, bolts of cloth, kegs of nails, button shoes, rolls of ribbon, a used violin for one of the younger girls, and dozens of shovels and hoes for the Indians.

The road to the south of Utah is a bleak and brushy prospect. But my curiosity and my excitement to be traveling toward a new life kept me chattering like the jays in the stands of junipers through which we drove. My schooling was inadequate, and my understanding of Joseph Smith's theology abysmal. I meant to remedy that, so as to be John's equal in all things, and had many questions. John was well known for his dreams and visions, and his ability to heal with the touch of his hands. He was a leader from the early days and had learned the ways of the Lord at the very knee of the Prophet, so to speak. There was no better teacher.

So I availed myself of the opportunity to begin to learn all I could before Salt Lake was out of sight. Truth to tell, it was my wedding night, and I asked weighty questions to keep my mind off what was going to happen to me. I was not sure at all how a man and a woman made a baby—but was willing to find out. Talking with John was easy as we drove along in the warmth of the buffalo robe.

"I am unschooled, sir," I said. "Will I go to hell because my mother was a Catholic in her heart?" At this, he laughed heartily.

"Not likely," he said. "When did she pass on?"

"I was orphaned on the trail in Wyoming. Father went first, but he was sick before we left England. His new faith carried him farther than I thought possible. He was just happy to die in America, I think. I know he died sure in the knowledge of the Lord. My mother converted with the rest of the family, but I confess I believe she died a Catholic in her heart. She called for a priest even as she froze to death. Will I go to hell for that?"

"No, my dear girl, when we pass on to the other side, the unbelievers will all have the opportunity to receive the revealed truth of Joseph Smith, and if they accept it they will be all right."

"I see," I said. It was a small comfort.

"Will I see her again?"

"Of course, and all your family."

"And we'll be Mormons?"

"Of course."

"As I said, I'm unschooled."

"Life's enhanced by a knowledge of the scriptures. All the mistakes that were ever made are writ in the Bible—not that mankind's ever learned from them. Now that God has found you, he'll teach you, and I'll help, if you'll allow it."

"I'll study hard," I vowed. We rode farther into the deepening of the dusk.

Far off the hills rose before us in a gentle white undulation. We had to stop soon for the night in a place of wood and water. Would it happen then? Would he take off my clothing? I tingled not from cold, but from anticipation. I also shook inside at the fear of it. I was told there would be great pain by Sister Kippen. I was told it was a nasty chore.

"John," I asked, to forestall the setting sun. "How can we be baptized for the dead? What if the dead don't want to be Mormons?" John's amusement was tempered with the seriousness of my questions.

"It's an opportunity for lost souls to become members of the true faith," he said. "All of our ancestors, lost in the darkness of the Apostate church, will be received by the Lord if one of their living relatives is baptized vicariously for them."

"But what if they don't want to be Mormons after they're dead?" I asked.

"As they'll be in heaven, I expect they'll be grateful, looking at the suffering of others." That didn't satisfy me at all. I thought it a curious practice—still do. It's a presumption and an arrogance and an insult to other faiths, but it was getting time to stop for the night in the snowy woods. I'd vaguely imagined a small hotel, a warm bed, and perhaps a glass of wine to be appropriate for a man and wife on their wedding night. Instead we stopped the team just as the stars were coming out, and were quite alone except for the howling of the wolves.

My husband was so very solicitous to me that night, caring for my warmth. I figured his attentions would not be a permanent condition. All of the women in Brother Kippen's house said once the honeymoon was over, your life was over. But years later John was still the same caring man. When we arrived at the place to build the ferry he was still solicitous, and tender, bringing buckets of cold water for me and Elizabeth. He drove himself to care for his family all his life. During the first days on the Colorado he hung wet sheets for shade, and piled rock upon rock for a house under the brutal sun so we could have relief from the harsh heat and cold. Even in our exile he loved me.

I remember he made a clever tent under the wagon that night, and built a fire so its heat made it warm as a house inside. He even cooked for me, as he always did on the trail when he had the time. We lay with our heads near the entrance under a pile of warm quilts with the buffalo robe spread on the ground. Overhead the stars and planets were so sharp and clear they were touchable, silent lamps observing my first loving of a man.

I can bear the cold better than the heat. I was naked next to him. I was not embarrassed with John, ever. Beneath all the turmoil in his heart, he held out for me a place of calm until the very end. A small place amidst the turbulence which he caused me, but overall there was always that place we shared without touch or word.

So for the first time in my life I lay with a man without clothing. And it was so sweet to feel his hands as they slowly swept up and down my body, giving me chills and a fire's heat not of this earth. It was unlike anything I had ever dreamed. The strength of him made me tremble, the hardness within me an impelling search for my center. Sparks arced from our fingertips. God surely knew what he was doing when he made the sexes. There's no stopping it, and as children are the purpose of this happy pursuit, it was always a blessing to me, and never a duty. So he took my breasts in his mouth, all the while tenderly holding me to the frozen ground, and at that instant it set off an incandescence that put the stars to shame, and ever afterward he knew, he knew when to nip my breasts and the stars flew down to me and blinded me and I cried out for the wonder of the experience.

Afterward, more peace than I have ever known. We lay and looked upwards, and he told me he often dreamed of being on the stars.

"We shall be a God with our own planet," he said. "I intend for my rule to be benevolent, if God thinks I am worthy to have a planet of my own. You know of that promise don't you, have you learned it?"

"I don't know what you mean," I said.

"The missionary effort seems to be weak, if they didn't tell you of that," he grumbled. "I must mention it to Brigham. It's crucial.

'God is as man once was, and man shall be as God once was,' he said.

"What? We are to be Gods?"

"And Goddesses. If we live a dutiful life, and keep all of the ordinances, and fulfill our obligations, we are promised the Celestial kingdom. It will be wonderful. And God will give the faithful planets of their own to rule. It will be a joy like nothing we experience on this earth."

"That is hard to believe," I said doubtfully in my after-glowing.

"I'm subject to many dreams," he said. "Many of them so dark as I cannot speak of them. But at other times, I see us there, all of us in heaven—Aggatha and Merry Berry and Polly Bean and sweet Rachel and all of our fine children . . . God puts us to hard tests, but in the end it will be worth it," he said with conviction. "I'll point out the relevant scriptures to you from the Book of Mormon."

"I look forward to that," I said, not meaning it. I was looking forward to something else, and by dawn I was not disappointed.

CHAPTER SIX

Waiting for word from John was agonizing. Beside any news of his safety, we had no food except that which came from the struggling garden and the small game the boys were able to shoot. We had not tasted sugar for months. John was going to bring back a load of lumber so we could start on the ranch buildings. There was never any suggestion that the children and I, or Rachel and her children accompany him.

About four weeks after he left, Rachel Andorra walked down from the Pools Ranch up on the desolate Paria, and we had a visit. I hadn't seen her for two months. If my face mirrored Rachel's face, we had aged frighteningly since we came from the settlements to the Lonely Dell. Sitting with Rachel, her blunt face burnt black by the sun, gray hair long and unkempt, I had the memory, like a sharp thorn, of our paradise in Harmony back in the sixties before the flood, and the persecutions.

Rachel and I played a cruel game with ourselves on her rare visits. Despite the ache it would cause us, we brewed nostalgia with our cup of tea, and regretted it later. Living in the memory is a cruel pastime. Rachel did not look well, and appeared to be coming on with the flux. She mentioned her children had sniffling noses and flighty temperatures. Rachel was firm in her conviction that we would someday return to Harmony to reclaim our homes and land. It was impossible, of course, but I could not say it, and John had never held out that hope to any of us. But she still believed it would come to pass. Looking at her I bitterly remembered the beginning of the end. The first inkling of our future was brought to Harmony by none other than Brigham Young himself. Seeing Rachel always set off in me uncomfortable reflections.

When you are in the presence of the Living Prophet of God, you don't tell him he has bread crumbs in his beard. I had to bite my lip to keep from pointing out the fact. The Lion of the Lord looked, more or less, like a disheveled sack of corn, and little of God's light was leaking from his eyes, or pouring from his lips as he sat in our little dirt-floored parlor at Harmony. When Brigham Young performed the marriage ceremony between John D. Lee and Emeline Buxton, he cut a finer figure of a man, but his brusque, impatient manner was the same. Our visitor from Hell was now in the next room, we women having been banished from his presence so he could get on with the work of destroying my husband's very soul. And as God is my witness, he brought the rains with a succeeding visit which forty days later washed our home at Harmony off the map.

It was a brief visit. His retinue of sycophants and favor seekers had gone ahead to Washington City, but his armed escort was bivouacked nearby in the cottonwoods along Ash Creek. That morning a rider had come ahead from Cedar City to announce Brigham Young's intention to stop off at Harmony before continuing on to inspect the Cotton Mission. When the Governor of the Utah Territory, the Indian Commissioner, and the President of the Church of Jesus Christ of Latter Day Saints all rolled in to one wishes to visit, I can assure you the dust flies and the linens are washed clean enough for angel's robes.

We were waiting by order of seniority in front of the odd collection of adobe walls, small orange brick houses and truncated wooden outbuildings that comprised our little settlement. I still felt a tether to Salt Lake City, and England for that matter, but for love here I stood on the red packed earth and awaited His Arrival. We are like a line of cattle, I thought, waiting to have our teeth inspected and our teats pulled. As I was the tallest, and the newest of John's fifteen wives, I was at the end of the line which made a jagged prospect of different heights as we waited in our best dresses under an early evening sky sweet as God's breath.

His carriage drew up in a dust cloud, yellowing the light, and then he alighted with a distinct groaning of steel springs. John looked to be fairly bursting with pride at the appearance of Brigham Young, at his line of wives, his droves of children who hid behind the skirts of the women with mixed sounds of titter and giggle. I, for one, was not awed as Brigham commenced a rapid greeting down the reception line. Aggatha, at the head of the line, face like a twisted sock, nearly collapsed with awe and pleasure, and so on the same reaction from each of the other women as he greeted them. He seemed to remember a few of the wives' names, which brought swooning delight, but when he came to me, and took my small hand in his massive paw I could see by the look in his eyes he had no more recollection of marrying me than he would have recognized a woman on the face of the moon.

When there are visits by people of importance, I've noticed the real party takes place at the periphery—amongst the groundlings, so to speak. I noticed that our plain finery was accented by the high color of rare beef on the cheeks of some of the sister-wives. Brigham's visit was no different. Aggatha and Rachel bustled to lay on a groaning board of food for the Prophet, while we lesser lights circled about his majestic presence like moths to the flame. The unexpected holiday brought laughter from the children at the special food served to them in another room.

After the Prophet and John were closeted to take care of the important business of men, we knew the party would continue without the restraint of Brigham's severe visage. Had I known the business at hand, even then, I might have taken a knife to the man's throat, right after I throttled my own dear husband for his meek submission.

After we trooped into the largest room in the fort, one with a wooden floor, we all sat down and waited for the Prophet to pray. In the coolish air the dishes of corn and beans steamed. A mound of mashed potatoes awaited his spoon. Aggatha's old sharp eyes kept us rooted to our seats down the long wooden table as we awaited the Prophet's selection of the food.

Aggatha was John's very first wife. She had aged ten years to his one, by my lights. I once asked Rachel about the bitter line of Aggatha's attitude, and she hushed me. "When you get to know us better, you'll learn our lives have not been so easy." I was learning, bit by bit, about my new family, and so far had mixed feelings. I also noticed, with a sense of growing disquietude, that each and every one of John D. Lee's wives seemed to carry some weight, some heavy and invisible dark drapery. I sensed that the burden or the bitterness or the fear was not necessarily directed toward their husband, but at some larger matter, the horror of which was to remain hidden from me for a long time. I noticed at odd times they would pause in their work, and stare bleakly at nothing before they collected themselves, and resumed the knitting and spinning and churning and washing. Even John's eyes, in our lightest moments together, naked as jaybirds, would suddenly cloud and dim until no light was left in him. It gave me an utter chill when that happened, and remained a mystery. The words Mountain Meadows never once slipped from their lips in my presence all those years at Harmony until the end.

Would he choose Polly's pickled beets, or Rachel's special apple butter? One of Louisa's leaden biscuits, or Sister Vilate's fat-back bacon. It was all before him to choose, and more. Ann Marie, ever the little scribe, sat with a tablet on her lap and wet the tip of a lead pencil with her pink tongue, leaving a black smear on her upper lip. I remember nothing of his prayer over the food, nor did I feel it tasted any better after he was done.

"I'm tired," the Prophet said to our astonishment, looking at our proud bounty. "I think I'll just have milk and mush, a word with Brother Lee, and be on my way."

Well, the insult was never forgotten. Old Aggatha, never known for her reticence to correct bad manners, said, "Sir, we have spent hours in the preparation of this food. You'll eat it, or leave."

John turned purple, then white. John's pride in his long service of Brigham Young he wore on his sleeve like a badge. He worshipped the man. We had noticed that Aggatha was getting buggy in the head lately, and her instructions to Brigham Young to eat her meal or leave was final proof.

"Aggatha!" John said with quiet alarm. "Please Aggie," he said. "I do apologize for her rudeness, sir. The cares of the past weigh heavily upon her at times. The hot sun . . . " he murmured vaguely. "Perhaps a lie-down, my dear." Rarely was John D. Lee ever embarrassed the way Aggatha embarrassed him that evening, but it was soon forgotten.

"Oh, no, let her stay, please Brother Lee," Brigham said. "Aggatha and I have known each other long enough so her correction of my manners is quite proper. It is I who should apologize."

"Aggie, forgive me for my sharpness. You have laid on a fine table," John said. "Please stay."

"I'm sorry, sir," Aggatha said, as if just realizing that she had not rebuked one of the children.

"No, forgive me, Ma'am," Brigham said expansively. "It's a fine spread of food, and evidence of the Lord's bounty and your family's industry. Sister Lee," Brigham said in his baritone which carried as if he were speaking through a trumpet, "it's just that the journey's put me off my feed. I apologize."

John still was a hue of many colors, but evidently the Prophet had taken no offense. He was not a master politician for nothing. "But if you would be so kind as to put up some of those beans and greens, I'll take them with me, and savor them like I savor the memory of you and your kind hospitality." Aggatha was not buggy enough not to be flattered right down to the ground by his smooth words, and soon all was well. Brigham did finally rouse himself enough to take a slab of beef the size of a shoe after he finished his milk and mush.

Brigham loved to laugh and dance it was told, but that night I saw no sign of a lighter side to his nature. The meal was quickly cleared, the children banished, the young men sent to the last of the chores, and we sat in the room by the light of fire and candles while Brigham picked his teeth, and John sat nearby beaming with pleasure at the comfortable little scene. He had no inkling of what was to come, and so was in the mood to dare suggest a glass of wine made from our very own young grapes.

"I doubt a little taste of spirits will kill me," Brigham said as John poured us all a thimble of the purple wine. He raised the glass to the low light, turned the little glass in his thick fingers, and brought it to his lips. Everyone but me, it seemed, held their breath for his pronouncement. "By Heaven, it's good," he said, bringing smiles and raised arms as we sampled the wine, not expecting it to be any other thing but good. He had said so. It was thin, and bitter, to my taste, but what did I know about wine? It was the second glass I had ever taken in my life.

"It reminds me of the vintage we raised in '45 in Illinois, Brother Lee," Brigham said. "Aggatha and Rachel must remember that vintage," he said, looking at Aggie and Rachel who sat nearest him on ladder back chairs. They were both bewildered. I doubt they had ever taken more than a glass of wine in their lives themselves.

"I do not remember the wine, sir," Rachel said, "But I do remember the fine brick homes." I almost knew what she wanted to add. Rachel was sharp with a penny, under John's tutelage. Nickels squeaked when a Lee parted with one. She told me that John was a wealthy man in Nauvoo, Illinois, before the mobs came over from Missouri. Millions of dollars of property was abandoned by the Saints without a penny of compensation from those who moved into them while the ovens were still warm.

There was no gauging the depth of my new family's enmity toward the people of the United States. The powers back east thought we were in a state of rebellion because we refused to take orders from corrupt anti-Mormon judges. They viewed us as a licentious people because of our obedience to the Holy Commandment of Polygamy. An army had recently occupied the Salt Lake Valley to tell us how to worship. Everyone knew it was possible for us to be driven again into the wastes of the Great Desert. But a young woman in love cares not for wars, or rumors of wars. I had much to learn.

"And I remember nothing but blood and mobs." Aggatha's outburst suddenly extinguished the easy lightness of the evening.

Brigham's arrival had affected her profoundly for some reason, had overturned the rocks in her memory. Her words stripped any veneer of happiness from the assembly as if a cold wind had torn off the door and swept the heat right up the chimney. As a newcomer, I did not then realize the depth of the sacrifice these people had made in the service of their God, and of Brigham.

"Yes," Brigham said somberly. "It has been a long, and trying trail to the Kingdom. But we are still here, are we not Sister? And stronger than ever." I looked at my husband, still perplexed at the odd turn the evening was taking. It was not like him to be so quiet, as if he had a vision of what was to come.

"I would propose a toast," John said, raising his glass. God, he was a handsome man, his hair shot with steel gray, his eyes grayer still as they reflected the firelight like glazed windows. I thought John's bearing and assurance as great as that of any Prophet old or new.

"To Brigham Young, a truer man never lived," he pronounced. "May he bless this family." Oh, the irony. I came to find Brigham Young's blessings a curse, his prayers a blasphemy, and his advice to John so self-serving as to sicken me when as I listened to it pour out of him like oil from the flask.

"Hear, hear," we murmured. In the moment I believed and agreed to the toast, and drank the thin wine with gratitude for having found myself at last a home in the everlasting bosom of Zion.

With a nod from his head and a smile, John made it known that we all were to retire. I left the table for my house which was still unfinished, and the others went to their own, some fine, some not so fine depending upon the materials available at the time of their raising. Polly Bean looked quite put out at our dismissal. Ann Marie's lips were black from the lead of the pencil as she recorded Brigham's prophetic utterance, "Good mush."

Obediantly, I rose to leave.

John said, "I think we shall hold our discussion at your home, Miss Emma. Would you please put on the tea, and then I think it best that you retire."

I tried to read John's eyes, and saw hidden messages. John knew there would be little privacy in a two-and-a-half room house, but Brigham seemed unaware of John's purpose in moving their meeting. My heart was a leap of confusion. Why should I be privy to these matters, the newest and least senior of the women among his family? True enough, I felt that John loved me as fiercely as I loved him, but an outsider would never guess it by his treatment of his wives. They all loved him—to one degree or other—and he treated them with the utmost respect, and as equally as possible.

As I left and walked along outside Fort Harmony's thick adobe walls they gave me the feeling of stability, of protection and of shelter. I missed my mother and father terribly. I still do. Four months after the night of the Prophet's hasty departure the rains began, but we had seen a flaming sunset, and eaten fine food, and had a Prophet in our midst, so what did we care about the weather?

It was apparent from the day of my arrival that Aggatha and Rachel and Louisa got favored treatment along the lines of seniority—better houses, clothes, and the choicest meats and vegetables from the fields and farm, but who could quarrel with that? Our religion is an earning religion. If you don't deserve, you don't get—either salvation or bread. As Brigham said to me at the time of my first interview with him to determine my marital status, "You do understand the order of the Kingdom?" To which I replied I surely did. Better shared love that a stroke of lightning and eternal loneliness, glazed windows notwithstanding

I heard the heavy tread of feet as the two men came into the house with the dirt floor and sacking for windows. Glazed windows and a wooden floor were some years away for me, I knew, but could not complain. Leaving Salt Lake City on the arm of the man I loved was enough for me. The rest of it was just plain living.

Before I retired I had set a small fire blazing in the stone fireplace, and had a pot of water in the coals. I also had brought from the large kitchen several platters of cold food, bread and jam in case the Prophet's appetite returned. I heard John making the tea, and then sitting. I tried to put the corn shuck pillow over my ears. Every movement I made in bed caused a rustling sound, as if mice were racing about, so I lay utterly still, and listened with eyes wide open to the night. I had drawn aside the sacking curtains, and the stars' cold glitter reflected off the small gold band I wore on my finger, and off the face of the glass which covered the portrait of John D. Lee and Emeline Buxton on their wedding day.

It was a father and son who sat before my fire that evening. In the manner of the olden times, Brigham had adopted John as a son years ago, and for years had treated him as such. It was a custom of our peculiar church, and it was practical—the more sons, the more the resources. Bound by love and faith, these arrangements moved mountains, moved a whole people across the plains of the country in an Exodus not seen since Egypt. It was an orderly march to Zion, with John and Brigham and all of the other Elders in the van. And they went singing into the wilderness!

Having walked much of it myself, I knew a little of their suffering, and could only wonder at the strength of their faith. They were walking into the unknown, whereas I was walking into a known and settled circumstance where we were promised shelter and an end to our journey. I sometimes think that we who followed were made of lesser stuff. Our motives were less pure, those of the wish for a better life over that of a burning desire for freedom. And we were not driven by mobs, but, perhaps, by less fearful desires—land, comfort, hope . . .

And lest I ever forget, it was Brigham Young who, by the sheer force of his personality, his formidable physical strength, and his indomitable will had carved this empire out of a savage wilderness. It was the Prophet Joseph Smith's vision which brought to the world the Restored Gospel, but it was Brigham Young who made it a reality. The Indians, some of whom were even that night camped nearby, were not savages, they were overwhelmed by smoking gunpowder, disease, and sheer numbers. I was the newcomer in their midst. So very much to learn.

"Do you remember the battle of Crooked River?" I heard Brigham ask John. I could hear them clearly, even the pace of their breathing, the snap of the juniper on the fire.

"I do," John replied, and I heard the puzzlement in his voice. "They took my sword," he said. "Burned my house." I had to see their faces. Words were not enough. With men words usually have to be taken at their value, there is little underpinning. But with

Brigham Young, I suspected, there was always a more subtle text, a motive which belied other motives which hid even further motives. The man, as blunt and direct as an ox, was ever sly as a fox. His only counselor being God, Brigham's purposes were often as obscure as God's own.

I must see their faces, or lose their meaning. I slipped from the bed as silently as I could and drew the quilt around my shoulders, and pressed my eye against a gaping crack in the new board wall. Until that night I never realized the extent to which my husband bent to another man's will. But then he bent again, I think, in a Meadow in Zion. These facts, however, lay over the horizon just as had the threat of Johnston's army which in no small part precipitated the horrible killing.

"You've built up a fine place, Brother Lee, a fine family," Brigham rumbled, the teacup in his paw perfectly balanced.

"Oh, yes," John exclaimed with delight at the compliment. "It's been hard work, but the rewards have been great, as God has promised.

"And what of your plans?" Brigham asked innocently.

"Why, my head is full of plans!" John declared. His enthusiasm was not that of a fifty-year-old man, but the dreams of a twenty-year-old boy just setting himself up in life. "There is the molasses mill which will have steel drums, and I'm building a large stone grist mill in Washington City itself," he said. "Right next to the large stone house that will go up at the same time as the mill. Some of my boys are going to trade horses as far away as Arizona we've got so many. I've developed a recipe for peach preserves in rum and molasses that I can't make fast enough. People drive for miles for a crock of it. The dairy herd on Pine Valley mountain is prospering. Half the young boys spend the entire summer with the herd, milking it, and then bringing the milk down where my wives turn it into butter, cheese, oh, it's wonderful stuff. The cheeses are yellow as the moon! I've a big enough family for a school, and am hiring a teacher. I've bought six lots in Cedar City and a shingle factory . . . "

Hearing this catalogue astonished me. John was a man with an indefatigable industry, with the additional gift of a golden touch.

I realized for the first time that he was relatively wealthy.

"I'm sure that's all well and good," Brigham said, conveying small admiration. I could see his face was set. And sad, for some reason. John's face fell with disappointment that Brigham seemed unimpressed, unenthused. "I'm pleased for you," he said, and sipped his tea. "But I've news for you that is not quite so pleasant, nor does it bode well for your prospects."

"Whatever do you mean?"

"Judge Cradelbaugh, some army officers, and other federal officials are on their way south with warrants for your arrest, and the arrest of others."

"No, President Buchanan's pardon!" John said.

"That is a fiction, and you know it," Brigham said irritably. "It's a general document which forgives our hit and run war against the approach of Johnston's army. That we choose to interpret it so it exonerates you and the others will never stand. They will not let it rest, John, and are going to smear the Church until the end of time if they are not satisfied that some justice has been done."

"I see," John said quietly, looking at his hands. His face then had just the beginnings of the furrows of time in them, and in the shadows they deepened into canyons. He bowed his head momentarily, and raised it. "May God forgive me," I heard him murmur.

"God will forgive you. But that will not satisfy the government. And in order to protect the Church, there are some things which I must do that pain me greatly, dear Brother."

"I'll do anything you ask, of course," John said. He regained his composure. I saw the light glance off his eyes in profile.

"Certain other facts have come to light over the past few months. With that, Brigham produced a paper and handed it to John who read it swiftly, and aloud:

Parowan
August 12, 1858
We have carefully and patiently investigated the complaints made against President William H. Dame, for four successive days, and are fully satisfied that his actions as a Saint and administration as a President have been characterized by the

right spirit; and that the complaints presented before us are without foundation in truth.

"This is a God-damned travesty!" John declared.

"Don't YOU DARE blaspheme the Lord in my presence!" Brigham said forcefully.

"Forgive me that, but I'll speak as I like against this lie. Whoever heard that Colonel Dame is innocent? He gave the damn orders sir, he gave the damn orders!" John suddenly changed before my eyes from dutiful son into an angry equal. "Look at these signatures. Traitors! Half of the men who signed this were there that day. They know this is a lie. They were in blood up to their knees!"

"That's not the way I understand it," Brigham said coldly.

"What do you mean? I told you every last detail of the massacre in the very first report I gave you to your own face. I rode day and night to bring you the truth from the beginning. It was a massacre, sir, a massacre! Or was it you who gave the orders to Colonel Dame?"

The accusation bled Brigham's face white. He rose to his feet and roared until it shook the board walls.

"How dare you accuse me of that?" he shouted. "I had nothing to do with it."

"But you sent George A. Smith to the settlements to spread such hatred and poison we were ready to believe anything about the emigrants. His words were your words!"

For a moment I thought the two men would come to blows. I shrank back, frozen within. This was the moment when the two men began their irrevocable breaking away from one another. There was a long moment of breathing silence, and I dared to look again. To be a master of men, one must first master oneself. Brigham was laying his head in his arms on the stone mantel. John stood looking at his broad back with his fists clenched. With a great effort Brigham raised his head and turned, now fully composed, although his face was scarlet under the grey-white beard. The two men looked at one another for endless moments until I sensed a softening, a truce. The shared memory of the past held them together for a season longer.

"Sit down, son," Brigham said wearily. "I will forget you ever said that. You are forgiven." I thought John was about to make a retort, and thought to myself, "shut up John Lee. You can't talk to a Prophet like that."

"My duty in this affair has always been to cover up any involvement in the massacre by members of the church leadership. It will ruin us—statehood, peace, everything. I will continue to cover it up until Hell itself freezes over if it will protect the name of the church," Brigham said. I wondered how John dared to face the Prophet's wrath, for his voice was deep as doom. "There are other facts. That affidavit, for instance. Jacob Hamblin's testimony. Others . . .

Jacob Hamblin?" John asked incredulously. "He was two hundred miles away.

What other facts?" John asked, trying now to calm himself. "For this group of men to exonerate Colonel Dame only means that they've been lied to. For the love of Heaven!"

"Don't speak aloud again of that horrible day. I cannot reveal other knowledge, or the source of it to you," Brigham said imperiously. At this John was on his feet, tearing the paper into shreds and then casting it into the fire. Brigham was restraining himself while John stormed around the room.

"There is no other source of knowledge. I was there! Treachery, sir. Calumny and treachery," he said over and over again. "My brothers have betrayed me to save themselves."

"I came as a friend to give you warning, Brother Lee," he said. "If I were you I would make myself scarce until they get tired and leave. You'll be all right when they go back north."

"You came as a friend, but not a father," John said, trying to hide scorn.

"You tread on ice, sir," Brigham rumbled. "I'm going to order the Stake Presidents to relieve you of any of your church responsibilities, and have the district withdraw your judgeship."

John turned away from Brigham, and faced me. It was terrible. The pain on my husband's face looked enough to break him. "I think I'm beginning to see. The others have turned against me, and now they've poisoned your mind toward me. They will lay the entire affair at my feet."

Brigham's reply was silence. Massacre? I was terribly frightened, and wished I could stop my ears and eyes. I'd never seen John so agitated. Calm and steady and cheerful was ever my husband until that night. And of course I was blind that night to the agony he had already suffered for his part in it. I would not know the truth for a long time, but it was so naive of me not to realize that it was the weight of the Mountain Meadows that he and his family would carry to the grave. Nor could I have guessed that I would join their dark processional.

"No, they have not poisoned my mind toward you," Brigham said in a low, even kind voice. "You will always be my son and strong right arm. We'll get it sorted out someday. The government is always our enemy. They have never protected our interests. But I must see to the face of the church if we are to survive in this country. That is my only duty. I mean to see Zion thrive and survive, John. And I may have to do some things you might not understand. Thus, by relieving you of your public duties, there will be less of a . . . reminder. Stay close to your home, and be prepared to leave at an instant's notice. There are a pack of new anti-polygamy bills in the hopper in Washington, and the federal officials in Salt Lake are already trying to impose their will upon us. I have to play the game, John."

"And I'm the pawn."

"No more than I."

"God, that we had stayed our hand, that awful day," John groaned, hiding his head in his hands. I felt queerly ashamed of him for an instant. Don't bow to this man, I thought, whatever may be the matter. He's bluff and blow, as far as I can tell, Prophet or no. Even then my ignorance was willful. I spun dreams instead of plans. Silly dreams of children and glazed windows, fancy balls in Washington City and long slow winter evenings with a fire in both the heart and hearth. I had allowed myself to think I'd found heaven in Harmony with my husband, when even at that early date I was approaching the gates of Hell. And Brigham Young was the gatekeeper. "I understand," he said finally. "What would you have me do?"

"Keep yourself out of sight. Rein in your industry. Be ready to flee if it comes to that. Judge Cradelbaugh will have a pack of coyote sheriffs with him, so I advise you to take to the hills."

"They can never find me, certain enough," John agreed. "But I feel like such a coward," he said.

"You are one of the bravest of the Saints, John Lee. I'll expect nothing less from you in the future."

"I will submit to your will," John said. "Pray for me."

"God's will, brother, God's will. I will leave now, and I recommend you do the same. My scouts tell me the federals will be in Beaver by the morning." Brigham rose, his shadow looming on the wall like a giant's shadow. John, a middling large man, was dwarfed by him. "Please convey my thanks to your family for the meal. Prepare yourself, John Lee, for I fear this may just be the beginning of your trials. This I prophesy."

And with that bitter prophecy he opened the door, called for his guard and buggy, and rode off into the night. I can't say we weren't warned. And there is this. John Lee came to my bed trembling, shucking his clothes in the wan light, his white skin gleaming. He came to me not out of a need for my body, but for the solace that a woman's body can give. His love was tender, sorrowful, and sweet. Afterward I kept waiting for him to speak, to confide in me. To abide in me. But he never afterward spoke of the conversation, nor did I ever ask him. He knew I had heard every word. Thus I spent a sleepless night wondering if my new husband had brought bloody hands to my body, but dared not ask. And in my silence, the war within my heart began its long, slow march. And within my within was growing our first child, but I had no heart to tell him.

CHAPTER SEVEN

I t's not home yet, is it?" I said to Rachel, coming back, aware of the empty green river. There was neither bird nor twirling leaf, wind nor cloud to register upon the timeless sense of the place.

"Do you remember, before the rains flooded us out, how many men we had working for us?" Rachel asked as we sat in the rock house that had most of a shingle roof by John's indefatigable industry, and my turning the shingle machine until my hands bled.

"Ten?" I ventured.

"Exactly," she said, her eyes turned inward. Try as I might, I was irresistibly drawn into the hopeless game.

"And the horses, at least a hundred," I mused, seeing them in the softness of the mind's eye. Funny, I thought, how our present need prompts memories of things once taken as unremarkable. "And cattle fat and sleek, and bacon pigs and figs from our own trees. We had flour then by the hundred weight," I said. I was hungry. If John was not returned within a fortnight we should have to butcher an old beef. Rachel would agree in an instant, and John would not upbraid us. Still, we must hold out as long as we could. The killing of a beef would set us back against the coming years.

"And yellow butter, and cheese," I said wistfully.

"Raspberry jam and strawberry tarts."

"Peaches and ripe melons."

"Hand-turned ice cream. Please," Rachel said, "you're making me hungry." She said it in a light voice, but her square face had hollow cheeks.

I poured her another cup of ephedra, or Mormon tea, for stimulation. But even that heart-pounding brew did not change our melancholia. I tried to change the direction of our ruminations, and for a time we spoke idly of the garden crisping in the sun.

As we sat in the long afternoon the usual high thunderheads began to form. Both of us fearfully, unconsciously looked at the boiling sky. A distant flash of lightning turned both of our faces to a parchment.

"And then it was all gone," she whispered suddenly, violently.

"Whatever do you mean?" I asked. Although I knew what she meant.

"The rains," she said. "Then Brigham brought the rains. It was Brigham who brought the deluge. The ice cream ran in the ditches."

It haunts her still. It haunts me to this day. Whether or not Brigham was responsible I'll leave to God, but it was ironic that the winter rains were late, and did not begin until first light on Christmas Eve that year. And welcome they were.

Harmony sat a thousand feet higher than the Rio Virgin valley to the south, and we expected snow to follow the rain at that altitude. I remember the beginning of the rains because John had spent the night with me, and we lay together under the warm quilts listening to the first pocks on the shingle roof, like little hollow bullets.

"May turn to snow later," John said. "Will make for a cleaner Christmas." He rose after kissing me lightly on the forehead, went to the window in his nightshirt and rubbed our breath from it with his hand. The glass squeaked.

"Uhmm," I replied, still in the warm bed.

"We'll have a wonderful celebration tonight and tomorrow," he said, and I heard doubt in his voice.

"What is it, John?" I asked.

He studied the gray sky for a long time. "The Lord is telling me something," he said, "but I can't make it out." By now I was used to John's dreams, premonitions and prophecies, most of which came to nothing. He could see other's futures, but could never see his own. "When this lets up I'm going to move Teresa Wright and her family out of the fort and into the house in Washington."

"She won't like that," I said. "Ugh, the spiders in that fort. Teresa has five children now, I guess it's time she has a proper house," I needled.

"She'd have had a proper house long ago if that is what she wanted," John said, a little on the defensive. "But she likes living in the adobe. Says the climate is even,"

"And dusty."

"Her looms require a great deal of space. She's a wonderful woman, Em. I think she's made most of the cloth we wear and the carpets we walk on."

"She is skilled," I said. "And I like her. I just don't like the idea of living in the earth like a mole."

"I no longer fancy it myself."

"She's pregnant again."

"Yes," he said. "Another blessing. Aggatha will have to live with you for a time after Teresa is moved to Washington," he said absently. "I'm going to tear that place down in the spring. Tear down the old. Did you know that Brigham himself gave me the specifications for the fort?"

I didn't know, and surely didn't care.

"I remember the day we paced it off together. I was for putting up wooden walls, but Brigham insisted on adobes. I told him we didn't have enough straw to make good adobes, but he would have nothing less, and so we built it as it stands."

"It's impressive," I said. I hated the place, but had never really had to live in it for long. The interior and exterior walls of the fort were the back walls of a sprawling collection of rooms where they lived long before I came to Harmony.

"Aggatha will not wish to leave those walls," I said. "Poor dear. She'll refuse to leave the fort until the day she dies."

"Yes," he said, preoccupied. Then he brightened. "Son Richard and his family will be here by noon I hope. All of my family together for the first time in who knows how many years except for the boys at works in the fields of the Lord." By that he was referring to his three elder sons in the missionary field, two of whom were in England—still a fertile ground for sowing the seeds of the new faith.

"A good soaking rain and a foot of snow will be a blessing come spring," he observed. "Let us pray the day," he said. I slipped out of bed to my knees, and he knelt beside me, as was our custom, and John gave a brief prayer of thanksgiving, then we were up to start the day's work. Work on the Lee place was portioned out, each to his abilities, and the storm clouds of Brigham's visit were still below the rim of our lives.

The Christmas celebrations were large and festive. Each household had been assigned a specific meal and item of food for the Christmas day supper to be held in the large communal rooms of the fort. One of the boys had shot a large deer, and it was my task to cook the venison, but we had slaughtered a fatted calf, a pig, chickens, a turkey and a goose. This year there was plenty of food, and all but three of the families were in some sort of permanent house along Ash Creek or on a rise behind the thick walls of the fort. John has worked all year on his peach preserves, a thick concoction of molasses, peaches, sugar and rum for which he was famous. This year there was enough for a taste to each man, woman, and child at Harmony after the Christmas feast.

The Lee family was large enough to sport its own band and choir, so a Christmas program was planned, and afterward a great dance was to be held. People from up and down the country were coming for the festivities. The falling rain that day did nothing to drench our spirits, but what had started as a gentle morning rain through the day steadied into a gully-washer.

Christmas morning was marked with mixed rain and snow, but light hearts and hands made it seem as if the sun was shining. In the afternoon the entire family gathered in the fort and exchanged little presents; we sang and clapped and then sat down to a wonderful meal. In the late afternoon, the guests began to arrive from north and south. The walls of the old fort thudded with the stomping of our feet until midnight. At midnight we served a late supper, and danced until dawn. There was no dancing for me, of course. I was seven months pregnant with Porter, and so dancing was not a good idea. It was a wonderful Christmas that in no way gave any sign that it was the beginning of the end for some of us.

On New Year's Day, it was still raining. All outside work had been stopped except for the caring of the livestock. We sat in our little warm settlement and waited for it to lift, still in much of a holiday mood.

By the fifteenth day of January it was still raining, harder than ever. There had not been a pause in the falling water since Christmas Eve. John was everywhere seeing to leaking roofs, shoring up some outbuildings along Ash Creek. He stopped in briefly on the morning of the sixteenth and said Aggatha would be moving out of the fort and into the furnished basement of my house. "That fort may wash away," he had muttered as he left.

By the third week in January, nothing was dry. Mud ran in rivers around the fort, around the stone foundations of houses, and had flooded my basement. Aggatha sat silently in my parlor, looking into the fire. Her eyes were filled with terror from having to leave the fort.

On the 27th of January, the large barn fell apart like a house of matches. The ground beneath it had literally liquefied. It was becoming a grim business. Although our houses were on stone, the saturated ground turned into a sponge-like bog. One heard the creaking of lumber when the wind was right. Snow and rain and fog; a dry world was hard to imagine. John and the older boys, especially 20 year old Richard, Rachel's oldest, worked day and night shoring walls, feeding livestock, digging drainages around the houses. With the loss of the barn, the milk cattle and draft horses stood hour after hour in the slanting silver-gray rain, slowly sinking from their own weight into the mud.

On the twenty-fourth, three houses fell into Ash Creek, dispossessing sixteen people. The creek was now a dark red river, and had cut a new course through the orchards, tearing out half a hundred trees, the twirling roots on the flood like so many arthritic arms asking for rescue. John had thrown up a series of wooden shacks with the lumber from the collapsed barn on the rise behind the fort, and those whose houses had collapsed clustered in wet misery around a large ironwood range that John had salvaged. They had to stack the wood next to the range for it to dry enough to burn.

The situation was becoming serious. I almost never saw John. My days were spent drying clothes in front of my fireplace, tending my children and Aggatha, and worrying. I nearly wore the glass from my windows with my looking at the sky. The rain had to stop sometime. The Book of Genesis got a good, fresh reading in those days.

"Are you making plans for an ark?" I asked John one day in a light jest.

"I've considered it," he said, and to my astonishment, saw he was serious. "I doubt there's enough dry wood left to build an ark," he concluded, leaving me chagrined. John—all of us—were becoming exhausted.

Two things happened on the 28th day of January. The sky lightened, and we thought the rain would stop. The sun broke out for five minutes like a wink of hope, and then the world was swallowed once again in darkness. A man came riding up the valley that day, and reported that Washington City had disappeared into the Rio Virgin. Reports from Santa Clara said that Jacob Hamblin's house had washed away, and that he had drowned. A false report, to my everlasting regret. We were now trying to retain our foothold upon the lower eastern slope of Pine Valley Mountain. We were fighting for our very lives.

The water was above the floorboards of my house, and we had to abandon it. John had a wagon pulled up to the front, and everything I owned, bed, table and chairs, was moved to higher ground where it stayed, uncovered, until it warped into firewood. Then it turned colder, but the rain did not turn to snow. John ducked in late on the afternoon of the 30th, and told me he was moving Teresa Write and her family out of the fort in the morning.

"The north wall has collapsed," he reported. "I told Brigham we didn't have enough straw. You'd best move yourself up to the shelter," he said, looking at the water lapping up through the floorboards at our feet. John's face was drawn, and anxious. The relentless waterfall was pounding Harmony into the ground. Would it never stop?

"We're going to be ruined, Em," he said. "The Lord must not like it if we get too smug and comfortable with our worldly goods." I saw the crumbling of Harmony was crumbling a part of his heart—our hearts. He was a proud man, sometimes a man hard to understand in his blind faith, but he cared as deeply any man I've ever known for the safety and welfare of his family.

"Yes, John, we'll move now," I said. "We'll never be defeated, John, by a little weather," I said, and got a smile from him. And so packed up the two boys with Little Winnie's help. We took Aggatha by the hand, and trailed up through cold, sucking mud into the miserable encampment where near to 40 souls stood under a leaking board roof covered with sopping canvas. Thus we stood, shivering and burning wet wood, even our prayers damp. Half of the children were sick, our medicines scattered in the rubble of the settlement.

I found a place some distance from the range and placed Winnie in charge of seeing that Porter was covered in the quilts. Then I went back into the downpour and sloshed down to the fort whose tan walls had turned black. Great gaps were in the north wall, but the rest of the fort looked stable. I went inside to the series of rooms where Teresa lived with her looms, spiders and children.

"Have the spiders taken to rafts yet?" I greeted her.

"Not yet," she said cheerfully. I hadn't seen Teresa in two weeks, and was surprised to see the reason why she didn't want to leave the fort. It was warm and dry, except for little mud puddles seeping beneath the back wall.

"Why, it's nice in here," I said. "No wonder you're reluctant to leave."

"No, John's right," she said. "The walls are crumbling on this side. I just have a night's work on the loom—I have to finish this cotton before it's ruined—and then we'll leave. John has already moved most out of our goods. Would you like tea?"

"That would be nice," I said, shivering.

There were two large looms at the end of the room, the shuttles being worked by Teresa's twin girls, aged fourteen. Two other boys, eleven and eight, were sitting in a corner engrossed in a game of some sort that involved a lot of pushing and shoving. Her seven-year-old daughter was sitting in her lap, a dark-haired little angel. The damp had made her hair a fright of curls. As we sat I looked overhead and saw a sagging roof beam. A thin sift of dirt fell from overhead upon the cotton in the loom.

"I'd don't think I'd tarry overnight, Tess," I said.

"I'll lose months of work if I have to take the loom apart and move it. It will unravel like a spool. Addie and Maddie and I will get it finished. We've been fine so far, but John said he had a dream, and when John has a dream . . ."

"We all jump," I laughed.

"And smartly," she joined, and so I left her, warm and apparently safe but with a bleak prospect for the morrow.

The first night in the makeshift shelter was endless. The rain never once paused; indeed, it increased in its intensity. Children whimpered, we prayed together and tried to sleep. John went from group to group with words of comfort, and was then back out into the weather hammering on more boards and patching holes. He hadn't eaten in days. Most of our grain was in the river, and half of the orchards were gone. The outbuildings were in kindling, and what was left of Harmony had slipped to the lower slope— a disastrous tangle of wood and wire and mullion frames. Earlier, three cows had been swept away in Ash Creek when the bank on which they were standing collapsed.

It was near to morning when we heard the rumble of Fort Harmony. Like the thump of a foot, or a deep, sonorous drum, and then high screams pierced the wall of rain. John and Richard were stoking the stove when we heard a cracking of timbers, and more screams. It was perhaps seventy-five yards distance from the shelter to the fort. Several other women and I ran out into the rain. John and Richard and sixteen-year-old Oliver went before us. Through the murk, I searched for the bulk of the fort that had been there in daylight or darkness since the day I had arrived. It was always a comfort, although John's skill with the Indians had long ago eliminated the need for the fort's protection. If anything, the fort was a protection from our own government, not the Utes or the poor Paiute or the even poorer Shivwits on the Santa Clara.

"Bring shovels," I head John order. Close behind I plunged and to my horror the fort was but a high heap of mud, with fragments of boards like bones sticking out of the darkness.

"Teresa!" I shouted, and John was on his knees, digging like a mad animal with his hands. We could hear the faintest of screams now, from beneath the earth, like voices of the dammed. Soon a dozen of us were digging with hands, shovels, and boards. The rain came down, and we dug. The rain fell, and we dug some more. By the time it was light enough to see across the valley, we had dug out the bodies. Teresa was found with her body covering Addie and Maddie. Their mouths were full of mud. We recovered the rest of the bodies within the hour.

We laid Teresa and all five of her children out with their faces to the rain. John was too numb for tears, I thought, as were we all. We could not bury them for the soggy ground. We covered them with cloth and rocks anchored with willows, and went back to the shelter where John led us in prayer. And all the while, the rain fell. John never forgave himself for not insisting that Teresa move. But a weaver is reluctant to leave her loom. Thus, they died with the fort. And all for lack of straw.

It rained for exactly a Biblical forty days and forty nights. For doubters, it's in the history of the country. The Rio Virgin tore up the Cotton Mission and swept it into the Colorado. It was as if the Mormons had never been there. But for a few standing stone houses here and there, up in Zion Canyon, out on the Santa Clara, as far as California all was ruin. It was thus John and the remnants of the Lee family began the task of burying and rebuilding. There was nothing else for us to do.

Our thoughts twined in the silence. Rachel's tears fell like the rains of our remembrance. We might drown in memory if we linger.

It was with sadness that I saw Rachel leave. I walked as far as the ranch with her so I could talk to the boys. She shuffled off into the dusk, her long skirt raising skirls of dust as the sun fore-shortened the canyon walls. A bleak alkali wind blew down the Paria. I watched her out of sight at the willow and mud dam.

The dam across the river was a project for a Sisyphus, and vital to our lives. The spring floods would take it away it an instant. Most of the garden at the ranch site was dead as the one at Lonely Dell.

I spoke to David and Porter, who looked as if they were having the time of their young lives, living independently as grown men with the livestock to tend, patching the dam, and exploring the wild places which surrounded us. David at fourteen had my fair hair and John's grey eyes. He was the leader, like his father. Porter, although a year older, was bookish in his manner, but keen all the same to sweat his young body in the noonday sun to bring feed and water to our livestock. It was a hard place for the boys, but they were young and healthy and had the sunshine itself in their smiles. Life was still an adventure for them, and I did nothing to spoil their game.

There was a chill in the evening air, and I wore a woolen shawl as I sat in the horsehide chair that John made for me to rest on while I watched the sun go down. The cottonwood leaves were the color of Spanish gold, the seep willows scarlet. I must confess to a loneliness that was so profound I was envious of the stones themselves for their companionship with other stones. If it were not for my darling Elizabeth, who had just turned a year, I should have gone mad for the wanting of company. John praises my self-reliance; perhaps it is true, but I am frightened of the alone-ness. David and Porter were adolescent helpfulness. It would have been nice to have the two older boys with us, but one was in England spreading the Gospel, and the other . . . in the grave. It has not been satisfactorily explained to me by the church authorities, or by John, or by God Almighty how one is to under-stand when a child precedes one in death.

A week later a rider came in, his horse lathered, near dead. It was Agatha's eldest son Heber who had ridden down from Skatum-pah with a letter from John. From the look on his face I knew the letter bore nothing but ill for us all. I calmly heard the bare facts of his news, fed the boy, and sent him back for home, thanking him for his long ride—five days in the coming and going.

I sat in the dooryard in the evening chill. From the heft of the letter, I knew I should have started to read it earlier, while there was still light. I turned it over in my hands whose roughness repelled me. I thought of England, and the soft soap and the kind water from limestone pools. The crest of my conviction had carried me here. The promise of a new life in a new world had amplified my faith, perhaps. Living on the frontier was a hardship easily borne, for love. But this? The supposedly unlawful wife of a man of a minority which the nation hates . . . I unfolded the heavy, oilcloth bundles of numbered pages, and recognized John's firm script.

CHAPTER EIGHT

Sept 8, 1876
Point of the Mountain

My Dearest Emeline,

They've captured me, Em. By the time you receive this letter by the hand of son Heber, they will have transported me to the prison at the Point of the Mountain near great SLC. I hesitate to relate to you the humiliation of the circumstances of my imprisonment. That I should be brought short at pistol point by a gentile after all these years galls me to the core, dear wife. I was promised by the church authorities, including Prest. Young himself, that no harm would befall me, that no enemies should find me. They must have been mistaken . . .

I was captured by the territorial Marshal while hiding in a pig pen in Panguitch. I was betrayed, of course, but I'll never know by whom, for my enemies are everywhere now that Brigham is doing nothing to hinder the federals in finding someone to punish. I don't know what to think of the matter.

I am not resigned to my fate. I am not at peace. In my spirit I have not abandoned you at the Lonely Dell. The future holds more loneliness and hardship for you I fear. I do not know the disposition of my case, or when I will be able to come home to you and the boys and dear little Elizabeth.

I have been charged with violating the polygamy laws which we knew would happen, but they have laid on to me the most heinous charge that I ALONE am responsible for the events at the Mountain Meadows. I will shoulder my share of the blame, but I will not shoulder the responsibility for initiating the terrible event. I had nothing to do with the decisions leading to the horrible massacre, for I must call it what it was.

They say—the federals under Judge Cradlebaugh—that they will let me go if I name the names of those who were there that dark day. I cannot betray them, else I betray my church brethren and my God. I cannot break my vow of honor.

The prison is a sunless place. Criminals, mostly young louts of low character, are my companions. What am I to do? I have spoken to no man nor woman yet of the facts and my recollections of that September day in 1857. When I ask myself to whom I may unburden myself in complete safety I think of your fidelity to me—no higher than some of my other wives— but in you I find an abiding love that I cannot quench, and find therein my refuge. I am thus decided to pen to you my thoughts and recollections, for they will be safe with you.

If the worst comes, and I am convicted, at least you will have this true testament. The proper disposition of this confession you shall have to decide when the time comes. It is a terrible burden, I know. In the meanwhile, I entrust you with my heart's truth. Be brave, Em, for they know not what they do, nor what I can bring down upon their heads if they do not treat me justly.

I see you sitting in our dooryard reading this. I know your moods, Em, better than I know the moods of my other wives. I can feel your heart beating for me across distance. There is no knowing the will of God in this matter. I am confused. Know this, then, in love I release you from your eternal vows to me.

If you wish, you may leave the Lonely Dell and seek your destiny elsewhere.

TRUST NO ONE WITHIN THE CHURCH, NO MES-SENGER OR SPOKESMAN! I know that Major Powell or some of his party will assist you if you wish to remove from there to the east, or go to California. I would even recommend to you that young Lt. Dellenbaugh, who is in your debt and is bound to lend you every assistance. Your safety and that of the children is uttermost in my mind. I know this is hard on you, and it tears me asunder.

It is my hope that you will stay at the Lonely Dell and run the ferry. The ferry will be our only source of income for the foreseeable future. I'm selling off what is left of the rest of my land to secure lawyers, and my other families must, perforce, fend for themselves, as must you. Without you at the ferry, there will be no money, and no means of getting any. But if you choose not to stay, I shall understand.

It is your choice, my dear, and whatever choice you make, I will rest with the knowledge that the things I write to you will remain in confidence until, or when, my fate is decided. Shall I keep my silence? Shall I remain faithful to Brigham and the others? If they will keep their faith in me, I shall keep my faith in them. I have written B.Y. with a plea for his assistance, but I am met with silence. I waver. I pray to God for strength not to betray the others.

Daily, General Maxwell comes to the prison and whispers in my ear to name the names, and thus set myself free.

I have no enemies to punish, but by the same token, I have no FRIENDS to shield either by keeping secret. I did not act alone, Em. We were all acting upon what we knew to be lawful military orders as well as serving the church. We considered it a religious duty—may GOD DAMN my blindness.

Joseph Smith said that we are not responsible for Adam's transgression. I must dispute that. In each man resides the sins of all men, and we are little better than beasts when the corruption of the flesh is unloosed. It is true of myself, as of the men who were with me that awful day. Men will corrupt any truth, this I now know. The purity of God cannot reside in man. His institutions corrupt the spirit. Is this true of woman's nature? I think not. Woman has some capacity that men do not have, the will to subdue the lust for blood.

I would suggest you hide these papers at the place of the white rock, bind them against the weather in oilcloth and bury them. Let no one follow you. And now I write to you in my heart's blood of the blood of the innocents:

Because you were not yet even arrived in this country, you must understand the times. There was fear, and anger that filled the Saints from the north in the Salmon River country to the red south deserts of Zion. Almost from the first, when the truth of the Restored Gospel was given to the world by our Prophet Joseph Smith, the United States had done their best to subdue us and our faith, had driven us into a wilderness where we flourished like the sage and Sego lily. All we sought was freedom to worship our God as we saw fit. The enmity of the enemies of the Church, from the President of the United States to the most common, misinformed Missourian, never slept. They drove us from Ohio and Illinois and Missouri to Zion where we began to raise up the Kingdom of God near the Great Salt Lake.

This endless attack upon our principles and our conduct induced in us a tension that was in our every thought, and it naturally caused some of the Saints to criticize Brigham and his leadership of the Church. In 1854, on account of general wickedness, backsliding, apostasy, adultery, murder, and thievery that was becoming prevalent among some of the Saints, Brigham Young called for a Great Reformation to sweep the church clean.

There was a call for a general rebaptism and rededication to the Gospel that summer, and in the prosecution of these goals, admittedly, there were some excesses. I thought the reformation ill advised. All true members of the church, man and woman, were required to stand before the church authorities and confess aloud to any sin, no matter how slight. We were required to take an oath of fidelity and obedience, and to *answer a list of questions to prove our faith to the church authorities. We were questioned by both those from Salt Lake and those who were our local authorities, the Stake Presidents, Bishops etc.*

Among the questions to be answered were: Have you committed murder by shedding innocent blood—or consenting thereto; Have you spoken against any principle contained in the Bible, Book of Mormon, Doctrine & Covenants, or any principle revealed through Joseph the Prophet or the authorities in the church; and other questions regarding stealing, paying of tithes, adultery, and personal cleanliness.

This reformation still had a strong grip among the people when, in 1857, just ten days before the massacre, General Apostle George A. Smith, after whom St. George is named, came south with a message for all the settlements. President Buchanan thought that Brigham Young asserted too much control in the territory, and the federal officials appointed over us thought we were in a state of rebellion.

So President Buchanan—using polygamy as a whipping post—sent Johnston and the U.S. Army toward Utah to 'put down the rebellion.' Johnston's Army was on the march toward Zion with the express purpose of exterminating us, as had been tried in Missouri, and Illinois.

There was a great fear and furor in the land. Brigham Young declared general martial law, and vowed a scorched earth policy if the army should ever reach Deseret. Out on the plains we fought a courageous, and successful guerrilla war that delayed Johnston. We were prepared to resist the government with our last breath and drop of blood. Brigham had a contingency to move us to Mexico, but we meant to make our stand in Deseret. This, my beloved, was all to uphold our constitutionally guaranteed right of religious freedom. My ancestors, including Light Horse Harry Lee, fought and bled for these freedoms. Shall we give them up again to the tyrant?

So, as a general authority, George A. Smith spoke for Brigham Young wherever he went. His message was Brigham's message: Prepare, resist, fight. Apostle Smith stayed with me at the house in Harmony during his tour, and we had many private conversations on this very subject.

"I have been sent down by the old Boss to instruct the Brethren of the different settlements not to sell any of their grain to the enemies who pass through Utah," he told me directly.

"I understand," I said, "Although some of the people resent this order, as it is the only means of their getting any cash."

"Would you feed our enemies?" he asked me. I did not reply. Then he said, "Brigham Young has received a revelation from God, giving him the right and the power to call down the curse of God on all our enemies who attempt to invade our Territory. Our greatest danger in the south lies from California. The people of the United States who oppose the Church are a mob, from President Buchanan on down, but it will be hard paid if their armies are to prevail against the Saints who have gathered here in the mountains."

"On that, I agree," I said. "The people are ready to fight to protect themselves."

You must understand the weight of his words, Em. Smith held high rank in the military, that of General, and was one of the Twelve Apostles. His orders were inspired of God, and it was my duty to obey without question or hesitation. I visited many settlements with him and he preached hell fire against any emigrants who tried to pass through the territory. I do say that after a few of his sermons I became bored, and visited among the people while he hurled epithets against the gentiles. Apostle Smith ordered the people not to sell the emigrants any food, or give them any shelter or comfort of any kind. We needed all we possessed if the big fight came with the U.S. Army.

One day, on the road from Fort Clara, we came upon old Moquis and his boys, who had blood in their eye. I interpreted as best I could, and told them that Smith was a big captain.

"Is he a Mericat Captain?" they wanted to know.

"No, he is a Mormon Captain," I said, "And he is a friend to all of the Indians." Then Smith gave them a general sermon *on how friendly we were to the Indians, and that we must help each other and drive away any 'Mericats who tried to pass through Zion. He did not need to use much urging. The Indians already knew, in their uncanny way, of the coming of the Fancher train. And so did Smith, but he did not deem to tell me of their approach.*

As we rode away, Apostle Smith said to me, "Those are savage-looking fellows. I think they would make it quite lively for an emigrant train if one should come this way." I had to agree.

"They will attack anything," I said, "including us."

"Suppose an emigrant train should pass through, making threats and bragging of the part they took in helping kill our Prophet, what do you think the Brethren would do?"

"I myself would seek out those killers and avenge the Prophet," I swore. "There is not a man in the country who would not aid me," I assured him.

"Do you really believe the Brethren would make it lively for such a train?"

"They will, sir, if they lack a pass to travel through Utah from Brigham Young, or one of the authorities," I assured him.

"Well," he said, "in all confidence, Brother Lee, I've had a conference with Colonel Dame and Major Haight of Panguitch and Cedar City respectively. They assure me the same thing." It was clear to me, by the time he left, that nothing would make Brigham Young or himself happier than to have no emigrants pass safely through the territory without an express pass from him.

I now believe, dear wife, then as I do now, that General George A. Smith was visiting southern Utah to prepare the people for the work of exterminating Captain Fancher's train of emigrants.

Events tumbled swiftly after General Smith returned north. He must have passed the Fancher train on its way south, but I heard nothing about that. Prest. Isaac C. Haight of the Cedar City Stake of Zion summoned me to Cedar City by messenger on the night of Sept. 4, 1857. I met him on a moonless night at the black iron works near Cedar where the Saints had poured so much of their fruitless labor in getting iron ore. We took blankets with us and lay under the furry stars, each one a testament to God's Glory. Isaac was the second in command in all of the Iron Military District set up by Prest. Young. Isaac had a small jug of apple brandy with him against the chill of the altitude.

"There is a train of emigrants, Missourians, on the way," he informed me.

"I've heard the rumor," I said, still wondering at what that had to do with me.

"A more Godless set of Gentiles never came through Zion," he spat. Isaac wore huge white side whiskers, which nodded in the faint light like the fanning wings of a chicken. I had to suppress a snicker—the effects of the brandy, no doubt. "Word from the town of Fillmore is that they are abusing every Mormon they come across. They are insulting the women, and letting their livestock trample crops. It is insufferable," he declared.

"Have they a pass?" I asked. You must understand, Em, it was impossible to travel in safety through Utah without a handwritten pass from Prest. Young in those days. Utah was under a state of martial law. More persecution was not to my liking after being run out of Illinois, and Missouri. I longed to avenge the Prophet's blood, as did all men in the Church. I still do. We were sworn to it. Isaac was one of the early leaders, along with myself, and had carried out many missions for Prest. Young on the trek west.

You may have heard the whispers of the Sons of Dan. Yes, I was the seventh member sworn back in the East, and I have protected the Prophet and the Church eye for eye when called upon. I began to suspect that the Sons of Dan in Utah were going to be called out.

"They need no pass," Isaac said with disgust. "They've over seventy men, are heavily armed, and we have no force able to stop their abuses. It is intolerable."

"I agree," I said carefully. My blood was up as he gave more

detail of their actions.

"They are poisoning springs, burning fences, leaving a trail of misery with the passing of their train. They defile the very ground of Zion."

"But, what is to be done?" I asked, angrily. The more he described the depredations of the Fancher train, the more indignant I became. For years we had suffered at the hands of the mobs. Now that we had ten years in Zion we were ready to repel any Army, as Prest. Young promised. There was no man, woman, or child that was not prepared to fight to the death to defend Zion.

"They said," Isaac muttered through clenched teeth, "they would return with soldiers after they got to California and string up Brigham Young and kill every damned man, woman and child."

"They will leave two corpses behind for every success," I said. "If they pass through Harmony and dare to touch my land, or family, or even my Indians I shall see them in hell," I vowed.

"Just so," Isaac said.

"It's best to let them pass through, though, and get rid of them," I suggested. "Keep them at arm's length, follow our policy of having no commerce with them, and they will want to leave as quickly as they can," I said. "If we stir up trouble, and they go to California and come back with another army, we'll be sore pressed. With Johnston so close, we can't defend a southern front when they invade the north."

"But don't you see, if they are allowed out of Utah, they will bring back a southern front."

"Just talk," I said. "If they pass unmolested they will have no cause."

"Brother Lee," he said to me vehemently, his teeth gleaming, "They say there is one man among the party who claims to have the very pistol that slew our Prophet."

"May God damn his eyes," I said, feeling again the awful pain when Joseph was gunned down at the Carthage jail. There was no one among us who were at Nauvoo with the blessed

Prophet who didn't wish to avenge the blood of our Prophet. "We should cut the man out of the train and give him his just reward."

"We must do more than that," Isaac said. "It is said by Kanosh, of the Corn Creek Indians, that the Fancher train gave them poisoned meat. They are taking to the warpath. They have sent a messenger asking for our help."

"In what way?" I asked.

"Yesterday there was a council of all the authorities. It was decided to arm the Indians, and assist them in every way. We'll give them provisions, ammunition; have the Indians give them the brush—his exact words—and if they kill all, or part of them, so much the better."

"But Kanosh and his Corn Creeker band can't handle a tenth of that number," I said. "They are not fighters, these southern Indians. They're too hungry most of the time to be fighters. Except amongst themselves," I added truthfully.

"We've sent word down to the Muddy and to bands across the Rio Virgin," he said.

"Who is your authority for this?" I asked. I well knew Brigham's policy of keeping the Indians fed, but unarmed. "If we arm them, sooner or later they will be turned on us. I don't like that at all," I said, becoming uneasy. "Has Brigham sanctioned such a course?"

"It's been decided," he said to me. "It's the will of all in authority. You need no more than that, do you Brother Lee?"

"Of course not," I said, feeling his rebuke. I cannot and could not conceive of disobeying the Priesthood. "THE PRIESTHOOD IS INCAPABLE OF LIES."

"Colonel Dame has ordered, and everyone has agreed, that we are going to let the Indians use up the whole train. I expect you to follow orders," he said.

I knew that I must obey, or die. Such as are we sworn from the time of the persecutions. But mark me, Em, I had no wish to disobey! My superiors in the Church spoke for God. It was not in my place to ask questions. Don't you see? There is no higher authority than God. To whom could I appeal for a more moral course?

"You will go back to your place at Harmony, alert your Indians, and recruit Karl Shirts as interpreter," he instructed me as the hours of our discussion passed, and the stars wheeled, and my thoughts were in turmoil. "Send your messengers throughout the south, warning them of the approach of the Mericats. Rise up the Indians, Brother Lee. We are their friends. Make them see that it is in their own interest that this party shall not pass out of Utah with impunity for their outrages."

"As you wish," Brother Haight, I said.

"I will send Nephi Johnson behind you to stir up a large enough force of Indians to finish them. We will give the emigrants a good hush."

"But what if Brigham disapproves of this course?" I asked, and let it be recorded I did ask such a question on more than one occasion.

"These are the orders given by the Council," he said, becoming irritated with my questions. "This will be an Indian affair. If the Missourians are massacred, no blame will be assigned to us. If it is played right. I am counting on you. No whites will be implicated in the matter. We can lay it on the Indians."

"But Brother Haight," I protested at last with some heat. "You know how the Indians will act. They will not stop at the men. They will kill all the party, the women and the children. You know we are sworn not to shed innocent blood!"

"Be still, you!" he roared into the night. I nearly reached for my knife, I was so startled by his shout. This was an unsettled man. "Oh, Hell, Brother Lee. There will not be one drop of innocent blood shed, if every one of the damned pack are killed, for they are the worse lot of out-laws and ruffians that I ever saw in my life! None of them are innocent," he shouted. The brandy jug was empty, I noted.

"As you wish, Brother Haight," I said.

We walked back to the town with blankets around our shoulders just at dawn. After breakfast at Brother Haight's he bade me leave and go about my duty. But before I left he said to me, *"Go, Brother Lee, and see that the instructions of those in authority are obeyed, and as you are dutiful in this, so shall your reward be in the kingdom of God, for God will bless those who willingly obey counsel, and make all things fit for the people in these last days.*

This missive to you is not to diminish my own responsibility, dear Em, nor is it to plead for any mercy, or ask for any pity. It is to unbosom myself to the one whose bosom I wish to be near, to be enfolded in some peace that I know I shall never have again . . .

The light failed me. It was so dark I could not see the pages in my hand. The night-chill of the desert had fallen, and I went inside the house. I knew I would not sleep. Did I indeed have the courage to finish the letter, or should I save myself by consigning it to the fire without reading another word? Wait for the sun, Em, I counseled.

CHAPTER NINE

Breakfast was ashes in my mouth; peculiarly flavored corn meal mush in milk and water. Worms. Nature is relentless in her displeasure at our pitiful habitations. I fed Elizabeth, and left the stone house and gazed at the empty river, the towering red walls, the cloudless sky of a powdery blue. There was no sign of life. Black vulture and black raven alike had deserted the sky. Though fall was upon us, the heat of the day would be brutalizing to the spirit.

I thus early set David and Porter to work hauling water for the parching garden, leaving Elizabeth in the shade for them to watch. The boys were ever mindful of the dangers. Then I repaired to a place John and I knew when we wanted to be alone; a shaded cove of white rock, a wind-scooped depression that fit the form as comfortably as a plush sitting-room chair. I set a gourd of water beside me in the sand. As agonizing as it was, I could think of no better place to face the truth than in this valley that so much resembled a stony Bekka. I closed my eyes in a brief prayer, and then began to read from the letter again:

I remember the weather Em, as clearly as if it were today. I rode toward the Mountain Meadows on a fine blood bay mare. Near Pioche, the sky had the clarity of still water, and a sweep of vastness that uplifted my heart. There was just a breath of cool from the Pine Valley Mountain, a hint, a harbinger of winter. The sage smell that the horses stirred underfoot was like a perfume. How could I know it was to be the last time that I would have the peace to contemplate God's beautiful handiwork, for my vision now is clouded in the nimbus of a dying sun.

At Harmony, the news reached me that the Indians I aroused had not obeyed my instructions to wait for white leadership. This, I knew, could lead to a disaster. A rider from Cedar City sent me thither with orders from Major Isaac Haight to try and restore some control over them. When I arrived at the meadows, I saw the Indians had stopped the train the night before, killing seven, and wounding sixteen of the miserable travelers. The Fancher Missourians were brave fighters, repulsing attack after attack, killing some of the Indians, and breaking the knees of others in close combat. Indian runners were sent out in a call for reinforcements, and thus was I ordered—drawn ever closer to the destruction.

I was told to pacify the Indians as it was thought that I had some influence among them, having taught them the rudiments of agriculture. Nothing could be further from the truth. They did as they pleased, and when it pleased them they heeded my instruction. When it did not, they ignored me. Nonetheless, my orders were to keep them from further attack until the authorities from Cedar City should arrive. I knew that if the Indians were, by some small chance successful, and broke the train's defenders up, there would be blood deep enough in the ground to make it mud.

Do you remember when we picnicked in the pine valley on the west side of the mountain? You remarked upon the cones of the extinct volcanoes, standing as sentinels between the endless Mojave and the Great Basin of the Kingdom of God.

Black rock nosed against fragile red rock, the sage giving ground to soap yucca, blue Sego bowing to the prickly province of the scarlet cup. Oh, I do remember your delight.

We passed near the Mountain Meadows that day, although I could not mention the place to you, and cannot think of the place today without a vile sickness invading my stomach. The meadow is spring damp the year 'round with tall grass, bordered on the north by thick juniper and scattered piñions. The train had been stopped by the Indian attack away from any cover. To the south a swale gives way to a lowering of the meadow where the red rock peers in cliff among the heat twisted black rock. It was once a beautiful place. I am told that to this day nothing will grow on the meadow, as if it has been sown with salt.

I found the Indians, Toquer and Walker's bands, Kanosh's and hardy Paiute all mixed up in a blood fever. They claimed the train had poisoned a well in their country and it had killed many men, horses and cattle. I later found this to be true. The Indians eyed with envy the fine cattle, horses and weapons of their enemies. They had succeeded in killing a number of cattle, and bloated corpses with wasteful roasts cut from haunches were scattered on the perimeter of the train. There was the smell of dry sage, putrefied flesh, gunpowder. As I only had the acquaintance of the Corn Creek and the Toquers, it was difficult to get the rest of the bands to pay me any mind. I was the only white man present that day, and I rode among the savages pleading with them in my broken tongue to desist until we should get clear instructions.

Brigham Young had made Jacob Hamblin missionary to the Indians. It was he who had some authority with the local tribes. But Hamblin was conveniently absent that day. Brigham had appointed me farmer to the Indians. What this day's work had to do with agriculture, I could not fathom. My pleas were punctuated by a Paiute who had his knee shot off, and was howling in pain throughout.

I saw they were intent upon another attack, and I begged them to desist saying the Mormons would aid them and would give them all the livestock. I reasoned that there would be fewer casualties. One of the primary orders I had been given by Haight was not to antagonize the Indians, for when the United States invaded they would be invaluable allies. When I saw it was of no use, I began to weep with fear and frustration. They were all feathers and fury, smelling of blood and rancid grease.

It was that day, a Wednesday I recall, that I got attached to me the derogatory nickname of Yawgetts or Yaw-Guts from the Indians. I carry it to this day, and it has done me untold harm ever since in my relations with them. I no longer speak with any authority to the Lamanites. They called me mockingly old Yawgetts, which means cry baby. They thought I was weak, as I confess I was. I wept before them as I pleaded with them to spare the women and the children.

The Indians were frustrated. The Fancher train was wealthy, and had equipped itself with stout wagons, which were drawn into a circle with the wheels chained together. From the east side I could see they had dug rifle pits under the wagons. The only drawback to their defenses was they had been brought short of water by the first attack, and were forced to leave the protection of the circled wagons and get water under volleys of poorly aimed fire from the braves.

The Wildcat Missourians were brave and expert marksmen with good rifles. I saw that their defenses would be impossible to break. But, as an example of the foreknowledge and careful planning which the authorities had made, I would soon learn that the instructions were to play the traitor to the race. For treachery it was to be, by my hand, that lowered the defenses of the surrounded settlers, and led them to their death.

Chief Toquer, whom I had labored with to teach his destitute tribe to grow melons on Touqer Creek, was dressed in his best buckskins, which is to observe that they were old, dirty, torn, and misshapen with age. His band was armed with small bows and a few knifes. They possessed among them one flintlock with no powder or lead. The other bands were similarly poorly armed, but they were ferocious in appearance, and *their anger was keen.*

On Thursday afternoon the men arrived from Cedar City. As God is my witness, those that I remember present were: Samuel Knight, Oscar Hamblin, William Young, John W. Clark, Karl Shirts, Harrison Pearce, James Pearce, William Slade Sr., James Matthews, Dudley Leavitt, William Hawley, William Slade Jr., and two other men whose names I have forgotten.

I reported to them all that had transpired, and was glad to have the burden of responsibility taken from my shoulders. I did not know at the time that a messenger had been sent north to Salt Lake City for instructions, but now know that it was a sharp play on the part of the authorities in order to protect themselves if things went wrong.

We parleyed all day among ourselves, and with each other.

"Such groans of the dying," David Lewis declared before us in the afternoon council. He was a witness at the Hauns Mill massacre back in Missouri when the mobs slaughtered tens of Mormon men, women and children. "Such struggling in blood I hope that none may have to witness, unless it is in avenging the blood of those that were slain, for truly they shed innocent blood, which must stand against them until it is avenged . . ."

Higbee said all of our justification could be found in Joseph Smith's Doctrine & Covenants, Section 98, Verses 23-32. We must forgive our enemies in meekness, he taught, and not retaliate. But after we have been driven four times, though they would still be more blessed if they could forgive again, "Verily, thine enemy is in thine hands, and THOU ART JUSTIFIED."

Many of us had been driven more than four times; Haun's Mill, the Martyrdom of the Prophet, and of his brother; the burnings and lootings by the mob, the soldiers of the state against us, the abandonment of the shining city of Nauvoo, the bleak trek across the desert west. We have been driven four times and twenty, some declared.

John Lott, his slouch hat in his hands, face licked by the morbid yellow light of the afternoon sun said, I hope to see the day when the blood of the martyrs will be avenged, and these damnable rebels make restitution.

And we prayed, and others bore their testimony:

"Their dead bodies were brought to Nauvoo, where I saw their beloved forms reposing in the arms of death . . . I then and there resolved in my mind that I would never let an opportunity go unimproved of avenging their blood upon the heads of the enemies of the Church of Jesus Christ. I hope to avenge their blood, but if I do not I will teach my children and children's children to the fourth generation as long as there is one descendent of the murderers on the earth . . ."

My God, how those words inflamed our hearts. By turns I was blind with rage and quaking with fear. I too had sworn the blood oath of vengeance. Before us was the present generation of the murderers, no matter, then, that the largest part of them were wholly innocent of the slaying of the prophets. It is what groups signify that enables us to resist them. If we give a face and personality to the enemy, we shall be helpless, I reasoned, thinking of the little girls in white dresses I had seen that morning who had been playing under the wagon, oblivious to the Indians hordes and the gathering Mormons on horses.

There were perhaps three to four hundred Indians camped around the ridge lines. The unblooded new comers were armed with rifles and fit to fight. If the Indians took the notion, they could by now have wiped us all out, Mormons and Gentiles alike so many were their numbers.

We killed a small beef for dinner and continued our discussion. Campfires threw an unholy red light upon the distant white canvas tops of the silent wagons. My heart went out to those people, and I became even weaker in my resolve. We decided to send a messenger back to Cedar City for further instructions, and I pleaded with the messenger—who was either Edwards or Adair—"Tell Haight, for my sake, for the people's sake, for God's sake, send more help to protect and save the emigrants, and pacify the Indians."

Along toward evening, the Indians attacked again. I heard the screams of animals, of terrified women and children from inside the wagon circle. I could not stand it, so I ran toward the scene. William Young and John Mangum were with me. The Indians whirled and began to fire on us! Three buzzing balls from their guns cut my clothing. One ball went through my hat and cut my scalp, blood streaming in my eyes, staining my vision. Another ball went though my shirt and put lead in the top-flesh of my shoulder. I was screaming at them to stop!

"Yawgetts, Yawgetts," they taunted me, and turned back to their attack. Finally Oscar Hamblin, who was as good an interpreter as Jacob Hamblin, succeeded in stopping them, but it was more from weariness and wariness that they broke it off rather than by any threats or reason on Hamblin's part.

On Friday morning several more men arrived; Joel White, William C. Stewart, Benjamin Arthur, Alexander Wilden, Charles Hopkins and a man named Tate. If evidence is needed that white men are as base as the red man, while we waited for news from Cedar City, some of the men sat in the shade of the berry heavy junipers, loaded their rifles, and spent the afternoon pot shooting at the train. It was disgusting to me. Alexander Wilden took the pains to fix himself a tripod of branches to steady his aim. He had a flask of whiskey, and he whiled away the time shooting indiscriminately until he was too drunk to reload his rifle.

The Clara Indians arrived, and wanting part of the booty, made a miserable attack and suffered one killed and three wounded for their troubles. In a fit of pique, they stole some cattle and left the meadows not to be seen again. I prayed incessantly. But no word came from either God, or Cedar City. Unbeknownst to me the Cedar City men already had their orders. I was deceived. There was no pretense of cutting out the offenders of our laws as they had passed through Utah. They meant to kill them all.

Thursday evening we held a final council. By now John M. Higbee, Major of the Iron Militia, and Phillip K. Smith—whose name is Klingensmith, Bishop of Cedar City—came into our camp with more armed men; Ira Allen and Robert Wiley of the High Council and many other officials Viz. City Councilmen *and attorneys, the adjutant to Major Higbee, blacksmiths and grocery men. All of them Mormons true to the faith, with belief in the infallible priesthood they all held. John Jacobs, a Captain of Ten—In all, I remember counting fifty four of my brethren in attendance at the meadow that night and the next day. In that, I bear 1/54th of the burden. Can one make those discriminations? Can one take a fifty fourth part of a man's life? When one hundred twenty seven men or women or children have died, does it make the sum of one hundred twenty seven deaths for each attacker, or one death, or . . . Ah God!*

These are the names, Em, these are the ones who, with myself, began to do the day's work of death. Men with whom I'd traded and worshiped and fought. To betray them would be to betray myself. To commit myself to the work at hand was to betray humanity. What must I do? What have I done . . . ?

I let the pages slip from my hands. There was more to read. The sun was a white blaze, and I shifted to the shade. I raised the cool clay jar of water and slaked my thirst. There was a salt taste to the water, and it was warm . . .

CHAPTER TEN

Looking at the unread pages, my hands began to shake as if they were not part of my body. I looked at the sheaves of paper as if they were blank. Quietly, locks slipped, and feelings like deranged black ravens crashed into places they did not belong. It was as if my mind was loosened. My grief expressed itself in laughter. I became, before sanity was restored by a soft voice, as benighted as a Shivwits woman grinding corn with bloody hands, and I cursed John D. Lee for his love, and his religion, and his God.

"Mrs. Lee, is it bad news?" It was Lt. Dellenbaugh who had somehow approached my private cove of stone and spoke, startling me out of the trance in which the written words in John's letter were hieroglyphs.

"I'm sorry if I frightened you, Mrs. Lee," he spoke softly, his fair hair bleached white as salt by the sun, his river men's clothes marked by Lieutenant's bars as the only badge that he was of Major Powell's party of explorers. I made to hide the manuscript beneath my skirt, but desisted, and blushed instead. "Your children told me I might find you up here. I'll leave you if you wish," he said.

"It is nothing. Stay a moment," I said to the man whom I had nursed back from the dead. He had been stricken by a mysterious illness, and Major Powell asked me to care for him. For days he was delirious, and I despaired for his life. John was away at the time exploring and proselytizing in the Indian settlements of the Moenkoeppi to see if we might settle there if the pressure became too great from the north. And to find more food.

"I'll share the shade," I said. It may have looked unseemly, but he sat next to me in the curved rock, his hard hip next to mine. Even with the sun, I could feel his heat.

To this day I blush at the memory of it. They brought him in a litter to the rock house about a week after John left for the north. One of his arms was listlessly dragging in the sand as they approached, and Major Powell reached down with his one good hand and held it out of the dust. Two ragged men, Mr. Satterswaithe and Mr. German, set the litter down and doffed their hats. For rivermen, they were schooled in manners, I always thought. Major Powell's influence, no doubt.

"Mrs. Lee," Major Powell said, his left shirt sleeve pinned as it always was to his shirt front. "We are at our wits end. I've dosed him with calomel, but he's sinking. Is there anything you can do? I fear he's going to die on us, and I can't afford to lose him. The fever just won't break. Hell—begging your pardon—he's got the entire geography upriver right here," Powell tapped his head with his one hand.

"I've some small knowledge of medicine," I said.

"It's the river fever, or something," Powell shrugged. "We'll pay," he blurted.

"That is unnecessary," I said. "Bring him into the house. It's cool in there."

"That's what we thought. The tents are furnaces," Powell said.

German and Satterswaithe grunted as they lifted the Lieutenant and took him into the house.

"Here, lay him on my bed," I directed, throwing on a fresh old quilt. "And if you have more blankets, I'll need them."

"You'll cook him like a sausage," German said, looking at the unconscious man. I learned there was great affection between all the men of the Powell expedition, but especially for the cheerful leadership of Lt. Dellenbaugh, who looked gray as ash. His body alternately shook and ran with perspiration, and then suddenly dried as if he'd been hung on a line in the sun. It was odd. I covered him, and sent Satterswaithe for water.

"Set some pans of water to warm in the sun, and then bring a bucket of the cold river water directly to me," I said as I took over the nursing chores. Men who can run unknown rivers unable to cope with sickness? It always confounded me. Helpless creatures withal. "And if you see my eldest son David about please send him to me quickly."

"Yes ma'am," German tipped his hat, glad to be away from the sick man.

"Anything at all we have in the camp is yours," Powell said. He too looked helpless. There was indeed little we could do, but the men seemed past trying.

"How long has he been like this?" I asked, burying the Lieutcnant under several layers of rather malodorous hides.

"Two days now," he replied.

"Have you tried the willow bark to reduce his fever?"

"I confess our botanist has been unable to find the right willows," he said awkwardly.

"Then send him up the Paria half-a-mile. He'll find a stand of green willows on the north bank."

"Yes, Ma' am

"I'm not sure that it's the river fever," I said doubtfully. "His skin should flush when he is not perspiring. Has he cut himself anywhere?"

"Not to my knowledge. As I said, wits' end," Major Powell shrugged. "Fetch more blankets like the lady says, Bill," he ordered. "I'll leave you now, Ma'am, and we are grateful."

Thus began an ordeal which I shall never forget. The young and healthy man was as sick as any man I'd ever seen. I'd seen countless Lee children stricken from one ailment or another over the years, and something in my memory was jogged when I saw the greyness of his face, but I could not place it.

Forty-eight hours later, in the heat of the afternoon, Lt. Dellenbaugh was still in a kind of coma. I'd sent David for fistfuls of feverfew, brewed it up and forced the liquid between the Lt.'s clenched jaws. Major Powell had draughts of opium and alcohol, but that I sensed was useless. Alternately I drenched his body with buckets of cold water, and then when the chills came I piled a mountain of covers on him and then covered him with my own body.

The Major toiled up from the camp to inquire of the Lieutenant's health every four hours. Already I was beginning to feel defeated. This was unlike any river fever in my experience, and there was plenty of the fever in the lower fields near the Virgin River where St. George was in the building.

Shortly after the Major left, and the boys were about their chores, the Lieutenant seemed to come awake, and then he screamed, and began to buck as if his muscles were steel springs that had lost their temper. He was quite mad. He tore off the covers and stood, naked, and made for the door. I tackled him by the ankles, and shouted for the boys. As I tried to hold him down I felt out of myself, as if I were not a participant. I was wrestling with a handsome, naked, muscular man, his large male parts flopping, and from a distance it may have looked as if we were in the tight agonies of love making. I blush, and confess, looking down, it aroused me, and figured when this passed, I'd better get myself to the cold river for a bath.

Luckily, Mr. German appeared to make his daily check, and saw my predicament.

"Lord God, look at that," he said. My dress was above my knees, and a button was torn from my dress front. In the heat I wore no underclothing.

"Help me, you daft fool," I said. "Hold him down or he'll break his neck." German put a broad knee in the middle of his chest and pinned him effortlessly. And then the attack, or the fit, or whatever it was over, and German lifted him back to the bed without effort.

"I'll leave you now," he said, his face flushed. Men do not like to see other men naked, for what reason I'll never know. Nor do they like being called a fool, but I had no time for niceties.

Oh, I'll tell it all. As I bent over his form to cover him with a wet sheet I looked at him, and in the nearly innocent looking, I may have saved his life. I had a curious shortness of breath. His body was still strong, the muscles defined in his arms, and thighs. A heavy down of blond hair covered his legs and chest and in the hollows under his arms. His hips were thin, clean, hairless except for . . . there. And it was the *there* that I looked, just briefly, just a glance as I began to pull the light sheet over him. What is this? I glanced at the empty doorway. Should anyone ever see me, oh, unthinkable.

I noticed, at the flesh where the long male part and the orbs of procreation joined, a purplish discoloration, a swelling inflammation. I pretended I was handling John, and wanted to close my eyes, but I could not. I lifted his member and pulled it aside and probed with my other finger into the loose sackworks. He was quite unconscious, breathing heavily—I could not straighten out my thoughts—and then I saw the cause of his affliction. It was something of a miracle. Had I not handled him—wished to handle him, may God forgive me—he may well have died.

Two swollen wood ticks were buried almost out of sight in the tender flesh scrotum, festered and sick as boils. There! Curious. Ticks were less common in the desert than up in the higher wooded mountains to the north. But there they were, a source of continual tick fever. I was too embarrassed with the nursing to call for help, so got down the flask of volatile medicinal whiskey, a razor, my vanity of tweezers, and performed some delicate surgery, praying no one would walk in upon the scene.

Tell it all. After I'd cleaned the razor and tweezers with the whiskey, the surgeon herself took a large dollop having observed its effects for a long time upon men's courage. After I stopped choking and gasping the courage was there quick enough, and I began the delicate task at hand, so to say.

I made an incision across the black back of the first tick, and then cut deeper. There was little blood, but, Lord, it must have been painful. Very carefully I excavated and separated, and knowing the entire head and body must be removed I took my time. I extracted the ugly insect, and saw it was still alive. It made me sick in the stomach. Confident now, I quickly went to work on the second tick, this one deeper. It too was alive when I withdrew it and dropped it in a dish.

Finished, satisfied with my surgery, I pressed a poultice on the two small wounds with my hand. Tell me about the power of life! As I settled the cool poultice, his member began to grow like a thickroot mushroom. I could have died. It was rising and clean and stout and I ached within and blushed within and covered him with a sheet and ran to the river as fast as I could. "Go sit with the Lieutenant!" I ordered Porter as he crossed the yard. He watched me with bewilderment. I ran down the beach out of sight and then threw myself into the river. The cold water didn't help for a long time.

His recovery was slow, but steady. The next morning when Major Powell came to see him James was awake and alert, and a little of his color had come back.

"Why, it's a miracle," he exclaimed. "Has the fever broken?"

"It is still with him, but the worst may be over," I informed him.

"Whatever did you do? I thought he would be a goner by this morning, pardon my lack of faith, Jim."

"It's all right Major," James said with a weak smile.

"In the course of my . . . washing him I discovered he had these buried in his vitals," I said, crimson creeping up my face.

I held out the basin for him to see the insects.

"I will be damned! Ticks. Did you see these Jim?"

"She showed me," James said, and more color came to his face than I would have expected.

"They were well hidden," I supplied.

"Indeed. Tick fever. Had you not extracted them he'd have died sure. You've done a miracle."

"Just a little cutting," I said.

"We are ever grateful," Powell said. "Well, Jim, she's saved you. You take your time now. I don't expect resupply from Kanab for weeks yet, and in the meantime we'll be exploring the Navajo country."

"I'd like to go with you," James said, trying to rise.

"Daft, all of you," I said, shooing them out. "When I think he's fit to join you he shall join you, and not before," I said smartly, hiding some pride in my patient's recovery.

"Yes Ma'am," Powell said, flashing a toothy grin from beneath his short black beard. "And we'll be beholding. I'll visit later Jim, when the sun's gone down."

So began what I can only think of as an guilty idyll, one which caused me much trouble at the time, but today I look upon it as the treachery of nature's dominion. I found myself having to fight down the unseemly thoughts. In another day James was sitting up in bed and eating solid food. By the third, he was able to walk and I helped him out into the dooryard where he sat in the shade and gazed at the river. Without their father, the two boys waited upon the Lieutenant hand and foot, and hung on his every word. When he gave each of them a small pocket knife he made them friends for life. He would sit and bounce Elizabeth on his knee for hours while she gurgled up into his river-green eyes with happy contentment.

Between chores I sat with him, and began to know some of the happiest hours of my life. He had an endless curiosity, and I found him able to draw out of me memories and knowledge I didn't know I possessed. And I gave as good as I got.

Explaining Mormonism is a chore, sometimes. James listened to me with a serious face as I told him about the Baptism of the Dead and the fact that we would someday be Gods and Goddesses on our own planets. His eyes, however, betrayed a deep, skeptical amusement. I told him of other curiosities—of the Golden Plates written in an ancient tongue which were revealed to Joseph Smith by the Angel Moroni. And that the Prophet could read this strange language using magic spectacles. "I see," was all he said.

One afternoon I asked James how he had come to know the Major and join the expedition.

"In the war," James said, his eyes distant. "I'd just graduated from the University of Pennsylvania. The war was two years old by then, and there was a great demand for cartographers. Huh," he smiled. "I never got near a map."

"What did you do then?"

"Fought, and killed."

"I'm sorry."

"No, I'd do it again. We saved the country, and destroyed the abomination of slavery. Or nearly so."

"Yes," I said. "The war was very distant in Utah. Two of John's sons served in California, but the rest of them stayed home. We were fighting then as well for our lives, but in a different way."

"The Major was in command of the Company when I enlisted. I was with him through to the end. Saw him lose his arm to cannon shot."

"It must have been terrible."

"Yes."

"Why did you stay with the Major?"

"Adventure, of course," he laughed, and I could not tell if he was serious or not.

"I'm a poor swimmer," I said. "Going down the cataracts in those boats would scare the life out of me."

"It has a treacherous heart," he admitted. "Sometimes, in the deep canyons, wet and hungry, I longed to be back at war. There was more lulls than fighting, mostly, but the river never quits, never sleeps. It will reach out and grab you in an instant. You can never turn your back on her."

"Her?"

"It's a her to me."

"That's odd."

"I don't have much experience with women, though. I could be wrong," he said. "The river has the quality that I expect women have."

"And what quality would that be?"

"Oh," and then he flushed. "Soft and liquid to look at—beautiful—but she has a hard core if you fall from any height."

"Surely dozens of women must fall for you."

"Not likely," he laughed. "Where we go there are no women."

"Worse luck for them," I jested.

"You're kind," he said, and I saw him wanting to take my hand, and suddenly realized the wrong turnings our conversation always seemed to take.

"I'm going for a bath now," I said. "Hotter than . . . "

"Hell's hinges," he said, and grinned his man-boy grin and the sun was twice as hot.

"I'll join you," he said, rising. "I'm quite ready for a bath myself."

"Not with me, sir," I said, and walked away before I said more.

The river was a woman, then? Her color was emerald this afternoon with coils of rust-red fans swirled down by some distant deluge. I waded into the water in the small cove downstream from the rock house where I always bathed. I shed my dresses and petticoats, and slipped into the cold water feeling it's embrace between my legs and breasts, cooling and cleaning, giving a rise to a sensuous langour, at which thought, thankfully, the cold water quickly dispelled. I was not a strong swimmer, and one did have to watch the level of the water as it could rise and fall in hours due to upstream storms or melting from the distant Rockies at its source. Rose and fell, coiled and swirled and sucked at the rocks and sand, a deep bellied thing if indeed it was a woman.

My thoughts were a thousand miles away, my mind seeking its own source. I thought of John, and imagined him in the cool mountains cutting lumber on the top of the world. I let myself drift slightly out of the cove where there were dangerous eddies that could suck boat, man or animal into them and spit them back out upon a malevolent whim.

I always stayed close to the shore, but my mind was not upon safety, and so I suddenly became aware that I was perhaps ten feet farther from the shore than I had ever strayed, and so began to strike for the shore, a little hiccup of panic shortening my stroke and breath. The next thing I knew I was farther from the shore than before, and moving downstream slightly, the sight of my clothes on the bank more distant.

The first small whirlpool tugged at my ankles and my head went under. I fought the panic again, and turned upon my back because I swim more strongly that way. Then I began to kick hard for the shore. But it was of no avail, and a second large evil coiling of water rose to the surface and grasped me for a final cold embrace. I thought of my children as I fought to stay on the surface, and then all thoughts left me and I began to scream until my throat seemed to rip apart.

Sound in the desert, on bare rocks and thin distance carries far. I saw James running as if he'd never been sick, shedding his boots and pants as he hopped on the bank.

"Hold on!" I heard him cry and he plunged into the water, a clean white knifing without a splash. He swam like a fish. I had been turned out of the smaller eddy into a larger one by the time I felt him tuck his arm under my shoulders and haul me to the surface. I clung to him and fought him in my unreasoning panic until he gripped me under my bare breasts like a vise. "Stop fighting me!" he ordered, and I went limp in his arms, exhausted and chilled. In a moment we were on the warm sandy beach and he sat me down. I was quite all right by the time he got me to the shore, and for my gasping for breath I was unaware that my single petticoat was plastered revealingly between my legs, my bare breast-tips wrinkled and high from the cold water. For a moment I didn't care, and he looked at me with something akin to awe, wet dripping from his chin, his bare legs and men's shorts also like a skin.

"Have your cuts healed?" I asked him queerly, and then we both burst out laughing until I was crying, and he was holding me, my breasts pressed to him and his hand under my backside and then we kissed. My hand brushed across the front of him as I pulled away, feeling the proud pole obeying no thought of the brain.

"Oh, stop," I said, and ran for my clothes and pulled them on, shame burning my face. In a moment he was beside me, fully clothed, stammering an apology.

"Oh, forgive me, Mrs. Lee," he pled.

"Of course I forgive you, Lt. Dellenbaugh," I said. "I think, however, considering that last little *tete et tete*, you're quite well enough to return to your camp."

"Of course I am," he said, pain in his eyes. "Thank you for saving my life."

"It was my pleasure," I said, and blushed to the roots of my hair.

"We'll never be square," he said. "That whirlpool was about to put you right back to shore. You'd have been just fine. I could have kept my feet dry, but I wanted to rescue you. I know the river. That's how she works. Aren't I the fool?"

"I shall always think of you as my hero in any case," I said. "But from now on I think it would be best if there were no James and Emeline. I am Mrs. Lee, and you are Lieutenant Dellenbaugh of the Powell expedition."

"I quite agree," he said, turning away, and I wanted desperately to call him back. Instead I said aloud to his retreating form, "I've got cows to milk."

And that is not what I wanted to say at all.

Now he was sitting beside me once again when I needed him most.

"A letter?" he asked, indicating the sheaf of papers. "I saw the rider come in. Is it bad news?"

"My husband," I said stiffly, "is in the penitentiary."

"Oh what a travesty!" he said, and turned to me, his face close. He took my hands in his, and his green eyes filled with sympathy. I gazed at the blond curls upon his head, the strong nose, the mouth cocked over teeth bone white against his sun-browned skin. I wanted him to tell me of his transcendent eastern sophistry, that there are shadow worlds with soft edges which do not echo the harder edges of this world. I wanted him to speak to me of green lawns and slow rivers, of lace and laughter, of books and politics, of bright paintings and delicate porcelains. In this sun-hammered place there was nowhere to hide. And I wished to hide in him, to let him love me until our heat turned the sand to glass.

"Is it because of, well, the polygamy?"

"One of the charges," I said.

"What a cruel injustice," he declared fiercely. "I hold that the Constitution of this country protects religious freedom whether it expresses itself in plural marriage, or by worshiping the night sky or the spirits of the woods! It is all the same thing. It is a damnable, unlawful persecution, a hunting for witches. I am so sorry for you and your family."

"Yes, thank you."

"You have done so much for me, I'll never be able to repay you," he said, suddenly conscious that we were holding hands, and let them go. We were the same age, but I knew that I looked like the Shivwitts women I had seen, old women by the time they were teens. His face, though sun brown, had youth's strength in it, while I felt the age of the rocks. At that moment, I was as close as I'd ever come to cursing God aloud to His face, may I be forgiven. "Is there any favor at all that I may give you? Accompany you back to the settlements so you may see him? Money? I can draw some pay from the Major."

"No, thank you, but no. There is nothing you can do, Lieutenant," I said. "I will not be leaving for the settlements any time soon. My place is here." I could see the bewilderment in his eyes.

"But surely you want to go," he said.

"He wishes me to stay here," I informed him.

"That's a hard piece of business," he said, working his jaw.

"This is our home. Someone must keep the ferry, and raise the children, and make sure Brigham's pilgrims don't get their feet wet. Please, now, I wish to be alone."

"I'm sorry. I'll leave you, then," he said quietly. He rose from the sand with just the suggestion of a courteous, old world bow. I watched his broad shoulders recede in the hot, quavering distance. When he left I wanted to run after him and throw myself into his arms. Instead I took another drink of the warm, slightly saline water. It was very many minutes before I regained the courage and composure to read on.

CHAPTER ELEVEN

The rest is sadly told, and in the telling of it I am in a peril of losing my own sanity, Em. That I should confess to my beloved of the crimes I've seen troubles my waking and sleeping moments. I loathe this prison, and am old and the cold damp penetrates my bones like knives. That I should suffer this discomfort for an eternity does not trouble me if only I could find forgiveness in the present.

Major Higbee addressed us by firelight. "It is the orders of the President, that all the emigrants must be put out of the way. President Haight has counseled with Colonel Dame, or has had orders from him to put them away; none who are old enough to talk are to be spared ."

When at last it came my turn to address the group, I told them that God would have to change my heart to consent to such a wicked thing as the wholesale killing of people. I made every attempt to reason with them, and I could see by their scowls how they disapproved of me. These are the men with whom I'd settled the country, and now they turned against me.

I've never been a man to have friends, but I never thought that of all these men, whom I'd treated fairly, could be so spiteful. I felt doubt. I was betraying the Priesthood, but made a last stab at holding my conviction. I was ordered to be silent.

"Brother Lee," Higbee said with sarcasm, "is afraid of shedding innocent blood. Why, brethren, there is not a drop of innocent blood in that entire camp of Gentile outlaws; they are a set of cut-throats, robbers and assassins; they are a part of the people who drove the Saints from Missouri, and who aided to shed the blood of our Prophets, Joseph and Hyrum, and it is our orders from all in authority, to get the emigrants from their stronghold, and help the Indians kill them.

"But Joseph Smith has told us never to betray anyone," I said. "The only way to get them out of that fort is by treachery, and I will have no part of it."

Silence. Only the snapping of the fire, the hostile, mayhap guilty look on some faces, but withal more anger with me for questioning authority. I, at that moment, and may God forgive me, weakened my unpopular objections. It was then that Brother Higbee gave me my orders.

"Your faith has never been questioned until this moment Brother Lee. There is one more test, however, so I may promise you the blessings of paradise. You will go into the camp under a white flag, and you will negotiate with them to surrender themselves into our safe-keeping. You will decoy them from their position, and arrange for their order of departure. Stress to them that we are acting solely for their own benefit, to protect them from the savage Indians. Do you understand?"

"I do," I said. I was bound to obey. I knew that the orders had come from higher up than Colonel Dame. Further, I was bound by a military oath of the Nauvoo Legion. To disobey a military order was punishable by the firing squad. I capitulated, hiding my tears from the white men. To do otherwise would have meant my own death in the night at the hand of my brethren.

We then knelt in a large circle, holding hands, and praying for God's guidance. I called upon heaven and angels and the spirits of men to forestall this tragedy. After the prayer I withdrew into the darkness and sat under a juniper, tears unashamedly coursing down my face. Footsteps told of the approach of the one man whom I felt was a real friend, Charlie Hopkins.

"I don't think I can do it, Charlie," I said.

"I think it will be all right, Brother Lee," he said to me, putting his arm around my shaking shoulders. "The priesthood is united in this thing. We do it for our survival. God cannot condemn us for that. There will be blessings upon you tomorrow. Did not Higbee say he had evidence of God's approval?"

Suddenly there was the approach of another man, a dim shape in the darkness, but I picked him out as Major Higbee, who had so insulted and taunted me for my weakness. Starlight shone on the saber at his side.

"Leave us alone, Brother Hopkins," he said, and Charlie tipped his hat, gave me a comforting touch on the shoulder, and left as Higbee placed his hands upon my head.

"Brother Lee, I am ordered by President Haight to inform you that you shall receive a crown of Celestial glory for your faithfulness, and your eternal joy shall be complete."

I was shaken, and was comforted. This was my life's conviction, the obtaining of the Kingdom of God both here on earth and in heaven.

"I will do as you say, Brother Higbee. But I shall do it with a heavy heart," I said.

"It will be a business upon which the Lord will smile," he informed me . . .

My water was gone.

There were but a mere few pages left for me to read.

CHAPTER TWELVE

There are no walls to the mind when it slips into madness. Figures wrought by horror danced in the heat mirage. A heaviness pinned me to the earth even as my spirit was clawing my breath to depart my body. In moments of lucidity my faith in God held no meaning.

I watched, and prayed for Lt. Dellenbaugh's form to appear and comfort me. Nothing but heat, and the hallucinations of a meadow in Zion shimmered in the distance like the floor of hell. I put the papers down, seeing blood stains upon every curvature of his pen, and cursed myself for having been so blind.

The signals were all there, had I but seen them for the looking. I cast back, and in the dancing heat mirages saw the rains, the horrible rains. And then in my unsettled mind's eye I saw the riders coming in the night with guns and torches rooting through our property in outrageous searches and seizures. Brigham was as good as his word. At midday on a fine fall day, with the light slanting low over the Pine Valley Mountain, a rider appeared from Cedar City saying Judge Cradelbaugh was on the loose, and headed for Harmony to arrest John D. Lee.

There was a sophisticated warning system setup throughout the south of the state to give notice that Marshals were on the hunt for polygamists. The territorial prison was full of men whose families were sadly left to fend for themselves. It was a cruel tyranny. Prearranged sets of signal flags flew from high bluffs, riders were sent out, and Indian smoke signals were used as subterfuge. Usually there was plenty of warning, and the Marshals had a hard job of it finding any polygamist who didn't want to be found. There may have been some, of course, who wished for nothing better than a little time cooling their heels in the pen just to get away from their wives.

I rememberthe day in late 1874 or perhaps 1875 when John, Louisa Wright and family, Rachel and her family, and Ann-Marie and Polly Bean were riding back home to Harmony in two wagons from Washington City and the county fair. My confinement with David was long over, but I did not feel the need for company or county fairs. My life had settled into a reward of work, raising David, doing the community chores, and beginning to put my house together. John had dug a basement for my fine new house, roofed it, and so we were to live until the upper stories were completed. It may sound as if we were living like tubers in a cellar, but that was not so. I had carpets, and lights from windows, and the house remained an even temperature despite the summer heat. John assured me the warming in the winter would be just as easy as the cooling, and I was quite content.

Several of the families still lived within the walls of the adobe fort, having in a patchwork fashion built rooms and dorms for the children. Outside the walls other houses were in various states of raising or completion. John was scrupulous to give each one of his wives their own desires, some for leaded glass, some for hardwood floors, others for extravagant fretwork on the eaves. His mills, his fields and flocks were growing by the day. It was a happy time, and most of the days passed without ever thinking of massacres or Indians or Brigham Young. We had our own church, and school at Harmony. David was a cherubic, tousle-haired boy with fat cheeks and a dimpling smile. John adored all of his children, and I admired the judicious hand he took with those who had reached the age of rebellion.

As young men will and must, the breaking away was not easy. John counseled them to stay at Harmony and build their lives around their own family, but if they wished to leave he bade them godspeed. Several of his older sons were on missions to England, of which he was proud. John preached each Sunday in his sonorous voice, sometimes moving me to tears with his love of God. Indeed, God's bounty showered upon us all, and I was happy.

My sister-wives slowly adjusted to my presence, and soon we were working together for the common good. Mind, it was not all sweetness and light, for there are always human squabbles as with any other family. Let's just say that when a squabble starts in a polygamous family, it tends to extend itself until scores of people have to have their say-so. It was just plain living, and I loved it all. John shared himself and his companionship as equably as he could. Of course, some of my sister-wives were of the temperament that less was better, but not Emeline Buxton Lee. I looked forward to seeing him day or night, and was seldom disappointed.

But o'er all, lay the shadow.

When the rider found John on the road with his wagons he warned him the Marshals were coming. John bundled Sarah-Caroline in the other wagon with Rachael and came on ahead to Harmony in some speed.

"Saddle Sadie!" he cried to Polly's fourteen year old, William. Then he rushed into the kitchen area within the fort. I came out of my cellar with David in my arms and went to see what the commotion was about.

"Back so soon?" I called to him.

"Back and gone, I'm afraid, Em. It's the federal fools out for exercise. I'll be going up to the Kolob fingers to cool my heels. Fetch me a side of that bacon, dear," he said. He seemed thoroughly unalarmed by the news that he was being pursued.

"Then you must hurry, John," I said, helping him assemble some foodstuffs. He filled a sack, gave David a chuck under the chin, kissed me breathless, and then was on his fine grey mare before the rest of the wagons hove into view from down the valley.

We were used to such alarms, but nothing had really come of them until now. No sooner had Sadie's grey rump disappeared across the valley than a cloud of dust rose to the north, and the government officers descended upon our home at Harmony like so many barbaric raiders.

I turned and saw Aggatha standing at the entrance to the fort. The wreath of her white hair shone in the sun, her nearly toothless mouth set in a straight line. To my astonishment, she was trying to load an old flintlock musket, the kind not seen since the American Revolution, and she was making smart work of it. The long rifle was too heavy for her frail arms to lift, so she held it in the crook of her arm. Soon all of us, perhaps ten women, two dozen young women and boys, and children in arms were standing in a nervous knot, not knowing whether to run and hide, or to stand and resist. Resistance, of course, was useless.

The first dust coated rider pulled his horse to stop in front of us, nearly knocking me over. I passed David to Little Winnie, daughter of Louisa, who sometimes helped me tend David, and grabbed the horse by the reins. I caught a quirt across the face, and a boot which sent me sprawling. I was more angry than hurt, and as Rachel stepped forward to help me I got up, went to Aggie and wrested the musket from her hands and leveled it at the big man with the moustache, having no real idea how it worked. Before I could figure out the triggers another man on horseback came bowling around the back of the fort and snatched it out of my hands.

"She was going to shoot you dead, Ezra," the man laughed, throwing the musket into the raspberry bushes.

"The whore," the man cursed at me. Soon we were confronted by a half dozen rough looking men who looked as if the ride from wherever they had come from had not lifted their spirits. From the center of the arc of riders a man rode out who appeared to be the leader and dismounted. He was tall, spare as a pole, and had an long waxed moustache white with dust.

"Who's in charge of this whorehouse?" he demanded of us generally, and was met with the only weapon we had. Silence. "Search the Goddamned place right to the basements, he ordered.

You people stand fast or I'll round you up and lock you up. Is that clear?" Silence greeted his demand.

The little posse had practice in their dirty work, for they spread out and began to loot the houses with a breaking of glass and flinging of furniture. Here came a child's pot chair into the yard, then a dress. They helped themselves to sackfuls of food and fruit.

"Not a sign of liquor," I heard one shout angrily—only John knew where the liquor was buried. "Damn Mormons."

"Get off this property," I heard Rachel demand of Mr. Moustaches. "You have no right."

"I not only have a right, but I've got a writ, lady," he said.

"We're friends of Brigham Young, I warn you," said Polly Bean in more of a snit than outrage. Polly was a funny girl thinking the axis of the universe was centered somewhere between the top of her chestnut hair and her gangly big feet.

"Shut up, Polly," I said, and she did. I will admit, she received instruction well, but it never took, as they say.

It didn't take but a few minutes to sack the place, and the men reassembled in the growing dusk.

"All right, which one of you wants to tell me where John D. Lee is hiding? Tell us now, and maybe we won't run off your stock, or worse," the leader said.

"Tell him nothing," Rachel spat at their feet. "Cursed men," she said with contempt. Another rough man made a move toward her, but Moustaches stopped him.

"That'll do," he said, and I could hear a weary resignation. "We'll never catch any of these Polygs or the murderers. They know we're coming before we know we're coming," he said with disgust. He mounted his horse and rode into the fort's walls, ducking low. In a moment he returned with a kerosene lantern. We stood breathless with fear. The man slowly rolled a cigarette and then lit it while the other men restlessly looked at us, and at the gathering of the night.

"We want to be out of here by dark, Ez," one of the men said.

"Let's light the place up a little," Moustaches said, carrying the lantern to the large barn full of the summer hay. Inside were a three of our draft animals, the mules, and several sheep. He casually tossed the lit lantern into the open loft door, and the dry grass exploded in the night.

We watched the barn burn to the ground, a towering yellow fire eclipsing the light of the yellow moon. Our bucket brigade had but three buckets. The screams of the trapped animals was a horror, the fire so hot we could not go near it to release them. It's a dry country.

We Mormon women are not known for our idleness, nor our timid hearts, but in this instance, and others, when the magnitude of events were far beyond our abilities, we turn to tears and prayer. Neither extinguished the fire, nor stopped the death of the animals. It was enough, then, that our children were unharmed, and our husband safe. But our love for our fellow man, our countrymen, continued to erode until it is no wonder that a sense of siege remained with us for all of our lives.

And I wondered about the fidelity of God to his Chosen People that he would allow us to be so persecuted, but suffering is life's salt, and we had the guide of the Jewish people as told in the Bible. The Jewish People had centuries of hideous persecutions, whereas the Mormons were a "people" for less than thirty years. By comparison, our experience paled, but that knowledge was of no comfort.

I was for some reason angry at John for abandoning us, for not protecting us. Practically, he had no choice. If captured he would be an utter loss to his family which needed his work, his guidance, his husbandry. And in my delusion, I thought he was hiding because he was a polygamist, for that is ostensibly what they were searching for. The federal net was cast broad for polygamists as well as for participants in the Mountain Meadows. When John finally confessed to me, it became apparent that his wives and children knew almost nothing about the massacre. Loyalty and secrecy run deep, and though John's soul was in daily torment, he continued to believe that he had done the work of the Lord.

Only Rachel, as the second senior wife, knew the secret hideout where John and other men went when the federals were roaming the countryside. Aggatha was nominally our leader in John's absence, but she was so frail as to be a figurehead. It was Rachel who took charge in his absence. Through the years of the Civil War the "visits" by federal officials were infrequent, but after the war they got to the point when half of the able bodied men in southern Utah were in hiding.

"I want you to come with me to take news to John," Rachel said to me as the sun was rising over the black ashes of the barn. "Someone else has to know where he goes in case something should happen to me." I do not know why she selected me, but I was only too glad to go with her to be able to see John. I thought he would comfort us. Our saddle horses were in a corral behind the fort, and spared the fire, so the next evening we slipped out and caught two and rode off into the night in search of our husband. Rachel led us on a circuitous route. David was left with Little Winnie's mother, Louisa, who was wet and nursing twins. Since my walk across America I had not been out much in the wilds, and found each shadow, each night sound full of menace.

We rode higher, and then struck east into the narrow defiles of Kolob's finger canyons, following a dim sandy trail under the mute white lantern of the moon. After what seemed miles, Rachel stopped.

"We wait here. They will find us," she whispered, but it was not until the first leak of the water-thin light of dawn before we suddenly heard a voice behind us.

"Adonai," we heard a gruff voice call from a rock above and behind us. I whirled in the saddle, startled.

"Gives us Life," Rachel answered in a loud, firm voice. She had taught me a series of passwords as we rode through the night, and I marveled at the cleverness of some of them, and the foolishness of others. I was learning that secrecy was as much a part of our lives as innocent conversation. With the stream of California emigrants coming through Utah we suspected spies were always among them, and we had to remain vigilant lest we reveal the whereabouts of our menfolk.

"Who goes?" the voice asked.

"It's Rachel."

"Who is with you?"

"Emeline Buxton."

"Wait, I'll fetch John," the voice said, and so we waited.

John came riding hard down the trail just as the sun was rising. I could tell by his posture that he was anxious. He rode alongside, reached over and gave us both a hug—Rachel first—and then told us to follow him closely. Two hours later, after a bewildering series of switchbacks through a forest of red rock arches we came to a three-campfire camp, and I saw a half dozen men finishing their breakfast, cleaning their gear, but it was the work of idleness. Some of the men had been hiding for weeks. I recognized some men from both Cedar City and Washington City, but they did not deign to greet us in any friendly manner. It was depressing. I felt as out of sorts and angry as the men who looked jealously at us, wishing for their own families.

John took us to a lean-to built of a flap of tenting, sat us down on some soft hides, and made us breakfast while Rachel delivered the news that several thousand dollars worth of feed and livestock had gone up in smoke.

John took the news calmly, but I by then knew the look in the man's eye, and there was a real fire there, one that would scorch barnboards. He insisted we give him a careful description of the man who had fired the barn. But he did not seem overly surprised at the news of looting and loss of the barn.

"Well, it's a good enough excuse that I get to see you both," he finally said. "The comforts of camping have lost their appeal. The man will regret his bent for arson. What other news have you?"

"We saw another fire down toward the Kelsey farm when we were riding up," Rachel reported. "I expect that is where they paid their next call."

"I want you to send young Robert up the Pine Valley mountain. Have him bring the herd down, it's time anyway. Robert and John Jr. are to take fifteen head of milking cows to St. George and sell them. Turn the money over to Aggatha. When I come back I'll go to Cedar City for materials. We'll buy what hay we can find, and set things aright. I had a vision of his happening, but the loss of a barn and the livestock—damn, my best pulling horses—is as nothing if you all are safe. What is that welt on your face Em?" he asked seemingly offhand. I turned to Rachel for a guide as to my reply. She shook her head negatively.

"The clothesline snapped at me," I said lightly. He studied me for a moment, looked at Rachel who hid her eyes in the ground.

"Very well," he said cooly. "They'll not be back, from the reports we've had. They will be sweeping up Long Valley to the east now. The others called him 'Ez', eh? I know just where to find them," he said cryptically.

In the late afternoon, waiting for darkness so we could return to Harmony, John and I went for a walk up through a stand of junipers and scrub oak. We climbed for a time, and then broke out on a ledge overlooking the valley below us.

"As I said, I had a vision of that calamity last night," he winked at me as we sat side by side. He dug in his pouch and produced a fine pair of brass binoculars. "These do aid the vision," he said. "I watched from here. I could tell it was not the fort or the houses, so I did not come down."

"You already knew."

"Yes, and it took some restraint not to ride down and shoot them all, but shooting won't work. They're coming, Em, and they won't stop coming. In another vision, or dream a week ago, the Lord disclosed to me my time is short."

"You must be mistaken."

"Perhaps, but I saw men in the shape of dark-winged birds. Hosts of dark creatures . . . The men in camp say that Brigham will not even entertain the notion of outlawing polygamy, and I won't have it myself. But the future may see things differently."

"Surely a legislature can't override God's law."

"No, but it could retire it until the people recognize its truth."

"I've never heard of such a thing," I said, shocked. "Were you there, when the Prophet had his vision of plural marriage?"

"I was in Nauvoo, but it came gradual, like. Joseph knew the reaction of the people would be less than favorable, so it came in secrecy. But I have seen the revelation," he said, in a voice of wonder. "God's writing by God's own hand."

"But the Prophet isn't God, John."

"Of course not, just his chosen voice. And it is a golden world that awaits us yonder. There won't be any barn burnings," he said, and I heard the seed of bitterness in his words.

"May I be so forward as to ask about Aggatha and Rachel?"

"What do you want to know?"

"They are so much . . . older."

"It was common practice for men to marry the elderly so as to afford them salvation and protection. Widows and the like. For those who could not find husbands they are not doomed to Hell or anything. They are just in a kind of ante-room of heaven until Christ comes and there will be plenty of opportunities for them. I've married I don't know how many women I've never lived with, or had relations with. Aggatha is the first. She was sixty when I married her."

"I see," I said, not clearly seeing.

"And it was my duty to feed them and house them and afford them whatever comforts I could. Aggie was brave after Crooked River. She ran a part of a mob off our farm by herself."

"She was going to shoot the man with the moustache with an old musket."

"I don't doubt it," John laughed, and became grim. "We'll see," he said.

"And Rachel?"

"Rachel too was sealed to me to afford her protection. I think she is sixty-five now, but she's borne me three children, and suffered as much as any woman coming out of Missouri. A fine woman, always true," he paused. I saw a whelm of doubt cross his face, and then anger as he reached up and drew his finger along the welt the quirt left on my face. "Clotheslines are tricky things."

"Yes," I said, embarrassed for my lie. Even white lies are black, no matter the intent of the lie.

"Another week, I'll be back. Damn!" He pounded his fist on the bare rock hard enough to crack it, and seemed not to feel the force of the blow. "I feel such a coward. Shall I give myself up, Em?"

"For polygamy?" I asked, startled. "Not likely."

"Ah, Lord save us," he said, looking into the setting of the sun. "I hope you never have to know . . . "

"Know what, John?"

"The future."

"We can't know the future."

"Some of us know the future, for we write it for ourselves. Be strong, Em."

"I will, John," I said, and he began to stroke my yellow hair, and I lay my head on his shoulder, the light gold and soft on the red rocks, the sharp smell of juniper in our nostrils. It happens, oh, it happens—his rough hands felt good as they touched my legs and ran up my flanks, and when our bare flesh and hands touched and touched and my breasts rolled out of my bodice wet and full of milk. I lifted them in my hands and offered them to his mouth. Ah, the slick wet of his tongue and the tickling of his beard against my nipples so good as to never be forgotten. John standing as he shed his clothing a dark shape against the setting of the sun as I hiked up my skirts and took him by his hard white hips and drew him into me my eyes open to the sky and the arches of heaven shaped to receive a stone thrust that went so deep and good I was lost in fires that had no smoke. Thus was dark-haired Porter Lee conceived on the summit of Kolob at the setting of the sun.

And I remember the swift swallows of gossip that flew through the country some weeks later after John returned. Never doubt we had our own circuit of opinion and information quite separate from that of the men. And it was not all idle gossip of children and crops and new dresses, but information of the heart, and information that sustained us. If the center of the world was in our husband, the orbit of our lives followed our own eccentric course around him, and we were our own selves despite all that the Gentiles will ever say about us that we are deluded slaves and whores.

I despise polygamy in all of its evil manifestations to this day. But then I was willing, and so God willed it for me to live until such time came when I should gain a different kind of freedom. The information we womenfolk had, even beyond our own circles, was usually much more accurate than the information the men possessed. The men told tales and stories which tended to gather an embellishment with each telling, while we women stuck to the truth. It is the truth that sustains us, sustains me even unto this day.

Silly Polly Bean got the news first in Washington City. Mr. Moustache was brought through the city on a litter in a wagon, beaten half to death. He was accompanied by an armed guard. It seems the man who had torched John D. Lee's barn, and struck his wife Emeline Buxton across the face with a quirt was caught off guard in their camp at Long Valley up in the Cedar Breaks. Someone had come out of the darkness, and gave Mr. Moustache such a thrashing he would spend the rest of his life with one arm permanently bent. I did not wonder where the quirt came from that John began to carry when he rode. It was a piece of leather which I recognized. But never a word came from John's lips as to how he may have acquired it.

CHAPTER THIRTEEN

Many people take refuge in their fondest memories, but I was having a hard time finding them this day. The sun was high, and hot. It hammered the ground, tried to dissolve the very shade itself in which I was sitting with John's book of the dead. Better the bitter memories than to finish this cursed confession, or whatever it was, I thought.

For several years after the barn was burned we lived in peace at Harmony, and then twin blows fell upon the Lee family; Brigham Young paid a visit to Washington, and the rains came, God help us. I should have known his arrival was harbinger.

Brigham was due to come south in September. It would be the third but not the last time I would see him in person. John's new house and flour mill in Washington were finished, and his prosperity seemed to increase with each day. My house was complete to fine glass windows with little warpage, and we had other luxuries—better food and shoes and clothes. The children thrived, and the Meadows seemed to be forgotten.

Most of the time I chose to remain at Harmony in my new house raising my children and working in the fields. Rachel too preferred to live at Harmony. In the summer some of the younger wives moved to Washington to occupy the imposing stone mansion John built near the cooperative cotton mill. Polly Bean had set herself up as mistress of the mansion, and put on airs to make me blush. She acted as if every day was a theatrical in which she was the star. Ann-Marie went with her, as well as Sarah Caroline. Poor Aggie had wandered off to some place in her mind in recent months, and was invalided within the old fort from which she had refused to move after all these years. Until John told me about Haun's Mill I never knew the reason for her fear.

John asked me if I would come to Washington City for the festivities, and I reluctantly consented, not really wishing to see Brigham again. Since his warning to John I distrusted the man, but let it sleep. Every time I heard John praise Brigham Young—which was often—I went into a depression. At the same time I knew one could not dislike the Living Prophet of God and expect any of God's mercies.

An undeclared holiday always occasioned the arrival of Brigham in the settlements in Zion. We prepared our finest clothes, cleaned our houses, and polished the furniture. The men cleaned stables and dressed up their horses with the finest tack. In the mansion it was all bustle. When Rachel and I arrived, Rachel took charge, as was her right. Polly's authority was usurped, and she was ever in a pique. She thought the Prophet was coming to see her, and no one dared disabuse her of the notion. She was so full of herself that when the next day the Prophet passed her by without a notice, she ascribed it to the rain which began to fall that day—another harbinger which would fulfill itself by Christmastime. "How could he see me in all that downpour?" she pouted.

In the event, Rachel took over the mansion and threw herself into the preparations for the great feast that we were to get ready for Brigham's arrival. All of John's wives loved the Prophet. I kept my own counsel, of course. The night before his arrival Rachel and Polly were in the kitchen baking. I was upstairs sewing a new dress for Little Winnie. All of the lamps in the house were blazing in the windows, a great extravagance. John was in a holiday mood himself. He was proud of what he'd built, he was proud of his family. That is ever the Mormon measure of one's standing with the Lord.

John was sitting in his stuffed leather chair in the parlor which faced the broad street. Outside, traffic was to-ing and fro-ing like it was the Fourth of July. Small boys were setting off fireworks in the south fields, lighting the sky. The town band was tootling down by the mill in a warmup for the 'morrow's concert. Even I was caught up in the good feelings, and I hummed as I stitched.

Then from downstairs I heard the sudden breaking of glass. There had been a storm brewing all afternoon between Rachel and Polly Bean, and it broke with a fury. John had a reputation for non-interference with the flare-ups between us. Usually we sorted it out among ourselves, but the noise from the kitchen brought John to his feet and into the kitchen like a flash, with me in trail.

Rachel was standing with an iron skillet in her hand, hefting it as easily as a dish towel. Polly Bean, hands on her hips, had her little bright red tongue stuck between her teeth. A smashed plate and a broken cherry pie lay on the floor between the old woman with the skillet and the saucy young actress. John stood there with a red face, debating whether or not it was a mistake for him to have charged into the negotiations.

"What is it?" he asked with surprising calm.

"Rachel has insulted my pie," Polly said, her eye lashes batting like fly whisks. John looked down at the pie and the broken plate. I thought he was going to go up the chimney.

"Rachel is in charge of this affair, Polly," John said mildly. "Pick up the crockery, apologize to your elder, and make your peace. Rachel, dear, that skillet does not become you. We don't have time for this fussing."

"I shall not!" Polly declared, and both Rachel and I gasped.

"I see," John said. John had never raised a hand to any of us, and rarely the children, but I thought if ever a time when the rod was meant for a wife, the time had arrived.

To our collective astonishment John fell to his knees and began to pick up the broken pieces of the plate. Soon I was beside him, then Rachel, and finally Polly joined us there on the floor. The sight of the big, solemn man on the floor picking up the broken plate suddenly caused me to erupt in a little giggle. Now I'm for it, I thought. Rachel had a laugh like a horse, and it started in her belly. She sat back on her rump and let go with a neigh. John looked at her, looked into his hands, and absently picked up a piece of the cherry pie, tasted it, and said, "The pie is fine."

Polly's little peal of laughter broke his stern resolve. I noticed the fine sheen of grey whiskers on his face under the bright lights. Outside, the band was passing by the house, playing a lively march-step hymn. Polly raised her hand in a mirror-practiced titter, and John D. Lee erupted in laughter of his own. Soon the four of us were rolling on the flagstones. We began to eat the pie that was free of dirt—Polly kept a fine floor—until it was gone. Finally John rose, went to the door, turned back and said, "Let that be a lesson." The door closed, leaving us looking at one another wondering just exactly what the lesson was.

I left Rachel and Polly to finish up, peace restored. I went into the parlor to go back upstairs and saw John had taken up his scripture again. He looked fine in the lamp light, perhaps a little bemused. I went over to him and put my arm around his shoulder and kissed the top of his head. He pretended to still be out of sorts. As I went up the stairs I heard him mutter, "A man knows better than to sort wildcats without a sack."

A messenger came to the house just as we were turning out the lamps. He reported to John that Brigham wished John to meet him on the trail in the morning, and accompany him as he entered Washington. It was a sign of high favor, and a signal to the community that John, despite his association with the Meadows, was still under Brigham's protection. It was the carrot before John felt his hard stick. We hadn't seen Brigham for years in the south, during which small signs of resentment against John surfaced in the community. I am convinced this was Brigham Young's insideous work with the conivance of local Church authorities. The federal grip upon the territory had strengthened, and rumors flew despite our apparent tranquility. John interpreted the pre-arrival meeting with Brigham as a good sign.

John asked Rachel and me to accompany him to meet the Prophet, but Rachel demurred. She had a subtle way of knowing when we wished to be alone, which was not that often. I doubt if they had slept in the same bed for years. Then John politely asked Polly Bean if she wished accompany us, a great honor, but to my surprise she too declined, saying her hair was not yet done to her satisfaction.

"Three hours, and I'd think sufficient," John said. "I can dress a dozen horses in that time." Polly's vanity always disappointed him. I do not know how often John visited her to fulfill his obligations, for she remained childless. Later, when she left him, I heard she bore a half dozen children for a horse trader who took her to California. In any case, I thanked the stars for her preoccupation with herself.

We rode John's finest saddle horses up toward Toquerville where the Prophet had spent the night. Little did we realize John was traveling the *Via Dolorosa* of his soul. It was a meeting which in the breadth of its treachery and hypocrisy was stunning. I think men and card players employ the phrase "blind-sided".

It was ten by the time we met the long entourage, the sun hot and high. Brigham greeted us with a wave of his hand, and beckoned us to fall alongside his carriage, one on either side. Brigham traveled far ahead of the dust, and so we were some fifty yards in front of the wives-and-other-baggage wagons. Brigham took favored wives with him wherever he went. Armed outriders were darting among the creosote bushes scouting for trouble.

Brigham was wearing a broad-brimmed hat which shaded most of his face. His dark suit looked hot and dusty, and his shirt was loose at the collar. The tassels from the buggy top went limp when he drew up and said, "John, tie up and sit with me a time." He ignored me as if I weren't a few feet away. It was a keen insult, but in the blindness of my husband when in the presence of Brigham Young, John didn't even notice. I was furious. Still am.

Instead of introducing me as decency dictated, John jumped down and tied his horse to the back of the buggy. Then he climbed up into the seat next to his father. He was like an eager child, and it disgusted me. I didn't even temper my thoughts. I did not care what they had shared before—God or hardship—no man on earth deserved such guileless worship.

Brigham snapped the whip over the backs of his fine dark horses and with a regal motion waved me back, indicating I was to follow along in the dust out of earshot. I was speechless. By this time John realized his neglect of me, and the insult, and I heard him say, "but she is my finest wife." Brigham ignored him.

"I'm sorry, dear," he said to me with a shamed face. "If you would excuse us for a brief time." My first impulse was to ride away as fast as I could, but something told me to stay. I obediently fell back. There was a little breeze, so I rode on the slight upwind, not feeling any guilt that I could hear their every word. I'm not by nature an eavesdropper, but where Brigham Young was concerned, I thought to play the innocent was sheer folly. I could have ridden a mile away and still heard the conversation, for when Brigham spoke it was always as if he were speaking to a congregation of thousands, and wanted those in the last row to hear every word.

"Thank you for meeting me," Brigham rumbled.

"I believe you'll find Washington City ready to welcome you," John replied. I became fascinated with the bouncing tassels of the buggy fringe. They resembled the state of my nerves.

"There have been some recent developments," Brigham said, "that will jeopardize the name and safety of the church, and perhaps result in the army taking over the civil government—or try."

"Sir?"

"Some faithful church members have written to me asking me to forgive them for their part in the Mountain Meadows. The government is intent on punishing someone, preferably me."

"That cursed place," John groaned.

"In their petitions for "'forgiveness'"—Brigham said the word with distaste—"they revealed to me some details that you neglected to give me when you made your first report."

"I told you everything," John protested. "We've been over this before."

"Different points of view have a way of disclosing different truths."

"And now you don't believe me?"

"You said it was the work of the Indians, from start to finish," Brigham said, his voice neutral.

"I did no such thing. I told you everything, including the names of those present. I even took it upon myself to assume much of the blame." I could hear John's anger in the rising. I'd wager for thirty years there hadn't been ten cross words between them.

"Others have come forward, and the government presses."

"What others?"

"One letter said the deed was ruining them, in that they could not sleep nor eat."

"It was horrid," John said.

"Do you know what I replied?"

"No, I don't." John said. I wished I could see their faces.

"I said if you are guilty and want a remedy 'a rope around your neck taken with a jerk would be very salutatory.'" I heard John gasp. "I have sworn to Governor Cummings that I will do everything in my power to see that the perpetrators of the massacre are brought to book."

"I see," John said.

"My hand is forced, for the greater good."

"You're going to cut me loose. For thirteen years you've allowed me to continue in the church, and I have faithfully served. Why now?"

"Many other particulars have come to my attention."

"What particulars?"

"I never realized the extent of your involvement."

"I told you every detail, for the Love of God. Why are you lying? I spared you nothing, not even my own involvement. And you've never said I must be cut off from the church until now." John's voice had taken a hard edge. "I told you the whole truth, with the exception that I put most of the blame on myself, when it should have gone to others. Let's set it straight between us, Brigham. What was done was by the mutual consent and counsel of the high councilors, Presidents, Bishops and leading men, who prayed over the matter, and diligently sought the mind and mill of the spirit of truth to direct the affair. If any man has told you to the contrary, your informant has lied like hell."

"Be that as it may, hell's soon to pay. A letter of excommunication has been drawn up, and will be delivered to you at your place in Washington."

"Apostle Smith made it clear that we were to drive out the invaders."

"He was speaking in figures. You must have misunderstood."

"He preached that they should die."

"You misheard."

"Of course," John said wearily. "Will you make it public?"

"That is the point," Brigham said.

"I see," he said. "When word of this gets around, no one will have anything to do with me, or my family. You will leave me exposed to every legal humiliation."

"You must be prepared for that. I cannot help it."

"I understand," John said with an empty voice. "The secret is safe with me."

"It is now out of my hands. Any further communication between us must be discreet, but I am counting on you for future works."

"Of course."

"I do not think it wise we enter the city together."

"No," John said absently, lost. I could not prevent myself from charging the horse abreast of the buggy.

"John?" I inquired. His face was that of a bewildered child. The pain made me wince. John was utterly devastated.

"Please leave us," Brigham ordered.

"I think I'll stay," I said coolly, challenging the Prophet whose face was in shadow. He ignored me.

"I'm to be cut off from the church, Em," John said.

"Understand, Mrs. Lee, I still have great work for John to do. I shall do everything in my power to protect him, but the die is cast."

"I see," I said, not seeing. "And what of his soul?"

"His soul is in jeopardy," Brigham said uncomfortably.

"Because you've put it there," I charged back.

"Em, hold your tongue," John ordered.

"I shall not," I said. "If you disfellowship John he will have no help, aid, or protection from the church. What you are doing is withdrawing your tacit approval of this business which you've known about for years. You're going to throw him to the wolves!"

"Get this unruly woman out of here," Brigham demanded.

"Don't you worry, sir, I'm leaving," I said, and kicked the horse of the flanks and left dust in both their faces. Brigham had just signed John D. Lee's death warrant.

John returned to the house alone, hours later. Brigham's entourage had come and gone through the city, and had not stopped at the Lee house. The women in their best dresses stood on the porch and watched him pass, expecting John to be in the carriage with the Prophet. And then they looked for him to be riding close behind. The hot food lay cold on the table. The afternoon lengthened. The concert down by the mill was over, and darkness gloamed the tops of the elms by the time John returned. I feared for his sanity. For him to be cut off from the church was the same as killing him. What had John done at that place to deserve such treatment?

We gathered in the bright front parlor reflecting all of John's wealth and industry. His face was grim. "We'll be returning to Harmony tonight," he announced to the questioning and anxious faces of his family. "Make your preparations. Douse all the lights, and close up this house. I will speak with all of you later." And then he got back on his horse and rode off into the darkness. We didn't see him for a week.

When he returned John gathered us together in the grape arbor at Harmony. The shaded arbor was heavy with black fruit, the smell of ripe wheat in the air. Near to the east the crimson monolith of Kolob rose in the evening sky like a majestic witness to God's throne.

Present that evening were Elder Mother Aggatha and Martha "Merry" Berry, Rachel Andorra, and young Lena Smith Lee. It so happened we were all pregnant except Elder Aggatha who was past her fruitful age, and some of us were happy and some of us were not. John read Brigham's message aloud to us. It was not written in his own hand, John noted, clutching at leaf and straw. Brigham

Young is too shrewd for that, I thought, keeping silent.

John D. Lee, of Washington County

Dear Sir: If you will consult your own interest,
and that of those who are your friends, you will not
press an investigation at this time, as it will only
serve to implicate those that would be your friends, and
cause them to suffer with, or inform upon you. Our
advice is to make yourself scarce, and keep out of the way.

"Well, what do you make of that?" Martha Berry puffed, her youth already beginning to be tamed by the work in the sun. "What investigation?" I winced at her demand, and looked at John, surprised that he was not rolling his eyes in exasperation.

"The federal government has finally enough power to press for an accounting of the dark occurrence," John patiently explained. "Some of the anti-Mormon newspapers in Salt Lake have said Brigham Young is an accomplice because he harbors and protects the guilty. I can save him with the truth, Martha," he said.

But what of yourself, what of us? How will you save yourself and your family, I wanted to scream aloud.

"Dark occurrence?" Martha said dully. "Whatever are you talking about?" It was then I realized they—we—truly did not know John's secret and his shame.

"There are some men of Salt Lake, journalists, who will see to it that my story is told with accuracy. I will not be forced to name names. But I have rejected the notion. These friends," he indicated the note in his hand, "fear that I will expose them, which I shall never do. This is Brigham's advice to me," he said. "And I must take it. I couldn't bear prison."

"As for myself," Sister Rachel said quietly, "I will be glad to leave. All of the new Saints in St. George look upon us as if we were criminals. They treat us so cruelly. Just the other night some of the children taunted my children with insults. Will the thing never die?"

"It will never die as long as men have tongue and memory,

dear," John said, his eyes briefly on the red monolith of Kolob. "I ask you all once again to forgive me for bringing this upon all of my family."

"What memory?" old Aggatha complained.

"I must tell you that I have been disfellowshipped," he finally announced. The shock was so profound there was a silence that lasted minutes. It was unthinkable to each one of his family. I had known, and was numb still. I sensed some of my sister-wives immediately withdrawing from him.

"I believe that President Young has suffered this to take place for a wise purpose and not for any malicious intent," John said. "My prayer is, may God bless him with light and with the intelligence of Heaven to comprehend the things of God and discriminate between truth and error."

"John?" How could he not be fulminating with anger? After all these years to be suddenly severed from all he held dear. I couldn't believe he would forgive Brigham. Finally I asked, "What do you mean to do, John?"

"We must quit this place," he said, pacing, smacking one fist into the palm of his hand. "The warrants on me for polygamy alone dictate that we, or at least I, as the gentlemen say, must make myself scarce."

"You mean leave Harmony?" Martha Berry said, eyeing old Aggatha carefully. "I could not bear to leave this lovely place. We've worked so hard!" And she, who along with Polly Bean spent more time at our big house in Washington City pretending to be society than the rest of us put together. I wanted to shake the daft girl.

"I'm afraid we must," John said.

"But where?" Rachel Andorra asked. "Can't we continue as the other families? We have ample warning when the marshals are about in the country. You can safely hide anytime you please."

"Yes," Martha said, "The others manage to keep safe. Why must we leave?"

"There is the other matter that hounds me," John said. He was always so patient with us when important things concerned us. When it had to do with workaday he could sometimes be short, and would brook no complaint. It stung, those times. I was confused, pregnant, lost really in the midst of this sprawling family when John spoke aloud those cursed words.

"Mountain Meadows," he said simply. I felt the talons of those words. This was the shadow world. It was becoming my affair.

"God help us." It was a collective murmur. One of those times when we sister-wives were of one mind, and one voice.

"I cannot defend myself without implicating the other brethren. This I cannot do, on my oath. My part, as you know, was not innocent. I am, and was that day, merely the instrument of the Priesthood. It was the will of God, and for that I cannot apologize. What I did was wrong, but I have sworn to protect the others. My conscience is clear. But I testify before you dear women and before my God, I shed the blood of no man, nor woman either. I am innocent of shedding innocent blood. I swear it.

"But for some reason, the others have turned against me. Someone is protecting them, but Brigham counsels me to flee. Brothers Haight and Isaac have fled for Mexico. I do not know if Brigham counseled this. But it cannot be held that Brigham ordered that terrible deed. To my knowledge, he did not. But I am not sure. It was Colonel Dame, and Haight who brought the orders. It was Apostle George A. Smith who whipped up the sentiment for blood in all the southern settlements. If any is to assume the whole blame, it is those three. In any case, for this reason, I must remove us to some other place of safety."

There was a silence then, not perhaps of assent, but resignation. And I knew some of the other wives would express their dissent by deserting John.

"Brigham Young needs someone to satisfy the federals that justice has been done. Back East they'll never forget until some of the Brethren are punished," I said. I remembered vividly the meeting with Brigham Young. The man's presence was ever in our lives. "This is Brigham's answer."

"You are free to go or stay as you wish," John said, looking at each of us. "I release you now," he said quietly, sadly. One desertion would break his heart, and there were many.

Of my ten sister-wives who were living at, or near Harmony, at least six deserted John—two by death—and have apparently abandoned me, though I still love them. But, in separate chambers of my heart, which I am free to visit or not, there is an abiding bitterness toward them that is salt. If I were to carry their burdens from room to room my back would break. My heart thus is dry as the land, and I have not the strength to visit other places which might exalt me in the vast space within that loved him.

Ann Marie and Lena and Martha Berry and Polly Bean abandoned John without a second thought the very next week. Old Aggatha chose never to leave Harmony. As she lay dying, her eldest son, named after Brigham, walked twenty miles to the top of Pine Valley Mountain to bring her a bucket of snow to slake her last thirst.

CHAPTER FOURTEEN

Not daring to think of the taste of cool, snow melt water, I raised the last few pages of my husband's letter. Even the sight of John's handwriting, once a comfort to me, looked as stiff and dead as the petroglyphs scratched on the surrounding canyon walls by a vanished race; a scrawl of menace.

THIS WAS THE PLAN: The emigrants were to be decoyed from their strong-hold under a promise of protection. Brother William Bateman was to carry a flag of truce and demand a parley, and then I was to go and arrange the terms of the surrender. I was to demand that all the children who were so young they could not talk should be put into a wagon, and the wounded were also to be put in a wagon. Then all the arms and ammunition of the emigrants should be put into a wagon, and I was to agree that the Mormons would protect the emigrants from the Indians and conduct them to Cedar City in safety, where they should be protected until an opportunity came for sending them to California.

It was agreed that when I had made the entreaty—or treaty—as we called it, the wagons should start for Hamblin's ranch up the valley with the arms, the wounded and the children. The women were to march on foot and follow the wagons in single file; the men were to follow behind the women, they also to march in single file. Major John M. Higbee was to stand with his militia company about two hundred yards from the camp, and stand in double file, open order, with about twenty feet space between the files, so that the wagons could pass between them.

The drivers were to keep right along, and not stop at the troops. The women were not to stop there, but to follow the wagons. The troops were to halt the men for a few minutes, until the women were some distance ahead, out into the cedars, where the Indians were hid in ambush. Then the march was to be resumed, the troops to form in single file, each soldier to walk by an emigrant, and on the right-hand side of his man, and the soldier was to carry his gun on his left arm, ready for instant use.

The march was to continue until the wagons had passed beyond the ambush of the Indians, and until the women were right in the midst of the Indians. Higbee was then to give the orders and words, 'DO YOUR DUTY'. At this the troops were to shoot down the men; the Indians were to kill all of the women and larger children, and the drivers of the wagons and I were to kill the wounded and sick men that were in the wagon.

Two men were to act as outriders to shoot down any who might escape the initial onslaught. The Indians were to kill all of the women and children so it would be certain that no Mormon would be guilty of shedding innocent blood. I took up my cross, and prepared to do my duty.

I recoil with disgust and loathing as I write this. I pray God will forgive me.

According to the plan, I was allowed inside the fortifications where the first thing I observed was the emigrants burying two men who had been killed in the night attack. They wrapped the bodies up in buffalo robes. *I was then told by some of the men that seven men were killed and seventeen others were wounded at the very first attack by the Indians the day before I arrived. Three of the wounded had since died, making ten of their number killed during the siege.*

As I entered the circled wagons, stinking of an invisible Judas skin, the men, women and children gathered around me in a wild, feverish consternation. Some felt that the time of their happy deliverance had come, while others, though in deep distress, and all in tears, looked upon me with doubt, mistrust, and outright terror. I noticed one woman, in a yellow-checked dress, the top of her bosom exposed to a suckling child, who just stared at me blankly, as if the world could no longer hold any more horror for her.

No language can describe my feelings. My position was untenable, awful. My nerves were unstrung, my brain on fire, dry tears ran inside me like drops of a carbolic. And then I could hold them no longer, and so amplified my name of Yawgetts, and I wept openly before them, stupefied with what I was doing. I wished for earthquake, for a terrible fire to fall upon me. Yet my false faith held when I thought of the terror the church authorities would visit upon me should I fail this mission.

I laid aside my humanity, Em, as reluctantly as if I were laying down my own life.

I delivered my message, and the emigrants agreed. They had no choice, of course. I ordered the children and the wounded men, some clothing and the arms, to be put into the wagons. Their guns were mostly Kentucky rifles of the muzzle-loading style. Their ammunition was all but gone, I do not think there were twenty loads left in the whole company. If the emigrants had a good supply of ammunition I do no think we could have captured them without great loss to ourselves, for they were brave men, and very resolute and determined.

Just as the wagons were loaded, Dan McFarland came riding into the corral and said that Major Higbee had ordered great haste to be made, for he was afraid that the Indians would renew the attack before he could get them to safety. I had to admire this cunning piece of subterfuge on his part. The Indians were perfectly concealed, and awaiting his orders!

I hurried up the people and started the wagons off towards Cedar City. As we went out of the corral I ordered the wagons to turn left, so as to leave the troops to the right of us. Dan McFarland rode before the women and led them right up to the troops, where they still stood in open order as I left them. The women and larger children were walking ahead, as directed, and the men following them. The foremost man was about fifty yards behind the hindmost woman.

I saw this much, but about this time our wagons passed out of sight of the troops, over the hill. I had disobeyed orders in part by turning off as I did, for I was anxious to be out of sight of the bloody deed that I knew was to follow. It was my duty, with the two drivers, to kill the sick and wounded men who were in the wagons, and to do so when we heard the guns of the troops fire. I was filled with loathing to shoot defenseless men. But they were guilty men. And I was sworn. No amount of blood, thought I, could replace that spilled precious blood of Joseph Smith. I was walking between the wagons; the horses were going in a fast walk, and we were fully half a mile from Major Higbee and his men, when we heard the firing. As we heard the guns, I ordered a halt, and we proceeded to do our part.

I here pause in the recital of this horrid story of man's inhumanity, and ask myself the question, is it honest in me, and can I clear my conscience before my God, if I screen myself while I accuse others? No. Heaven forbid that I should put a burden upon others shoulders that I am unwilling to bear my just portion of it. I am not a traitor to my people, Emeline, dear, nor to my former friends and comrades who were with me on that dark day when the work of death was carried on in God's name by a lot of ordinary men who had become deluded religious fanatics.

All of the small children were put into the wagons, but now I remember that there was one little child, about six months *old, who was carried in its father's arms, and it was killed by the same bullet that entered its father's breast; it was shot through the head. I was told by Haight afterwards, that the child was killed by accident, but I cannot say to the truth of that. In any case, it was dead.*

When we had got out of sight, and just as we were coming into the main road, I heard a volley of guns at the place where I knew the troops and emigrants were. Our teams were walking fast. I first heard one gun, a pistol, and then volley after volley of mixed fire.

McMurdy and Knight stopped their teams at once, for they were ordered by Higbee, the same as I, to help kill all the sick and wounded men who were in the wagons, and to do it as soon as they heard the guns of the troops. McMurdy was in front; his wagon was loaded mostly with the arms and small children. McMurdy and Knight got out of their wagons; each one had a rifle. McMurdy went up to Knight's wagon, where the sick and wounded were, and raising his rifle to his shoulder said: "O Lord, my God, receive their spirits, it is for thy Kingdom that I do this." He then shot a man who was lying with his head on another man's breast; the ball killed both men.

I also went up to the wagon, intending to do my part of the killing. I drew my pistol and cocked it, but somehow it went off prematurely, and I shot McMurdy across the thigh, my pistol ball cutting his buckskin pants. McMurdy turned to me and said: "Brother Lee, keep cool, you are excited; you came very near to killing me. There is no reason to be excited."

Knight then shot a man with his rifle; he shot the man in the head. Knight also brained a boy of about fourteen years old. The boy came running up to our wagons, and Knight struck him on the head with the butt end of his gun, and crushed his skull. By this time many Indians reached our wagons, and all of the sick and wounded were killed almost instantly. I saw an Indian from Cedar City, called Joe, run up to the wagon and catch a man by the hair, and raise his head up and look into his face; the man shut his eyes, and Joe shot him in the head.

The Indians then examined all of the wounded in the wagons, and all of the bodies, to see if any were alive, and all that showed signs of life were at once shot through the head. I did not kill anyone there, but it was an accident that kept me from doing it, for I fully intended to do my part of the killing, but by the time I got over the excitement of coming so near to killing McMurdy, the whole of the killing of the wounded was done.

May God rest their souls. There is no truth in the statement of Nephi Johnson that I have heard who accuses me of cutting a man's throat. I did not do it.

Just after the wounded were all killed I saw a girl, some ten years of age, running towards us, from the direction where the troops had attacked the main body of emigrants; her white dress was covered with blood. And Indians shot her before she got within sixty yards of us. That was the last person I saw killed that day.

About this time an Indian rushed to the front wagon, and grabbed a little boy, and was going to kill him. The lad got away from the Indians and ran to me, and caught me by the knees; and begged me to save him, and not let the Indian kill him. I told the Indians to let the boy alone, and took him up in my arms and put him in the back of the wagon and saved his life. This little boy said his name was Charley Fancher, and that his father was Captain of the train. He left Harmony before I brought you home as wife, and our secret did not allow us to speak of him in your presence. I believe that he is today known as Idaho Bill, a notorious outlaw, but I cannot swear it.

After the parties were dead I ordered Knight to drive out on the flats and throw out the dead bodies and he did so. Then I ordered Knight and McMurdy to take the children that were saved alive, (sixteen was the number, some say seventeen, I say sixteen) and drive on to Hamblin's ranch.

While going back to the brethren, I passed the bodies of several women. In one place I saw six or seven bodies near each other; they were stripped perfectly naked, and all of their clothing was torn from their bodies by the Indians.

I walked along the line where the emigrants had been killed and saw many bodies dead and naked on the meadows. I saw ten children; they had been killed close to one another; they were from ten to sixteen years of age.

I do not know how many were killed that day. But I am given to believe, including those who died at the hand of Stewart at Richard's Springs, would make the total number one hundred and twenty-one.

When Major Higbee spotted me he said, "Lee, the boys have acted admirably, they took good aim, and all of the damned Gentiles but two or three fell at the first fire."

Major Higbee ordered me to search the bodies for valuables, which sunk us to the nadir, if that is possible—we descended from savage heathen killers to body robbers. I refused. So Higbee, Klingensmith, and Wm. C. Stewart rifled the corpses and kept whatever they found. There was not much money, I was told.

An hour later we were all assembled, men with blood dripping from pants legs, hands, shirts. WE then swore a solemn oath of secrecy not to tell anyone, even our wives, of this day's work for the rest of our lives! We also took the most binding oaths to stand by each other, and to always insist that the massacre took place at the hands of the Indians. We vowed to keep our secret from the entire world.

I was dead tired, having been sleepless for five days. I fell under a juniper and laid my head on my saddle, and went into the troubled stupor of the living dead who people my dreams.

The rest is tedious detail. A making of soap. A washing of hands and conscience. The necessary rationalizations which must attend every sin. I cannot continue, darling Emeline. This is all my courage can write. As I have asked God to forgive me, so I ask you to forgive me. I have lived in a sunless place since that day, so why should I fear the sunless walls of prison? I release you dear, praying for your safety. If I am able, I shall write to you soon. Perhaps Brigham will cut me loose. My love, please go to the children and hold them for me, tell them I love them as I love you.

Your husband,
John D. Lee

CHAPTER FIFTEEN

Lt. James C. Dellenbaugh took me from the river men's camp
as diplomatically as he could manage under the circumstances. As I laid down the manuscript everything was torn loose
within me, the rage clashing with sorrow, the anger warring with
love. It was a terror that held like the poisonous, implacable bite
of the Gila serpent. And it was just as deadly to the spirit.

I found myself in my bed. My dress was in tatters, my hair torn
in tufts which left bald places on my scalp. My face was blistered
with sun and the bites of sand fleas. I had lost one boot.

The face I first recognized was that of Lt. Dellenbaugh, although
I was aware of the voices of the boys outside the rock walls. There
was a cool evening breeze blowing the flour sack curtain I had
placed across the bare window opening.

"Miss Lee, can you hear me?" I heard across a haze of distance,
his voice like a voice lost in a canyon, reverberating in a search of
its author. I felt a large hand lift my head, and then the cool wash
of a wet cloth on my face. I still bear the tiny scars from the burning
of the sun that day.

"Yes," I finally replied, seeing only his head and shoulders in silhouette against the pale purple of the evening sky. "I don't understand," I said.

"You were confused," he said softly.

"What?"

"Sleep now, I'll sit with you until morning."

"Yes. Sleep, the water must be carried in the buckets. The little girls in white dresses . . . "

My dreams were staged upon a mountain meadow. I saw John, my husband, his hair turning to snow, his hand raised as if warding off blows. I spoke to him, calmly, "There is no need, there is no need," I told him, and he looked at me as if I were a stranger. There was in his eyes a madness. He did not recognize me. And there was a smell, like rich wet powder of copper, a stench of loose bowel around which were laced like tendrils the odor of strong roses, red roses without stems, floating upon dry grass, and I reached for John's hand but he would not take it. I followed him, and found myself stepping across shrouded forms wrapped, curiously, like the Egyptian dead, in coarse linen, mouthless and faceless and I remember dreaming that I should ask John for his knife so I might cut places around their mouth and eyes and nose so they could see and breath, or even speak of the knowledge they now possessed.

In the watercolor wash of a lavender dawn I saw Lt. Dellenbaugh sitting on the dirt floor, his back against the wall, sleeping lightly. I was perfectly sound now, in my mind, except there were places of a vanished memory. I recalled setting down the manuscript in the sand and being sick. Beyond that, nothing of the entire afternoon or evening. The Lt. sensed me awaken, and I saw him open his eyes that, in this light, were green as river pools. He rose, and took my hand.

"The boys?" I asked. I sensed Elizabeth beside me.

"I've set them to hauling water to the garden. And they showed me how to feed her," he said. "They didn't like the work, so I bribed them, I fear."

"Yes?"

"A ride on the Major's boat. We have to cross supplies this afternoon, and then we shall be leaving down river."

"Oh," I said, and looked at myself, the torn dress, and felt the pain in my scalp and on my face. "I don't understand what happened to me," I finally said.

"You stumbled into our camp in the late afternoon. You were quite out of your senses, I'm afraid."

"I don't remember. Why?"

"I don't know, you were talking in gibberish. The sun must have overtaken you. It happens," he tried to reassure me. I felt acute shame.

"I made a spectacle of myself?"

"I think the men understand," he said. "The sun melts the best of us."

"You brought me home?"

"I thought it best.

"Thank you." And then I placed my hands on my face. They came away wet from the weeping blisters. "My God," I murmured. And then I remembered the last lines I had read. The image of the corpse-littered meadows brought more tears. I was exhausted. John's confession was vividly etched upon my memory, and I could tell no man ever what it told. "Yes, the sun. I must have dozed off, and the sun turned, and turned . . . "

"The sun can do terrible things," the Lieutenant said reassuringly. "Are you all right?"

"Yes, I'm fine," I said, rising, feeling the weariness in my arms and legs.

"I'm sorry for the inconvenience."

"Inconvenience? There is no inconvenience. If I could stay, I would stay, but I must go."

"Thank you," I said. "I'll be fine.

"I'll try to call upon you before we leave in the late afternoon. The Lava Rapids are ahead of us, so we'll camp upstream and run it in the morning's light."

After he left I stayed in bed, trying to compose myself. The Lieutenant's tenderness moved me, made me feel a need. Could I ever hold John D. Lee in my arms again without loathing? That is a question I would have to make a peace with, or put away, or I would have to put myself away from him and his church and this utterly God-forsaken place.

It was all I could do to summon the courage to walk to the river men's camp in the afternoon and tender my apologies. I'd washed and mended my dress, and covered my scalp with a white cloth cap. I was ashamed of myself and my momentary refuge in what can only be called a madness. The horror of John's words would not leave me, but neither would the necessity of salvaging the esteem of the river men, for they had been kind and helpful and a source of hard cash to us for the little services they asked me to do such as mending and sometimes cooking for them in their camp.

How I admire the river men. To cross the west deserts in search of freedom is one thing I do understand. But to cross for the sole purpose of exploring the unknown dark labyrinths of the canyon of the Colorado merely for the sake of knowing, well, it confounds me.

I knew that Major Powell had lost two men on his expedition in 1869. The unfortunates should have stayed on the river with Powell, but they climbed out of the canyon and disappeared. There was no doubt the Indians killed them. Lt. Dellenbaugh told me one of the reasons for Powell's return was to find the two men, or determine their fate, and rescue them or bury them. John D. said it was common knowledge they were dead. Some clothing of the men had been seen on some of the tribesmen. John admired the Major for his loyalty to his men.

Polite acknowledgments were made toward me as I walked into their midst. I saw some embarrassment on their rough-bearded faces, but also some sympathy. These eastern men did not understand how the Mormon men could leave their wives scattered and alone. Their fires were out, the ashes scattered. Four sturdy boats were loaded to the side boards—gunwales?—with supplies. The Powell expedition had brought much-needed cash over the seasons to places like Kanab and the other settlements. Hamblin got rich from them, though he would deny it. Major Powell even let us use one of his boats for a ferry in the early days at the Lonely Dell.

Major Powell saw me and walked over and saluted casually

with his one good hand. The empty sleeve was pinned to his blue shirt. He had a kindness in his eyes. Despite the enmity of the citizens of the United States toward us, and toward anyone associated with the Mountain Meadows, relations with Powell and his men were always cordial. My cooking may have something to do with that state of affairs.

"Mrs. Lee, I hope you'll be well until your husband returns. I'm sending over some extra foodstuffs for you and your family."

"That won't be necessary, Major," I dissembled. "But I'm grateful."

"No room for them anyway," he responded. "Tell John D. we've appreciated his help. I'm going to recommend to Congress that your 'Lonely Dell' be placed on the official maps of the United States Survey as 'Lee's Ferry.' Tell him that, will you?"

"Yes, it will please him. But I've come to apologize to you and your men for the, ah, spectacle that I seem to have caused."

"I've seen some of my strongest men become helpless at the blows of the sun. There is no need for apologies. You had us worried. You must wear your becoming bonnet at all times," he advised, and I had to smile at this small flattery standing as we were in hot sand under a white sky.

"I've brought some young melons to take with you," I said and offered him a small sack.

"Why thank you, Miss Lee. You and your family will not be forgotten." He turned and looked at the river, and I saw an expression in his eyes, a fearful fascination, and resolve. It was the river man's look. The only look we Mormons get when we see water is a calculating look—some would say cunning. How to get the precious stuff out onto the dry land is our only thought. Over the years, I'd come to love the river as one loves a pagan god. And to hate it in like measure.

Major Powell gestured to Lt. Dellenbaugh who stood some distance away, watching us.

"Please escort Mrs. Lee back to her place, Lieutenant," he ordered. "This lady should never go abroad without escort," he said, and turned away, leaving his meaning twisting before me. Flattery or condemnation of my husband? Sincerity or irony?

Manners, or mendacity? I'll never know.

The handsome young Lieutenant linked his arm in mine as if we were on a city street, and we toiled as dignified as we were able, considering walking in sand is to look as clumsy as the promenade of a duck.

When we arrived at the rock house the boys came running. They'd been across the river in a small boat with the Lt., and were excited to see him again. I shushed them away after they said their goodbyes again. When they were out of sight, the Lt. looked into my eyes, not seeing the blisters and the horror, for he was blind in the manner of men. I had the impulse to confess to John's confession. To blurt out the terrible truth. To give it to someone else. But I could not. In what peril had John placed us with his secret? How could one have faith in a church which used the instrumentality of murder to protect itself, no matter the threat. A church which professed itself to be Christian. In no place of scripture had I ever learned that cold blooded murder of innocent men, women and children to be an enterprise of a soul's salvation.

James Cameron Dellenbaugh stood before me, his eyes intent. I felt my eyes close. The nightmare for the moment dissolved into a red haze, and I felt his hands on my shoulders, his lips on mine, deliberately soft, masculine as leather, and then he was gone.

It was not the kiss of a friend, and I felt my skin color high as a scarlet cup. My impulse was to run after him, to beg him to take me with him down the unknown river, anyplace. The danger of the Colorado seemed as nothing to the bleakness of the future. Who knew how long John would be in prison, or if he would ever be released? How long must I live like a burrowing animal in windowless houses of brittle rock? And all for a God who, day by day, was becoming less benign, and more an indifferent avenger.

I stood on the shore and waved to the little procession of white boats as they disappeared into the swirling turquoise of the river's bend. Red silt ran in sinuous swirls and curled down the river like twists of hair, like ribbons of rust in the green water. As the future is always unknown, I wondered if they, in their fragile river boats, were heading into a wilderness darker, and more unknown, than mine.

And then I was left alone, faced with more knowledge than I ever wanted. After the boats disappeared down the river, I carefully buried the manuscript at the white rock cove. I felt as if I had been beaten with a knotted well rope. I found my missing shoe in the sand some fifty yards from where I had been reading that book of the dammed. I absently set the boys to work, hefted Elizabeth on my back and climbed to point where I could see the chasm which had swallowed a man who caused in me feelings I dared not entertain, not even in the most secret alcoves of the heart.

How does one begin to unlove a man? How does one begin to know a man beyond his actions? I realized that some of my heart was descending that river. By the reading of John's confession my life's course had been altered in ways I could not yet imagine. I looked down at the lonely house and beached ferry from the high promontory and saw the boys brushing out a horse. John's sons. And at the little girl in my arms. I was stunned at the thought of John luring the innocents to the slaughter. Throughout the day I kept looking at my hands. These hands that had held and caressed John D. Lee with all of the ineffable tenderness I possessed. I realized the nights I had lain with him I had lain with a stranger. His confession of cowardice had so deeply shaken me that I thought I should throw myself into that river, and be washed to the sea.

Book II

CHAPTER SIXTEEN

It was nine months after they took John to the prison in Salt Lake City. If ever time pressed, and if work is a balm to its passing, then I should not have reckoned the weary length of the months. The work of keeping us alive kept me busy every waking moment, and time's tread was wearisome beyond the measure of mere hours. We'd fought the flash floods that washed out the dam on the Pariah, and had to show for it but a mud puddle behind the earthen plug of sticks and wattles. It was a hopeless task.

Before the snows came in December, light and cool as feather down at first, then driving and bitter in January, we should have starved had not John, by what means I cannot guess, been able to dispatch from his place on the upper Paria a nine-mule train loaded with flour, molasses, raisins, slabs of smoked bacon, blankets and some cloth for Rachel and me, clothes and trinkets for the children's meager Christmas, and cloth pants for the young men.

In curious moments of a dark winter night I thought of Lt. Dellenbaugh, images of him in his blue wool shirt, his lips pressed to mine, but pushed them away and consoled myself with general worry for their welfare on the treacherous river down which they had disappeared like solitary leaves on the flood. Loneliness can stretch the skin across the bones. Loneliness can canker the heart, leave it vulnerable . . .

After the Powell Expedition left, I knew Sister Rachel would be frantic with worry over John, so I resolved to walk to the Pools Ranch and tell her the details of the news. Son Heber said he had stopped briefly with the gist of John's capture, and then had hurried on to me. When I consider the insignificant human commerce at this lonely crossing, hopeful families in wagons sent by Brigham to the Arizona missions, raiding Navajos, prospectors and fugitives, the tally doesn't amount to twenty or thirty people in the past three months, discounting Major Powell's activity. But Rachel was more isolated than I. My heart went out to her, and knew she must be suffering the same heartache upon the news that our beloved husband was in the hands of his enemies.

I could not leave the boys alone, so I told them to prepare for the long walk to the pools. Lonely as I was, I could not imagine walking these many miles for a visit as Rachel was wont to do. My David was a lanky lad with a tow head, his father's full nose and stern mouth—and icy eyes. His voice was past adolescent cracking, and he was proud that he was the token head of the family in John's many absences. Porter, a year younger, was dark from the black Irish side of my family. A little thing I'd never told John about was that side of the Buxton family line. The people on that side were not discussed much at our place in Middleshire. I overheard my father, before he died, telling my mother whose family it was, "I wonder how the Mormon elders will think of us if they knew your family was not known for paying the King's taxes?"

We set out for the Pools in the darkness of the summer morning. It was a fifteen mile walk up the banks of the desolate Paria. The trail was twisted, and we had to walk down scalded gullies full of vitriolic blue clay. Even the shadscale would not grow on that cursed earth. The boys carried baby Elizabeth for long miles, as I was nearly too weak to carry myself. My breasts were thin, the milk bitter. Four-winged salt brush and scorpions were the only observers of our toil up the river beside the horrid turkey vultures who circled overhead. Their black wings against the cloudless blue sky looked as if they were shadows thrown up against heaven.

We did not arrive until the early evening for, good sense had prevailed. John's admonition not to walk in the heat of the day came to me at a good time. So we crawled under the skinny shade of a clump of creosote bushes. I was achingly tired when David shook me awake and I saw the sun low in the west like an ripe orange which came from California at Christmas. I've eaten two of them in my lifetime. The thought of a sweet, juicy orange tortured me and tantalized me for many miles. By the time we were within a few miles of the Pools the water gourds were empty, and we were sucking sour tasting stones for moisture.

Rachel's boys heard us coming and ran out to greet us with unconfined joy. We had come across a scrawny cow in a mud flat in the river bottom, so we drove it before us toward the Pools. Rachel was delighted to see us—and the cow—and celebrated our visit by lighting her last hoarded candle stub. I stepped into the poor room and could see starlight through the roof of brush. But it was cool relative to the outside air as she had hung a wet sheet over the doorway. She had baked a loaf of bread for their supper in the outside oven built of clay. She had not the luxury of an iron stove; another reason for my pity, and some measure of guilt.

I told her the briefest recapitulation of the news in John's letter. Who but she would know better the details of the massacre, I thought. She was at Harmony throughout the period of turmoil. But when I had the chance to speak with some of my other sister-wives, they knew next to nothing of the part John had taken. And after delicate probing, I saw Rachel was entirely ignorant of John's participation at the Mountain Meadows. It was only rumor that reached their ears and fed their anguish in the days right after the horrible deed. John had taken in the young boy whose life he saved and he lived with the Lee family for a time. What kind of man was it, I wondered, who had participated in the slaughter of the boy's father? I had to erect bars to those rooms of speculation, lest I go mad myself. I found it to be a terrible task telling Rachel of John's incarceration, but spared her any detail of the horrors that had been revealed to me by John's own hand.

With the children gathered around—her three, my two boys, and baby Elizabeth—we ate the freshly baked bread and a withered melon, and prayed and wept. Rachel was beyond consolation. Her having to leave the lovely, fruit-heavy place at Harmony for this dry wilderness had broken her heart, and it was past mending. And if we were not weighed down enough with our feelings of desolation and abandonment, just at the time the last of the candle stub was guttering, and we had talked ourselves out, the Navajos came riding out of the moonlight, like ghosts, wearing coats of white ash, their horses black as the shadows.

It was a raiding party, and their whoops in the darkness drove us into a clutch of fear. I knew they were up to mischief because they did not come directly to the hut and beg for food. Rather, they circled the poor hut, the hooves ringing on the hard earth. We waited within like cowards, and after a few minutes I was seething with resentment. I was sick of their taunts and threats from previous times at the ferry, and told Rachel and the children to stay in the house, and I would go out and try to make a peace with them. Rachel begged me not to leave, and we had no means of defense but our wits. There was John's heavy horse pistol which I was damned if I'd carry on a foot trip to anyplace. My mouth was dry when I stepped out and saw the men, hard smoky wraiths in the white light of the half moon.

When I stepped out, armed only with prayer, they stopped their mad circling and drew up in a line before the house. There was light enough to read the Bible by, and I counted at least ten braves. I recognized one of the warriors, a young man with a devil's scar on his face which grizzled under the face powder. His face was mobile with savage thoughts, and the scar winked and flashed ominously.

"What do you want?" I demanded. "We have no food." I showed them my empty hands.

"We eat beef," he grunted, gesturing to the small herd of malnourished cattle gathered in the brush corral. It is a measure of the fear they held of the white man's vengeance that they even bothered to ask.

156

"If you kill a beef John Lee will punish you," I said. And then I changed course. "We are women and children alone. Don't you protect your women and children? Make a camp," I said, "and in the morning we will bake bread for you, and give you a melon." I could see him considering my offer. They could have taken all of the beef, and slaughtered us where we stood, but they knew if they did, John Lee and Jeb. Hamblin's wrath would be merciless. "I beg you, camp and sleep."

Many of the young warriors didn't like this proposition, and they muttered and cursed and shook their rifles from which hung feathers and tassels of dyed cloth. The man with the winking scar finally spoke to them, and with surly expressions they dismounted and hobbled their horses and threw blankets on the ground. I knew perfectly well that, sometime in the night, some of them would try to slip into the house, and who knew what lust for blood or a woman they held in their hearts. If I did not do more to settle them, I knew we were still in imminent danger.

I withdrew into the dark house, and saw white faces clustered in a corner. Rachel had as many of the children in her arms as she could gather. "What are we to do?" she asked. "They will come after we are asleep, and murder us. You know they will," she said, a shrill of terror in her voice. David, the eldest said, "I have my big knife. I will protect you." He was so brave it broke my heart. And then I saw the Lord show me the way, for my prayer had been incessant. Men are slaves to flattery at any given time of the day or night; were not the Navajos men? They had as much honor, in their own fashion, as did we white people. I knew what I was going to suggest would appall Rachel, but it was the only thing I could think of that might save us.

"Gather your blankets, and come outside with me," I ordered.

"What?" Rachel gasped.

"Don't you see? We must place ourselves under their protection. They cannot harm us if we appeal to those sentiments."

"Those sentiments do not reside in their hearts," she protested. "This is folly."

I do not know how it is that my authority superseded that of Rachel. My youth, perhaps. My stubbornness. She was tired, and afraid, and lost. I gathered up such quilts as we had in my arms and told them to follow me.

We stood in a vulnerable knot, our faces shining from the big brush fire the Navajos had built perhaps a hundred yards from the corral. I could hear their hungry muttering. An occasional shout, full of threat, was directed toward us, and then their faces went slack with astonishment as we marched, single file, arms full of sleeping apparel, toward their fire. I walked directly up to the scar faced warrior, and looked into his black eyes which reflected yellow, snapping flames.

"We are placing ourselves under your protection for the night," I said. "We are women and children. You are so strong and brave and there are so many of you we know you will protect us from the dangers of the night." The brave's eyes were confused. Here we stood, placing ourselves under his protection. I had him. His honor was at stake now.

Busily, I ordered the children to spread their blankets around the fire in a bit of presumption that still brings awe to Rachel's voice when she tells it. After the children were tucked in, I gave the collective men my most innocent and adorably trusting smile, and laid down and went to sleep. When I awoke I was met with silence. They had left in the night, silently, and not a hair on our head was harmed, the beef were still in the corral, and next to my quilt lay a small figure or amulet carved of wood which I treasure to this day.

CHAPTER SEVENTEEN

On a late forenoon early in 1876, I heard the creaking of a wagon, and human voices that did not belong to the Dell. The sound came from the trail down the Paria, and I went out, glad for the company and a little ferry business. Our second crop of melons was in, and we had fresh vegetables to sell. Even the buds on the peach and plum trees had bourne small, succulent fruit due to our diligent watering.

As John had foreseen, the ferry supported us, just barely. Brigham's pilgrims, and especially the gold-fevered miners, were a source of cash and trade. I'd managed to send fifty dollars to John since his confinement, and the spring travelers to the Mexico and Arizona missions also brought a trickle of ready cash.

The river was high all of the spring, a thrusting, scouring brown and red tongue, and the boys and I had to struggle to make the ferry crossings. By now, however, I was considering myself something of a ferry woman, and could cross twenty people with their livestock in a day if other backs were willing. Some of the travelers expected to sit at their ease while the boys and I manned the oars and sweep, but most fell to with poles and took the oars from the youngsters and we made fast crossings.

"Hallo the ferry," I heard a deep man's voice hail as the wagon and team hove into view from around the point of rock where our sieve of a dam was still holding.

"Hello yourself," I said to the man on the wagon who'd hailed me, "and welcome to Lee's Ferry." I saw a woman beside him on the wagon seat wearing a hat shaped like a Conestoga top, her face in full shade, and I got a deep pang of envy. I thought the woman would not cross the river but she leave it behind, if I was any student of John's horse trading abilities. I also felt, somewhat wistfully, that I had no idea of fashions, or trends or news of England in many months.

"You're Sister Lee," the big man stated as he stepped down and smiled at me. A welcome gesture of a welcome guest.

"You've come to cross," I said. "It's a fine morning for it."

"Cross nothing, Sister Lee, we've come to take over the ferry for you."

He could see the visible surprise on my face, and he laughed as he helped his wife step down. She was a small woman, her face still covered by the scoop of the hat. "This is my wife, Zitha," he said. The little woman stepped forward and shook my hand briskly, and then turned her face to inspect what was to be her new home. A flash of sun found its way across her face, and I saw a sharp nosed woman whose eyes bespoke disappointment at the appointments of Lee's Ferry. "How do you do," she said, and looked at the rock house in more disbelief than surprise.

"Warren Covington," the man said. "John D. Lee, with the assistance of Bishop Coates of Cedar City, and the support of some of the other Brethren who shall remain without names, have sent us down here to take over the ferry so that you may go north, and tend to your business."

What business, I wondered, and saw the embarrassment on the man's face.

"I've a letter," he said, "from Bishop Coates." "It will explain things."

"Well, unhook your outfit and put your stock in that brush

corral," I said, covering my emotion with the motions of business. "Sister Covington, come into the house and out of the sun. And I meant to say when I first saw you, that is the most handsome and practical hat I've ever seen."

"The hand-carters made them for the crossings, and they've become quite the vogue again in Salt Lake City," she said, with just a rouge of hauteur.

"They were not worn when I crossed with a company of handcarts," I told her, out of some spite, or pride.

"Just a moment," she said. She went to the back of the wagon and climbed up and I heard her rummaging around and then she came back out and handed me a paper bag. "Here, your husband bought this for you, and wanted us to bring it along to you."

I could not hold back the tears as I opened the bag and saw the hat with the great scalloped brim for shade. It was blue, with a red ribbon for a tie, and inside was a scrap of paper in which John wrote, "Come quickly. I love you and need you in the time ahead."

So I had a new bonnet to wear to the trial of John D. Lee.

The letter from Bishop Coates was brief, and to the point. "We've made arrangements for you to attend the trial of Brother Lee. He has requested this. If you do not tarry you can be in Cedar City by the day the trial commences".

I had traded for a mule and a horse from a group of miners just a week previous, and the thought passed my mind that God had prompted the transaction, for I had no means or plans to travel. I had resigned myself to dying at the Lonely Dell. All of John's houses, carriages, and property were long gone. I suspected sharp lawyers were taking advantage of John's helpless condition, and saw the opportunity when I went north to get them straightened out if need be.

The mule was a scatter-eyed caution, as are most mules, but a slap or two on his backside and he would allow one to ride or pack him. The horse was a little Navajo Pinto. I wondered, in the midst of the bustle of readying myself to travel north, whether or not I should take David and Porter. Brother Covington said either way was fine with him. I made the rational decision that they should stay; they would be of great help. I also made an emotional decision that they should stay at Lonely Dell, for what young man wishes to see his father tried for wholesale murder? They were sorely disappointed. There was no consoling David, but he fought back some manly tears when I promised I would try to bring back with me a tooled leather belt which he had been coveting ever since he saw one on the waist of a miner. I'd tried to buy the belt from the miner. He wanted more than money.

I traveled alone with Elizabeth, stopping off at the Pools Ranch to tell Rachel of the new developments, and that John had promised to send someone to help her if she wished to come north. I could tell she was in a jealous mood, for she had got a letter from John via the Covingtons, but she did not share it with me. "I'm to go to Kanab, and wait there for the outcome," she informed me. "But that is his wish, and I fear for your safety on the trail," she said through tears. "A train will pass through from Arizona in a month, and I'll come north then."

"I'll be all right," I assured her with no conviction. Truth to tell, I was terrified of being alone on the sixty or seventy miles up into the Kaibab timber country where sometimes the Utes came to war with the Navajos, and wild bears looked upon mules as windfall delicacies, or so rumor had it. Travelers also reported the mountain lion crop was commensurate with the size of the deer of which there were plenty that year to our great benefit and health.

After I left the pools, I rode along on the little Pinto with a golden -haired toddler who rode in a sling fashioned after a Navajo papoose, and led the mule packed with what meager necessities I thought to bring. I had only one dress of black silk in which I dared present myself, and worried many miles about that state of affairs. I had some melons and a handful of corn meal, some coffee, and a few articles for toilette. I had plenty of time to think, clopping along with the sun-illumined vermillion cliffs to the right, and to the left the chasm of the Colorado in its twisted, shadowy canyon, which had carried James toward the Pacific seas.

I toiled along through the day, rising into the Kaibab wilderness. I realized, when I finally tethered the horse and mule under some pine trees, and placed my tattered bedding on the soft, fragrant pine needles of the forest, that I possessed a certain peace. It may have been the sight of wildflowers, the lupines and the larkspur and the smell of the pine. The chattering of the pinon jays kept me company and put me at ease. The months since John had been in prison had given me time to think of the future. But the opportunities were bleak. I could only resolve to do my best to see that he had adequate, lawful representation. I could only give him the comfort of my love, and the assurance that come what may, this one woman of the ferry would be with him until the matter was resolved. After that . . . I dared not give that eventuality any thought at all.

As I rode I began to nurture a deeper ground of resentment than I thought myself to be capable. I resisted it as unbecoming my own mind and spirit, but it was a black, pervasive seed that needed little water but tears, and little sun but that which came in dreams.

Brigham Young's power over every detail of our lives since the day he had married us seemed to be an oppressive pall. It was unclear to me if Brigham was taking the position that John D. should be a scapegoat for the deeds of the others—I don't know what to call them. Saints? Avengers? Butchers? My John, a butcher of women and children . . . Why, after twenty years, did Brigham allow this trial to proceed? He had covered for John and Klingensmith and Higbee and Haight for so long, why now? Federal pressure had always been there to find and punish those responsible for the Meadows. John had written me that he sent a stream of letters to Brigham for an explanation, but Brigham's reply thus far had only been silence. And this from a father, and from one for whom John would lay down his life.

How I prayed for the strength to present myself to my husband with the same fortitude with which he had faced the condemnation of the church and the people he loved. I was beginning to feel the small needle and seed of bitterness against the church, forgetting its truth. I was adrift. I had been out of contact for so long with any semblance of civilization, of commerce and gossip and formal worship—I was a new child coming into a new world. In an irony, I realized I was already beginning to miss the peace and stolid magnificence of the Colorado's canyon.

I wondered if Lt. Dellenbaugh ever thought of me. Elizabeth

was wrapped in the Navajo blanket beside the small fire, asleep. The horse and the mule were tethered some distance away in a glen of green grass. I sat with my back against the trunk of a large Ponderosa, looking into the fire, my stomach grumbling. Dozing between nightmare and fantasy I imagined that I was with James in the English countryside, a place of gardens full of red roses and women in blue silk dresses. We were taking Mooalong tea and sweet English biscuits. James was telling me of a painting he had seen in Philadelphia. I shook it off, stirred the fire, and fell back against my tree once again. It was a chill night. I was a little ashamed of my fantasy. It was unfaithful to John. How deeply did God reach into our thoughts, I wondered fearfully.

I must have fallen into a deeper sleep. The fantasy that was conscious dissolved. It was then I had a disturbing, fitful dream. James and John were both standing in the green river, as if to baptize me, and they were quarreling. I stood on the bank, and I was naked, the sun burning the tops of my breasts. I asked them not to quarrel, for I said I loved them both. They looked at me, and then both beckoned me into the river. I went to them and they each took a hand, as if to immerse me. I shook my head, and broke away from them and swam away, baptizing myself. I saw underwater their manhoods waving in the current, limp as river reeds. In my dream I felt the cold river between my legs as if the river were entering me like a man. Then the river became a pressure, a weight, and I awoke with a small start, not knowing where I was.

The pressure was still between my legs, and the weight was still in my lap. The fire was a bed of glowing coals, and I looked down, and saw a pair of slitted, glowing eyes looking into my soul with the eyes of Satan. I was being punished for my fantasy. The rattlesnake, seeking warmth, had slithered across my legs while I slept, and curled on the top of my skirt in the hollow where my legs were joined. It had settled in for a mid-summer's nap. Its body was thick as my upper arm, and in the red light I saw a hump in its middle and knew it had a rodent in its stomach. It can't be hungry, I thought, in that curiously disembodied state I enter when I am panicked enough to scream. It won't hurt me, I reasoned, but my starting from the dream had awakened it. The snake was very annoyed.

On my heavy skirts the snake had coiled, and now it raised its head to strike. I froze, breath stopped. I tried to look toward Elizabeth, to see if she was safe, but I could not break the gaze of the snake. It's rattle tick-tick-ticked in slow warning. Its dual tongue divided the dry air, testing, tasting, and I knew I was a dead ferry woman.

Prayer? I was too petrified to spit, let alone pray. What if I should be struck, and die? Elizabeth would lay beside me, and die too. She would starve, or when the mountain lions and the wolves came to feed on me she would be small game, a morsel. The impulse to pray became a silent curse.

I remained as still as I could, thinking God perhaps would want to cause me to sneeze. Someplace in the Bible it said the faithful could handle serpents and not be harmed, but I'd make no wager. In what seemed hours the snake decided his warm nest was not going to move again, and so seemed to settle back into a deeper torpor of warmth and digestion. I did not know what to do. Should I quickly roll? Stand? Scream? I peed my dress. The warmth flooded me, and the snake seemed to enjoy the added heat as much as I was mortified. He seemed to settle into a deeper calm, or sleep, or whatever it is that snakes do in their brainless menace.

The dawn was approaching in a grey filtering stealth, the chill of the mountains deepening. We die just before dawn, I'd heard. The situation lasted long enough for me to loosen a particle of my fear, and I did pray to God for deliverance. His answer for me was nature's answer. My little Elizabeth, as was her wont, woke up with a hungry baby-squall. She never was a child to gurgle and coo in her awakening, but was ready for breakfast the instant her eyes flew open.

Her lusty little cry instantly brought the snake out of its dark reverie. It half-coiled, whirled, and cocked its triangle of a head and fangs in the direction of the noise. I saw my opportunity, its head was pointed toward Elizabeth, and I sensed it was ready to move. Although I was numb in arms and legs my hand slowly reached out, and then quick as the snake itself I had it behind its head like I'd seen men hold snakes. I stood up, screaming, holding the writhing snake at a distance. It coiled around my arm, a blood stopping squeeze, but I managed to unravel it and then snapped it like a whip. The head stayed in my hand, and the body went whirling into the rising sun. I threw the head of the snake into the ashes of the fire, went to my knees, and threw up from my stomach the river water I had swallowed in my dream.

I took up Elizabeth and held her for a long time before I was able to begin to move again. I built up the fire and we sat by its comforting warmth. I gave Elizabeth a sore breast, and then some mush which we shared. "Elizabeth dear," I said to the little girl in my arms, "we are both due for weaning. We'd better get used to it."

I knew I should not tarry, but for the balance of the morning I fed small branches into the fire. The carcass of the snake lay down the hillside. I made a cup of bitter coffee and gave my attention to Elizabeth. My delight. A bright-eyed child who was beginning to speak in syllables that conveyed her love, although unintelligible to anyone but her mother. How could I protect her? If I did not understand John, how could she ever hope to understand?

I did not want to linger in the place of the snakes another night. But before I left I committed an act which left me wondering how quickly I was going to hell—or mad. How to explain what I did next? Quite deliberately, yet without a conscious thought, I went to the saddlebags on the pinto and extracted the Book of Mormon which I had from the missionaries in England. It was a prized possession. I had carried it across America in the pocket of my skirt, and I gave it much careful reading in the early years. And then life got in the way, and I only glanced at it on Sundays. I never could profess to understand the convoluted history in the Book of Mormon. I turned it over and over in my hands. The book had a power which I never before suspected. It moved some men beyond their reason, their humanity. It made their eyes burn. Joseph Smith's vision was full of endless, brutal wars. If it was true that Christ visited the Americas after his Resurrection, then his message of peace had gone missing like it has in the rest of the of world.

I sat before the fire and, page by single page, tore the coarse paper from its binding, and fed the pages to the flames. They made a dark smoke. The Chapter of Nephi curled up at the edges like a black fist in the yellow flames. Moroni's golden trumpet was smelted to dross. I was not burning history, but fantasy. This book was the only object upon which I could express the growing rise of gall in my throat. Page by page. And then the worn black leather cover turned to white ash, making a Pagan smoke. I did not bother to extinguish the fire as I packed and left. The book and the men who believed it had set my entire world on fire.

In the early evening, with Kanab in sight down in the valley, I put the dream and the snake out of my mind. Some of the rooms in my heart were filling with grotesque furnishings. I knew I must keep them tightly shut, and double locked. If it were not for my ability to hold things separate in my heart, I should have gone mad years ago. I could not banish the thought that in the few letters I'd had from John D. he had, in each missive, implored me to leave him. In his last letter—in which no further detail of the massacre—he again told me I was free to leave with a clear conscience. Of his fourteen living wives, eight had deserted him.

I am not one to quit anything.

After two days of lonely travel marked without further incident, I arrived in the settlement of Kanab, and stayed overnight with the family of John Stewart. How was it, I wondered, that John Stewart could live so freely and openly a hundred miles from Cedar City, and not be molested by the law? I wanted to visit with Martha Stewart, a kind woman with dumpling cheeks, to probe her feelings about the business of living with a man so heavily implicated in the massacre. It was like trying to converse with a brick. Secrecy and ignorance are comfortable bedmates. I reluctantly left Elizabeth in the care of Martha, but thought it best she not be near the scene of the trial. It would disappoint John not to see her, but it was best.

I took the trail up through the Cedar Breaks, along with a team of wagoneers who were taking lumber from Skatumpah to Cedar City. They were rough young men, and knew who I was, and where I was bound. I could hear their snickers, but ignored them.

Ever since I'd come into the Lee family, I'd noticed that the new converts to the church who had come west had heard of the

Mountain Meadows. And they were appalled that "we" could participate in such a thing. The veil of secrecy had slowly crumbled over time. One could not hold the guilt far from the heart. Families of the known participants were tainted, children taunted, business ruined. Except, I thought for years, it had nothing to do with me.

When we finally left Harmony it was with some relief, because our neighbors hated the wives and children of that murderer Lee. Once the word spread that Brigham had excommunicated John, the family became invisible until it was convenient to vent some anger or mischief upon us. How little they knew of the sacrifice John D. and the others had made so they could plant their cotton and erect their white temple in peace.

I arrived midmorning after two days crossing the breaks. The teamsters became bored with their banter, and ignored me. Cedar City was a marvel to my ferry woman's eyes, for in the intervening years it had indeed grown to something that resembled a city. It had been years since I'd seen row after row of houses with glassed windows and curtains of every description, from sacking to silk. There were houses or cabins on every lot, shade-spreading green trees and patches of grass and great gardens bursting with plenty. The streets were abustle with wagonry, freighters and buggies. Now that the railroad had come as far south as Fillmore, Iron County had become a magnet to commerce, if I may say that.

I was quite dazed by the scene until I recognized the courthouse, and was brought back to a chill realization that I was on no holiday. I wanted to bathe, and shop, and take tea and biscuits in someone's parlor. I wanted to rest.

My husband was within walking distance of me, but I could not present myself to him in this condition. I had to buy a suitable dress, and underclothing that was not made of Red Rose flour sacks. My face, under the great arch of my new hat was, I knew, brown as a bear's hide, dry as a pan and marred with sun cankers and ticked with blisters. I was probably a horror to small children, and thought John would be disappointed with me. I was between tears and terror, feeling the cold looks and the murmuring of those idlers who stood on street corners and measured me.

I had not given much thought as to where I should stay. As I drove down the busy streets, some one or two people recognized me. I saw Sister Robinson, who was a frequent visitor to Harmony, but I had either changed beyond recognition, or she wanted no part of any of the mass murderer's family. I soon found that to be the case.

It was not long before I became aware that the flood of new emigrant church members in all of Utah thought the trial of John D. Lee was wholly proper, and was needed to set things right with the history of the church. Even the old pioneer families, when I stopped to inquire of lodgings, seemed embarrassed to see me, and dissembled and were obviously in fear that they would be singled out as sympathizers if they showed me any kindness. In the unaccustomed geometry of straight streets and lines, I felt like a pariah in a strange and dusty labyrinth of hostility.

After inquiring, I found the large white house of the Cedar City Bishop who had written me the letter. I thought if anyone could help me, it would be he. I tied the horse to a stone post with an iron ring in it and walked up a genuine sidewalk of cement. Pansies with wilted faces bordered the walk. I ascended to a broad porch that had a setting swing hung from the ceiling, and longed to sit down in the shade and watch the traffic and drink lemonade and gossip—but gossip of what? I knew nothing of the lives of these people.

My knock was timid. The door was tall, with an oval glass beveled on the circumference so that it reflected a rainbow of deep colors that lit my face as if by the footlights of a theatrical. It was eerie, this great wood house that displayed the wealth of the Bishop therein. Wealth—fine houses, horses, and many wives— usually signified a high church position, whereas poverty, I'd come to learn, was thought to be the result of a fractious spirit toward the church and its iron strictures. One obeyed and prospered. One disobeyed at the peril of prosperity, and sometimes at the price of one's life. Do you think I write this without thought? I knew without a doubt that Brigham Young used blood atonement as an instrument of policy against those who were perceived to have transgressed against the church. My husband had sworn to it in his letters to me, with names and dates. Blood atonement was not only prevalent in Illinois and Missouri, but is a practice used to this day if the offense is serious enough. If browbeating and shunning and scorn do not keep the troublemakers in line, the knife will do the job. I know this to be true.

A tidy young woman whom I assumed was one of Bishop Coates' wives opened the door.

"Is Bishop Coates at home?" I inquired, feeling shabby in my faded and patched green dress. The young woman's face appeared as if to have never been exposed to the sun, and her smooth ivory hands went protectively to her throat.

"Who is inquiring," she asked, and I saw the fear in her eyes.

"Mrs. Emeline Lee," I said.

"Of course," she said. "Just a moment, and I'll see if the Bishop is in." And with that she shut the door in my face, and I waited without on the shaded porch like a supplicant.

Manners seemed to have suffered in the modern times which had passed me by, I thought, or perhaps it was the result of the arrival of telegraph and the coming railroad. In a moment the door opened again, and towering over me was a large man of early middle age—which is to say my age—who wore a face full of bristly brown whiskers. He also affected a set of small pince nez which made him seem ridiculous. Those tiny spectacles perched on his big nose made his face seem large as the lid of a Dutch oven. But what surprised me was how young he was to be a Bishop of the Church.

Age and authority are hand in glove in the church, and in most institutions, I suppose. When Brigham Young usurped the power from the Prophet's family after his martyrdom, the only qualifications to become the prophet, seer, and revelator of the church was He who had the highest most seniority. Thus time in service qualified one to be a Prophet, which, to me, is suspect. This is all to say, Brigham was the master of the mob, the manipulator of men and women alike. The mantle of Joseph Smith's authority, I've always thought, should have stayed with the blood family, but Brigham and his Council saw their main chance at power, and have held it ever since.

"I'm sorry to intrude upon your day," I said, "I'm Mrs. Lee, and I thought you could give me some information on the state of the trial, and where one might find lodgings for the duration of these . . . proceedings." I was surprised at the formality with which I was able to address him. I was used to talking to Indians, children, and mules. My speech was full of "cant's," and "aint's," and "don'ts" when at the Dell. Now I was using the speech of my father and mother.

"Won't you come in, Mrs. Lee," he said. I noticed he did not address me as Sister Lee, as was the custom in all situations. The man was cool, but at the edge of cordiality.

"Thank you," I said, as he stepped aside. Coates was a full six feet tall. The woman who answered the door was waiting in the hallway, and gestured to twin doors which led to a formal parlor. It was a room of English excess, and I was dazzled by the lace and velvet and porcelain bric-a-brac that sat on every shelf. There was a handsome mahogany sideboard with a real silver service upon it from which I saw steam rising, even in the warm air.

"The tea was just ready," she said, glancing at me now with more curiosity than fear. She had a sweet oval face framed by a tightly woven nest of braids that circled her head like a garland. She was small and fine featured, but one noticed first the strikingly violet colored eyes, bright as bits of glass through which she appraised one as if through a jeweler's loupe. It was only when she glanced at her husband that her eyes became opaque, guarded, and silent. "Won't you sit down, please, and I'll leave you to your business," she said.

I sat in a velvet softness and waited with my hands on my lap as she poured the tea. I felt foolish, wearing the great flying buttress of a bonnet, but did not know if I should take it off or not. My hair would be a sweaty fright, so I decided to keep it on so as not to alarm them, good form or no.

"Was your trip pleasant?" the Bishop inquired politely after his diminutive wife had slipped from the room. The question revealed his vast ignorance of the world south of Cedar City. A hundred miles of primitive trail with a mule and pinto was not pleasant. He had a pronounced Cockney accent with semi-educated pretensions. I marked him fresh off the boat. How had he risen to such a position so new from the old country, I wondered.

"It was," I said.

"I'm sorry about your trials," he said, and then caught his blunder. "I'm sorry. I meant to say, your tribulations," and his face went crimson and he pulled his tiny glasses more firmly upon his nose, tilting his head backward in embarrassment.

"The Lord will see us through it," I said. "Have you seen my husband?"

"Ah, no," he said. "I've not had the opportunity." Or the inclination, I suspected.

"I see."

"He's just arrived from Salt Lake under escort."

"And what is your interest in the matter, Bishop Coates?" I asked.

"Well, none, if you wish to know. I'm merely acting upon instructions from higher authority. I was charged with seeing to your replacement at the ferry, and getting you up here for the trial. How that was arranged, I do not know. I trust the Covingtons were satisfactory?"

"Oh, yes, for me," I said. "For them, well, only time will tell." I remembered my last glimpse of Mrs. Covington, who never took off her hat, looking forlorn as a lost pup when I left the Dell.

"Well," he said. "I want you to know that I am a neutral in this matter. I've no facts, and I do not participate in common gossip. The law will decide the matter of your husband. My instructions are to see that you were present, and that your lodgings are provided. To that end," and here he paused and looked toward the closed doors, and said softly, "Olivia, would you please come in?"

The beautiful little woman appeared as the doors opened quietly.

"Yes, Charles?" she said. This is rehearsed, I thought.

"Please join us now for tea," Coates said, and it sounded like an order although it was couched in tones of politesse. She took a seat in a small wingback and looked at me, this time with open, friendly curiosity.

"I am so sorry for the occasion which prompts our meeting,"

she said, poising her cup of porcelain toward her pert mouth. I saw a swallow-swift glance toward her husband, as if testing the propriety of her words. He merely nodded.

"Yes, well," I said. "Do you know of any place I might stay for the, ah, duration?" I asked.

"Olivia has found a small cottage—really a small house, for you. It is old, but comfortable I'm told."

"It is the best I could do," Olivia said, and I saw some embarrassment.

"The cost?"

"Oh, no expense to you, Mrs. Lee," he hastened to say. "It is church property."

"I'll not be a burden to the church," I said firmly. "I'll pay my own way, and not be beholden."

"I'm afraid it's all that is available," he said a little stiffly.

"Then I'll pay a rent, and we'll be square."

"If you wish," he said. His eyes, as do the eyes of all men, explored my bosom, hair, eyes, ankles in that flicking glance that one must practice to see. Evidently what he saw pleased him, for he smiled briefly, slapped his hand on his huge leg, and said, "Olivia will show you to the place, and see that you're comfortable. If you should need anything at all, then she has been instructed to assist you." He rose, thought about shaking my hand, rubbed it along his leg again, and left, closing the doors behind him.

There was a moment when the ticking of the gilded clock on the small fire place mantle matched the beats of my heart, slow and deliberate. I could sense the curiosity of Olivia as to what kind of woman would be wife to a man accused of heinous crimes, but also a genuine sympathy, as if she too knew some kind of burden. And at odd flickers of our eyes' meeting, I thought I saw an eddy of pity.

"How many sister-wives have you?" she suddenly asked, her voice small, and timid.

"I sometimes have to remember," I said with a chuckle. "Before the troubles, I believe John D. Lee was husband to about fourteen or fifteen wives. They were all blessed by his husbandry until . . . this."

"I'm the sixth of seven," she said, in a small voice.

"The Bishop seems a fine man," I said.

"Oh, he is," she said hurriedly, and I recognized a bold lie when I heard one. There was another unaccompanied beat or two of the clock works. "I've seen your husband," she confided. "And I don't believe the things they say of him. Any reasonable person could see it was impossible for him to have done the things they claim. He'd have to be six or seven men to be in all of those places at once. I know some men in this town who were there that day, but are too cowardly to admit it." I was utterly surprised by her bold opinion.

"How does he look?" I asked earnestly.

"I would say he looks worn, I'm sorry to say," she said. "A fine, handsome man. It's hard to believe . . . " And then she flushed to the roots of her hair. "Oh, I've no business being nosy, and I apologize."

"There is no need," I said. "What's to be will be. My husband has admitted his presence that awful day. The question is who is responsible, who gave the orders. My John was obeying lawful orders from both the militia and the Church. I would suggest that is earthly authority enough for any action he might have taken that day. The real perpetrators are not on trial this week. I mean to remedy that, one way or the other," I said, and it was at that moment that the small darkness was spawned in my heart, spreading like a heat into my loins, setting my heart to an erratic race. "Yes," I said aloud to the thought. "I mean to remedy that by any means at my disposal. Does not God depend upon the hand of man to do his work?"

She looked at me, puzzled by my cryptic remark. And I saw what I must do as clearly as if it were written in a book.

"Let me get my hat and I'll take you over to the old Sorenson place," Olivia said, breaking my troubled thoughts. "I've cleaned it, and got some linens and food from the church storehouse. You'll be comfortable. Come on, you'll see," she said, suddenly excited. I found myself liking this young girl immensely. Her innocence was troubled, but her enthusiasms, I could tell, would carry any burden of those she chose to be her friends. Little did she realize that day her life was to be changed as irrevocably as was mine as I came to my decision in the elegant little parlor on a side street in Cedar City, Utah, one hot day in July.

CHAPTER EIGHTEEN

I hitched the rented team to the borrowed buggy for my first trip to the Iron County Courthouse. I wished to arrive with some semblance of dignity, or at least a frontier formality, to ward off the stares of the city. Olivia had taken me to my small, paintless house, which was more than adequate for my needs. The luxury of glass windows was enough. It had one room with a small iron stove, table and chairs, and a small frame bed upon which were piled fresh linens and a quilt. There was a clean wooden floor, another amenity I enjoyed.

After I had unpacked my few things, and we had taken the mule and the pinto to a nearby stable for boarding, Olivia took me to the ZCMI mercantile where I spent $17 on underclothing, some full skirting, and a new dress of finished cotton from the mills in St. George that was somberly brown with black cuffs and neck. I still wore my Conestoga bonnet as if it were a badge. Olivia was helpful, friendly and warm. I took a bath in a galvanized tub full of cool well water, and was then ready to go see John. Before she left me, Olivia paused at the door, her face working with some decision.

"I shall accompany you to see your husband," she announced, "if that will make you feel more at ease. The jail is a rough place. Two ladies," she emphasized, "may temper the situation."

"That is so very kind of you, Olivia, but this is a walk I have to make alone," I said, touched by her bravery. "I don't think the Bishop would approve in any case."

"I don't ask his permission for everything I do," she said with half a brave, defiant little pout, but I didn't believe her for a moment, and my affection for her only increased.

I drove to the jail with my head held high. I had shed the bonnet for a severe bun of braids. As I was bathing, I had an impulse to cut my waist-length hair, some act of penance or defiance or some gesture that things were to be different in the matter of John D. Lee who had at least one willing wife to stand by him and assist in his defense. I dismissed the thought as petulant. I remember the many times John buried his face in my hair and said it was like the veils of heaven. I blushed, there in the tepid bath in the remembering. Remembering happier times when work was a blessing, love a gift, and life no burden at all.

My arrival at the jail had not gone unnoticed. It was hot, the late afternoon sun descending like my spirits as I contemplated the iron bars on every window. A small crowd of rough looking men, some soldiers, a few sadly assimilated Indians, and a knot of idle boys were gathered along the sides of the stone building, some standing on the wooden porch, others in the dusty street. I also recognized several town officials from the old days when we had great commerce between Cedar City, our place at Harmony, and Washington City.

I tied the team, with no offer of assistance, and ascended the steps. Fortunately, I had kept the buggy whip in my hand. The instant I opened the door and peered into the smoky dimness I was repelled by the odors of slop jars, tobacco, and unwashed men. The room was large, nearly empty and echoing, with shadows from the bars on the high windows slatting across the floor like lines which dared me to cross into this bastion of steel and foul smoke. The Iron County jailhouse was positively medieval, I thought, and then I heard a deep voice from the gloom.

"There's one of John D. Lee's whores. Wonder what she's here for?" the voice asked, and was met with snickers and guffaws.

Without a flicker of thought I let the tasseled end of the buggy whip fall to the floor, and then lashed it across the face which belonged to the voice. The whip caught him on his whiskered cheek and bony nose, instantly raising a red welt laced with birdshot droplets of blood. As I was raising it for a second blow, my hand was caught in a firm grip. "No need for that, Mrs. Lee," a man said. "Get on the hell out of here, Parley," he said in a voice of quick authority, and the men, laughing at the man whom I had struck, moved smartly toward the door. I was so angry I couldn't speak for a moment, and if the man who held my hand had released it, he'd have gotten a lash for his troubles too.

"I'm Quinn, Sheriff Short's deputy," the man said, releasing my wrist. "I apologize for those remarks."

"They weren't yours," I said. "I'm here to see my husband."

"I can allow you half an hour," he said with a note of apology.

"So briefly? I haven't seen him in more than a year and a half," I said.

"Let's see how it goes. I'm sorry, but I'll have to witness your conversation."

"Damned outrageous," I said.

"Orders," he shrugged, taken aback at my words. "It's up to you."

"I'll see him now, if you please."

He led me to another door that had an iron plate fixed to thick oak. He produced a large key, fitted it in the heavy door and swung it open, allowing me to pass before him. He smelled like the jail. The sun had slipped below the height of the windows, so everything was in shadow except for one thing. I saw a white crown in the dimness, a luminescent crest that seemed to give forth a light of its own. And then a pale apparition appeared beneath the glowing crown, and I saw John's face, wreathed in a smile that put the blazing star of Kolob to shame.

I went to the door of the small cell, noticing that the other two cells were unoccupied. I looked impatiently at Deputy Quinn, who paused just a moment, and then unlocked the door to the cell. In an instant I was in my husband's arms, frozen by his heat, smelling his smell, feeling his cleanly shaven face against my cheek. We were polar magnets, repelling and attracting, and I was breathless, and then I was crying, and then we were both crying.

"I'll leave you alone," I heard the deputy say quietly, and heard him walk down the corridor from the area of the cells, and close the door. When I heard the lock, John released me and studied my face.

"At last, at long last," he said, holding me closely, and then at arm's length, "Your hair, let it down."

"I can't," I whispered. I wondered why I did not find the sight of him repugnant, but I did not. I searched his face for signs that he was a criminal—he himself had confessed it. I wanted him to tell me his letter was but a dream, and only I had dreamed it. John would sense in a moment that his distant act had altered my whole present reality. But the man who stood before me was the man with whom I had thrown my lots in this life. Had I the strength? I did not know.

"I suppose not," he said, grinning like a boy. "Come, sit, let me see you." We sat on the rough iron cot that creaked with rust upon which was dirty sacking filled with corn shucks. We held hands for the longest time. His were softer than mine, now, after nearly a year and a half in prison. I was conscious of it. He was not.

"The trial is tomorrow?" I asked, not sure.

"So they tell me," he said, leaning back, and I saw he was feigning a look that was meant to show me he was unconcerned. In fact, he had an air of serenity the foundation of which escaped me. Then there was a lengthening silence. His face slowly began to twist with apprehension. The serenity crumbled.

"I should never have placed upon you the burden that I have," he said quietly.

"Better knowledge than ignorance," I replied.

"Why have you chosen not to leave me, Em?" It was a question for which I had no answer.

"I love you John, despite . . . "

"What I have done?"

"Yes."

"You may leave and I'll not blame you or condemn you."

"I could leave you, but I won't. I have sworn before God."

"You have full knowledge, and you still love me?"

"I don't know how to stop loving, John. It is a thing I've never learned. But the knowing has changed me."

"How could it not?" he grasped my hands in his, and looked into my eyes with a hint of the old fire. "And before God I swear I believed we were justified. I was mistaken."

"Are we not to condemn the sin, but love the sinner?" I replied.

"But that is the business of Saints," he said.

"No, it is the duty of love."

The prison had done a damage to his spirit I could not comprehend. He was so very alone, and vulnerable, and lost. To abandon him would be unthinkable. Mothers stood by their hanged sons, weeping at the foot of the gallows. Wives stood by their husbands though Hell and Heaven would not have it. I looked at him and saw a man on the snowy streets of Salt Lake, a billow of frost coming from his mouth as he spoke, "I was present at the Mountain Meadows."

It was then I should have abandoned him, not now. But we cannot alter our thoughts, or banish our emotions. Thoughts and feelings are but another layer of skin. They cannot be flailed or flensed and made to disappear. I knew that I must throw up iron barricades in the rooms of my heart, and burn the map to the passageways. I must, for the time, remain as I was; the wife of John D. Lee, for better or for worse.

"I shall stand by you come what may, John," I finally said. And with that statement my heart turned black with fear. The poet was right: The world is too much with us, late and soon . . . "

And so there we left it for a season. There was yet the business of saving his life.

"The jury selection tomorrow will be critical," John said. And with that practical matter I locked myself tightly against the coming storm, and gave him my full attention.

"Mr. Bishop informed me yesterday he thinks the jury will be composed more entirely of Gentiles who'll wish to hang me. That is the government's plan. However, if Church members are seated, then it will most likely be in my favor."

"It is his job to see otherwise then, isn't it? But I sense the shame and the hostility here, John," I said. "They need their sacrifice to assuage their own conscience."

"But you see, if my defense is that I was following ecclesiastical and military orders, it is those who gave the orders who are, at least, equally responsible. Brigham Young cannot allow that, and he will instruct the faithful to vote for acquittal."

"It is so terribly complicated. How can it end?" I said, trying to keep despair out of my voice.

"It can only end one way," he said quietly, and held me closer around the shoulder. His snapping, steel grey eyes were appraising me, my strength.

"If there is justice," I began, but he interrupted me.

"There will be justice only for me, dear Em, you must reconcile that. I have made my peace with God, but not yet with man."

"It is your decision," I said. "You must reveal the others, the names in your letter."

"No."

"Who is more important?" I asked, fishing for a different subject. I had been over the tangles and the ramifications of the affair so many times my head was a spindle upon which was tangled yarn. "The jurors or your lawyer? Is he a good one? When can I meet him, surely before the trial."

"Ah, my angel, he's the best. A Gentile, of course. Brigham would excommunicate any Mormon bold enough to defend the notorious John D. Lee."

"Is he from the East?"

"He's from Pioche, Nevada, of all places," John said. Pioche was a small mining town just to the west of our old home in Harmony. "And he believes that I am being made the scapegoat as surely as I believe it myself. Not only that, dear one, Mr. Bishop says that my trial is really an attempt of the federals to get at the higher members of the church who ordered the massacre. He is only too willing, in my defense, to forward that purpose. While I shall surely be convicted . . . "

"No!"

"You must face it, Em. If they don't hang me, they will put me in the darkest hole in perdition. That, however, for my part would be just." I saw large tears in his eyes through the film of salt that washed my own.

What he said, I could not dispute.

"But what I did cannot be undone. There would be some satisfaction if Brother Brigham is shown to have covered up the affair for the past twenty years. I cannot prove that Brigham directly ordered the affair. I told you that I rode to Salt Lake City soon after the . . . action, and told him in complete detail as to what had happened, and who had participated.

"I can testify that once he learned this, from my own lips, he approved of it, and said so both privately and publicly. He swore me to secrecy again. That is, after he got over the shock." John said wryly. "Brigham knew the location of the Fancher train the moment they stepped into Utah Territory ."

John's face was solemn, twisted with a confusion of the intricacies in which he found himself entangled. "But," he brightened, "With Mr. W.W. Bishop's convictions as strong as mine, we'll make a formidable defense. I don't expect he'll allow me to speak in my own defense. But, he's the lawyer. I think you'll like him very much, and I commend him to your trust."

"But what of the others? Surely you won't be alone in the dock?"

"Oh, they've issued indictments against Haight, Higbee and the others, but most of them have got themselves scarce, or thankfully are dead. Brigham has sent Colonel Dame to England on a mission of indeterminate length. No, it's me that will satisfy both the church and the United States."

"That is not justice."

"There was no justice that day at the Meadows. You must understand that. I am grateful that you'll mourn me. Few others will."

"There will be no mourning just yet, Mr. Lee," I said. "If Bishop can prove you were merely following the orders of not only the military commanders, but of the priesthood of your church, how could you be blamed for it all? Why, if you had disobeyed they would have shot you! And disobeying the priesthood was unthinkable, and you would have atoned with your own blood for your disobedience! What else could you have done?"

"I could have refused, and paid with my own life."

And that, God help me, I could not dispute.

"If it was to be done again I would gladly lay it down. But in those days, in those times, I did what I thought to be the right thing, in the name of the Lord.

"If I'm to tell all I know in open court, Em, the Destroying Angels, my friends," he added with sarcasm, "would have me dead by the next sun. The only thing that has kept me alive so far is my refusal to reveal names. Oh, the government has tried to persuade me to implicate the others, and I've been tempted. Brigham will not even acknowledge my existence, and I'm an adopted son. I've served him for thirty years without a question in building up the Kingdom of God. At the risk of my life. I'm bitter Em, and don't know how to quench it."

"Well, lawyers will have their day. If they don't prove satisfaction there are other means," I said bitterly. John looked at me quizzically for a moment, and then passed off any reaction to my implied threat.

"Bishop's the only hope I have, Em. Treat him fairly. He's been not only kind, but very trustworthy. While he is not sympathetic with my actions—who could be—he believes that the blame and the punishment should fall upon the men who ordered the deed."

"As do I. I know, somehow John, that you must forfeit something. It makes me die inside. I've worn out the ears of heaven with my prayers."

"Perhaps that too is your answer, for here I am. Nevertheless, I am prepared, and so must you be prepared for the days ahead."

"If you trust a lawyer with your life, that is a high recommendation," I said, reserving my own right to judgment. I knew that if I detected the slightest falsity in the man when I at last met him, I would see to it that John had another lawyer in an instant. I would delay the trial, do whatever I could to see that he was fairly served.

I was not long in the waiting, for there was the sound of a

mechanism, the key in the outer door, and then two silhouettes. The deputy, with his hat, I recognized. And there was another, whose face was covered with a slouch hat, made of the finest beaver, for the dying sun had now spread into the upper windows like a crimson wash.

"Visitor, Mr. Lee," Deputy Quinn announced. "Your lawyer." With that he turned and left, locking the door behind him.

"I believe you're Mrs. Emeline Lee," the man said, taking off his hat, and extending his hand through the bars. Bishop, I saw, was dressed all in black, a formal frock coat, dark pants, black boots with a high polish. The front of his shirt affected a flat lacework and a black string tie. He looked more like a gambler than a lawyer, I thought, but they are one and the same at times.

As he turned his face in the dying light toward John, he briefly smiled, and I saw nice even teeth behind lips that were full, even suggesting intemperance, or indulgences of the flesh. But his smile was genuine, and winning. He had a sharp nose, and wore a goatee black as his boots. His eyes were a direct, kaleidoscopic hazel in the light, turning with color as do the crystals in the viewing end of that device. He wore a pair of round, gold-rimmed spectacles that softened the sharpness of his features, lending to his face an air of lawyerlyness which was some small comfort. And his briefcase—black—appeared to be stuffed with work.

Overall, my first impression was that of a cunning fox, until I saw him for what he really was, in the last days; he was a lawyer all right, but he had the soul, and disposition of a poet. I later learned he was thirty-five. A more curious man I've never met. And one to whom I'm eternally beholden. I fully expected to need him later in my own defense.

"I'm afraid some documents have come into my possession which must have your attention, Mr. Lee," Bishop said, hefting his briefcase to his knee and opening its clasp.

"What's this?" John asked. He still had his arm around my shoulder in a familiarity in front of a stranger that I was unused to displaying. However, under the circumstances, I would have stood in the public square undressed with him if he had asked.

"This is a copy of the letter you told me about, but which you said must have been destroyed. The prosecution is offering it into evidence in order to exonerate Prest. Young."

"The letter of November 20?" John asked glumly. "We were told it had been lost."

"Well, it has been found, if it is the genuine article, and not a forgery. Only you can tell me that," Bishop said, extending the paper through the bars. It felt odd being locked in the cell with John, and his lawyer standing on the other side of the bars as if he were the jailor. John studied the document, but the light was gone.

"Deputy Quinn," John called. "We need a light in here."

"That'll be ten cents," I heard shouted back through the heavy door.

"Damn him," John cursed. "I've not been able to read at night for six months." He looked at me sheepishly. "The only thing that doesn't cost is the bed. You'll have to come back tomorrow, Bill, for I've no money."

"Here," I said, digging into my shoulder bag. I thrust a handful of bills into John's hand which he examined closely. I could see that he was losing his sight. I'd noticed upon first seeing him that his eyes, the color of storms, had a film over them through which the man inside was having to peer, as if through cobwebs, or a cotton gauze. I did not remark on it.

"Damn them all to hell," Bishop suddenly blurted, heading for the door. "This is unconscionable!" he shouted, making the iron bars ring. The door opened and the Deputy, with a dim oil lamp entered.

"Lights is ten cents to prisoners," he said to Bishop.

"And twenty five cents for meals and how is a prisoner to pay for it?" Bishop demanded. "I got the fees waived for Mr. Lee while he was in prison. He is a full ward of the state. I expect the same treatment in Iron County."

"See Sheriff Short," Quinn grunted, withholding the lantern with his other extended. Bishop dug into a pocket and slapped a dime into the man's hand, snatched the lantern, and turned his back on him.

"Leave me alone with my client, Deputy," Bishop snapped. His voice held a righteous anger in it, and that was, to my ears, oddly reassuring rather than upsetting. The man had some sand. He brought the lantern near the cell door, and tried to fit it between the bars. It would not go, so he held it high with one arm while John, holding the document close to his eyes, studied it. In a moment John handed it to me, and nodded.

"That is a true copy of the letter," he said. I swiftly read it as John's lawyer shifted the lantern to his other hand and held it for me to see. "Emeline, I wrote that letter at the specific instructions of Brigham Young. It was nearly dictated to me."

Harmony, Washington Co., U.T.
November 20th, 1857

To His Excellency, Gov. B. Young,
Ex-Officio and Superintendent of Indian Affairs:

Dear Sir: My report under the date May 11th 1857, relative to the Indians over whom I have charge as farmer, showed a friendly relation between them and the whites, which doubtless would have continued to increase had not the white man's been the first aggressor, as was the case with Capt. Fancher's company of emigrants, passing through to California about the middle of September, last, on Corn Creek, fifteen miles south of Fillmore City, Millard County. The company there poisoned the meat of an ox, which they gave the Pah Vant Indians to eat, causing four of them to die immediately, besides poisoning a number more. The company also poisoned the water where they encamped, killing the cattle of the settlers. This unguided policy, planned in wickedness by this company, raised the ire of the Indians, which soon spread through the southern tribes, firing them up with revenge till blood was in their path, and as the breach, according to tradition, was a national one, consequently any portion of the nation was liable to atone for that offense.

About the 22nd of September, Capt. Fancher and company fell victims to their wrath, near Mountain Meadows; their cattle and horses were shot down in every direction, their wagons and property mostly committed to the flames. Had they been the only ones that suffered we would have less cause of complaint. But the following company of near the same size had many of their men shot down near Beaver City, and had it not been for the interposition of the citizens at that place, the whole company would have been massacred by the enraged Pah Vant. From this place they were protected by military force, by order of Col. W.H. Dame, through the Territory, besides providing the company with interpreters, to help them through to the Los Vaagus. On the Muddy, some three to five hundred Indians attacked the company, while traveling, and drove off several hundred head of cattle, telling the company that if they fired a single gun that they would kill every soul. The interpreters tried to regain the stock, or a portion of them, by presents, but in vain. The Indians told them to mind their own business, or their lives would not be safe. Since that occurrence no company has been able to pass without some of our interpreters to talk and explain matters to the Indians.

Friendly feelings yet remain between the natives and settlers and I have no hesitancy in saying that it will increase so long as we treat them kindly, and deal honestly toward them. I have been blest in my labors the last year. Much grain has been raised for the Indians . . .

There then followed an accounting for wagons, implements and etc., including a sum for John's services.

"This is the letter that Brigham Young forwarded to the Government as a means of placing the blame on the Indians, and so to hide the actions of the Mormons," Bishop explained to me as I handed it back to him.

"He will have to explain that to the jury," I said.

"Of course, but who will believe that it wasn't one of John's own efforts to protect himself and the others?" Bishop glumly said. "However," he brightened, and withdrew the lantern. "I'll be challenging the jury selection tomorrow. It is likely to be a tedious affair."

"We'll not miss a moment," John said wryly.

"If you don't testify, and name the others, they will surely convict you, John. I warn you for the last time." Bishop's voice was calm, but carried a fervent plea. "Your only hope is to do that, and appeal for clemency when it comes to sentencing. I'm sorry, Mrs. Lee, it's the best we can hope for."

"Mr. Lee will decide that in due course," I said, looking at John, who just nodded his head silently. "In the meantime, we must do all we can to see that those responsible for setting this in motion are brought to book," I said. "I am at your disposal, Mr. Bishop, for any assistance. I am quite adept at letters, if you should require any copying of documents or such," I offered. "I wish to do all I can to assist you in John's defense."

"That kind offer may be accepted," the lawyer said, placing his hat on his head, giving the brim an insouciant rake. "With that I'll leave you alone."

The Deputy showed me out of the jailhouse just as the deepening dusk had sunk into blackness. I stood on the steps and surveyed the dark, quiet streets. Lights were on behind glassed and curtained windows of comfortable homes. There was the ruffian bark of coyotes in the distance answered by indignant dogs in closed backyards, making me homesick for the peace of the Lonely Dell.

I had the team returned to the livery in the late afternoon when I saw that Deputy Quinn was not going to make me leave. Thus, in the darkness, it took me a moment before I determined the direction of my little cottage—shack—and began to walk in that direction, perhaps eight blocks.

John had changed in that dark prison. He had shrunk. I looked up at the disclosing stars, felt a sense of hopelessness. The question would not leave me, waking or sleeping. How could I face this? How could I bear it? It took a great discipline of mind not to see myself floating down a green river with Lt. Dellenbaugh, away from all this horrible trouble. I remember on the handcart trail my father saying to me, "Step by step is what gets you to the end of your journey, not thinking about it, Emma." And I repeated that like a litany, not thinking of the trail or the trial ahead. Step by step. Do what is in front of your face. What could one woman do to change the course of the future? Perhaps the answer had come to me in the parlor of the good Bishop Coates. I shivered.

My father's advice kept me from going mad then, and with the uncertainty that lay ahead like a threat, I knew that I had to steel myself to the inner core, or I would break. There was no future. My life was ending. I never remember cursing John D. Lee for what he had done to himself, and his family, and his name, and to me. I did not feel any self pity. What was this compared to Haun's Mill? Just one woman's small drama played with a script written by others. I had sworn before God to stand by my husband whatever may come to pass. But it was hard—God was hard. I stiffened my back, ignored the stares, the scorn, the open hatred as I walked the street as if I had not a care on the horizon.

The summer evening air was cool enough for a shawl of which I had not. I passed down a boarded sidewalk along the main street which had hissing, blue flamed carbide lamps on the corner of every other block which deposited sickly yellow pools of light. A few cafes were open, the Cedar Hotel dining room appeared to be full and I was passing hungry for a delicious meal of garden vegetables and a piece of fresh meat. Coffee with sugar as much as my teeth could take. Cake. Candlelight.

I passed by and looked at the warmth within and hurried on. As I came to the corner where I would turn the two blocks to the street where I would reside, I heard a voice call my name from the doorway of a small cafe. I was momentarily startled, and reached for the small derringer in my handbag which I had carried with me to take into John's cell in case he asked for a weapon. I had been carrying the .44 derringer since I came to civilization. In the wilderness, I never bothered to go armed.

"Mrs. Lee, a word please," the voice said as a man stepped from the shadows and I saw the signature slouch hat of W. W. Bishop, attorney at law. "Won't you come inside and have a coffee with me, or something to eat? The Ashleys are known to be sympathetic to Mr. Lee. You must be tired after your journey, and the prospect of the days ahead." I did not hesitate.

"Of course, Mr. Bishop, thank you. I've wanted to speak privately with you to learn all of the details of the defense." I stepped past him and we entered a small room with bright Chinese lanterns over red check-clothed tables. There was a chin-high serving area upon which were plates of pies made of fresh fruit, coffee, and, of all things, golden globes of oranges from California.

I was famished. We sat at one of the tables near the window. Three other tables were occupied, one with a small family, one by a single man who looked to be a gentile drummer, and one by a single woman who looked as if her trade was on the streets. After dark. I was scandalized, but upon a quick, rueful reflection, was reminded that the whole of the nation viewed me—as a plural wife—as little less than a woman of the evening streets. A delicious irony that instructed me, once again, to withhold all judgment of my fellow men who are not declared to be my enemies.

A hefty, red-cheeked woman puffed from behind the high counter and took our orders. I ordered peach pie, and coffee. Mr. Bishop, laying his hat on another chair, ordered the same. "And an orange, please," I added. "I dreamt about juicy oranges on some of the hotter days on the Colorado," I explained. He smiled sympathetically.

"I can imagine the hardship," Bishop said, and looked for the first time at me with searching eyes, as if to fathom trust, or intelligence, or threat from me. My gaze apparently satisfied him, for he smiled, and pulled a small cheroot from his vest pocket, his eyes puzzling at me for permission to smoke. I nodded. It was the first time in my memory of Utah that a man ever asked permission to smoke, chew or spit in my presence.

"What can you tell me of John that he might wish to conceal, thinking to protect me?" I asked him frankly. He studied me for a moment.

"Mr. John D. Lee is one of the most courageous men I've ever known, Mrs. Lee. He has suffered in a silence while being assailed by his own church and the federal government. How he has resisted for so long is testimony to his character."

"How do you mean?"

"Did you know," he smiled, "that after your husband was arrested and being transported to the prison in Salt Lake City that his jailers got drunk one night and he stood guard over them until the dawn? He could have disappeared as easily as smoke, but he had given his word he would not escape. John could have disappeared forever in this country, yet he forsook it."

"I didn't know that, but I am not surprised. John is truthful to a fault," I said. "That is a virtue I sometimes question."

"One person cannot hold all of the virtues. But I would hold that choosing truthfulness over, say, sloth to be commendable," he grinned, rather than smiled. Such a simple stretching of the cheeks can do wonders for a person's mood. I was grateful.

"John was practically running the prison by the time he was brought back down here to southern Utah," Bishop chuckled. "He had gardens, began to teach some of the boys to read and write, many kindnesses."

"Yes," I said. "He wrote me of that."

"Did he tell you that the warden extorted five dollars a week from him for the privileges of teaching, gardening, and cleaning stables?"

"That is unconscionable."

"Yes. And for a few more dollars they let him sleep outside the prison walls. He never tried to walk away. That is where your hard earned ferry money has gone, mostly," he said.

"But your fees? I thought . . . "

"I understand perfectly well there will be no fees, Mrs. Lee," he said. "Not that I'm wealthy. In fact, I'm just about broke. Perhaps when this is over I'll recoup some of my expenses with a lecture tour, or other public attention. And I have an interest in a small silver mine over in Pioche that is promising. No, what I do for John D. Lee is what my conscience impels. The government is going to make this a trial of the leadership of the Mormon Church. I am their willing accomplice, for it is my—his—only defense in the end."

"Brigham Young will not stand for it," I said. "He controls everything."

"Including the jury," Bishop said. "No Mormon will vote to convict John D. Lee if so ordered by Brigham Young. Brigham still wants to maintain the fiction that the church leadership is innocent. That's why there'll be a fight over the jury. I must confess something to you, Mrs. Lee, and hope you will not hold it against me. For I have another motive in defending your husband."

"And what would that be?" I asked.

"My only sister is married to a High Councilor of Brigham Young, with Brigham's connivance. She was threatened, cajoled, and coerced into joining Kimball's polygamous family. I view the church as an enemy of freedom, both temporal and spiritual. She has recently written me, and begged me to have her back, saying her life is a living hell, but she cannot get away from the hold they have on her. She is terrified to leave, and terrified to stay.

"If I can prove that high church officials condoned the massacre, or if they did not condone it, concealed from the public as to who was responsible—which they have clearly done—then it is safe to say every other perfidious technique they have to justify their kingdom on earth is suspect, and evil. Anything I can do, Mrs. Lee, to bring the light of truth upon the tyrannical hold Brigham Young has upon the territory of Utah, I will do." He paused, as if waiting for a righteous reprimand. I have no stomach for righteous indignation.

"Survival is not evil," I said quietly. "I have been a member of the LDS faith, Mr. Bishop, since I was sixteen. What you cannot understand is that the faith is pure, the Prophet true. It is what men do to corrupt the principles, not the principles themselves. So I will join you in condemnation of Brigham Young, and his obedient tools. But I ask you please, do not question the beliefs of my church."

"I care not a fig for your theology, Madam," the young man said. "But I do care about freedom. And that means freedom to worship, which is denied by commission and omission among the people in the Utah territory. They fled the states in the name of religious freedom to build a kingdom in which only the official religion is tolerated. A so-called Gentile dare not speak out against the church . . . "

"Upon peril of their own lives," I finished for him.

W. W. Bishop studied me in silence, and then with a swift nod of his head proceeded.

"You know nothing of the pressure that has been brought to bear upon John while he was in the prison in Salt Lake?"

"It would not be like him to worry me thus," I said.

"Then you should know something of it," he said, toying with the cheroot between his fine, thin fingers. "There was General Maxwell of the Army, and the warden. They pleaded with him over the months to reveal what he knew. If he would implicate Dame, Haight, and the others he was sure to get a swift trial, and possibly exonerated with a mild sentence. He kept his silence, although he was suffering in prison. He was cold, hungry, and in ill health. Did you know that? He could have walked out of that prison months ago."

I felt my face go pale. John had hinted of nothing like that, no deprivation was ever mentioned.

"And he would not have survived to see the next sunset. They would have shot him in the back. No, I did not know of those pressures," I said, feeling the anger rise in my gorge. How could Brigham allow such treatment of his lifelong friend and servant, his bodyguard and stout right hand? With a word he could have ameliorated any bad conditions at the prison which John would have to endure. "It is outrageous!" I fingered the derringer in my handbag, trying to conceal my growing hatred. Common decency would not allow such treatment. The question had to be asked.

"Why did not Brigham Young come to his aid, even see to his comfort? A word from Brigham moves mountains."

Bishop snorted smoke from his nostrils, mixing a chuckle of scorn with a down turning of his mouth.

"Brigham Young," he said, shrugging, "Answers to no man. He is a law unto himself."

"Brigham Young is subject, as are all men, to one inevitable law," I said. "He shall not destroy my husband. If Brigham Young wishes John D. Lee to become the sacrificial lamb slaughtered to atone for the sins of many, he himself shall atone. I swear it."

"Mrs. Lee," Bishop said, studying me intently. "If, for a moment, I believed what you just said, I would not stand in your way. But I'd advise you never to speak that thought again to anyone."

CHAPTER NINETEEN

My husband's trial began on a hot July morning in Beaver, a small town just to the north of Cedar City. The sudden change of venue was mostly to give as little attention as possible to the proceedings, although the move caused only more furor and public interest. Mr. Bishop was furious. John D. was sanguine, and said he looked forward to a change in scenery. Thus I had no place to stay, and did not know what I should do. It was an impossible distance to travel by buggy each day to and from Beaver. I was in a despair as I packed my few things. John D. had been transported the previous evening, and Bishop had rushed after him, sending by a boy messenger the bad news that the trial had been moved.

I had withdrawn from my small trunk the only article of clothing which became me, I thought. It was a dress of black silk, with black lace at the throat. I was saving my new store-bought brown dress for what occasion I knew not. I wore no adornment. The black dress I had worn occasionally to funerals, and once to a general church conference in St. George months after I was married to John, but it had remained in my trunk ever since we had left Harmony for the Lonely Dell.

As I was preparing to leave, a timid knock came to the door, startling me. Into the dim lantern-light stepped Olivia Coates. She presented herself in the cool pre-dawn and announced that she would accompany me to Beaver City that day and thereafter every day. I was astonished.

"How, pray, did you get permission to do this kindness?" I asked as we bundled into the buggy and set out along the darkened streets.

"I've been sent to spy on you," she informed me, her eyes wide with confidence. "The Bishop sent me on orders from someone else," she paused, and raised her eyes, like the gesture of lifting a finger to the heavens, "Higher up."

"I have nothing to hide," I said. "Why should you tell me this?"

"Because you are friendless and alone and because I admire you for standing up before all of the hosts of the church and the men," she said solemnly. "I shall do nothing to betray you," she said. "Confide in me or not. I'll be your company if you need me, and will assist you in the necessaries if that is all you require. It is my duty," she said.

"But what of your duty to the church?" I asked, suspicious.

"I was not asked if I wanted to join the church, or to be married to Bishop Coates," she said with a youthful, petulant defiance. "It was the wish of my father."

"So you rebel by helping me?"

"No, I merely act upon my convictions that the church is no more infallible than the men who run it. Perhaps," she said with widely arched eyes, as if astonished at her own revelation, "I shall be your Mrs. Cooke."

There had been, I recently learned, a great scandal involving Brother Brigham's 19th or 27th wife—no one knew exactly. Probably not Brigham Young himself. Apparently he had pursued Mrs. Ann Eliza Webb—a divorced woman—with a vengeance, and caught her, to his everlasting regret. She had left him several years ago, fled from Utah, and had taken to the lecture circuit with a venomous anti-polygamy agenda. Her expose of life in Brigham's polygamous household caused a national furor which was still simmering. President U.S. Grant himself attended one of her lectures in Washington. Brother Brigham, I'd heard from Olivia, was apoplectic with rage over her betrayal. The then leader of the Salt Lake City anti-polygamy group, Sarah Cooke, had helped spirit Ann Eliza away and into fame—or infamy. Mrs. Cooke was a companion through those travels, and if Olivia wished to cast herself in such a role, well, I had other things to worry about than spies.

"I don't think I will require such a service," I said, "But your companionship will be most welcome."

"Thank you," she said sweetly.

"Are you certain this won't put you in peril?" I asked.

"Perhaps peril is where I wish to be," she said cryptically, and offered me a piece of bread which she pulled out of her enormous carpet bag.

It was a long, rough ride north to Beaver that morning. But as the sun rose over the hills that were covered like a thick carpet with green junipers, I felt some little hope rise with it. Olivia was charming. She chattered to me about the fashions of the day, the dances and the goings on in that part of the state. It was wonderful distraction. But under her young woman's enthusiasms I sensed a deeper current, a reserve, a secret. She was well read, and informed, I learned, and I enjoyed her company. It was clear she held her husband in fear from the little hesitations and editing lapses when she came near her home life in our conversation. In time her cares became mine, and mine hers, but that was in the future, God bless her.

By the time we arrived at the mud-hole-gone-dry that was Beaver settlement, there was a large crowd in front of the small building that was to be used for the trial. Mr. Bishop was dressed for the first day of the trial in an exceedingly handsome and formal black broadcloth suit with a snow white shirt and one of the new ties that disappeared into the vest. Compared to the others assembled there that day in the rude room of the small courthouse, he appeared to be proud, and confident, and purposeful. I knew better. The federal officials looked as they were supposed to look, carrying about their persons an air of tedious officiousness, a solemnity which was suitable, and a faintly condescending manner toward the Mormon bumpkins and Bishops, hicks and hayseeds, murderers and polygamists. The Judge, a man named Boreman, was clearly at the service of the prosecution. The prosecutor, Sumner Howard, was a middling man of middling intellect, or so it appeared. In his prosecution he had a dry, dusty voice that somehow mitigated the underlaying outrage of the crimes of which John D. was accused.

That first morning no women were admitted to seats. At Mr. Bishop's insistence the judge allowed ten women to be seated thereafter, which subtly changed the language and the tone of the trial, to John's benefit, I thought. The room where the trial was held sat little more than fifty people, including officials. It was crowded, and by the time of the opening statements there was no breathable air.

John was brought into the room last of all by Sheriff Short and Quinn, the deputy from Cedar City. He looked frail. He looked old. But when he saw me his face came alight, and a broad shaft of sunlight lit his head like one of those engravings of Saints in a moment of beatification. He was dressed in a suit that was much too large for him with the weight he had lost. His head was held high, and I thought his spirit was on the same plane, but his body was bowed by the months in prison. My heart broke again at the sight of him, but at the same moment I felt a thin line of bitterness firm my lips. When I searched the genesis of this affair, all I saw was the hidden hand of Brigham Young.

I sat near the small defense table, next to John and Mr. Bishop. There was much muttering by those from Cedar City when they saw Olivia Coates sitting behind me dressed plainly, almost severely. The judge was freshly from Washington, I learned, and from the outset the spectators and the participants saw that he had one purpose in conducting this trial. John D. Lee, it became apparent, was merely a side show. What the government wanted to reveal by these proceedings was that high officials of the Mormon church had been the author of the Mountain Meadows massacre. They would get to the fate of John D. later, Bishop assured me.

This became clear when the indictments were read. John D.'s name was not the first. The government had many of the facts of the massacre available through years of investigations and secret deals. The indictments included the principal author of the outrage, in my opinion, Mr. William H. Dame, of Parowan. Next was the name of his close confederate Isaac C. Haight. Then John D. Lee's name was read. Every eye was upon him. John M. Higby, George Adair Jr., Elliot Wilden, Samuel Jukes, P.K. Smith (Klingensmith), and William Stewart. So it was to become a trial *in absentia* of many of the participants in the massacre. The problem was, only John D. Lee sat in the dock. The others were dead, or in hiding, or had been excommunicated like John so as to remove blame from the church.

Brigham had engineered many of the disappearances of the witnesses, and perhaps, cynical as I was, he had arranged some of the deaths. Blood atonement is a quick and ready instrument for the purchase of silence, or revenge. The victim's own shed blood washes away his sins, and he may be saved. An abominable notion. Only by Christ's shed blood may we be redeemed. That John D. had not yet fallen to Brigham's knives was perhaps because he had some feelings toward John. It was at B.Y.'s instruction, after all, that we fled to the Lonely Dell. But when it came a choice, Brigham needed some symbol to lay up to the people of the United States that Utah was a place of justice toward all.

Then came the selection of the jury. The change of venue had upset some plans for jurors, but the new location was probably prearranged. It was a select group. Of course they knew they would be summoned. There was no aroma of fairness in the entire proceedings. The majority of jurymen were Mormons who had been ordered to vote . . . Guilty or Not, neither I nor the assembly, nor, seemingly any of the lawyers knew which way Brigham's puppets would dance.

Mr. Bishop glanced at me when the jury selection was complete; eight faithful members of the Mormon church were seated, and four Gentiles. Mr. Bishop, I could see, was gratified. He was not, however, at all happy with Federal Judge Julius Boreman, an avowed hater of Mormons with the reputation of looking "the other way" if it served his purpose. Rumor had it that Judge Boreman had been instrumental in convincing the so-called 27th wife to publicly leave Brigham Young and sue him for divorce. Any blow that could be struck against the Church, legally or extra-legally was, in Bishop's characterization of the judge, justified.

Boreman was a tall man who wore dandified clothing and had an air that was anything but judicious. But he had the full support of Washington including the Congress and the President. Bishop hoped that Boreman's zeal would lead him to appealable mistakes when it was all over. I held no such hope.

John studied the faces of the jurors. He knew some of the men who were sitting in judgment upon him, whether as friend, acquaintance, or merely as a brother Mormon. His firm gaze caused many of them discomfort. I could not tell the mood of the room, filled as it was with newcomers to Utah, curious as to the facts. Many could not believe their fellow members capable of such an act; clearly it was the Indians, as the higher authorities had assured them. And John D. Lee was a renegade.

It was apparent that Brigham had seen to it there was no one to bear witness against John—and thus the church. The word had gone out that no Mormon was to testify as to those events. Therefore, the prosecution paraded an ineffectual string of second-hand hearsay. Robert Keyes, a little mouse-faced farmer who lived near Pioche, testified first. His testimony was simply to establish the fact that the massacre had occurred. My stomach revolted within a few minutes of his words. The silence that fell upon the room roared with horror.

"And what did you see at that time?" Prosecutor Howard asked.

"You understand, this was three weeks later," Keyes said, dipping his small head. "And I saw a miracle."

"A what?" said the astonished prosecutor. "Please just describe what you saw."

"Well, the Meders was all, like, winter brown by then," Keyes said. "Poking out of the ground was an arm, or a leg, or a bit of clothing. Wolves had dug 'em up," he said. There was the sound of a quiet cry in the back of the room. I felt dizzy, and glanced at

John, who was watching Keyes unflinchingly.

This was the first public airing of the massacre in twenty years. Previous inquiries by the government had been met with unanimous silence. It was never clear, over the intervening years, whether President Buchanan's pardon for Mormon outrages as they tried to stop Johnston's army applied to the participants of the Mountain Meadows. In Brigham's eyes it did. In the Gentile's eyes, of course, it did not. There was still a justifiable sense of outrage and revenge; witness my husband before the bar that morning. Oh, the Church had conducted a few token hand-washing inquiries and then advised the witnesses to make themselves scarce. Thus my trip to the Colorado River.

"Go on," Howard said quietly.

"There was one thing I'll never forget," Keyes continued, looking at the ceiling as if the scene was thereon painted. "It was the body of a woman, nude, without clothes. She was so beautiful. She was so beautiful that neither the wolves, nor the vultures, nor the heat of the sun defiled her body. And this is three weeks later, mind."

"That's outrageous," Bishop said rushing to his feet. "This has no bearing on the matter at hand. I've heard the same myth for twenty years. This is evidence?"

"It's a fact," Keyes snipped before the prosecutor cut him off. "And nothing won't grow on the ground to this day," he added to the mythology before the prosecutor excused him with embarrassment.

The second witness also described the killing grounds, although in a more circumspect manner. Even so, the entire courtroom was shaken by his descriptions.

Finally, in the early part of the afternoon, the star witness was brought before the court. It was Phillip Klingensmith, a friend and neighbor of many years to our household, and an upstanding member of the Church. Some years earlier, in a mood of stricken conscience, Klingensmith had confessed to the crime in Pioche, and it was written down and signed.

I remembered Klingensmith as a robust man, full of vigor, fair-complected with a clean shaven face and light brown hair. He visited Harmony many times, and I always thought him to be a fine man. Klingensmith's picture was, according to John, mostly true, under the circumstances. Now Klingensmith sat in the witness box a frail man, who looked like a stick in the wind, a skeletal old man nearly bald, but sporting a chin of whiskers that looked like a sage bush.

Klingensmith was our witness, although he hated the fact. His previous confession clearly exonerated John, I thought.

"So Mr. Lee was not present at the meeting in Cedar City when a discussion took place as to what action, if any, should be taken against the emigrant train?" Bishop asked.

"Not as I recollect," Klingensmith admitted.

"But it was proposed to kill them all at this meeting, was it not?"

"Yes sir, it was. But many were opposed to such an action."

"So what did precipitate the action if the house was divided?"

"Orders, sir," Klingensmith doggedly said. "We had orders to equip and muster and prepare for field operations as the law directs."

"Who gave that order?"

"Isaac C. Haight."

"He acted alone?"

"No sir. I believe his orders came from Colonel Dame, of Parowan. His words were he had 'orders from headquarters to kill all of the said company of emigrants except for the little children.'" At this the cadaverous man paused, and I saw tears welling at the rims of his eyes, which he brushed off quickly.

"And not from John D. Lee?"

"No sir, like I said, he wasn't even there at the time. It was only later that Haight sent him south to see if he could forestall the Indians. His official title was 'Farmer to the Indians.' It was thought he had much influence with them, but that wasn't true. No amount of missionarying can convert those heathen. They wouldn't listen to him in any case because the Missourians had poisoned some of their friends, and they had blood in their eye. God almighty himself could not have forestalled their vengeance."

"Mr. Klingensmith, did you not hear a conversation between

Colonel Dame and Mr. Haight the day of the massacre?" Klingensmith looked doubtfully at Bishop, and nodded.

"Yes sir," he said.

"What was the substance of that conversation?"

"Well, it was the evening of that day," Klingensmith said. "Colonel Dame had just arrived from Parowan at the Hamblin ranch, about six miles north of the meadows."

"What happened?"

"At the ranch I heard Isaac Haight and Colonel Dame having words."

"An argument?"

"Heated words, like."

"And . . . ?"

"Haight was mad. Colonel Dame told him he was going to report the killing of the emigrants to Brigham Young. Haight said he'd better have a look before he reported anything, so we rode back . . . there. It was a horrible scene, they, I mean the Indians, had done a great butchery. Parts of women and children's bodies . . . " at this Klingensmith took a full minute to recollect himself, and then he went on, not looking at John.

"What did you hear them say?"

"Well, Colonel Dame was mortified, you might say, at the destruction he saw. Many of the bodies had not been buried. All of them had been stripped by the Indians. Colonel Dame was ghostly pale, even sick at the sight.

"'Horrible, horrible!' he kept saying to himself. 'Horrible enough,' I heard Haight reply to him. And then he said, 'But you should have thought of that before you issued the orders.'"

There was a murmur through the crowd at Klingensmith's revelation.

"Go on, Mr. Klingensmith," Bishop commanded.

"Well, Colonel Dame said, 'I didn't think there were so many of them—' To this Haight said, with some heat, 'It's a little late for that now. The fact is, it is done. And by your orders. Now, what do we do next?'

"Then, they were quiet for a time, watching the men working at burying the bodies. Nephi Johnson rode up, and Haight asked him, 'What do you suggest we do here, Brother Johnson?' 'Do you really want to know my feelings on the matter,' Johnson asked. 'Of course,' Haight said. 'Well, this is what I think. You have made a sacrifice of the people, and I think we should burn the wagons and turn the cattle loose for the Indians, and go home like men.' Then President Dame said, 'We must report this to Brigham Young.' So Haight asked him how it would be done. Dame said, 'Just as it is. I will report everything.' It was at this point that Isaac Haight became more upset. He was more like furious. He was shouting at the Colonel. 'You know that you issued the orders to wipe out this company, and you cannot deny it! You had better not try to deny it! If you think you can shift the blame onto me, you're fooled. You'll stand up to your orders like a man, or I'll send you to Hell cross lots.'" Klingensmith paused, looking helpless. "When he cooled down, Haight told Col. Dame he'd better address the men, so he did."

"What did Colonel Dame tell those men that evening at the Mountain Meadows, Mr. Klingensmith?" Bishop asked him gently. The audience was by now beginning to realize that the memory and the crime were as fresh in the minds of the participants that day as the day it happened. Gentile reporters were so riveted they stopped their scribbling when Klingensmith continued. They were wondering what any man could say to temper the minds and souls of the men who had just committed an act of mass murder.

"He told us that we was privileged to have been a part of avenging the blood of the Prophet. The most important thing was to keep the affair a secret, and blame the Indians. That we should not discuss it among ourselves, or with our friends or wives, no one. We should blot it from our memory. And then we formed a circle and made a most solemn and secret pledge before God to go to the grave with our secret."

"And why do you now reveal this, Mr. Klingensmith?" Bishop asked.

"My reasons are my own," Klingensmith said firmly. And with that the Judge adjourned the trial until the following morning.

I confess at the time that I did not understand all of the proceedings. Perhaps that was deliberate on my part. How should this end?

It was Mr. Bishop's responsibility to keep ever in the mind of the jurors that John D. Lee was acting upon orders from his superiors, both military and ecclesiastical. By the afternoon of the second day of the trial, these facts seemed to be established, some exonerating, some damning; John was not at any of the councils which decided to act against the train; it was also clear that John had done his best, by argument and pleading to dissuade the Indians and then the white men from proceeding with the attack. On the one hand it earned him the scorn and a nickname from the Indians, and on the other it caused his own brethren to doubt and mistrust him, branding him a traitor to the priesthood until he complied with their plan. He had pled that the Mormons escort the emigrants back to Cedar City and safety from the Indians. He was alone in his attempt to stop the massacre.

However, John D. Lee did act as the Judas Goat, the witnesses agreed. He did persuade the poor people to lay down their arms and place their fate in the hands of the Mormons. According to the orders—from Dame to Higbee to Haight—it was John who was the instrument that disarmed them and led them into the cursed valley. He told them the order of march, the men in single file, the women and children separated from them. He led them into the valley of the shadow. A sweet place of juniper and pinon and sage. As John believed it was not only God, but man's will that this was to be done, how could he have acted otherwise? To what other authority could he have pled?

His own conscience is the silent answer, the one that no one, even I, spoke aloud, neither defense nor prosecutor. It is John's unyielding destiny that he could not, or would not appeal to the authority closest to his heart: simple human justice. Mercy upon the innocents. John still insists he was under the idea that they were only going to cut out the perpetrators of the killing of the Prophet, and those that had broken the laws of Utah as they passed through the territory. He suffers the dreams of the damned, he tells me with his eyes, although he keeps a cheerful countenance. I love the man. And I hate the man who did not listen to the counsel of his own heart. A witness tells of John's mercy toward the orphaned children, as if that could mitigate the deed. I die inside with each thought. I feel distrust corrode the love. I feel not pity, or sympathy. Is loyalty enough? How can I bear it?

The trial closed the end of the second day with the characteristics of a "Mormon Storm." All "sound and fury, signifying nothing," which, translated to this country, means fuss and threat and great winds, but not a drop of water. After the jury was closeted, John was led away to his small cell, but they had not chained him. Sheriff Short had replaced the Deputy from Cedar City, and showed me a kindness when, coming up to me as I left the building, said, "Mrs. Lee, I just want you to know that my hand in this is my duty. I bear neither you nor your husband any malice in this affair. If there ever was a man facing his responsibility with courage, it is your husband. He will take his medicine."

The third day was a curious example of how justice can be draped to please the needs, desires, and predilections of her suitors. If the audience was becoming confused, so must be the jury. The witnesses that day heard the approved version of the Mountain Meadows. And it was with the collusion of the defense that the jury heard the Mormon Church's official whitewash. Sworn statements and affidavits establish—had they not been fabrications and prevarications—the Mormon elders were rescuers, nothing more.

The Gospel according to the rabble rouser George A. Smith, who was as culpable as anyone *in absentia*, was—The Indians attacked the train of their own volition on Monday, and the massacre occurred the following Friday; Nephi Johnson, the Indian interpreter, and some other white men arrived on the scene on Wednesday, but they found the Indians ready to fight them too, and thus retreated to Cedar City. There was no explanation forthcoming about how the women and children were separated from the men, nor of John's part in any of it—indeed no white men were present. The judge's incredulity was expressed in speechless anger.

Isaac C. Haight and William H. Dame—the two men who should have been tried long before John D. Lee's name ever came up—were said to have arrived at the scene on Saturday! They gave the bodies a Christian, but hasty burial in shallow graves, from which the wolves had great pickings. There were, it was agreed, over two hundred Indians present. Thus the pact of silence continued in the face of Klingensmith's testimony. For twenty years the curse of the Mountain Meadows had lain like a black shroud over the people and the town of Cedar City and the environs of southern Utah.

John was furious, but silent. He had told me and Bishop that a private court had convened in August of 1858 and, in a handwritten note, absolved William H. Dame from any responsibility! It was the same note Brigham showed John when he visited Harmony. The first signature was that of George A. Smith, now called a Saint, who has a town named after him. Liar! Isaac Haight said 'Nothing has been done here except by your orders,' according to Klingensmith. Now, like a good obedient child, he also signs the paper exonerating the man who gave the orders! It was confounding to John and others, but in the curious shift that justice wore that day, a harlot's revealing gown and a drapery of classical black, no truth would ever emerge. I despaired. The jury was instructed and repaired to their deliberations in the late afternoon. I was exhausted, John was barely able to conceal his fury his own . . . impotence in the face of a solid wall of lies. John understood Bishop's unwillingness to have him testify, so John kept his face of silence while underneath he seethed.

Mr. Bishop assured me that the jury would be back within an hour, but he bade me go to my rooms and wait for the news. I lingered for the hour, and then another. "They have to acquit. I'm sure Brigham Young has so instructed to protect the church," he told me, his brow anxious, his finger nervously drawing along his moustaches. "They have proved nothing. If it's hung, it will be a mixed blessing. It will be hell on John, for he'll stay in prison until the next trial, and God knows when or how that will occur."

"They will acquit him. They clearly see who is to blame," said I, wishing the hope to be real. Knowing it would not.

"If the eight good Mormon brethren can prevail over the four Gentiles," Bishop said worriedly. "Has Brigham put out a whisper that if the Gentiles vote to convict, they'll die before the next sun?"

"Anything is possible with Brigham, I've learned," I said. "And anything is possible if they convict my man without others bearing the responsibility likewise."

"I've cautioned you against loose talk," Bishop said quickly. I ignored him.

"I'll go to the jail to sit with John," I said.

"Emeline, they have forbidden it. They are convinced we've hatched a plot to break him out. He's under double guard. Brigham's work, I suspect. I'm sorry. Please go to your room and try to get some rest. I'll let you know the moment there is news. They may deliberate far into the night. The judge has directed them to return with a verdict, no matter how long it takes. I don't know."

"Then I will busy myself with prayer, Mr. Bishop," I said, and felt as if I would collapse in the street. Olivia helped me to my room.

I had been able to secure a small room in a decrepit boarding house in Beaver city. Olivia elected to stay with me in her office as spy-turned-double-agent, as she promised, and was sleeping beside me on a small, low cot. The wait was unbearable.

Night fell, and then fell deeper. Every sound tricked my ear into hearing the sound of footsteps coming to announce the jury had spoken. I was unable to sleep, I thought, but then found myself in a tangled dream that was populated with winged creatures. There were clouds of sparrows, like brown sand raised on a storm, winging thither on whimsical currents. These were replaced by a black mass of grackles, hateful, eye-pecking birds who moved across the sky like storm of black hail. I struggled for the calming vision of a summons of white swans on the Mersey, stately as monarchs, adrift upon life's placid river. John D. Lee was killing me inside, and my dreams were the echoes of my waking hours.

I awoke, my bedclothes damp.

"Are you awake, Emeline?" Olivia asked me quietly, laying nearby. By the starlight I could see her hair loose on the pillow, her eyes open, her hands folded on her chest as if she were laid out for a funeral viewing.

"Dreams," I said.

"This waiting must be an agony," she said.

"Time has stopped," I whispered. "Thank you for being here, Olivia."

"Your loyalty is beyond my understanding."

"Loyalty and duty and love get mixed up sometimes," I said.

"I can learn how to be a woman watching you."

"I doubt that very much," I said, smiling in the darkness.

"How can you still love him, if all the things they say are true?" she whispered.

"It is a different kind of love, now," I said.

"How is it different?"

"I feel a shadow between us. I find a breach between what I felt and what I now feel. But then the memories bridge the chasm and I don't know which side I'm standing on. It is difficult."

"His other wives have abandoned him, I've heard," she said, lifting herself up on her elbow to look at me. I lay quietly. "And he is not the only one who should be in the dock."

"No."

"Does it hurt so much?"

"It feels as if I have entered a familiar house, but all the furniture has been changed. The pictures are different—things are missing. It is the same, but different. You are lost, yet you know where you are."

"Yes, I understand that," she said.

"As for the others, that is their choice," I said. "It's the help-lessness that's hard."

"People will never understand you feeling this way," she said. "They would think you should hate him."

"Love and hate lie side by side in every breast," I said.

"I suppose they do," she said. "I do understand helplessness. I had to leave my home, because I was helpless to prevent it."

"You're anything but helpless," I smiled in the darkness. Once free of the stern hand of Bishop Coates—under the silly guise of her spying for him—she had revealed herself to be a feisty child, quick to question.

"I was living in Provo when Bishop Coates spotted me on the

street. He was fresh from England. His family had some wealth. He was driving a fine buggy, and had hired a driver, that's how wealthy he was."

"And you fell in love with him?

"Not likely," she laughed. "He stopped the buggy and sent his man across the street and asked for my name, which I did not give him. Boorish."

"I've noticed he does tend to carry himself with some sense of self-importance."

"Three years ago I was attending normal school in Provo, preparing to teach. We had an orchestra, and I sang in it. We traveled once to Salt Lake and gave a concert in the Arbor House. My mother died years ago, and I was raised by my father, a colder man I've never known. He didn't like me. Only sons, he thought, who could hold the Priesthood, and do a man's work were worth anything in his estimation. I think he practically sold me to Bishop Coates, although he would deny it to the rooftops."

"So Bishop Coates courted you?"

"No, he showed up one day at my father's house with a high church official whose name I shall not mention. He is the official who said that he had enough wives to whip the whole United States Army, and they would make short work of it.

"Coates announced to me that he was there 'to bring me my salvation,' at which point I laughed in his face. He didn't take it kindly. Pompous ass."

"My," I said mildly, so grateful to have the dark room lit by this bright girl's light, even if her tale was a sad one. "What happened then?"

"My father told me to get my things together, as I was going south to Cedar City to be the sixth wife of Bishop Coates. I kicked the Bishop in the shin before I stormed out of the room. I think the pain of my blow set off something buried in his head. The pain I had hoped to deliver to the man gave him pleasure, as I was to find out."

"Pleasure?" I said. My thoughts were thoroughly off the trial with this curious revelation. Gave me something to think about.

"Yes. But the slap my father delivered for kicking the Bishop was not pleasurable. He was furious. I had no choice in the matter. Oh, they tried to tell me how lucky I was. And overall it was my duty to obey my father's wishes. It was never good with the Bishop. Never. I'm off men forever."

"I doubt that," I said. Pleasure from pain?

"Has Mr. Lee ever struck you? Beat you," she asked curiously, almost distantly. "Whipped you for his own pleasure?"

"Never! The thought of it," I gasped. "Pleasure?"

"Bishop Coates has a cane of Chinese bamboo. The welts are just beginning to heal since I've been spying on you—at this she laughed—It is not pleasurable, I assure you. He only did it to me, and none of the other wives, I think."

"Oh, no," I said. "That is unspeakable. You should have reported him to the Stake President. On second thought, that probably would have got you nowhere," I amended.

"Beyond the humiliation, I'd have gotten a lecture in obedience from the stuffy old shirt fronts," she said. "May I tell you something else more intimate? I can't understand it. I need to understand things."

"If you wish to confide further," I said, uncertain.

"Once he went out in the night and brought back another woman."

"What?"

"All of the wives live in a dormitory near the house. He sent for us at his pleasure. We took turns staying at the house to cook and clean and . . . "

"Yes?"

"One week when it was my turn to . . . serve him . . . he went out and brought back another woman, one whom I'd seen on the streets before. A night woman."

"I was raised in Liverpool," I said. "I know of them. Poor creatures."

"He made the woman watch . . . while . . . he was beating me," and at this the girl broke into sobs that tore at my heart. "And then he ordered her to beat him! I had refused, so he beat me until I couldn't move. It was the most horrible hour of my life. He squealed with pleasure at the pain."

"Unspeakable bastard!" I said, and I meant it, I was furious. I couldn't picture it.

"I'm planning to leave him at the first opportunity," Olivia said.

"As well you should. I could use you at the ferry if things don't turn out," I suggested to get off the subject. "If it's solitude you seek. In light of what you've said, and it stretches my imagination, I think a divorce is your only recourse. What you say is unthinkable. It is perverse."

"I'm grateful. What I have to do is petition Brigham Young for a divorce. Do I need a lawyer to do that?" she wondered.

"I don't think so," I said.

"You've met Brigham, haven't you?"

"He married us," I said.

"Really? Is he a good man?"

"He's is the author of this from the opening page," I snarled before I could catch myself.

"It's hard for me to imagine. People think he's a Saint or something. But he's done everything he could to put Mr. Lee in peril, from what I understand at this trial, and from my conversations with Will."

"Will?"

"Mr. Bishop," she amended.

"Brigham Young didn't have the decency to give John a scrap of bread or a word of comfort or encouragement while he was in that awful prison. A Christian would have done so." I was tired, wishing her to be silent.

"He's caused you much pain."

"Yes. It is one thing to defend oneself, the faith, the territory, but to stir up the Saints using the mouthpiece of George A. Smith, to whip up the people with a frothing xenophobia is to be responsible for what followed. The government should have Brigham Young in the dock, not John D. Lee."

A thoughtful silence darkened the breathing room. I had spoken too frankly.

"Emeline?"

"Yes, dear."

"If it turns out bad, I will be with you," she said. "I think the

Bishop knows I am not spying on you. And I think he knows that I will try to get away from him at the first opportunity. But I have no way, or means just yet. So I'll be with you if you like when I am able."

"Of course," I said. "Thank you."

"If it turns out bad I think I would wish to kill Brigham Young," she said.

"Stop that kind of talk," I said, soul freezing. Could she read my thoughts? But like a girl her thoughts had passed quickly to another subject, one more dear.

"I understand he is liberal with divorces, though," she said hopefully.

"He's liberal when it suits him. One word from Brigham Young could free my husband."

"I don't think so, I'm sorry to say," she said. "But one day I'll go to Salt Lake and lay my case before him. He wouldn't throw me out of the church, would he?" she asked, as if the thought had just occurred to her for the first time, which it hadn't. She had a way of surprising herself when she opened her mouth. "I don't know what I'd do if he refused. But I need his blessing. Oh, it's a mess."

"I don't think you would be disfellowshipped for a divorce from a man who treats you badly," I said with no conviction.

"I would miss the singing most of all," she said, and a cool night wind belled the curtain. "If he denies me, I don't know what I should do," she murmured, and slipped into her dreams.

I waited out the hours, seeing the face of each juror, wondering how long it would be. What influences may be wrought in that room of which I had no inkling. I thought I'd had my share of hell on this earth in the past few months. And I wondered the worst. Why was it taking so long? Surely that was a good sign. Mr. Bishop would have come by now if there was any news. When would they decide the fate of John D. Lee? When would they decide the course of the rest of my life?

And I could not help myself, may God forgive me, for having thoughts of John that were not loyal, or loving, or even charitable. How could he have been so fanatical as to disobey every instinct of humanity? How could a priesthood have such power? John often said he had visions from God. Where was God's mercy that day, then? How could I continue to ever look at him the same? If he had not killed, then he had made possible the killing. He was responsible. Oh, I knew he suffered, and repented. But was that enough?

My very soul was cleft, and there was no place I could find to hide. There was no comfort in prayer, no solace in scripture. I had to see it through, and didn't know if I could retain my sanity. That is how I spend the balance of the night. That is what peopled this woman's mind. May God forgive me my transitory weakness, my weakening faith, my loosening of love. But in this anguish, it never once occurred to me that I should abandon him. Better to die, than to abandon my husband. And had the situation been reversed, John D. Lee would not have walked away from me in a thousand years. That is our meaning.

It was near the dawning when the door to my room was thundered upon by male fists. I saw darkness through the window. Dawn was just a stealthy breath, and I heard Olivia scratching a sulphur match to light the kerosene lantern on the floor. When the lamp was lit, I saw to my astonishment that Olivia had produced, from beneath her bedclothes, a horse pistol the size of her forearm. And I saw she meant to use it. I remembered the derringer, and placed it in my hand, and cocked the hammers on both barrels, pointing it at the door.

"Please see who that is?" I said calmly to Olivia. Her violet eyes danced in the yellow light. I saw she was terrified, and wished she'd never heard of Emeline Lee.

CHAPTER TWENTY

Thus began the interval, the short season of reprieve, of a sunless Limbo, a place between Heaven and Hell. It was not an Angel of the Lord at the door with the news. Olivia opened it to the flushed face of Mr. Bishop. He was obviously long on strong drink, and he waved a sheaf of papers in her face and pushed into the room without a by-your-leave.

"The news?" I asked, lowering the derringer. Bishop looked at it with some surprise, perhaps remembering our conversation in the cafe that night.

"No need for that, Mrs. Lee," he said. "Have you thanked God for the telegraph lately?" Bishop asked, making no sense.

"Have you prayed for forgiveness for being drunk?" I asked in return. "We are, as you see, in our bedclothes. A polite messenger would have been more fitting, regardless of your news. And I see you're drunk."

"As four pigs with wings," Bishop said, his grin lopsided with a conflict of emotions. "I have a surprise for you." With that he gestured with a sweep of his arm toward the open door, and out of the darkness strode my husband, his white hair glowing in the lamplight, his face tentative, bewildered, and then transfixed with delight upon sight of me.

"A miracle," Olivia declared, dropping the horse pistol to the bare floor. Bishop scooped it up with wonder in his eyes at the lovely girl who dropped it. As he unloaded it his look changed from wonder to open adoration. John stepped into the room, and then into my arms. Olivia gathered up her blankets and made to leave, trying at the same time to shepherd Bishop out of the door. A small crowd had gathered below, and voices were raised in argument.

Curious, how at such moments, the underplay of living proceeds without regard to circumstances. I saw W.W. Bishop realize, for the first time, the beauty of Olivia Coates, seventh wife of Bishop Coates of Cedar City, and remembered thinking, 'Oh, Lord, you play the devil when it comes to love.' The thought passed, of course. I was stunned by the sudden feel of my husband in my arms.

"Stay, stay," Bishop said, laughing, holding Olivia off, appraising her with eyes wide.

"What is it John?" I said at last. "What has happened?"

"It's a little small in here," he said. Already I could feel his authority as a man, a leader coming back to him. His release from jail seemed to have allowed him to regain some of his old manners and confidence, although I was in a shock of unreality. "I propose, Mr. Bishop," John said, "That we take the downstairs sitting room of this establishment, rouse the innkeeper, lay on some refreshment, and explain to my wife the fact of the Lord's deliverance, temporary as that may be."

"Lord nothing," Bishop said. "Good horse trading, and Brigham's willing compliance. By all means, come downstairs and I'll be ready for you," Bishop said, waving the papers again which I could now see was a number of Western Union telegraph messages.

"I'll leave you to dress," John said, bowing to Olivia, and then my husband looked at me with such a mischievous gleam in his eye I saw a boy, flush with the tickle of first love.

Downstairs a fire was going in the small pot belly stove. On the lid was a steaming kettle of water. Mr. Burns, the landlord, busied himself with serving the four of us, and then excused himself, slyly leaving the door ajar. I did not care, in my excitement. How could it be a secret that John D. Lee was out of jail?

"Mr. Bishop," I said. "I take it my husband has been acquitted? Indeed, you seem to have wrought a miracle." I could see John was still a little bewildered, perhaps in shock at the pleasantness of the surroundings after months of iron bars and stone walls. Bishop took a drink of the black coffee and shook his head negatively.

"Next best thing," he said. "It was hung, eight to four, as we expected."

"Then it isn't over," I said. I could not hide my bitterness.

"There is no reason for John to go before the bar ever again, if that is his decision," Bishop said solemnly, looking at John.

"I don't understand," I said.

"I've managed to arrange a bail," he announced with triumph, waving the sheaf of yellow Western Union telegraphs. "It is unprecedented to get the judge to agree to bail, given the nature of the crimes of which John is accused."

"Bail? That's wonderful," I said, gripping John's hand. I could see how relieved and pleased he was, but he was also confused by this rapid transformation from prison bars to a nearly genteel sitting room.

"It was Brigham's doing," John said serenely. "Bless him." I looked at John D. Lee as if a lunatic stranger.

"You can't be serious," I exclaimed, shaking my head. "He's not lifted a finger for you in all this time. How can you say that?"

"Let me explain," Bishop interrupted. "Brigham, yes, by miracle of the wires, has indicated—through his clerk George Wallace that he would not object if John were freed on bail. Don't you see? It's an open invitation for John to get out of this country and live free the rest of his life!"

"Impossible," I said. "The papers are full of calls for vengeance," I said firmly.

"Yes, the government is furious, but they've been beaten by Brigham and his faithful jurors. Why would another trial bring a different result?" Bishop said, barely stopping himself from flashing me a wink of his eye.

"The bail? How will we raise it? How much is the bond?"

"Twenty thousand dollars," Bishop announced. I was awed by the amount.

"Who? How?"

"Some of Salt Lake's leading citizens have subscribed to John's bonding, including General Maxwell, Judge McKean, and Sheriff Short himself. It took a veritable blizzard of telegrams to arrange it."

"They are not afraid he'll flee in the night?"

"Perhaps they are willing to pay that price," Bishop said archly, "if John should disappear to live out his life to a ripe old age. It will quiet the country considerably to have this behind us. Brigham needs to treat with the federals, and vice versa. There are still the questions of polygamy, statehood, jurisdictions," W. W. Bishop waved his arms, and then he did wink at me, bold as brass, "and business, after all, must go on. The trial is a national sensation, and besmirches Utah. John can live a long life if he stays judiciously out of sight."

"But not out of mind," John said with an apologetic chuckle. "I do crave a hot bath. Thank God for those men, whoever they are. I need free air, or I shall not live to any age at all."

"But when would a new trial occur? What would be different?" I asked suspiciously.

"We'll have to see. It is Brigham Young who is really the key to this. The government is disappointed with the results of this trial. It is up to them to conduct another trial, but who can promise any other result? As long as Brigham can load the jury, the government cannot get at him. Brigham wishes the matter to be dropped, as we all do. Then John can remain on bail and free for the rest of his life. Only federal pressure can get another trial. I won't give them any excuse. I've already filed several motions to stop any further legal proceedings against John. That will tie them up for months. Delay, delay, delay. A satisfactory end, all things to be considered." Bishop was clearly delighted to have his notorious client out of jail, but not by any measure as happy as I.

"Yes, time is what's required," John said. "I need time to

regather my soul, my strength. Dear, loyal Emeline," he said sadly. "They'll have me in the end."

"No. We can go down to the Moenkoeppi and live with the people there. It will be thirty years before there is a law in that country. And we can still operate the ferry at the Dell. Why, there is no way we could not know if someone was coming after you. You have too many friends. You're free, John. And free you shall remain."

"I'll never be free in this life, Em," he said, his eyes clouded. Then he summoned a smile. "But, for the time, I thank Mr. Bishop and these gentlemen for their labors, and wish for a bath, and some sleep, and then, by heaven, I want to get on a horse and ride till my backside protests. With you at my side, Em. We'll go to Kolob, and watch the sun's rise and the sun's set, and forget for a season all of our troubles. Does that suit you?"

"That will be my pleasure, Mr. Lee," I said, unable to hide the tears whether of joy or grief I do not to this day know. The chambers of my heart were labyrinthine, exits and passageways a chiaroscuro of confusions, the very night o'er clouded with the omen birds of my dreams.

Leaving Olivia in the hands of Bishop Coates distressed me. I asked her to accompany John and me as we "fled" from Cedar City, but in her wisdom she knew we did not need a third party to accompany us. Coates, it turned out, offered—begged—her to return to his house, but she refused. Mr. Bishop kindly arranged for her to travel to Pioche, Nevada, and stay with his widowed aunt. Olivia and I did not spend much time saying goodbye, but wept and held one another, and I teased her about her prospects with the handsome young attorney.

I thought perhaps the lawyer and the lady would come to some future arrangement, but they barely saw one another while she was in Nevada. Will Bishop was in high demand as an attorney, partly as a result of his notoriety in defending the mass murderer, and spent most of the time in Washington working on John's appeal, and in Texas where he worked on a case which earned him a great deal of money. Olivia wrote to me she found the aunt agreeable, saw little of Mr. Bishop, and worked for a time in a dry-goods store until she could petition Salt Lake for a divorce.

Thus began the season of a strange idyll. That same day we set out on two fine saddle horses lent to us by one of John's friends in Cedar City who were not ashamed to recognize his friendship. The hubbub in Cedar City, as we rode in from Beaver that afternoon, was high. Word of the hung jury had passed quickly as a grass fire. It was a mixed reception. There was the slightest hint in the shops, now, of acceptance of John with the jury's verdict. As in the case of the man who lent us the horses, some few others acknowledged our brief stay in the city.

We provisioned, and then set out in the light of a lowering sun for the long ride back toward Kanab via the canyons of the Kolob, the spires and towers of the Zion wilderness where the Patriarchal domes stretched to heaven. There we hoped to linger in the green fern glades of the Weeping Rock , and bathe in the gentle summer flow of the turquoise heart of the Rio Virgin. It was John's intention that we should visit all of his scattered wives and children. Those, that is, who still acknowledged his husbandry and patrimony. But for now, the warm sun and flowing waters would suffice. It was no accident that tomorrow we would sojourn to a place called Zion.

We made our first camp in the shadow of the soaring, free-standing arch on the rust red shoulders of the Kolob monoliths overlooking our old home at Harmony. The rigid symmetry was breathtaking, the hole of blue sky large as a heathen God's eye. Among the towering rock were fragrant piñions whose nuts were sweet, and which had attracted the grey jays whose squabbles amused us for their domestic similarities. Far below us lay Harmony, its fields shining in the dying sun.

"It saddens me we can't go home, John," I said, gesturing to the place that had been Harmony.

"It was hard in the leaving," he said.

"They call it New Harmony now, I do believe,"

"Yes, I've heard." At that moment the jays broke the silence in a particularly noisy squabble overhead.

"They remind me of Brother Svensen and his seven wives," John remarked. "The jays are peaceable by comparison."

"But you seemed to have kept the peace among us," I said. "Mostly," I added. He laughed.

"Oh, there are always going to be jealousies and imagined slights. I tried to treat you all equally. Favoritism is a weakness, but now that I've been abandoned I guess I can declare it now, Em, you've always been the one closest to this old heart. And when the end comes . . . "

"The end has come, John," I insisted. "You must flee."

"Would you go with me if I fled?" he asked, studying me hard.

"I do not know," I confessed. And indeed I did not know.

"Well, you shall never have to make such a choice," he said. "I'll not hide, and they'll come again."

"That is a . . . damn fool attitude, Mr. Lee!" I declared. He ignored my outburst and regarded me with a quizzical expression.

"They'll come again," he repeated. "Prison kills a man," he said quietly. "I've seen strong young men wither to sticks, men with the fire of the Lord reduced to quivering and cursing His name. I can not describe for you what it does to the soul, Em. Perhaps the hardest was the thought of you and the boys and Rachel in the wilderness for my sake. The other families are settled well enough, but to abandon you . . . "

"We were not abandoned," I said. "You were taken away. Rachel, I fear, has suffered the most."

"We shall see her in Kanab, and I shall do all in my power to set things right with her," he said, looking at me tentatively.

"Of course, you must spend all the time you have with your other families."

"But for now," he said, putting his arm around me, "we'll have the time we missed, and not remember what it was we've lost," he said.

He placed his hand on my shoulder and I froze inside. The sun felt cold. The moment had finally come. I'd not lain with him for what seemed an eternity. I had not forgotten the urgency of a man's love—no less than my own. In my dreams I had taken and given love to many-faced wraiths, sometimes John, sometimes James Dellenbaugh, and sometimes by the Indian I had fed on the banks of the river. When I had those dreams I would wake and run out of the house and fling myself into the river to dissolve and cool the dreams.

I would do John's bidding—I wanted to do his bidding, to feel his lust—but I did not think I could bear it. John knew my agony. He did not try to take my body, or tease me out of my clothes, or demand his rights as a husband. I think we both knew, upon reflection, that the last time we had made love the night before he left for the north had been the last time in our lives, and I did not know if it was a relief, or a curse, or a blessing. Within me still flowed the heat of my body, and now it must be forever stilled.

John knew this as well as I knew it. If he were to run his hands along the inside of my thighs would they leave a trail incarnadine? His confession to me made his guilt a reality that was visible. Had his hands so stained me the countless times we had pressed our nakedness together so his skin was my skin? He knew it could never be the same—that I could never give again as I had—and so some part of us was finished. With what we were to face in the future, a sweaty coupling would solve nothing. Had we made love on the blanket on the rocks in the dying sun it would have left us both with an ache that would never go away. If we had rolled naked on the rocks for the rest of the month it would have solved nothing.

Had he insisted, I would have disrobed. But he did not.

He took my hand and examined it. I lowered my eyes. I thought I had been wrong—he was going to have me—but then he reached out and stroked my hair as tenderly as if I were a child. I thought his hand would fall to my breasts, but instead his lips brushed my forehead, and he stood in the red sun and looked up at over-reaching apex of the arch above us. "I wonder if a man can see heaven better from the top of the arch? I've a mind to climb it," he said.

"No!" I exclaimed. "That is dangerous."

"It can't be much more dangerous than having your life held in the palms of a lawyer," he said, smiling even though he'd lost the world.

CHAPTER TWENTY-ONE

We traveled publicly throughout southern Utah visiting family and friends. John never had the intention to elude justice, argue though I did with him to flee to safety. He refused to listen. "I'll not run, nor hide. My freedom is more precious to me than any other thing. But I am not a coward, no matter how they paint me," he said.

We conducted a discreet, though personally satisfying tour visiting with his remaining faithful families, renewing our friendship and kinship, caching up on the birthing and the dying. It was a good time for John. His robustness reappeared, his laughter, his smiles. But he never could hide the pain in his eyes from me. Answer me this. Why, when I did not know the extent of John's involvement, and the bloody details of the meadow in Zion, did I never before see the pain in his eyes? It was always there for anyone to see who cared to look. Love's blinders, the prisms through which we filter our own heart's desiring, are the only answer. The kindness of our own vanity.

It took some thawing of the other wives when it was clear that

John was traveling solely with me, and had lived with me alone for so long. But the facts of his imprisonment, and the impending darkness of another trial tempered their enmity, and we had sometimes cool, sometimes cordial visits. To each son and daughter, wife and sympathetic friend, the advice was uniform. They all begged John to never again place himself at the mercy of the government.

"The irony," he told them all, "Is that we were—every man-jack of a Mormon—be he cutthroat, candle maker, or soldier, pardoned by President Buchanan in 1858 when they negotiated to allow the Union Army into the Great Salt Lake Valley without a war. It was amnesty for all, and we were assured that applied to any who may have been involved at the Mountain Meadows. That's how we were able to live at Harmony and prosper those many years," he reminded them.

"If the United States breaks its word with the sovereign Indian nations for the past hundred years, then they will break their word to anyone. The conclusion," at this John smiled wryly at one of our gatherings, "is that we are no better than the Lamanites. I've never thought we were, but our treatment is as bad as any native tribe ever received. At least some of the tribes were offered land and food and clothing. We got extermination orders and no quarter anyplace we ever tried to settle."

The leave-takings were enough to wrench the heart. Uncertainty dogged us. I looked with dread upon our reunion with Rachel, who had removed to Kanab two weeks after I went to Cedar City. Perhaps she could prevail upon him to go to the Moenkoeppi. When we arrived in Kanab we went directly to the house where Rachel and her children were staying. The house belonged to Wm. Stewart, one of the more active participants at the Meadows that day. Iron piled on iron. Why was he not in the dock? I had a joyful reunion with my small and precious daughter, and John was delighted to see her.

I cannot tell what transpired between Rachel and John over the next two days, as I was not privy to any of their conversations, nor did John ever divulge to me what passed between them. At meals Rachel was subdued, but of seeming good cheer. John was over-

joyed to be among his children, and so the days passed. It was at
Kanab that a letter from W.W. Bishop caught up with us. John
handed the letter first to Rachel, and then to me after supper one
evening, and seemed to doze off as we read it.

*... March 11, 1876 ... it is my opinion that you will not be
retried until next April at the earliest. It appears that the
government is making no vigorous preparations, and I do not
think they intend to try you ever again. Now that you are free
on the secure bond you can most likely wear out your days as
you see fit & praise God that will be an end on the matter.*

*You ask my opinion, should we have a new trial, as you seem
to insist upon. Would we have Judge Boreman again? I say No!
A Thousand Times No! Exhaust all we know of the law,
management, trickery and corruption before we permit the
case to be tried again before one who is so thoroughly opposed
to the defendant as we know Boreman to be. Any fate is
preferable to that of failing, and that in the place where you
know the ambush is laid for you ...*

"Well, that is moot, now, is it not John?" I asked, looking to
Rachel for support. I must admit to naggery, for I never let an
opportunity arise that I did not suggest that it was in John's best
interests to disappear from the territory of Utah for all time.
Rachel seemed not to comprehend John's difficulty. She had been
the wife who, next to myself, was unwavering in her support. Her
selfless devotion put mine to shame. She had suffered the
hardships of the Hegira from the United States. She had froze and
burned and starved for her faith, and now the toll was due. As
much as it pained me, I observed that Rachel was, well, addled.

"John knows best," she murmured time and again. This led me
to speculate that John did not really consult with her as to his best
course. I pressed for flight and peace. John adamantly held hope
for a new trial, for justice. The only way justice would be done
would be to hang him, I continually reminded him. "Em, you've
had my neck stretched so many times I feel like an ostrich."

"An apt comparison, Mr. Lee," I said. "With your head stuck in
the sand. Rather I wish you were a garrulous blue jay rather than
a silent stone. It will save you John," I urged.

"Let it be," he suddenly snapped at me, and I felt ashamed of myself. It was his burden, his life. It was his silence that would doom him.

But what of me, my heart cried out. What of you, foolish woman, it answered. There are yet rooms of the heart you've never entered, never dreamed could exist. Dare you open them? Silence! I resolved not to speak of it again, but that diminished with each day with the pressure I felt for him to be in Mexico.

While we were in Kanab, and before we departed for Lee's Ferry and what I hoped would be a southward direction until he reached the tip of South America, a suspicious character appeared with a letter of introduction from Will Bishop. His name was Donavan, and a more disreputable character I've never met. However, I became his ally for a brief time, much to the displeasure of my husband, and this caused a strain between John and me which made me furious with him beyond all counting.

I was far gone from the church and the government. I no longer cared. Of course I had to continue to live the fiction for John's sake. He would never forgive me for losing faith. It was something I would have to arrange within my own conscience. Even at this date, John had a pathetic faith that Brigham Young would absolve him and make some reparations and by some mysterious act restore John to full fellowship in the church.

John sent letter after letter to Brigham Young in that period, the content of which I can only guess. I hope they were not letters of beggary and self-pity. No, John had little of that. He was so grateful to be out of prison I could see each breath he drew was sweet. He was almost childlike in his delight with flowers, sunsets, and the works of Mr. Shakespeare. On the other side, John was a man as pigheaded as a block of stone. It was maddening that he wasn't already swallowed up in the south. I was sick of his principles. How could he hold faith in a man who'd sold him down so many rivers I had lost count? The man who'd sold him south had sold me and my family and our future. Brigham Young had a lot to answer in this life or the next.

Mr. Taggert Donavan presented himself at Mr. Stewart's house in a plaid suit—grounds enough to dismiss any man at the door. I answered it myself. He grabbed my hand and pumped it vigorous-ly, and I thought for a moment he was going to offer me a cigar and slap me on the back.

"I take it you are Mrs. John Lee," the man said without so much as a tip of his odd bowler hat. Under the dust I could see his clothes were expensive, but in such taste as to turn the stomach. Green waistcoat—also plaid—yellow tie, and a high collared blue shirt. Patent leather boots. And flaming red chin whiskers. He made me dizzy.

"Who, are you?" I asked him coldly.

"Taggert Donavan of New York and San Francisco, agent to the stars," he announced, slapping a calling card in my hand.

"And what stars would those be, sir?" I asked him, ready to shut the door in his face, but his boot was already in the door. I was ready to stomp on it when he produced the letter.

"It's from your Attorney Mr. W. W. Bishop," he said heartily. That naturally gave me pause.

"I'll take it," I said. "Wait." I took the letter from his hand, and shut the door in his face. Retreating down the hallway and into the parlor where John was reading and Rachel was sitting and staring vacantly at the curtained window, I handed the letter to John.

"Who was it?" he asked, taking the letter.

"A drummer with red whiskers," I said, wondering if my eyes had gone bad. "What does it say?"

"Let's see here," John said, glancing at the brief note. He had acquired some magnifying spectacles in Kanab so he could read. "It's from Mr. Bishop. He advises that we talk to this man, and listen to his offer. He read the letter aloud to me and Rachel.

Dear Mr. Lee:

Mr. Taggert Donavan, who bears this letter, may present to you an opportunity you may wish to consider. Knowing your dire financial circumstances, at least hear the man out. It may well be that this course of action will result in more favorable public opinion toward yourself which we may use if a new trial should ever occur. However, John, I am entirely neutral on the subject, and would not influence your decision in any way. My regards to Mrs. Lee I am Yours obediently & Etc.

W.W. Bishop

"That's all it says." John was puzzled, wary.

"Shall I show him in?" I asked.

"Of course," John said. "It's impolite to leave strangers on the porch."

"Not this one," I muttered and went to let the man in.

We settled him with tea in the parlor. He tried to bounce an awestruck Elizabeth on his knee, but the colors frightened her. John himself had to disguise a smile at the sight of the man.

"Are you a drummer, sir?" he inquired.

"No sir, I am opportunity," Donavan replied.

"Let's hear it," John said. "They're few and far between these days."

"I've represented Miss Lilly Langtry and Mr. U.S. Grant," he said. "And I've come to represent you, sir, to make your fortune."

"I'll hazard I've made and lost more fortunes than you have neckties, sir," John said. "Represented to do what?"

"Why, to perform, sir, to perform before an adoring public." Somehow Donavan's booming voice had stirred Rachel from whatever vacant reverie she was inhabiting. She got up and left the room after a hostile glance at the man. I saw John sadly shake his head.

"How do you mean?" he asked.

"I'd like to take you back east on the lecture circuit, sir. There you will be able to state your case, tell your story, expose the church. I've got it all arranged."

"Lecture circuit?" I said. "That's preposterous." As I have said, I speak sometimes without due reflection.

"Now, Em," John said mildly, but I saw the storm in the building on his lined face. His hair was pure white by now, which made his grey eyes seem as stones in snow.

"With your recent notoriety, and the hung jury, I can assure you, Mr. Lee, that America is waiting to hear your version of events. And that's the truth. I'm offering you a chance to tell your story, and get paid handsomely to boot. What do you think?"

"I think that is outrageous," John said before I could open my mouth.

"Let's not rush, John," I said, my head spinning. Suddenly this selfish woman saw New York and Philadelphia. I saw carpeted salons, a return to Liverpool and lights. But what I really desired was our safety. This might be our one and only chance. I degraded myself with that momentary lapse—Adam's legacy. Is self-preservation a sin? John shot me a stern glance. I'd overstepped. It was his affair, not mine.

"I've got it all approved," Donovan said.

"Approved by whom?" John asked. "Even if I were interested, which I am not, the conditions of my bail are to stay within the territory of Utah. I intend to do so."

You fool, I thought, hiding my angry look.

"You have friends both in Salt Lake and back in the east, where the money is," Donavan winked broadly. It was almost a lewd gesture.

"I have no friends," John snapped back.

"Oh, but you do, sir. The prison warden speaks highly of you. The men in Salt Lake City who are not allied with Brigham Young are your friends. I have arranged for you to be accompanied by two officers of the court if you should decide to go east on the lecture circuit. They will vouch for your return to Utah, should it be required."

My heart leapt. Mexico had little appeal to me. I was tired. Perhaps this would be our chance to get away, to have the means to find a place away from the west where we could live in peace. I was, in my weakness, ready to change my identity and my name and my faith to be done with this nightmare.

"That is highly irregular," John said suspiciously, and then I saw the possible trap.

"It is," I said. "Why would officers of the court consent to this?"

"They are powerful men, Ma'am," Donavan said, pressing his case. "It suits them to your benefit. They wish the story to be told far and wide. All is required to be told is the circumstances, not necessarily your own personal involvement. You'll prosper, sir.

Kings may wish to shake your hand. You could make thousands upon thousands of dollars from a tour. I was the agent for Miss Eliza Webb on her lecture tour. She made fifty thousand dollars."

That sum made me gasp. John blinked several times and then stood up, seeming to fill the room with still rage.

"I would never degrade myself thus," he said. "You would use me to destroy my faith, my church and its leaders, and I will not have it. I am loathe to accept liberty and favors from those not of my faith. And even if I would, the moment I stepped out of the territory I would be shot in the back for jumping my bond," he said with contempt. "I may be a simple man, Mr. Donavan, and a friendless fool as most say, but I have not lost my powers of reason. Now leave us if you please, so we can wash the bad taste out of our mouths."

"But John," I began to protest.

"The very least you could do is let me live or die upon my own terms, Mrs. Lee," he said, and the bleak chill in his eyes froze me to my seat. In that one brief instant I felt a deep thrill of hatred. I was but an observer of this play, not an actor. Who was the author? Why were not the others in John's situation? Why must we bear it alone? John's blindness filled me with fury which I could scarce contain.

I thought John was going to physically throw the plaid suit out of the house, but his courtesy and manners returned as quickly as his anger at me died.

"Forgive my manners, sir," John said. "Mrs. Lee will show you out."

At the doorway Donavan turned to me and said, "Mrs. Lee, I'm sure your story will sell as good as his. You would be famous. What do you say?" Whereupon I grabbed him by the green waistcoat and propelled him backward off the porch. As he picked himself up out of the dusk I thought he was going to charge me, instead he said, "You Mormons deserve every last thing you got coming to you." And fled down the street, not out of sight for a long distance.

John's refusal to get out of Utah began to break my strength. We remained distant from one another on the journey back down to the Colorado. But I could not stay angry with the man for

holding to his principles any more than I could resolve the bifur-
cation of my heart. Love and hate in separate rooms take barriers
of great will. I could not cut off my own feelings, but I still manned
the barricades. As the miles passed by, and we got back into
familiar country, we slipped into familiar roles. In time there was
a mute truce between us. It was our custom in the Lee family,
enforced by John's strong will, that once decided, the matter was
dropped, no matter the decision. If you lost an argument, you held
no enmity. It's the only way love can live. Husbands and wives
have a way of speaking without words. Once we were away from
the last settlement on the upper Paria we were at peace with one
another. We loved but did not touch. There was a kind of peace
that I felt as dread.

My boys were overjoyed with our arrival. The Dell looked not
so much lonely, but more like a refuge, a home. It was not a pile
of rocks and brush and sun-seared sand, but an oasis, albeit a dry
oasis away from the river. The comparison of the landscape to that
of the land of Moses and Jesus struck me again as we sojourned
down the banks of the dry Paria; a withered landscape of lavender
cliffs and cinnamon sands. There was a beauty so severe it took
away the imagination.

The landscape at Lee's Ferry is the one thing I have encountered
on this earth whose shapes and forms approximate the notion of
infinite creation. The ocean is bounded by shores, the desert only
by the sky. One took this land as it was, on terms that light and
shadow dictated. There was mystery in the silences. Mystery in
the Raven's hoarse penetration of the void. Our voices echoed like
lost souls, the clipping hooves of the animals a syncopation of
some ancient, alien rhythm; absolute harmony was in the creatures that scurried on clawed toes, or crawled on sliding stomachs
with the blood's heat dictated by the sun, not the heart. It was a
place that waited to destroy the unwary, the unwise, the unb-
lessed. It was there we tarried for a season.

They came to the Lonely Dell for John D. Lee in the dead of
night. Sheriff Short and a posse of federal marshals had a rumor
that John and Rachel and I, with our children, were fleeing to the

Indian settlement of Moenkoeppi, or even to the safety of Mexico, where we would disappear forever.

They came in the very darkest part of the night, when the stars were a blizzard of frost-like light, the Big Dipper tipping its cup around the pole star. The dogs barked at the sound of the footsteps. Sheriff Short had tied his horses upriver and walked the ten-man posse toward the ranch house where the boys were staying. The boys, young men, David and Porter, struggled to get away to warn their father, but they were bound and left under the care of a man while the posse came its stealthy way to the rock house at the Lonely Dell and tore us from our bed of peace into the nightmare of the world.

CHAPTER TWENTY-TWO

Although we were not aware of it at the time, the Mountain Meadows massacre was the subject of exhaustive speculation, rumor, suspicion, charge and counter-charge for years across the United States and beyond. The eastern newspapers, and the telegraph which fed them, inflamed the anti-polygamist sentiments of the nation, and pilloried Brigham Young's failure to bring to justice the participants of the Mountain Meadows. These two issues were the major obstacles to Utah's annual applications for Statehood. And the knowledge that Utah Territory was a vast Theocracy in the grip of one man did not sit at all well on the stomach of the American public.

It always struck me to cross-purpose that the history of the Church was a quest for isolation from the world in general and the United States in particular. Yet at the same time, Brigham and his sober-slatted emissaries eloquently appealed to the very brothel which they condemned for the privilege of having a place in the sordid crib that is the U.S. Congress.

John's silence was compromised over the years by others who

sought to protect themselves. It had fallen to John to be selected by the Prophet, Seer, and Revelator, to shed Atonement blood. Thus, at the second trial of the notorious criminal, perjury was so openly flouted as to embarrass even the *Deseret News*, the Church's ink-curdling organ of obfuscation and self-justification.

The air in Cedar City had changed again. Hostility was palpable as dust. In the past three months the church had been at work getting the stories of the prosecution's witnesses straight. The San Francisco papers and Mr. Greeley's *Herald-Tribune* had eager scribes present who scribbled every last horrible detail of the proceedings. Two days after John was delivered to the jail by Sheriff Short—with me in trail—I saw Bishop at last and he was full of indignant fight. But he was under no illusions this time as to an outcome.

"This trial is a different trial, I warn you," he told us grimly. "Every eligible juror in the country has been warned that they must vote for conviction if they are seated, John. The busybodies sent south by the general authorities have been abroad in the night. Brigham has passed the word. I have it on certain authority that more than one man has been warned that he is a candidate for a blood atonement if he should fail his duty.

"I must warn you both," he declared as we sat together once again in the same gloomy cell, on the same bed with the corn husk mattress and rusting web of springs, "that this trial is a foregone conclusion. The government has decided it is fruitless to go after the high church officials, Brigham Young being the most prominent. Silence and lies are all they've got regarding Dame, Higbee, Haight and the others. No, John, sadly, both the church and the state will be satisfied to convict you, and be done with the matter."

"That is a damned outrage," John insisted time and again. "Convict me of the crimes I've committed, but for God's sake will no one else have to answer?"

"They've made it clear, John, that if you will confess, and name names, you'll get off with little more than a mild rebuke. I've had that from the back room brokers that do their business between the barrooms and Brigham's Beehive house in Salt Lake City. I think the government will stand by their word. It wouldn't be amnesty. Perhaps they would sentence you to the time you've already served. But, you must be clear on this, John. If you do not speak, you will be surely convicted. And this conviction will result in your execution. After all," Bishop said rather coldly, "they have already excommunicated you from the church."

It was at that moment, in the dimly lit cell, sitting next to my husband, that I took leave of my senses, much as I had when Lt. Dellenbaugh left me that day in the grotto of stone, filled with the bloody vision of John's words as he described that awful day. I felt as fevered as if I was sitting in the brutal July sun on the banks of the Colorado. And then time lapsed into an ether of greyness. Space, dimensions of the floors, ceilings, the very air itself became luminous, and began to warp, as shadows became as sinuous as a nest of snakes. I heard John's words to Bishop clearly in the midst of this frightening spell.

"Sing my song to save myself, eh? I'll go to my grave with the names, Mr. Bishop. However, bring me paper and pen in quantity, for I've much to say to the white soul of paper. After I'm gone, my honor will no longer be at stake. As long as I live I will honor my vows. However, Mr. Bishop, you will find in Emeline's possession a full accounting of that horrible event by my own hand. And it is the truth. If you would be so kind, please draw up any documents you think necessary to insure that they are kept secret and safe in your keeping if the worst happens. What you do with them will be no affair of mine. If it is your decision to publish them abroad, for profit, then I'll expect my family to share. I'll be standing before God, as He is my only judge. I haven't the slightest fear of punishment from the Almighty. I have been given blessings by every major figure in the Church ensuring my salvation. My error was in following blindly the orders of a man whose only purpose was to ensure the survival of the Latter Day Saints. And a noble work it has been.

"The orders to kill them did not come from me, and I held against any such action, and I killed no man, woman, or child. Do as you will with my confession after I'm gone. If, by some miracle I am set free, the documents will be returned to me, and I shall see them into hell's fire."

"As you wish, John, but let's see if we can't allow hell's fire to rain down upon the other guilty. I'll get you the articles you require, and will guard them with my life. I shall insist, however, that they will see the light of day if the worst happens. You must allow me that."

"I'll be past caring," John said from that echoing place outside my head as I sat, quietly, as if stunned by a lightning bolt or a blow from a hammer in the fist of God. This was the first time, perhaps, that the reality, the sheer enormity of John's fate had come to me. I thought myself to be strong, and now I knew I was weak.

I found myself some forty-eight hours later in a bed in my rooming house above the Ashley Cafe where I had stayed before. My first sight was of the sweet oval face of Olivia Coates, which creased with delight at the return of my senses, and concern over the loss of them. Olivia had rushed from Pioche to be with me. I was grateful to her for her sweet disposition toward me and John, at great risk to her own reputation and safety. It seems she was always there to assuage my concern.

"Oh, dear, you're with the living again," she said with a bright voice. "You gave us all a fright." I was still dazed, but after lying quietly for another few minutes Olivia began to chatter. "Doctor Rich, that addled old quack, has ascribed your condition to the strain," she informed me. "He further advised that you should avoid any further . . . aggravation. By that, of course, he meant for you to remain away from the trial."

"The trial! My God, what day is it?"

"Tuesday, September 14," she said. "You've been quite out of your head for two days."

I was up in an instant, and then fell back, my head swimming with nausea. "I don't think it's the strain at all," she said. "In my opinion, and that of Dr. Blankenstaff whom John sent to you after hearing that Doctor Rich had made his useless diagnosis, is that you're suffering from an attack of the river malaria. To judge by the fever and the symptoms, I'd say that is a correct diagnosis, although that pompous old Dr. Rich ascribed it to female hysteria."

"I don't think it really matters," I said. "I must wash, and get to the courthouse. Thank you for coming."

"Of course," she said, and I loved her for her unquestioning support. As she helped me wash and dress I could see that she was troubled by more than my troubles.

"What is it?" I asked. "You seem to have the weight of the world on your shoulders. Is it your husband, the Bishop? He disapproves of your supporting me."

"He asked me all about the events at the first trial, whether there were any secrets that he should know that I'd got from you. I refused to answer any of his questions. He has threatened church censure. Brigham will never grant a divorce if I am censured."

"Oh, you poor dear girl," I said, genuinely alarmed for her.

"Poor dear nothing," she announced, a smile breaking over her face. "I'm to be free, for he has thrown my possessions into the street!"

CHAPTER TWENTY-THREE

John's second trial was in Cedar City. The jury of twelve were peers indeed. Every last one of them was a member in good standing in the Mormon church. The significance of that was lost on no one. John D. Lee was in Brigham's net now, as he was foolish enough not to flee when he had the opportunity. Let the affair be closed, Brigham had decided.

It was reported by the rumor that passes for news that Brigham Young had declared within the hearing of his counselors—including George A. Smith—that John's sacrifice was like unto that of Nephi of the Book of Mormon. In that holy scripture—truly a tale told by an idiot, in the judgment of my last years—Nephi is ordered to do some deed, but in order to accomplish it he must murder the ruler, Laban. Nephi, naturally, was reluctant to commit the shedding of blood. Brigham is said to have said, quoting, "It is better that one man should perish than that a whole nation should perish in disbelief." The damage to the church, over the years, must come to an end, he had decided.

The issue before the court was succinctly put to the jury in Mr.

Howard's opening statement.

"The Mormon church is not on trial here today, nor its leaders," he told the jury on the first morning of the trial. "The only case before you is that of John D. Lee. Did he commit the murders at the Mountain Meadows? We say yes, he did. He planned and executed the massacre in defiance of the orders of his superiors to let the emigrants pass!"

At this John came out of his chair, his fists balled, his face contorted with anger.

"Lies, lies!" he shouted, and had to be restrained by Mr. Bishop and the heavily armed bailiff. Mr. Howard looked at the prisoner with delight. Surely this display showed that John D. Lee was an uncontrollable hothead capable of any crime. Bishop was as angry as John, but his words of objections were reasoned.

"The weight of the evidence is against such a charge," Bishop rejoined, but the Judge blithely waived him quiet.

"It was on his own responsibility," Howard said, pointing a finger at John, "in defiance of orders from his superiors, and in conflict with the teachings of his own church against the shedding of innocent blood."

At this blatant lie John rose in a towering dignity. His presence was so commanding there fell a hush over the courtroom. No one made a word to stop him from speaking. He looked as if all the fires of all the prophets of the Old Testament were burning within him. He quoted from Leviticus in a deep, demanding voice:

> *"And Aaron shall lay both his hands upon the head of the live goat, and confess over him all the iniquities of the children of Israel, and all their transgressions and all their sins, putting them upon the head of the goat, and shall send him away by the hand of a fit man into the wilderness. And the goat shall bear upon him all their iniquities unto a land not inhabited. And he shall let go the goat in the wilderness."*

The roar of authority deepened in John's voice.

"I have spent my time in the wilderness. I have been cut off from the church, and from all my family and from all of my friends.

So be it. But, before God, I am innocent of those charges, and damn you all who accuse me! For twenty years you have hidden the truth, and now you must have your sins washed away by my blood. Very well, have it. The rest is all calumny and lies and deception. I am guilty of following my God and his representatives, nothing more. May sleep fail you all as you contend with your own conscience!"

The room broke into a bedlam as John took his seat. Shouts broke out calling for his death. Other voices washed in a tide of angry assent. John's declaration had charged them all of the guilt, and they would not have it.

Judge Boreman quickly had John removed under guard, and adjourned the trial until the next morning. "And if your client speaks out of turn again," Boreman warned Bishop, "I'll have you in jail for a fortnight!"

It was at this turning that my fearful decision, till now nascent in its purpose, turned into the purest of resolve. While the lawyers droned in scales of increasing acrimony, I let myself focus upon what was to be done.

Whatever the outcome of John D. Lee's trial, I thought to lift the yoke of Brigham Young from future generations who should come to Utah Territory, and know only the tyranny of the man by history books. Brigham Young, at 66, was in a blossom of health. John was in chains, and dying by inches in his captivity from which Brigham had the power to release him. Brigham's prosperity was the envy of those who knew that he used his money and the church's money as if they were one and the same. John D. Lee, at Brigham's request, had gone into the wilderness, sold his houses and properties, and had done Brigham's every bidding, and he was a pauper as a result. It would be a simple matter in the execution. In my increasing will to do that which I must do, I saw the how of it.

For years Brigham Young had traveled south to his palatial home in St. George to enjoy the winter sunshine of Utah's Dixie. With him trailed, like a Pharoahnic procession, his retinue of selected wives (concubines), hangers-on, counselors, sycophants, office-seekers and armed escort. It was apparent that he would not show his face south of the city limits of Salt Lake until the Lee decision was rendered. His distancing of his own knowledge and involvement for the past two decades would not allow him to make any comment, or appear to be interested. If he should not come south, I would go north to find him. If he should hide I would discover his hiding place. If he should surround himself with armies of angels or demons, I would find my way past them until we came face to face at last for the reckoning of the tally sheet. In my purpose I saw myself as both avenger and liberator. I saw that one deed would change the course of history.

CHAPTER TWENTY-FOUR

These are the names of the handpicked jury: William Green-wood, John E. Pace, A.M. Farnsworth, Stephen S. Barton, Valentine Carson, Alfred J. Randall, James S. Montague, A.S. Goodwin, Ira B. Elmer, Andrew S. Correy, Charles Adams, and Walter Granger.

Olivia, quite openly breaking with her husband and his family, sat with me for the next three days in the courtroom that was packed with humanity, crowding the benches, some even lap-sitting in unseemly fashion. The walls were three deep with spectators, and small boys hung from open windows in the middle blush of the golden Indian summer.

There were seven witnesses through the three day trial. John sat silently, and listened, but there was no sign of an outburst such as he had on the opening day. I saw him sinking by the hour into a pit of depression as he watched those he had loved and respected and obeyed parade before him with lies dripping from their lips. Curiously, there was no venom in the lies. Rather, they were told with shamed faces, and hesitating ellipses.

The first witness was Daniel H. Wells, a tall, taciturn and respected man whom John had known since the early days of the church. In 1857 he was the commanding officer of Brigham's Nauvoo Legion which had been reactivated at the threat from the federal army. His testimony was merely to the effect that John was no longer in the military at the time of the massacres. "He had been a major," Wells said, "But at that particular time, I think not. I think he had been superseded." That was a lie.

Bishop immediately elicited from him an admission that John D. Lee's name was on the military rolls in Cedar City at the time. On another matter, Wells testified that he thought Lee spoke the Indian language on a simple level, but he was not fluent. However, he could make himself understood, and "he was considered to have some influence with them." Wells testimony seemed harmless enough, but it stung John that Wells had even agreed to appear in his prosecution.

The next witness was Laban Morrill. He had never been at the Mountain Meadows in his life. He testified that John was not at any of the meetings in Cedar City when the action against the emigrants was discussed. John never did have a voice in the council that condemned the Fancher train. However, he made it clear that instructions had been given to Lee by letter that he was to go to the Mountain Meadows and keep the Indians from molesting the emigrants until help should arrive. This John did to the best of his ability, at the risk of his life.

Joel White was the third witness that day. It was an increasingly warm day, and John remarked to me as we had a breakfast of bitter coffee in his cell before the trial started, "Weather's going to change, Em. By afternoon there'll be a clouded sky."

White's testimony was inconclusive, I thought. Howard tried to elicit the fact that John had acted alone and against the orders of the military. White said they had met John on horseback near Pioche and he was told to go pacify the Indians. John supposedly replied, "I don't know about that," or "I'll have something to say about that". In any construction, that was not incriminating. Of course, the jury was already of one mind. This was mere window dressing.

"Were you present at the Mountain Meadows at the time of the massacre?" Howard asked.

"Yes, sir," White replied. It was here that Bishop made a blunder by not demanding that White name the names of those present, and to describe his own actions. Bishop waved me away as I whispered furiously in his ear. "This is the first time you've had a chance to pin them down," I said. "He will only lie," Bishop said back, and I noted with deep alarm the resignation in the voice of the attorney. My heart sank.

The fourth witness broke John's heart into smaller fragments. Samuel Knight was the driver of the second wagon full of the wounded, women, and some children. "And did you see John D. Lee that day?" he was asked.

"Yes sir," Knight said, his head hanging, mumbling words so that he had to be asked to repeat himself which he did in a more incoherent whisper. "My wife was not well and we'd been staying at the Hamblin ranch north of the Meadows. She couldn't take the heat on the Santa Clara," he explained. "I saw John after the Indians attacked the emigrants, and he pointed out to me the bullet holes in his shirt and hat. He led them in the attack, and them holes was from the emigrant's guns." John folded his hands, tears running down his face, shaking his head negatively.

"He led them in the attack and they drove them back," Knight continued his damming statement. "Klingensmith, he ordered me to bring my wagon which we loaded up with weapons and gear from the emigrant camp."

"How many people?" Howard asked.

"I think there was two men who were wounded, one woman, and, I think, some children," he mumbled. "I was on the ground holding the team steady," he said, his voice lower, a sure sign of a deeper lie. "I think Lee killed the woman," Knight said. "Lee struck the woman with the butt of his gun, but the team was so fractious I couldn't be positive what went on."

"Who else was present?" Bishop was on his feet, restraining John who was quivering with rage.

"I don't remember?"

"Surely you must," Bishop insisted.

"I was busy holding the horses."

"So you didn't see a thing?"

"No sir, the horses . . . I got no idea who was there."

"Come now, Mr. Knight, a man's life is in the balance. He is your friend!"

"Well, "Knight gulped, fishing in confusion. "There was some Indians who jumped out of the brush about that time. But I'm almost positive he killed one woman."

"Are you lying, Mr. Knight?" Bishop demanded.

"No sir," came the inaudible whisper. "I think he killed one woman."

"Do you know that for sure, what with your difficulty in remembering?"

"Yes sir, I do," Knight said.

Samuel McMurdy's testimony followed.

"Who ordered you to go to the Mountain Meadows, Mr. Mc-Murdy?" Howard asked him.

"I was ordered to take my wagon and team down there by Higbee," McMurdy said.

"And what happened?"

"Well, John, uh, Mr. Lee told me to drive up to the camp where we loaded the children. My team went first, and we went fast, as I wanted to get away from the Indians who were riled up bad. Lee was walking between the first and second wagons, and I heard him say, 'Halt!'"

"Go on," Howard said solemnly, tucking his hands in his vest pockets.

"I think I saw Lee draw a gun, a pistol, and shoot a woman," McMurdy said, not looking at Lee. This was the incident of John's misfiring pistol. McMurdy's lie was unbearable to John. "I was too busy with the team to see much."

"But you're sure you saw him kill a woman?"

"Yes sir," McMurdy said.

"Yours," Howard said to Bishop in a regal gesture.

"Mr. McCurdy, you saw this with your own eyes, although you were busy with the horses?

"Yes, sir."

"You yourself did not help kill anyone ?" Bishop asked him in a cold voice.

"I had nothing to do with it at all."

"Then you did not raise your hand against anyone at that time, or do any of the killing of the emigrants?"

"No."

"And you were not slightly wounded by John D. Lee's pistol misfiring."

"No. I believe I am not on trial," McCurdy said stiffly.

"I ask if you refuse to answer the question?" Bishop demanded. McCurdy sat silently, his face working.

"I demand an answer," Bishop thundered.

"I do not wish to answer," McCurdy said.

"Do you know whether everyone of the Fancher train was killed?"

"I don't know."

"What about those in the very wagon you yourself drove?"

"I don't know," McCurdy said defiantly.

"Order him to answer, Judge Boreman," Bishop said in exasperation. Boreman peered at Bishop as if he were a stranger.

"If Mr. McCurdy doesn't know, he doesn't know. Witness dismissed," he ordered.

"I expect it will be over today, Em," John said to me in the evening gloaming as we sat in the cell side by side, possibly for the last time, I thought. We sat until the Sheriff came and told me it was time to leave. Bishop was out all hours trying to find someone to counter all of the damming testimony. If Haight, or Higbee could be found.

The next morning the first person I spotted when I entered the courtroom shocked me. It was Jacob Hamblin. What possible business could he have here except for the satisfaction of seeing John D. Lee hang? After the incident at the Lonely Dell, without my ever speaking to John about it, relations between the two had cooled to enmity. They had quarreled over Indian affairs, livestock, land, everything that once bound them. In Hamblin's eyes, once Brigham had excommunicated John, then it seemed to Hamblin that John could be treated little better than an Indian.

The fact remained, however, that Jacob Hamblin was not present at the massacre, and was not bound by any oath of secrecy. I had a terrible feeling when I saw him. And he looked at me with such hatred I wanted to take out the derringer and put out his eyes.

Nephi Johnson was the first witness that day. He was a young man at the time, now old and bent with the black secret, and had a memory as selective as the other witnesses. He is the one who overheard Haight excoriate Dame for cowardice and told the participants to bury the dead and get on with their living. As he was himself a fugitive—kept well informed of anyone looking for him by the church authorities—he had come to town under a special dispensation. In that, the prosecution gave him an amnesty for the duration of the trial, after which he was fair game for capture and would be tried for the same crimes as the others mentioned in the original indictment.

"I was up the side of the hill, and only saw the massacre from a distance," he insisted time and again, but when pressed his memory was faulty. "I did get my orders from Haight, who told me to go see Lee. I saw Lee fire off, and saw a woman in the lead wagon fall. Then Lee and some Indians were throwing bodies out of the wagons, and I thought I saw Lee making the motions, as if he were cutting someone's throat. It was him who seemed to be giving the orders."

At this there was a roar from the spectators' throats. John shook his head again, and then bowed it, his hands in his lap. It was more mortifying than any human could bear. For myself, I was stricken with a numb horror, a dread of John, and of the Church, and of God. How could he allow this?

"Who else was there, Mr. Johnson?" Lawyer Howard asked him

"I don't want to bring in any names," Johnson said.

"Well, who gave you the orders?"

"Lee."

Why, if Haight, Higbee and the others were John D. Lee's superiors, did they not take charge during these events?

"He acted like a man that had control."

"Did you not think at the time that John D. Lee had absolute control of everything there?"

"He acted like it."

"Your witness, Mr. Bishop."

"What do you believe about it?" Bishop said. His question was met with silence. For over thirty minutes Bishop cross-examined Johnson. It was like trying to elicit information from a stone. It was hopeless. And it became even more bleak as Howard stood and called the name of Jacob Hamblin to be a final witness against John D. Lee. I thought with a sickening lurch that he would have his revenge this day for my rejecting him so many long months ago in the rock house. It seemed as if it had occurred in a past life. Bishop had no clue as to what Hamblin would say, and was completely taken aback. He protested and objected for half an hour before Boreman silenced him with a threat of contempt.

Hamblin drove the final nail into John's heart. Hamblin was allowed by Judge Boreman to repeat the most damming hearsay. He was allowed to make a speech, more than anything else. If the spectators were ready for John D. Lee's blood, the reputation of this great friend to the Indians and the church left no doubt at all. His testimony, if it can be called that, began in an innocuous manner.

"I met John D. Lee in Fillmore as I was coming south to home. He was riding for Salt Lake City to report to Brigham Young of the massacre. He told me he had tried to restrain the Indians, and for that was called Yawgauts by them. Mr. Lee insisted that he was carrying out the orders of William H. Dame, although I don't know if that is true.

"When I got to my place I organized a party of men to go bury the dead whom the wolves had scattered from their shallow graves. It was horrible. Such a sight I've never seen. The women were beautiful, what was left of them. There must have been 120 bodies all told."

The spectators were hanging on Hamblin's words, for his reputation was nearly as great as that of Brigham in the south. And then he began his hearsay tale, a lie of whole cloth.

"What else do you know of the event, Mr. Hamblin?" Howard asked.

"There were two young ladies who had escaped the first volleys in the massacre. They were very beautiful," Hamblin said again.

"How do you know this if you weren't even there?" Bishop shouted, and at a signal from Judge Boreman Sheriff Short and his Deputy Quinn clapped hands on his shoulders and sat him back in his chair.

"Not a word from you, Mr. Bishop, or I shall have you removed," Boreman warned him. Bishop's face was purple, John's white as his hair. Echoes. Everything was an echo.

"Who told you this?" Howard asked him.

"I was told this by two Indian chiefs whom I have never known to lie," Hamblin assured him, his eyes sweeping the audience, and then they fell on me, and remained there. Cold, unwavering, filled with hatred. "Lee was there, and he asked one of the chiefs what he should do with them, the women—girls actually. Well, the other Indian killed one of them, and Lee killed the other."

"From where were these young women brought from?"

"From a thicket of oak brush, where they had concealed themselves. The other Indian shot one of them, and he cut the other's throat."

"Who cut the other's throat?'

"Mr. Lee."

And there it was, the final betrayal which so inflamed the audience and the jury that John was doomed to the extent that answered prayer could not save him. By the time Hamblin was through I was crying, remembering the look of lust in his eyes, the hatred, the cold satisfaction as he mouthed the lies, his eyes never leaving mine.

Bishop was hopeless, but still defiant as he summed up the perfidy and perversion of justice that had taken place that week.

"I will point out to you, members of the jury," he said solemnly, "that we have three witnesses who testified that Lee had killed one person, a woman, and might have killed others. We have one witness who said a woman was killed by a blow from the butt of a gun; another witness says that she was shot with a gun, and another also has her shot, but said that she was in the lead wagon, in which only children were riding! Now comes Mr. Jacob Hamblin with a most convincing tale—although he was two hundred miles absent. It seems now, instead of Mr. Lee killing one woman, which he did not, he has killed four, and who knows how many more if the church can bring forth more witnesses to do their lying.

"No other white man has been named as participating in this horrible act. Is that possible? I find it incredible, as must you. We further have a hearsay testimony that Mr. Lee is in the oak brush cutting throats. Which is it? What is the truth? None of it I say! If you convict this man, you must convict those who gave him his orders, including those who fomented this savagery by their inflammatory marshaling of God's avenging host which, I say to you, is none other than Brigham Young and the entire Mormon church!"

It was at that juncture that Judge Boreman signed to Sheriff Short.

"I am placing you under arrest for contempt of the court," he announced amidst the furious babble of the righteous. William Bishop was lead out of the courtroom shouting his outrage. My anger, my sorrow, and my shame seethed within me until I thought I would scream aloud to silence the demon mob.

After order was restored, it was with a sure, smug, swift marshaling of inconsistences that Howard proceeded to lay upon John's head the sins as if it were ordered, logical truth. There were no fifty white men there that day. By the time Howard was finished, John D. Lee was responsible for planning and executing the murders in defiance of his orders from his superiors both temporal and spiritual.

John sat in a profound silence, looking at Hamblin now, ignoring the proceedings. Had he the means, there would have been an actual throat cut that day, and I would have handed him the knife and held his coat. "Such a thing I have never heard of before," John told me afterward of Hamblin's damming lies, "that I cut a throat and the Indian killed the other. The old hypocrite thought that was his chance to wreak his vengeance on me for his own sharp trading, swearing away my life for a few horses and acres of land."

John would never know the truth. Would Hamblin have been a friend thereafter had I lain down for him that day? Would I do it this day for him if it would put things right? I cannot answer. I cannot say. The heart's chambers are a maze from which there is no exit. Death to all of them, I said, and say so now.

The jury deliberated less than an hour. Guilty of murder in the first degree. Judge Boreman immediately sentenced John to death by either hanging or execution by firing squad as if the choice he offered was a pearl of great price.

I watched them lead John out of the courtroom, this time in small chains around his wrists and ankles. Dark wings beat the air in the room, invisible to all except myself. The echoing had ceased, and I heard the mundane sounds of feet scraping the floor, of the chains in their metallic jangle, of voices of every shade of emotion, from anger to fear to fury, and then I heard another voice which was as familiar to me as was the sound of the river, or my husband's voice or my childrens' singing. Although the jury's voice was false, some place in my heart knew that John's guilt was plain. I hated him for it, and then hated myself for hating him. And it was all to end, and I would be alone with only his legacy of salt. I was not sure I could go on.

"Miss Emeline, I am so sorry for you," the voice said, and I turned and looked directly into the green eyes of Lt. James Cameron Dellenbaugh. Outside, the setting sun was ringed with a halo, and a pack of sun dogs tracked across the sky, hunting the last of the summer.

CHAPTER TWENTY-FIVE

We thought you lost, Lieutenant," I said, after unsuccessfully trying to hide my surprise, my blush, and my joy at seeing him again on the courthouse steps after the awful sentence had been passed. It was like a stroke of sun. "And then the papers said you'd reappeared. I am glad to see you."

"And I am so sorry fo you, and for John," he said.

"It isn't as if I wasn't prepared," I said. I wasn't prepared at all.

"But it is good to see you," he smiled softly. He looked leaner, his handsome face sun-darkened, his green eyes more distant perhaps, reflecting the trials they had experienced on the final passage down the Colorado. There was a fine fan of tributaries around his eyes from the sun on the water, and he looked more my age now, than his own.

"I've been reading Major Powell's accounts in the popular press," I said. "It must have been a grueling experience."

"It was that, and more," he said. "I was on my way to Salt Lake City with dispatches from Major Powell to Fort Douglas when I heard of this . . . travesty," he said. "If it is not an interference, I am prepared to return to Cedar City after my ride north and support you in any way I can," he said.

"I don't know what to say," I said. "Why would you do such a thing?" I asked him solemnly.

"Because I owe you my life, and would willingly lay down my own if it would help you."

These . . . noble sentiments—he looked so sincere, as if he were blinded by something in his heart. His pledge startled me, and I remembered the salt stains on the faded cloth of his uniform and the look on his face as he brought me from the delirium of the sun and the blood that rinsed my vision on the day I read John's first revelations.

At that moment Mr. Bishop came down the street, having been held in jail for over an hour, his face bleak, withdrawn. Upon the sight of Olivia I could see him raise a genuine smile before the enormity of the trial's result came across him again. After the introductions, Lt. Dellenbaugh spoke to Mr. Bishop.

"Would it be possible for me to see Mr. Lee?" he asked Bishop quietly. "There is something I need to ask of him." I looked at him curiously.

Olivia, at my side, was nearly open-jawed at the handsome lieutenant who was dressed in his military uniform. It was the first time I'd seen him in such attire, and he stood apart from the dusty rabble who left the courthouse in babbling knots after hearing the sentence of John. "Is there any service I might lend to you, Mr. Bishop?" he asked solicitously.

"If you're in the helping business," Bishop said, "and as you're a soldier, then you could read the military's mind for me. It is the military who've pressed for vengeance in this matter beyond endurance. What are their sentiments regarding this utterly unjust penalty of death? Can you tell me that?"

"No, but I shall try," he vowed. "By the by, Major Powell sends his compliments," the Lieutenant said to me. "He asked me to tell Mr. Lee that whatever the result of this trial, he still holds him, and you, in the highest regard."

"Thank you, and thank him," I said. The emptiness I felt had begun to seem bottomless, but the sight of the strong man did lift my spirits some. He was always a comfort to me in ways that I cannot describe. He had that presence which made one feel that he could hold off any disaster with a smile from his lips, or a blow from the sword he wore at his side. I am not a romantic woman, but the image of him wading through a crowd of bearded Mormons, sword slashing, did give me pause at my own . . . need for justice.

We had a calming tea at the Ashley House afterward, with the Lt. at my side, Olivia at Mr. Bishop's side, and the Ashleys, whose kindness and sympathy had increased with the duration of my stay at their lodgings. And then it was time for the Lieutenant to leave.

"I shall stop by and visit with Mr. Lee before I depart," he said to Mr. Bishop who just nodded his head distractedly, and gave him a handwritten note to Sheriff Short for his permission to see the condemned man.

CHAPTER TWENTY-SIX

While I waited for the appeals I stayed on in Cedar City. Olivia lived with me now in the small house. Her breaking away, or her expulsion by the Bishop, was the buzz of the community. The Lee trial had been chewed over so many times there was little else to say, and if there were any partisans left in his cause I didn't know where they had gone. Rumors persisted that a band of his family were organizing in the mountains to break him out of jail, but that was nonsense. His family was scattered to the winds, his few friends too frightened of repercussions to speak out. If John had any friends left, they were those who wished him to confess in public the names of the others. Their motive was not friendship.

Olivia held her head high as she ran a few errands between the house and shops, and she did everything she could to avoid the annoyed and embarrassed Bishop. Olivia was a blessing for her company. I never understood fully why she took up my cause and chose to stand beside me, but youth's idealism is like a strong spring shoot of grass. No stopping it short of pulling it out of the ground. The plain fact was, John D. Lee was guilty of culpability, and as an accessory to murders multiple, but he was the only one who was punished. The injustice boiled within me day and night, and, curiously, Olivia's sense of justice seemed as injured as mine. One morning Bishop Coates appeared at the door, his fist heavy upon the wood.

"Who is it?" I called, thinking the hangman had come.

"It is Coates," the man's deep voice shouted. "I will see my wife now, or break down this door." Olivia shrank back into the room, went to the small bed in the corner, and withdrew the horse pistol. She raised it at the door, cocked it with both thumbs, and then calmly indicated to me that I should open it.

"No, I'll fetch the sheriff," I said, but Olivia just smiled grimly.

"He'll never lay another hand on me," she said. "He's beat me for the last time. Open the door, please." I unlatched the door and stood back, trying to lift the derringer from my purse which hung on a peg nearby.

Coates stormed into the room, a bulk of rage. Then he caught sight of his young wife who held the pistol with steady hands. The bore was pointed directly between his eyes. "But, but . . . " he sputtered, and then whirled as he heard me cock the two small hammers of the derringer. Confronted thus by two ladies with pistols, and enough cause to use them, the good Bishop stumbled backwards and contented himself to stand in the street pleading his case to passersby.

Had it not frightened us so, it would have been laughable. She feared her husband and wore out her pen with letters of appeal to Brigham Young for a divorce. Bishop Coates would not let her go. Coates had threatened a violence upon me if I did not try to persuade Olivia she should return to him. He sent me threatening letters which I never showed to Olivia, his lost wife. We avoided him as much as possible, but he was a respected man and thus a constant threat. If John had not been nearby, we both should have fled for our safety.

Until now I had done my best not to pry into Olivia's troubles. God knows I had enough of my own. It isn't that she was reticent to discuss matters with me, it was as if the complexity of her problem still hadn't been solved to a point where she could discuss it and make any sense. I saw clear enough that Brigham Young was going to be her biggest problem. I could see her own immense struggle with the position in which she had placed herself. By now people had begun to shun her and openly remark that she was a traitor to her husband and her faith. A more serious accusation cannot be imagined then, or now. A shunning by the Mormons is an experience not seen since Salem, by my lights. It is a freezing of the blood to walk down the street. The worst part is that they will not even acknowledge your existence on the street, nor step aside, or lift a finger if you were dying in that same street.

Olivia passed many hours of our waiting time reading. She told me that men had come from monkeys, according to Mr. Charles Darwin, and after I was finished with my hysterical laughter at the notion, she explained his theory to me in some detail. It had its appeal. The strongest do survive. Perhaps it was true that we came down from the trees. God knows we acted like it often enough as a race.

"But by what leap did the awareness of God get into monkeys?" I asked her.

"He doesn't say," she said. "I guess God made the monkeys and then commanded them to get about their business." Her laughter pealed on the smoky roof beams. "But considering the behavior of Bishop Coates, I'd say that women came from superior monkeys."

"We are but God's small sparks," I said. "Not monkeys."

"If you say so," she said, and studied me with those intensely colored eyes for a moment, her face solemn.

"I admire you so very much," she suddenly said.

"And why is that?"

"Your strength, your loyalty. I wish very much that I could have remained loyal to Bishop Coates."

"It is risky for you to leave him and take up your fate with me. I'm doomed, you know."

"Nonsense," she exclaimed. "I tried to run away from him twice before we were married. He beat the stuffing out of me. Although I didn't choose my own fate, I did take my vows seriously, else I would have run away again, before he brought me south. I was resigned, and the church elders gave me hours of instruction until they had me believing that Coates would be the best thing that ever happened to me. They threatened my soul, you know, if I did not marry willingly." She paused, for a long moment, fighting tears. "They make you believe you are doing something of your own volition after they talk to you long enough."

"Yes, when the missionaries came to our rooms in Liverpool, I was overwhelmed by their notions. They just kept hammering, and then I began to believe. My father, you see, had to believe, or die."

"I wonder if it's all true," she sighed. "My life's aspiration is not to be a lap dog of a supercilious Englishman, I can tell you that. I wanted to sing in the opera in San Francisco. My professors said I had a fine enough voice to try."

"The man is ill," I said.

"Inferior ape," she muttered. "He made me do things I didn't wish to do, and I don't mean extra washing." I waited. How to probe that statement?

"Watching you hold your head high in the face of the contempt of the people gave me courage to leave the man. I thank you for that, Emeline, from the bottom of my heart. I don't know what will happen to my soul. Brigham Young will be able to tell me."

"Brigham Young may never get the chance," I said, and I think she took my meaning.

"Oh," she said in a small voice, and we left the matter in the keep between us.

Another event developed while awaiting John's appeal. The citizens of Cedar City, shamed and angry, drew up a petition to the military governor of the Utah Territory, pleading for John's life. It was a gesture which surprised us, and gave John some heart, though no hope.

The appointed day drew near, the 23rd day of March, 1877. Spring in the south of the Utah Territory—with the Indians nearly destroyed and the train track closer by the day—draws a flux, an effluvia from the north. Those with the wherewithal, frostbitten and weary, faces grey as slush from the streets of Salt Lake and the deep snows of the Wasatch Mountains, come to seek the sun of the south. They arrive by buggy and by train, by horseback and by foot, seeking the solace of Zion's bosom. In the spring the fragrance is the breath of heaven. The soap yucca flowers hang like waxed white fruit, the scarlet cup cacti so vivid one can see them from far away, like points of firelight in the darkness. Leading this procession to St. George and the Virgin River, like the Sun King himself, would come Brigham Young with whom, one day soon, I'd vowed to have an appointment.

Lieutenant Dellenbaugh finally returned from Fort Douglas with a critical piece of information. He rode out of a storm with a letter from Mr. Bishop who was in Salt lake working on appeals. The letter was an official copy of a letter written by Lt. Colonel Sweeney at Fort Cameron. It was a reply to Governor Emory and his query as to the military's position regarding the death sentence passed on John D. Lee. Governor Emory was trying to test the waters after the petition from the people who demanded that the life of John D. Lee be spared. We were all thunderstruck by the petition of the people to save John's life.

Mr. William Bishop struggled to the end, armed with the people's entreaty which James purloined. Bishop was indefatigable in trying to save John's life. The petition gave John as much comfort as the promise of heaven. It had been circulated a month before the date of his execution, and was signed by a total of 514 persons! That was nearly the entire population of southern Utah. It pled with Governor Emory to spare John, and outlined the extenuating circumstances of the war fever of 1857, the Indian's righteous wrath at the Fancher train. It said in closing: "He is but one of many who are equally guilty with himself of the crime . . . Said Lee is thus made a sacrifice to atone for the whole crime . . . to suffer death upon the testimony, connivance and prosecution of those equally guilty, or more guilty, than himself . . . "

Five hundred and fourteen signatures!

John somehow knew it was futile, but the fact that so many were willing to acknowledge the collective guilt, and would not suffer to see John alone punished, well, I know it eased him to where he was going.

God was so distant in my thoughts in the latter days that I would not think of Him, nor entreat Him, but rather scornfully, in my heart, cursed his Being, if ever it was.

On my daily visits with John—I was allowed an hour—we tried to prepare ourselves for the inevitable, and I tried to hold out hope for him, but he was resigned, as, I think now, was I. My sincerity was hollow, my hope a gall of irony in the face of the 23rd of March.

"The Governor's reply was politic," I informed John, "in that he said he appreciated the situation, but would not interfere. Mr. Bishop sends word that he will try to get back from Salt Lake before . . . to be with you . . . when . . . Mr. Bishop cannot prevail," I said, my eyes dry. I had no tears left. My breasts felt dry, my mouth full of sand and bitter alkali. "I've a wire from him in Salt Lake. The federal courts will not interfere, nor issue a stay. The petition made no difference," I said bitterly.

And on another day, one of the last. Mr. Bishop returned to Cedar City for the carrying out of the sentence. Then, out of a late winter storm, which was remarkable for its fury, rode Lt. Dellenbaugh in with the purloined letter. He carried with him my last real hope for a stay. It was not a new hope, but it was in writing, which made all the difference in my eyes.

Lt. Dellenbaugh had, at some great risk to his career, intercepted the reply to Governor Emory's inquiry as to the military's posture regarding John D. Lee's imminent execution. It was addressed to Lt. Colonel Douglas of the 14th Infantry. He was the Commander of the "occupying force" in Utah.

Once again we convened in the parlor of the Ashley House as we had the day the Lt. appeared and John was sentenced. It was still snowing, but inside it was warm, almost cheerful with the smell of wood smoke and tobacco smoke and the coiling of steam from the tea cups. Mr. Bishop pondered the Colonel's letter. The empty hope that I held in the letter only seemed to depress him even deeper.

Considering the age of the prisoner and the long time elaps-

ing between commission of the crime and conviction, I would recommend clemency only on condition of making a full & explicit statement of all the facts and circumstances attending the commission of the crime, substantiating his statements by proofs, and fixing the responsibility of his actions upon the proper person or persons . . . and disclosing the names of his accomplices, with a full substantiated statement of the extent of their participation. This I have been informed the prisoner can do, and if he will do so, I would recommend that his life be spared and his sentence be remitted or commuted.

And there it was in black and white written. The words "remitted or commuted" leapt out on the page, and I turned to Mr. Bishop with hope flaring.

"If there is anyone to whom John will listen, it is you," he said to me at last. "With this clear statement, well, he may at last be persuaded to speak what he will not speak. It will save his life. And it may give him his freedom. But the man seems determined to keep his vow. God knows this offer has been made before."

"But never as clearly. Never in writing, thanks to Lt. Dellenbaugh. Perhaps this will sway him," I said. "I can't thank you enough, Lieutenant. We might never have known. And John must certainly believe this. It will save him! I will go to him now," I said.

"He is not here," Mr. Bishop said softly. "They removed him an hour ago from the jail, placed him in a wagon, and are transporting him to St. George. The day after that, he will be taken to the Mountain Meadows for the execution of his sentence."

CHAPTER TWENTY-SEVEN

Judge Boreman, with an act of deceit as cruel as it was cunning, took two weeks of John's life away from him. Fourteen days of living erased by a penstroke. In our lives, fourteen days was eternity. Judge Boreman had pronounced from the bench that the execution was to be carried out on March 23, 1877. The place of execution was to be at the Point of the Mountain south of Salt Lake, because it was heavily garrisoned by the occupation army. It was a ruse of which we had no inkling.

Mr. Bishop had been summoned to the courthouse the previous hour. There a clerk—a clerk!—informed Mr. Bishop there were rumors that a group of our family and friends and supporters were plotting to try to effect a last-minute rescue of John. The sentence was to be executed tomorrow. It was a cruelty beyond bearing. I was stunned until Lt. Dellenbaugh took charge and saw to it that we were on our way the fifty miles south to St. George within the hour.

The trip to St. George was made by horseback, and in great haste. I was furious with this subterfuge and blamed Mr. Bishop for his not sniffing out this cruelty. And the final crushing irony was that John's execution was to be in the Mountain Meadows, a stage upon which the props would be ghosts and the players unwilling actors. It was a plan of final humiliation, a theater of the sort that appeals to the common masses, and it was hatched by devils.

Had I dared to approach anyone to try to mount a rescue effort? I knew no one I could trust except Olivia. I remembered my dangerous outburst at the Ashley Cafe those many months ago. Mr. Bishop saw that my threat was perfectly serious, and not just the bitter wish of a hysterical woman. And he had not protested, but I had never spoken to him or anyone else of my intent again. But a rescue party of armed men? No, it was impossible. There was little I could do but seethe in the heart with anger at Brigham Young and the United States, and silently grieve at the passing of each second of each hour.

As we plunged down the rocky road that led from the heights of Cedar City into the warmer valley of the Virgin and Santa Clara rivers, with St. George at the junction, spring was suddenly upon the land. It was as if we were in a different country. Kolob's massive sandstone shoulders were mantled with snow, but as we rode at a breakneck speed toward the red cliffs of Harrisburg and across Quail Creek, I could see sprays of green leaves budding on the cottonwoods.

As we rode past the little settlement at Harmony—now called New Harmony—I tried to avert my gaze, for I could not bear to see what our home looked like. But look I must. The man who had bought it had improved it until it looked like Eden. Had I tears left, they would have been shed for the loss of that beautiful home and the happiness I had there—when? A hundred years ago it seemed. My body ached from the pounding ride, but my anger at this subterfuge of trying to execute my husband in secrecy was a sustaining fire that allowed me to ignore the pain and outride the men.

As we topped the last dark ridge of black rock that capped the red sandstone above St. George, I saw the white temple rising amidst a flat of orderly green like a sentinel of all that which I had begun to loathe. The spire was like an obscene gesture. It betokened the insularity, the superior smugness of those who think they hold all truth, which leads to the darkest of actions because they are so anointed.

St. George was becoming a lovely little town. There were substantial businesses and large brick homes standing amidst brush-roofed shacks laid out in orderly squares. Yellow forsythia exploded on the eye, and there were nests of tulips as points of color along the muddy streets. There was the tang of growth, and hope, and a coiled energy in the air which was enforced by the arrival of the escort of soldiers who had John D. Lee locked in a box on a wagon.

We were able to locate where they were holding John by the assembled crowd. I found him in a dark windowless room with weeping rock walls. It was a sort of root cellar. And this within sight of the white temple.

"I can't see that it matters much. A week, a day . . . It's not as if I'll never see another spring again, Em, dear," he said to me after we were alone. There was a candle on a wooden box which shone on his face, which was one of complete composure. The yellow light, too, revealed a wink of humor in his eyes. "In heaven, I suspect, one can wish the weather as one pleases. If you're in the mood for spring, why, all you have to do is declare it. The season will change as fast as the hands of a clock's resetting."

"My inclination is to join you tomorrow, if you can summon the seasons," I rejoined lightly. "But I would choose the harvest time, the gold and the green and the time of dancing."

"And your wish would be my heart's desire," he said. "But you cannot even think of that." He was serious now, coldly serious. "You will go on, and with courage."

"I cannot apologize for what I feel," I said. "What will this life be without you?"

"It will be as fine as ever!" he declared. "You are a young woman with the harvest years just beginning. I cannot face what I must face with any courage unless I have the assurance that you will go on. You must raise our children to be fine sons and daughter of the Church, and live your own life as God will lead you."

"Yes, John," I said meekly. The enormity of what was about to happen had given rise in me a despair that I cannot describe. And then he broached a subject which we had avoided since my first visit to him in a jail in Cedar City.

"I have no means to provide for you, you know," he said quietly. "My other families have found havens of their own. Rachel is in Kanab, Sarah with her sons in Skatumpah. As for the others, well, I did what I could. Brigham will seize the ferry. He will claim it always belonged to the Church which I think is not just. But there is nothing to leave you, Em, except this . . . legacy of . . . sorrow.

"You must be practical, and remarry soon. You are most intelligent, and you will find someone to secure your future. I am deeply sorry I cannot provide . . . "

I saw John begin to weep. Tears rolled down his broad, high cheekbones and blurred his eyes. He quickly swept them away, looked around at the dark rough stone, "I'll be glad to see the sky for a while under any circumstances."

"Oh, John," I said. I was exhausted. In truth I had not given any thought to the future. I had no home, no money, no real family. I was marked wherever I went, or would go, unless I were to travel far, and go under a false name. That, I vowed, I would not do. My heart sat upon its divided mood contemplating the razor line between love and hate as pure as fire. I saw myself sitting in the darkness, as if I were apart from myself. I was a woman who had lost weight—my appetite was gone months ago. My skin had taken on the pallor of the same sickly whiteness that I had carried with me in the slums of Liverpool. The lines around my mouth had deepened until they resembled twin cuts from a scythe.

"Please, John. The letter from the Colonel. In writing. The words commute. Governor Emory . . . If you recant . . . "

"I can not," John said, gazing at me with misted eyes.

In one instant's thought I longed to take a pistol to my own head and go with John to a place where the streets were always lit, the seasons summoned with a wish. A place where fair children, having served in life and died a dutiful death, were playing in green fields illuminated by the shining presence of God.

Then the next warring thought came into my mind, and I

wished to take the pistol to the breast of Brigham Young and blow him to hell. I wanted to beard the Lion of the Lord in his spring den and feed him to the coyotes. I wanted with the fullness of my heart to send him to a place where there was only one season, that of the Inferno, where the damned slaked their thirst in a lake of red and yellow fire.

"Em, I commend to you Lt. Dellenbaugh. We have talked and corresponded. He is a fine young man, and I know he feels deeply for your welfare. He is a sincere young man, and would do any woman well in this life even if he is not of the Church."

This revelation was so startling that my tears stopped, and I looked at him as if he were in delirium. But he seemed not to notice.

"I know your faith has wavered, and I cannot blame you. What you've been through would weaken anyone. But, I would testify to you that the Church is true, and is our salvation. It is men who have corrupted its purity, not God. My faith is unshakeable. I stood watch over the Prophet in the darkest days of the Church. However, I cannot speak for your own heart, though I would wish it to be as one with my own. You must follow wherever your heart leads you after I'm gone. I'm sixty seven years old. I've had a good, rich life. There is a just God, and a forgiving God, and one day you shall join me in eternity. But from the time I draw my last breath, your life is your own again. On the other hand, you were always so independent I guess it always has been your own. A man never owns a woman. You must live now for yourself and our children."

"I always have, John," I said. "And I've loved you since I saw you in the church, and afterwards under the warm robe in the freezing snow. I've loved you without a reservation in my heart. But I must ask you to submit. I demand it for the sake of your children. Will you not speak to save yourself?"

I saw the deep cutting pain cross his face. I was ashamed of myself.

"Forgive me. My word is all I have left that is as precious to me as are you and my family. If I were to speak, my sons and daughters would carry my curse for generations. If I were to break my vow to my brethren, even if they have broken theirs, my name would be a curse to those who carry my blood. No, I cannot. Better to die in truth than live branded with the name of coward, and traitor to church and friends. Forgive me, I cannot." He paused, and searched my eyes. And then he said, wryly, "Besides, Em, my "former associates" would have murdered me in my own cell long ago if I had spoken. Not that I have kept silent on that fear, but one doesn't really want to hasten to the Lord as long as there is air to breath and a lovely woman to gaze upon."

"You sheer flatterer," I smiled. "You old fox. I love you." He gave me a quick little laugh, stood, held me, and kissed me, and bade me leave him to be alone with his God. At the door I paused to look at him again. His eyes were flowing now with tears.

"At last," he whispered, "I shall be free of the little girls in white dresses."

CHAPTER TWENTY-EIGHT

There was a small crowd of people gathered in the pre-dawn darkness around the house where John had been held overnight. Fingers of cloud were beginning to obscure the desert stars, and the coming suffusion of light revealed the day to be grey with a cold and rising wind ruffing the caps and capes of the onlookers.

That some of John's friends would try to effect a rescue I knew was impossible. But still I scanned the crowd, and the horizon, and the sky for some help. Lt. Dellenbaugh, dressed in civilian clothes, stood close by me, his face solemn and smooth shaven.

Into the rising wind went the first wagon, which held an escort of deputies and mixed soldiers. In the second wagon, under the guard of Sheriff Short, was John, dressed in the best suit of clothes he owned, and more soldiers. I followed in a buggy driven by Mr. Bishop. Olivia was in the back of the buggy sobbing quietly. Over the months she had visited John like a daughter and had come to love him. Lt. Dellenbaugh rode his horse. The next wagon carried the official witnesses to the execution and other important officials. The firing squad brought up the rear, riding in a wagon whose wheel was crooked, and creaked with every turn.

I had tried to buy a new dark suit for John, but he laughed it away. "Old clothes for old men," he had joked, buttoning his vest while I straightened his black tie. "And after it's been ventilated by the boys, a new suit won't be worth much. I never did understand burying in Sunday finery, which is perfectly suitable for wearing by the needy on another day." The black, thin cloth hung on him like a rag, he had lost so much weight, but the luminosity of his hair and face drew the eye to him like a polestar.

People fell back as we drove out of town, some hiding their faces in shame, others shaking their fists in a vicious satisfaction. It was reported that Brigham Young would not come south until the matter was accomplished. I'm sure it was an inconvenience for him to have to linger in the cold in Salt Lake until John D. Lee was gone.

The ride to the Meadows was made in a cold silence except for the jingling of harness and Olivia's soft sobbing. At last we drew over a small rise and looked down upon the scene. Our buggy drew alongside John as he alighted, looking over the land with clear eyes. The wind ruffled his hair. I got down and took his hand while the soldier stood respectfully nearby.

"I don't recognize the place, Em," John said to me, looking over the landscape. "The floods have done it in. It was a beautiful place, then." I looked over the small valley and saw great, water-riven gullies. It looked as if the land had been torn by the claws of a demon. The Mormons and the Indians had deserted the place because of the ghosts said to live now among the thin brush and withered trees and blasted scrub oak. It was as ugly a place as I've ever seen, and I've seen some God-forsaken landscapes down on the Pariah River. The Mountain Meadows was a place arranged to depict a hell on earth.

I knew that thirteen years ago a troop of soldiers had erected a monument in memory of the slain. Upon the monument was the inscription, "Vengeance is Mine Saith the Lord." The next spring, or the spring after, on Brigham's annual trek south, he deliberately took his entourage through the Meadows, saw the monument, and ordered it torn down. While he watched the horsemen pull down the stones he said, "Vengeance is Mine Saith the Lord—*and I have taken a little of it.*" There are witnesses to his utterance. Was that an admission? Now the monument was just a pile of rubble a little ways beyond the newly dug grave and the white pine coffin. There was a curse upon this land, my eyes told me. It was a place that was as still as a summer day on the desert, although a chilling wind whistled eerily across the wagon tops. In the imagination, and thus very real, I smelled the corruption of the dead in my nostrils. The desolation was complete.

Sentinels were posted on the flanks of the ridges above the Meadows to forestall the imaginary rescuers, and preparations were started. The wagons were lined up so as to form a protective screen. We stood some distance away, watching in silence. There was little to be said, or done. A few of the curious were held back from the protective screen of the wagons. Some were drinking. Some were praying.

At a nod from an officer, a man stood apart and read the sentence and the court's order. Prosecutor Howard stood nearby, but I could see no satisfaction in him. John's hand was warm in mine. The wind swept the hair from his forehead, and ruffled the black tie at his throat. He gave my hand a soft squeeze, and then let it go and walked toward the pine box.

"Is that a photographer?" he asked, pointing at a young man who carried a large box on a tripod. The Hon. Sumner Howard nodded that it was.

"I want to ask a favor of you," he said to Howard. "I want you to have that man take a photograph of me, and, if he would be so kind, furnish a copy of it to three of my wives, Rachel A., Sarah C. and Emma B." With that he sat down on his own coffin and arranged his face for the photographer who nervously took the picture and then retreated after shaking John's hand. While he stilled his body for the camera, John looked at me. It was a look of love and farewell.

"Do you have any last words, Mr. Lee?" the officer in charge asked after aligning the firing squad to his satisfaction.

"I do, sir," John said, standing, and then addressed the audience in crisp, clear tones that allowed no doubt that his words were his final truth. It was about 10:35, and the wind had died.

"I have but little to say this morning. Of course I feel that I am upon the brink of eternity; and the solemnities of eternity should rest upon my mind at present. I have made out—or endeavored to do so—a manuscript, abridging the history of my life. This, I have decided, is to be published under the auspices of my attorney and good friend Mr. William Bishop of Pioche, Nevada Territory. In it I have given my views and feeling with regard to all these things.

"I feel resigned to my fate. I feel calm as a summer morn, and I have done nothing intentionally wrong. My conscience is clear before God and man. I am ready to meet my Redeemer and those that have gone before me, behind the veil.

"I am not an Infidel. I have not denied God and his mercies.

"I am a strong believer in these things. Most I regret is parting with my family; many of them are unprotected and will be left fatherless . . . "

John paused then, never looking at me, but at the top of the Pine Valley Mountain clad in green pine and white snow.

"When I speak of these things they touch a tender chord in me . . . " And here his voice caught, and he faltered, but soon regained his courage. His voice rose with a righteous timbre in it that quieted the horses.

"I declare my innocence of ever doing anything designedly wrong in all this affair. I used my utmost endeavors to save these people.

"I would have given worlds, were they at my command, if I could have averted that . . . calamity, but I could not do it. It went on.

"It seems that I am to be made a victim—a victim must be had, I understand, and I am it. I am sacrificed to satisfy the feelings—the vindictive feelings—, or in other words, am used to gratify other parties.

"I am ready to die," he said softly, his voice falling again, but his eyes remained the steel grey that was the sky. His voice grew again. "I trust in God. I have no fear. Death has no terror.

"Not a particle of mercy have I asked of the court, the world, or officials to spare my life. I have said it to my family, and I will say it today, that the Government of the United States sacrifices their best friend. That is saying a great deal, but it is true—it is so.

"I am a true believer in the gospel of Jesus Christ. I do not believe everything that is now being taught and practiced by Brigham Young. I do not care who hears it! It is my last word. It is so.

"I believe Brigham Young is leading the people astray, downward to destruction. But I believe in the gospel that was taught in its purity by Joseph Smith, in the former days. I have my reasons for it.

"I studied to make Brigham Young's will my pleasure for thirty years. See, now, what I have come to this day. Evidence has been brought against me which is false as the hinges of hell, and this evidence was wanted to sacrifice me. Sacrifice a man that has waited upon them, that has wandered and endured with them in the days of adversity, true from the beginning of the Church. What confidence can I have in such a man? I have none, and don't think my Father in Heaven has either."

John paused, and looked at each one of the faces in the crowd. He looked slowly, carefully, and without rancor or recrimination. But he did not look at me. We had said our goodbyes. Olivia was becoming uncontrollable, and someone, Mr. Bishop I think, took her to the other side of the wagons. I could not summon tears. I hung on my husband's last words. "By God, he isn't going down without having his say, is he?" I heard one of the bystanders whisper to another, and the answering grunt.

"I regret leaving my family; they are near and dear to me. These are the things which touch my sympathy, even when I think of the orphaned children. I did everything in my power to save that people. Having said this I am resigned, and I ask the Lord, my God, if my labors are done, to receive my spirit."

And finally his eyes caught mine. For the last time. He smiled, and lifted his head in wordless adieu.

"The hour has come, Mr. Lee," the officer said. Mr. Bishop had arranged for a Methodist minister to pray with John. I did not know him or hear the prayer. They were together a few minutes, and then the minister left, his eyes flowing with tears. Then John walked to the firing squad and shook each one of the stranger's hands, as if pardoning them for doing their duty.

"Marshall Short? I ask one favor of the guards—spare my limbs, and centre my heart." Short nodded, and I could see he, too, was struggling with his emotions.

"Do you wish to have a handkerchief over your eyes?" Short asked.

"No," John said. "I shall be fine, by and by. Then John sat back down upon the coffin as if for the photographer again.

"Ready!"

The firing squad shoved home the bullets and raised the long rifles.

"Aim!"

"Shoot the balls through my heart, boys, don't mangle the body, if you please."

"Fire!"

CHAPTER TWENTY-NINE

It was to that beautiful but haunted place, at the mouth of Rock Creek, that I went with my children and the brave Olivia after John was buried in Panguitch.

Local folks had begun to refer to this canyon of vivid, monumental cliffs and scarps, with its scatter of small settlements, as Zion Canyon. The Rio Virgin flooded blood red in the spring, and then settled into a tranquil, liquid emerald necklace threading through pools and white water rills lending its color to the leaves of trees and stands of willows. The rough log cabin and plot of land was offered to me by a friend of John's who told me that he felt it was owed to me. I cannot disclose his name in this place.

With two nearly grown sons, and my daughter now a lively little toddler, and with Olivia's willing heart and hands, I had enough help to put the place in order. We planted a crop of vegetables, melons, beans and one of wheat with the aid of the mule and the pinto, and I tried to settle into a semblance of living. The forbidding canyon had become a homeland and a refuge for a curious mixture of protestors against the Church's policies of control over individual lives. It suited me well. The Bishops were forever visiting the little threadbare settlements with their noses close to the ground for a whiff of scandal or apostasy. They shunned me and my little household completely. It was a blessing. Had Zion more open land along the river it would have been populated from wall to wall. Show a Mormon dry land and nearby water and you'd better hang on to your fence lines. As it was, it was a refuge where dark gods warred overhead in the monsoonal summer thunder heads, ever disdainful of the souls of men.

In Zion, the reverberations of the firing squad rang in my ears. The representatives of the press would not leave me alone. They came from as far as New York and San Francisco. I found them perched behind trees, hidden in clefts, crawling from beneath rocks. Privacy was impossible. In the meantime, in May, after the planting, I determined to ride alone down to the Lonely Dell to see what ghosts or demons may there be embraced, or put to death. So I took the children, in the dark of night, to Kanab and left them with Sister Rachel and went for a long, wandering sojourn back towards the Lonely Dell. I did this out of some sense of nostalgia, some need to reaffirm that my life had not been a dream wherein all had been shadow, but did hold its hours of sunlight and laughter. Sister Rachel, by any kindness, was gone in her mind, but her children tended her with love and care. I tried to speak with her but she did not recognize me, so I left Kanab for the trek back . . . home.

It was while at the Lonely Dell, looking at the nearly abandoned rock house and the ferry works that I missed John's living so keenly that I was stunned into an ennui of hours, an inactivity of many weeks passing without my noticing them pass. Lee's Ferry was a busy place now, run by faithful churchmen who did not know me. Slowly, in my passage back up the Kaibab and into Kanab, my anger grew large enough to oer'shadow my grieving, and I returned to Zion fixed in my heart's purpose. There was no room left in me for love, I thought. I was locked within, shuttered and bolted in the heart against any emotion but that of my purpose.

How many degrees of guilt are there before the law? I know not. John's intention was to kill helpless men. I found it a curious sense of chivalry that they left the killing of the women and children to the Indians. Did the fact that he shed no blood exonerate him, or can you be tried and damned for thinking, for nearly doing? If so, then I was damned for what my thoughts held. These endless agonies cut worm trails through my being, leaving castings of a growing, remorseless fury. Man cannot live without justice. He may live without love, but not without justice. That is the history of all time.

I remembered John telling me that women had not the place in the soul which inclined men to seek war or spill blood or thirst for vengeance. As I no longer prayed, I no longer bothered to ask for the truth of that. I knew better. I'd seen women in the streets of England stab and claw and fight as much as any man when it came to surviving. I'd seen women bound for the Arizona mission as strong as any man, as ready to kill as any other human. So little do men ever understand.

It was the second week of August. Due to the plentiful and placid waters of the Rio Virgin, and the hot desert sun, the crops were in early, turnips and potatoes and plenty of fruit from the orchards. We dried the fruit, stored the vegetables underground, picked the tall corn and ground it into meal. The boys scythed the wheat and took it to the grist in Washington. I could not bear to visit the towns. It was the injustice of the hostile staring, not the act itself, that kept me reclusive.

Olivia had slowly adjusted to the tragedy. She had become melancholy, and had taken up a heavy correspondence with Mr. Bishop trying to fathom the depth of the intrigues and motives that led to the death of my husband. How this young woman could identify so much with me remained a mystery until I remembered my thoughts on justice while on the trek to the dell. Her melancholie was in part due to her inability to gain her Bill of Divorcement from Brigham Young. By alternate days she was sunny, and then sunk into a depression from which even Elizabeth could not tease her. I worried for her and her sanity. She seemed to nurture great secrets, the content of which were a mystery.

The replies to her letters to Salt Lake City put her off to some indeterminate time in the future no doubt due to Bishop Coates having changed his mind about losing this lively little rebel. The good Bishop Coates had made several nearly furtive trips from Cedar City to woo and court his estranged wife, but to no avail. She would have no part of him. Called him a cruel, lecherous, stuffy old coot to his face, and shooed him away as bothersome.

Apostasy seemed to follow me wherever I went. Olivia openly spoke against the Church until I warned her to silence, or we would have been driven from Zion. Brigham's refusal to see her left her alternately seething and then days passed by in her indifference.

We set ourselves to days of industry. Two women and two boys and a small girl. I had a guide. The indefatigable John D. Lee had taught me well. We cleared brush and grubbed stumps. We sowed wheat and planted trees. We rigged a handy system of irrigation from a small spring off the river, and the garden flourished. In our work was our salvation.

Olivia was a girl of endless curiosity, and she asked every stranger who mistakenly stopped by at our farm if they had any books. She had accumulated a small library, and with spare money bought books. She had a Shakespeare and a Dante. She would read from Dante by candlelight in the evenings, and when she came to the circles of hell even I got the chills.

And there were two adolescents who needed to learn to read and write, and by heaven they sat up straight in front of her every day for two hours or she would box their ears. David was always more interested in the farm, but Porter was like a well, so deep was his thirst for knowledge. In months he was reading and writing as well as I, but David, his voice cracking with maleness, one day informed both Olivia and I that he was through with learning. And that was that. Elizabeth was doing her letters better than David by the time he quit, but I too knew when to quit. David had learned a lot about horses and leading them to water and Etc.

Olivia corresponded frequently with W.W. Bishop, and I sensed a great, but not terribly serious affection between them. Bishop had written to me that in a few years time he would see to the publication of John's confession, and would share any proceeds with me if any. I promptly wrote back to him and told him I would not take a penny. He could throw the money into the pit, as far as I was concerned. To think that one should profit from the experience was an unspeakable breach of decency, to my mind.

One evening as we sat inside from a chill wind, Olivia asked me if I intended to marry again. I said I didn't think I ever would. I asked of her the same.

"Unlikely," she said with some sadness. "I'm beginning to realize the extent of your feeling of helplessness the past year. Always at the whim of others, mostly men."

"There are general characteristics of the species that need changing, but never will," I said.

"Indeed," she said. "If Brigham Young has the time to tend to beehives, surely he can find the time to give me a divorce. You see, we wait upon men all our lives. And they damn well know it, too," she added.

"The church and the government are wheels within wheels," I said mildly.

"Yes, they seem to forget our lives pass faster than we can keep up, and before we know it, we're gone. How can I get on with anything until I'm free?"

"Go to a civil court," I suggested. "You don't need his permission, you know, not really."

"It's on my conscience," she said, pleasing me for the strength of her character. "One cannot walk away from one's vows even if they were taken with reluctance."

"But you've lost most of your feeling for the church. Will it matter so much?"

"Oh, I know, asking permission from him seems a contradiction. But what of my soul if it's all the truth?" she asked, her voice haunted, and I understood. How very deep the fear of God ran in our lives. How very wrong, I thought, but did not say.

Although I had never spoken aloud against the Church to anyone, and never indicated any feelings towards Brigham Young, it was apparent to any observer that I had quit the Church. Olivia was openly scornful, saying a church that would suffer the death of an innocent man to clean its own skirts was no true church. I allowed, out of some exhaustion, my boys to attend the Grafton ward meetings, but I had made it clear to the Bishops that they were never to set foot on my place or suffer the consequences of Olivia's horse pistol or my Derringer which I kept as clean and oiled as a jeweled watch. Olivia, quite unwittingly, was the instrument in getting me close enough to the man to kill him dead.

On the fifteenth day of August, acting Captain James Dellenbaugh rode across the river and into the small yard in front of our cabin. I had been expecting him from a letter the previous week. When he arrived the boys were in an excited, jump-about happiness. Lt. Dellenbaugh was a man they could admire. He brought them presents, knives and shirts and such. He brought cloth for new dresses, and Olivia and I were able to clothe ourselves decently for his visits. On one visit he rode across the river leading two fine horses he had bought from the army. The boys were delirious with dreams of cowboying, and worshiped him with a shining devotion.

I had spent many hours explaining to my sons and daughter the circumstances of their father's execution, sparing no detail or nuance, and they seemed to accept it stoically except for the shadows in their eyes at the mention of his name. John D. Lee's name was freely spoken in my household. Not with any reverence, or shame, but simply in the manner of a departed husband and father whom God had called prematurely. I had nothing to be ashamed of, nor did my children, I assured them. However, the Lee name has become a curse and anathema in the southern mission and through the territories. The Lee name taints the enterprise and opportunities of the boys and their families even unto this day.

How his children can keep from cursing him—perhaps they do in their secret hearts—for leaving them his legacy is beyond me. But I know they loved him, even if they will suffer to bear his name for generations to come until God decrees that no more male children are ever born into this family.

Lt. Dellenbaugh was now posted in Fort Douglas in Salt Lake

City, having finished with the business of the Powell expeditions. He had gained some fame in the Army, and Major Powell had mentioned him several times over the past three years in dispatches for his courage and unfailing devotion to duty. James had written to me that a Captaincy was pending. I suspect that Salt Lake was the nearest posting he could find that allowed him to be within correspondence of me and my family. He came to the place in Zion once quarterly, an occasion that grew in significance until it became a holiday for me and my little family.

Lt. Dellenbaugh's expected arrival always quickened some life in me. I confess to bathing more carefully, and even rouging my cheeks. It was impossible, of course. How could I love him, or better the question, how could he love me? Who was I? I was used up. I was tortured with my plans, preoccupied by the questions of the good and evil of them. I was a creature whose eye palled at sunsets, whose nights were filled with terrors such as the gods in Zion visited over the brush and canvas roof of the cabin. It was only in his presence that I saw the tranquil beauty of the river, the unimaginable infinity of shapes that the wind and water had carved into the pliant rock; the sculpture garden that was Zion. He refreshed me. He gave me thoughts that I dared not entertain. He was becoming a reason to go on with the living in the face of the darkness of the recent past.

It was late that midsummer evening when he arrived. The heat was pouring forth from the rocks and monuments, but cool shade advanced across the narrow canyon in long imitations of the towers which cast it. I had letters by the week from James since the death of John in March.

In April, June and in August he managed leave from the army to make the train ride as far south as Milford, and then he came on horseback to the Zion Canyon to visit me and Olivia and the children. He arrived hollow-eyed and exhausted. He left, if I may say, as refreshed as a spring morning. He slept in the small hay barn with the boys on those visits. His faithfulness to me never ceased to move me, but I could not love him for his gratitude alone. And my body felt as dried as the corn withering in the summer heat. Yet. Yet . . .

The next morning, after a ride and a romp with the boys, James and I and Olivia took the wagon hitched to my faithful mule for a ride to the jade-walled coolness of the weeping rock where we planned to picnic. This was a place of fauns and ferns, a grotto of shimmering waterfalls which cooled the air to that of a near winter's chill. Welcome, now, in August when the thermometer which Major Powell gave to John so long ago read a popping 115 degrees, five degrees short of its limit.

Olivia, in deference to our privacy, left our picnic spot after we had lunched upon cold tongue and fresh bread, blackberries which we had picked from the brambles along the stream, and cool buttermilk in a crock that sweat with cooling. We sat on the old quilt while Olivia wandered in and out among the weeping over-hangs until she disappeared around a bend, and then we saw her in sunlight silhouette, walking along the river.

"Shall we walk or sit?" he asked me, laying back, his hat over his eyes.

"As you please," I said.

"I'm too full to move, but I'm also chilled. Let's get a minute of sun."

"You'll need a nap against your journey tomorrow."

"I daren't miss a moment with you," he said shyly, rising, taking my hand and leading me out into the sunlight where we sat on the smooth ledge, our backs just in the shade.

"At times like this I forget," I said to him. I caught the flash of Olivia's white skirt among the willow trees.

"Time will at least round the edges of your . . . experience," he said at last, taking my hand, looking into my eyes. I saw there a reflected sheen of the Colorado, of faraway places, and then an immediacy in them which held me still. He took me in his arms, and kissed me with a soundness, and a passion which was al-together breathtaking. And, for a moment I did forget, and folded myself against him, needing to feel the smooth contours of the man, wanting to plunge myself into his very body, to lose myself in his very being. I longed for his hands upon my breast, my flanks, my whole soul. I had to draw back then, or I would have been lost. But in the next instant he rescued me.

"Will you marry me?" he said as I pulled back, his hands holding my shoulders, his eyes a crystalline intensity.

"Oh," was all I was able to reply. I had never dreamed the man would wish to marry the shamed widow of a cursed man. Perhaps, in the slowest moments of dawn, the thought had flickered through my mind, at which moment I would rise and busy myself to forestall such thinking. These were dangerous phantasms. I truly had never taken the . . . hope? . . . beyond those brief instants of . . . longing. And now the man whom I'd come to . . . love . . . and depend upon, had asked me to share myself with him.

"Spend the rest of time with me," he said, forgetting the Mormon Church and its eternal marriages.

"That but I could, James," I said at last. "It is impossible."

"It is not impossible," he said in an iron voice. "It is not only possible, it will fulfill my heart's dream."

"I would bring nothing to you, James, I have nothing to give," I murmured. "I'm a worn woman, homeless, with a family to support, and a name that is a curse upon the lips of people."

"How can you be so blind?" he demanded, and slammed a fist upon the rock until I thought the ledge would cleft. I was startled by his anger. "I love you, Emeline Lee. I've loved you since the moment I laid eyes on you on the banks of the Colorado."

"Your debt for my nursing is long ago repaid," I said, blushing.

"Now you're being coy," he said angrily. "I've harbored love, not gratitude. Will you have me? I'll be good for the boys. I'll leave the army and we can go to any place you wish, if you'll say yes."

"There is little room left in my heart," I said.

"The heart is a vast mansion," he said, his anger vanished.

"I don't know, James," I hesitated. It would be cruel to say yes, and a dagger in my heart for the rest of my life to say no. I loved the man.

"I've killed men in hand to hand combat, and I've seen places on the river that only God should see. I've bowed to no man ever, but as you see, I'm begging on bended knee," he said with a wry smile.

And the daft man was on his knees, sun on his shock of light hair. He looked so funny I had to laugh, and then I began to weep.

"No, I cannot," I said. "In time, and perhaps in the future I will consider it. But you will not have me when the time comes. You will never be able to forgive me."

One would have thought ice water did run in my veins. But my thoughts were always elsewhere. It was a preoccupation long before the Mountain Meadows seeing the torture Brigham Young had caused John and his family with his cat and mouse games. Some have said I have a serene exterior. No, I lived in a fury toward Brigham Young that was years in the building.

Brigham Young may not have believed that Adam's transgression tainted his royal person with the burden of Original Sin, but by my Catholic mother, I was so stained. I was prepared to lose my life and the love of James in a sin of great commission. To my mind, B.Y. had sold his rights to Heaven, and gained his rights to Hell.

James was not a man of a weak disposition, for my refusal of his proposal of marriage finally caused him to grin as he dusted off his knees. He held me and we kissed. "Emeline Lee," he said, "It's like going down the river, I warn you. There's no quitting her. You'll have me in the end, and I've no inclination toward another. Whatever it is that holds you back, I'll wear it out, and wait it out."

And for that I loved him even more.

CHAPTER THIRTY

D amn the man!" Olivia said aloud on a busy Salt Lake City street corner. Her exasperated declaration brought to a halt several passersby who stared at her with undisguised shock. Had they known the man to whom Olivia had directed her curse in a public place, they would have taken her to jail forthwith.

"Watch your tongue," I cautioned her harshly under my breath. "You'll see us lynched." I looked at her, saw her press her lips together in a silent assent. "Let's get the *Tribune* for the morning's report," she said, and we continued on down south Main Street looking for a news vendor. "Perhaps they'll tell us whether he's sick from chicken broth or whiskey."

I had to laugh at Olivia's irreverence, and noted her lovely countenance was darkening with each passing day. Her mood progressed from a bubbling hope to a kind of despair within an hour's passing. I was worried for her health. She was irrepressible in her quest. The cancellation of our appointment was a difficult disappointment.

The Bill of Divorcement that was necessary for Olivia to be free of Bishop Coates had to be signed by Brigham Young. That a man with so many affairs still had the time to meddle in the very most private parts of the lives of the people in Mormondom still astonished me. He found the time to deal not only with the issues of statehood and war, but the very minutae of our public and private lives. As Coates was a Bishop, Brigham had to pass judgment on Olivia's suit against the Bishop.

It was a curious circumstance. Polygamous unions were not recognized by the Territorial Government. However, at the time of Olivia's sealing to Bishop Coates, Brigham Young was a bona fide territorial official, and thus her marriage legal. Olivia insisted that she be sundered from Bishop Coates both ecclesiastically and temporally. And the time had finally come. Or so I thought those were her motives.

The letter arrived in mid-August. Olivia was notified by Brigham's secretary, one LeGrand Richards Esq., that she was to present herself before Himself at the Beehive House near Temple Square in Salt Lake City. The meeting was to be at 2 o'clock p.m. on the 30th day of August. James had departed from Zion for his return to his post at Camp Floyd the very day before, or she should have accompanied him north.

There was little time to make the arrangements for such a journey. When Olivia asked me if I would accompany her, I assured her that it would be my pleasure. How could she know that I hoped she'd make such an offer. If she had not, then I would have invited myself. I had always planned to make my visit to Brigham Young when he came next south to his winter residence in St. George. Being in Salt Lake would be more fitting to my purpose. More symbolic that we should meet at last in the seat of the Kingdom in the very shadow of the rising temple.

If I had any chance to get past the guards of Brigham Young, surely this innocent young woman could prove the key. It was very likely that no one would ever recognize me. As her companion and advisor I could not be kept from an audience with him. It was the opportunity I had waited upon for many months. I made the preparations in as much haste as Olivia, and then we were off in the rattling old buggy on the dusty trail to Cedar City, Beaver

City, and then to Milford and the train which would take us the rest of the way.

I'd never been on a train in my life. It has much to recommend it as a means of travel. The tracks paralleled the trail John and I had taken south on our honeymoon so many years before. Olivia chattered away, and I found the sensation of riding so swiftly quite exhilarating. I watched Utah pass by without raising so much as a backache or getting soaked from passing showers. Near Salt Lake the tracks crossed the road leading west to Fort Douglas, but I turned my face toward the smoky, eastern windows of the car and shut my eyes. Upon our arrival, we secured lodgings in an inexpensive hotel near temple square and met our first obstacle; Brigham Young was temporarily indisposed due to illness. And there was another problem which Olivia would not let rest until she had her way.

I privately decided I would not attempt to see James. It was a wrenching decision. Although he did not know it, we had said goodbye the day he proposed. A letter from prison would be his payment for his devotion. I wanted to throw myself from the moving train for my duplicity, my treachery. A visit would only hurt him more deeply than he was about to be hurt, but Olivia chattered about my good fortune—as well as the exciting opportunity to visit a fort. It would be so very cruel to visit him and pass inconsequences of weather—indulge in the subtle tease of pleasures that I had allowed in my dreaming moments. But then to go away and . . . do what I had to do . . . it was impossible. I fully expected to be taken into custody immediately afterward. There would be no avoiding it. There would be no escape. I would, most likely, follow my husband's fate before a firing squad. When I finally told Olivia of my decision not to visit James she figuratively went through the ceiling of the room in our hotel.

We stepped out of the noonday sun and into the shade of a small Gentile tea shop at First South and Second East and took a table. It was hot, and the tang from the distant Salt Lake mixed with the dung of the streets and the smell of steeping Pekoe. Olivia fanned herself with an advertisement while I looked at the front page of the city's two newspapers for reports of Brigham's health.

"Ah, he is convalescent, according to the *Deseret News*."

"They would say that," she nodded impatiently. "What a shock they'll have when they learn their Prophet is not immortal. He's an old, very old, wicked man."

"They say it's just a troubled stomach. He ate green corn and peaches for lunch and is expected to resume his duties within a few more days."

"Such a meal would trouble my digestion too," Olivia said, sipping the tea. A small mist of perspiration skimmed her upper lip. Since our arrival in Salt Lake a full week ago, she had become more agitated with the canceled appointment, while I became more calm with each passing hour. The time would come.

We had showed ourselves at the gates of the Beehive House with bare hours to spare on the appointed day only to be informed by a mutton-whiskered young man, a second secretary or something, of the Prophet's indisposition. He informed us that he would reschedule Mrs. Coates' appointment if we would inquire again as soon as the Prophet returned to his office. This left us adrift, and short of money having to continue living in a hotel suitable for two unaccompanied ladies.

"The *Tribune*, however, reports that the illness is much more serious, and might be fatal," I said neutrally.

"Wishful thinking on the part of the Democrats," she said. "Please God, let him live long enough to affix his signature to my pleading," Olivia said in mock prayer. "If he dies on me who knows how long it will be before a successor is chosen. I'll have to start the whole proceedings all over again. It will take years. I'll never be free."

"Well, if he should . . . pass on, you'll be free in some sense of the matter, won't you? And it isn't as if you've restrained yourself," I said, teasing her. "The blizzard of letters from a certain lawyer in Pioche seems to've kept your mind off Bishop Coates." Olivia blushed, whether from the warmth or my words I didn't know. "In any case, we'll just have to wait it out."

I had mixed feelings about the frail health of Brigham Young. On the one hand his demise would lift a burden, and keep me from the act, keep me out of prison, or worse. On the other, there would never be the satisfaction of seeing him brought before the heavenly bar.

The city was a blunt shock to both of us. I had not visited any place larger than Cedar City in twenty years, though I had seen drawings in the magazines and listened to travelers telling of the growth of that place until it exceeded all imagination. I felt as provincial as I must have looked. A farming widow come to see the sights in God's city. What the Latter Day Saints had been able to do in twenty-five years astonished any visitor, be they from the sophisticated East or the cities of the Pacific coast. Even the famous English explorer, Sir Richard Burton, who had lived in Africa and among the Arabys, commented favorably upon Brigham and the order of things in the Kingdom. On the other hand, Burton had no objection to polygamy. Visitors saw what Brigham wanted them to see. Nothing more.

The marvelous Tabernacle was roofed with a turtle-backed golden dome, and the stone walls of the great white temple were rising ever higher nearby. Temple Square was an impressive collection of granite buildings with green lawns and ornate rings of flowers along the clean walks. In the next block, however, the place was as much as any city, cleaner perhaps than Liverpool had been, but a noisy place withal full of drayman and drummers, stray dogs and dithering commerce men. The streets were dirt and dung, and in August one wished for the clean, pure-smelling heat of the desert.

We had idled for three days, following the progress of the Prophet's health while taking long walks throughout the city to see the curiosities. There were many men on the streets who were soldiers, but few of them were in uniform. Fort Douglas was eighteen miles distant, and a daily coach and many freight wagons went back and forth so it would have been easy for me to get there had I the courage. Olivia never let me forget how near Fort Douglas was.

"I don't understand," Olivia said time and again after I delayed letting James know of our presence in Salt Lake. "He will be heartbroken if he learns you've been here and you've not even tried to see him, or at least let him know you're here. I shall send a message and tell him myself," she declared.

"No, please, don't. In good time," I pleaded with her, and she saw the extent of my feelings. "We shall stop off at the Fort on our return, and have a good visit. Let's attend to business first."

"But he loves you!"

"Yes."

"Well, then? You've got to get your mind out of the past and into the future. You're a beautiful woman. I'm sure Mr. Lee would urge you to remarry," she said. "I don't understand you at all."

Olivia and I had heated words almost every day over my decision not to visit James. I did not want to see him because of what I was about to do. I wanted him to remember me half dressed on the ledge of rock over the river, before I decided to become: an assassin.

"You have ice water for blood if you get this close to James and don't see him," she said hotly. "I'd never forgive you, and neither will he," she said.

Olivia was incensed as we strolled the streets, taking in the sights. My reluctance to visit James may have been a deeply unknown wish within me that the sight and feel of him would change my mind.

If I succeeded—and succeed I would—I would never in all likelihood see James Dellenbaugh again. There would be no wedding for Emeline Buxton Lee. I am not sure to this day but that I was still so angry with John D. Lee for his willingness to pay the price, I needed to lash back at something. May God forgive me, but without truth, I cannot live. There was only one room left in the house of the heart. The rest of the rooms were wreck and ruin. I decided the remaining room was too small to hold a future. The future was too large.

But the heart is ever a betrayer of the head. As a consequence of Olivia's withering persuasion, I finally consented to what my heart wished to do in any case. As cruel as it would be—a goodbye really—I had to see James one last time. I was ashamed of myself for my reluctance, but it was simply not yet the time for an explanation. I was sure that if James had a hint of my plans he would stop me even if he had to place me under arrest.

In the early morning we rented a buggy and pair of fast trotters at some expense, and drove toward Fort Douglas. By midmorning we were at the gates of the Fort, causing a great deal of excitement, fuss, and consternation. Olivia and I were shown to the office of the Commander who received us politely and bade us wait there until they could locate James.

Major Connors knew well enough who I was, but it was John the army was always after, not his women and children. James had long ago announced to his superiors he intended to marry me. In any case, had Major Connors kept me waiting at the gates, I'd carried myself with pride for years in the face of the world's scorn, and no snub or smear could ever touch me again. I did have ice water in my veins. It was but a short time before James came bursting into the office, his blue tunic soaked with sweat, his hair a dishevelment. He looked wonderful.

"I suppose I should have telegraphed," I said as he swept me into his arms.

"Oh, what a wonderful surprise," he said, letting me down, and then he gave Olivia a back-cracking hug of her own. We went to the empty officer's mess where a steward with a soiled jacket served us refreshment of tea and sour pie. Young officers were hanging in the windows. Someone as beautiful as Olivia among all those young soldiers almost caused a riot. After tea she discreetly rose to leave us alone, and went out to the porch where she held court, flattered to the tops of her button shoes at all the attention.

"I never thought to see you here," James said happily, holding my hand. "Why are you so downcast, darling, aren't you happy to see me?"

"Of course I am, James. The journey, it's tired me out."

"And how long will it take you to finish your business?" he asked.

"Not long, I think," I said.

"Let me see if I can get leave," he declared. "I'll accompany you to the city," James jumped up as if ready to ride at that moment. He fairly bounced about the officer's mess with the sudden idea. "We could have a wonderful time. We could go to the theater!" he exclaimed.

"I don't think so," I said. "There is time enough."

"Well, if you don't want me to go," he said, and I saw he was crushed. I noticed small shoots of grey at his sideburns. I was James' senior by a handful of years, and as men are said to age much faster than women, perhaps we would be of a dying age together. The thought singed my heart. I should not have come.

"You're sad," he said as he sat down and took up my hands again, searching my eyes. "What is it Emeline? What's wrong?"

"I guess I'm worrying about the results of Olivia's interview." Now I had become a liar to the man I loved. I'd never lied to John in my life. "If he refuses her I don't know what effect it will have on the girl. It will crush her."

"I don't know how often I've advised her to engage a lawyer," James said with annoyance. "There's nothing Gentile lawyers like better than to represent divorces to Brigham's courts. It drives them to a blue-blazes distraction that anybody would think of divorcing a Mormon man." And then he paused, and searched my eyes. I could not hold them.

"That day you said, 'if you will have me.' What did you mean? Of course I'll have you. I'd have you under any circumstances. You could go to prison and I'd still have you," he said in jest, and unable to say the truth I broke completely, and wept.

Olivia came back into the echoing room when she heard me, and lit into the innocent James.

"What have you said to her, Lt. Dellenbaugh?" she demanded, putting a protective arm around my shoulder.

"I don't know," he confessed, anguished and bewildered. "I would cut off my hand before I'd cause you pain, Emeline, you know that," he said.

"I'm all right. It's the heat. I don't feel well," I said, and I did not feel well at all. I felt like dressing in shrouds, and pulling the grass over the top of my head. I wanted to be in the Celestial Kingdom where there was no pain. Where my family lived in brick houses with glass windows, and my children were happy, whole, and safe. I wanted to go there soon. James would never understand. It was cruel to lead him on that we would have a future.

"I'll drive you back to the city," he said.

"No," I said, recovering. I had to live a little longer. I had to be strong. Seeing James had only strengthened my resolve. "I'll be fine," I said, "by and by."

On the Saturday came a report in the *Deseret News* that the Prophet was fully recovered, and was expected to appear in the Tabernacle for the Sunday meetings, and perhaps would even speak.

"I want to see the man's face, see what kind of mood he's in," Olivia said.

I resisted, fearing the sight of him in a public place would move me to a premature act that was bound to fail. His bodyguards were a group of burly men who were quick with their guns, it was told. This was not a public business, but a private one. Even so, my curiosity got the better of me. I had the presence of mind, however, to leave the Derringer in our room six blocks distant from the Tabernacle so as to forestall any impulsive decision.

We attended the afternoon meeting at the golden domed Tabernacle. The crowds were stifling. Thousands, it seemed wished to see the Prophet and hear him speak. We took seats near the center. Brigham was in rare form that day. I'd read his speeches in the papers many times, but the written word gave no hint of the man's power of speech and presence.

Brigham was particularly exercised that day about many things. He demanded obedience to the Word of Wisdom, fidelity to friends, and spoke against the evils of the Gentile influence. Nothing new here, I thought, sitting amidst the throng, sweating and silent and doing my utmost to remain calm. His speech, recorded in the next morning's papers was typical—the 66-year-old Lion of the Lord roared and sermonized for over two hours.

"With regard to the young men who think of getting married and choosing from amongst the daughters of the east you must be aware of the risk that you run if you take a wife who does not believe in the Gospel . . . Perhaps in other things she might be as good as many of our western girls, the course of some of whom I cannot recommend . . .

"The time has come when the Sisters must agree to give up

their follies of dress . . .

"We shall discard the dragging skirts and for decency's sake those disgusting short ones extending no lower than the boot tops. We also regard 'panniers' and whatever approximates the 'Grecian Blend' a burlesque on natural beauty and will not disgrace our persons by wearing them . . .

"Instead of hunting gold we ought to pray to the Lord to hide it up . . .

"And as for the cheap novels which are these days being imported into Zion. I should be very foolish if, because I had a poor appetite I took to making my meals of poisonous herbs and berries because they tasted sweet or were otherwise palatable. Novel reading appears to me very much the same as swallowing poisonous herbs. It is a remedy that is worse than the complaint . . .

And soon until I felt as if I'd been in church for a month. The Lonely Dell had many advantages, I thought with nostalgia, foremost of which was the lack of the opportunity to listen to preaching.

Afterward, we strolled until the evening cooled, but the moisture in the air had increased over the afternoon until the city was like a Navajo sweat lodge. Olivia was in a pensive mood. "He did seem to be in good health and spirits? That will improve his mood," she said. After a cold supper we went back to the boardinghouse and held a brief discussion of our finances. Between us, we could afford to wait another week, and then we should be penniless.

In the midst of this troubling discussion there was a knock at the door. Olivia answered it cautiously, as we were expecting no one. A young man in a fresh white shirt and scrubbed face handed her a note, and left without a word. She opened the note and passed it to me. It was a summons the next morning at nine o'clock for an audience with the Prophet, Seer and Revelator of the Church of Jesus Christ of Latter Day Saints. I prayed to God he did not know who her companion was when we presented ourselves for the . . . reckoning.

CHAPTER THIRTY-ONE

A wet August heat had settled upon the city during the night. We bathed and dressed in an awful atmosphere of moisture which seemed to fill the lungs, making breath difficult. The hint of the sun slowly filled the sky behind the soaring Wasatch Mountains with light the color of a gray-wash over textured paper, as if it were a watercolor. I dressed in the same dress I had worn to the execution. The full-length black silk with somber brown velvet borders was set off with a spray of white lace at my throat. For some reason I removed the thin gold ring that John had given me so many years ago in this same city.

The sun's fullness blasted the streets when we stepped out of the hotel. To the west, what once had been a clear sky was filling with bruise-colored thunder heads, and one could hear the rumble of distant lightning rolling out of Cottonwood and Emigration Canyons. We had been mostly silent through our morning break-fast of tea and toast. Olivia was dressed in a lovely dress she had made from a green sateen that James had thoughtfully brought to her in the early summer.

We were within easy walking distance of the yellow-walled Beehive House, which it was reported to have cost Brigham $50,000 to build twenty years ago. Brigham's wealth was a great source of scorn in the pages of the *Tribune*. The purse of church and state were all one to him. Wealth would not protect him this day, I vowed, nor the Lord Himself. The Derringer was safely in my large pocketbook with leathern sidewalls. I had loaded two fresh cartridges. My nerves were placid, and the heat brought no perspiration to the small of my back. Olivia looked wilted. She smiled at me wanly, her violet eyes dark from the dimming light of the sky.

The storm was becoming more threatening, and I foolishly wished for an umbrella, which I hadn't carried since the day I stepped onto the *Charley Buck* so long ago in England. I thought of England, and wished I had the wherewithal to return there some day. But these thoughts had to be pushed away. The image of John standing in silhouette against the doorless house as he greeted the morning on the Colorado flashed across the eye of my mind, and I blinked it away.

Olivia handed the note to the guard who was dressed in a foolish imitation of a military uniform at the iron-gated entrance to Brigham's home and offices. It was from this place he had governed Zion, housed and schooled his platoons of wives and children, and sallied forth to build up the Kingdom of God on this earth. The guard had a pistol on his hip, but paid no real notice to the two modestly dressed women—mother and daughter—who had appeared for their appointment.

"Up the stairs and to your right, Ma'am," he said to me in deference to my age. Olivia smiled and we walked along the broad walk and up a set of stone steps. The double doors were tall, painted a pleasing yellow with white trim. Inside, the floors were of plain joined pine, polished to perfection and dotted with rag rugs. It had a frontier plainness I thought, the house, until we opened the door upon which was a shiny brass plate which read: Secretary to the President, LeGrand Richards.

Richards' office was as plush as a Pasha's harem, with colored rugs and brass fittings and heavy curtains. But instead of the smell of incense there was the smell of stove oil and sanctimony. Olivia handed the note to the man we assumed to be Brigham's secretary, but were surprised when he showed us into another office, startling for its plainness. Whoever had decorated the Beehive house could not make up their minds as to plainness or pomposity, so it was all a confusion to the eye and senses.

"Mrs. Coates?" said a greying man of handsome face. He was dressed in a formal black day suit, and he stood and shook both of our hands. "And this is?" he inquired of me.

"Miss Emeline Buxton," I said, my heart in my throat. It was a risk I was willing to run. I would be who I once was, but not the same. Mrs. John D. Lee would have brought armed guards in an instant, I knew, but had failed to forewarn Olivia of my name. She looked at me in astonishment and then appraisal before giving me a quick wink of a colored eye to say she understood the use of my maiden name.

I scanned the plain room and saw a brace of pistols sitting on a side table. They looked to be ready for instant use. I clutched my handbag, and wondered if we were to be searched, but thought that foolish. The Kingdom of God, for all of its crises, was in a relative peace now, and Brigham's life had not been seriously threatened since the execution of my husband. There remained a band of hotheads who still chafed at the affair, mostly Gentiles, but for all Brigham was loved as a demi-god hereabouts, and the guard at the front gate did not seem suspicious in the leastwise. I was received. It was going to be done.

"President Young will give you a little more than ten minutes," Richards spoke to Olivia. "I've gathered all of the correspondence concerning your case, and he has read it. Just state your case, and await his decision. I assure you it will be from God's wisdom that he decides. He is a fair man." Richards looked at me suddenly, and I thought I saw suspicion there, and then I was sure of it. "Do you wish to see him alone?" he asked the supplicant.

"Oh, no, Mrs. . . . . Miss Buxton is my friend and advisor and I need her support," Olivia said, flashing those violet eyes and Richards forgot whatever thought had clouded his eyes. "She's widowed!" Olivia suddenly blurted, and my heart sank. I wanted to kick her shin, but Richards was distracted again by a sudden flash of lightning and a following slap of thunder which shook the window panes.

"Is that a fact," Richards said, studying me again. "Well, the President has been ill, so please be prompt with your business." He checked his pocket watch and went to the another set of double doors. It was precisely nine o'clock a.m. I am unable to segment time in its orderly measurement. For, truly, the one minute was an hour, and the next clock-telling minute raced within my reckoning as brief as the beat of a heart. The ornate, sword-like hands of the clock moved, I am sure, with the precision of God's eternal universe. But to me, it had all of the disorder, and erratic motion of a nightmare.

9:01: President Brigham Young was sitting behind a large desk, a stolid dark bulk in the dim light of the room. He wore a Prunella suit with white shirt and black string tie. A lamp had been lit against the lowering sky, and the long, narrow room was in a half light, and the muttering thunder seemed to be amplified within the confines of the room. He rose somewhat unsteadily, a very large man, the lamp shining wanly up into a round, stern face. I saw no recognition, merely impatience.

"You are Mrs. Coates?" he asked of Olivia. It was more of a demand than a question.

"Yes sir, and this is Emeline Buxton, who is my friend and advisor in this troubled time," Olivia said with a small curtsy which wanted to make me giggle.

"Buxton? I used to know a Buxton family, I believe. From Wyoming," he said with certainty. I thought I had been caught out, but had to smile inside at the man's mistaken confidence. "Are you from thereabouts, Sister?" he asked, beckoning to two straight back chairs in front of the desk.

We sat, and I nodded negatively, saying, "No, sir, I've never been to Wyoming." I enjoyed lying to the man. Both of my parents were under the frozen Wyoming sod. I wondered if he was going to inquire once again, as he had done at my prenuptial interview, how I crossed the icy streams, and wondered if I should repeat my tale of removing my shoes and stockings before crossing. I hated him for the superficiality of this moment, or was it merely an attempt at good manners? In any case, Olivia needed a signature on a piece of paper, and I should bide my peace until the moment came to blast him into Hell.

9:02: "State your business," he said bluntly, looking at Olivia with eyes that seemed suddenly vague, opaque. I looked more closely at him and saw the tinges of illness on his skin. He had a sickly color, a yellow and green hue that bespoke a poisoning within. He did not seem well, but then he had just suffered an illness, and the man was at an advanced age. The same age as John. They had once been brothers, and father and son, of similar strength and vitality save for one irredeemable fact. The one still lived and breathed. The other had the vitality of the heart and my hope torn from him.

"I've come to seek your permission and release from marriage to Josiah Coates, of Cedar City," Olivia replied firmly. "That is, sir, if you would be so forgiving." To that moment I had never realized to what an extent she was an actress. She seemed a different person. She had the presence of a trial lawyer. God knew how many hours she must have rehearsed and prepared herself for this conversation.

Brigham waved at a sheaf of letters on the desk before him.

"All from Coates. The man still holds powerful feelings for you. Did you not vow for better or worse? Did you not bind yourself to him in solemn vows for all of eternity?"

"I did, sir. But under the conditions of his fidelity to me and my sister wives," Olivia said, and I saw a startled, complex move of emotions pass under his stern visage.

"That is a strong accusation," he said at last. And then his voice matched the distant thunder, and I felt my hands seek to unclasp the handbag. It was happening all too fast. Minutes. Olivia must restrain herself! She must have his signature. "Miss Buxton? Advise this young lady to carefully choose her words. Has she considered Bishop Coates has upon him no hint of impropriety?"

"She will speak as she pleases," I said, shrugging with what I hoped would appear an innocence. Then he looked at me in what I thought to be a full recognition. This was replaced by a regal irritation. He was not known for his patience.

"All reports from Cedar City testify to his good, wholesome moral character."

"Then you have been misinformed," Olivia said. I laid a hand on her arm and gave her a look that subdued her. "There have been instances in which Mr. Coates has not shown full faith in his family."

"And what do you mean by that? Are you making an accusation against the man? One that will stand the scrutiny of witness and true testimony?"

"I merely mean, sir, that we had difficulties beyond those that are normal between a husband and a wife."

"Well, did he beat you then?"

9:05: Olivia looked at me.

"Yes, sir, with a Chinese bamboo," she admitted. "More than once," Olivia said, astonishing herself with the recollection.

"A strong rebuke from time to time of a wife by a husband is of no consequence. In fact, it is his duty," Brigham said. "Did he starve you, make you wear rags?"

"No sir, I was well provided for in physical necessities. I do not wish to go into the details. Suffice it that our differences have widened into an unbreachable gulf. There can never be any hope for reconciliation." She looked at him with defiance.

"Well, Mrs. Coates, reconciliation is exactly what I recommend. I also admonish you to get on your knees and pray for forgiveness, and that the man will have you back. I know of you and your treachery to the Saints!" he said, pointing a thick finger that included both of us. My hand slipped into the bag, and I closed my fingers around the cool mother of pearl butt of the deadly little gun. "You shall never have a divorce from the Church, or the courts in this territory. I'll see to that!"

The blood had drained from his face, and his agitation was like that of the storm which had descended upon the city and beat heavy-leafed branches against the window panes. It was dark as the Day of Judgment in the room. I thought I could smell his sickness from his breath as he made to stand.

"I know your story, Mrs. Coates," he charged. "It tells an

interesting tale of your treachery to Bishop Coates. How you openly chose to disobey him and attended the trials of John D. Lee. That you befriended the wife of the man and made no attempt to conceal your sympathy with the apostate Lee! That you have betrayed your Church. No, Mrs. Coates, you shall not have your freedom by my hand!"

9:06: I was utterly rooted to my chair at his outburst. He was going to absolutely refuse Olivia's plea. It was one more reason, if reason I needed, to begin to withdraw the carefully loaded Derringer. Before me was a towering rage of righteousness that I vowed I would blast to hell. But from the corner of my eye I saw Olivia suddenly stand and begin to fumble with her hands into the recesses of the voluminous carpet bag she carried for a purse. And then I saw the dull gleam of the horse pistol that I thought she had lost months ago. It was enormous in her small hands.

"Olivia, no!" I cried as she raised the pistol and pointed it at Brigham Young. There was a tremendous flash of lightning that lit every line in our faces, and before the thunderclap Olivia shouted at him, her face a dark fury.

"May Satan greet you as a brother," she said. "I'll divorce you from this life, you wicked man. You're through running other people's lives!" she cried.

I struck her hand hard just as the Prophet clutched at his stomach, groaned, and fell back onto his chair. Then he rolled heavily to the floor with a loud crash. Olivia looked at me with a blaze of fury still trying to cock the pistol and point it at the fallen man. I slapped her hard across the face, wresting the pistol from her, and stuffed it into her bag just as Secretary Richards flung open the door and rushed to the Prophet. A guard was steps behind him. Olivia and I shrank back into the shadows. I thrust my small handbag into her purse and clutched it to my chest. Brigham Young was gasping, and writhing with pain.

"Send for the Doctor!" Richards ordered, his face fearfully distraught. "You ladies must leave at once. The Prophet has fallen." It was 9:09.

CHAPTER THIRTY-TWO

B righam Young died two days later of the Cholera Morbus at 4:00 p.m. on the 29th day of August, 1877. He was surrounded by his family, and is said to have uttered some prophecies through the fog of opiates which the doctors administered to him in his last two days of pain. The learned medical men of this modern time write that he died from a ruptured appendix. A bullet from either Olivia or myself would have been more merciful, for he suffered mightily until at last God or Satan received him.

It was reported that he experienced moments of lucidity, but never mentioned the details of what happened that day. There was never a whisper of it. Brigham went to the grave with the knowledge of the attempt on his life in silence. More likely, at the moment of Olivia's blazing anger and drawn pistol, he was experiencing such pain as to not recognize his circumstances. Or, perhaps, he didn't even recognize the threat of death when he was stricken down by other means. The sudden onslaught of his illness was a Godsend. It has freed me at last of hatred, and an act of irredeemable savagery. Of that I repent. Of that, I am grateful.

And I thank God for his Providential sparing of me to find some later happiness which I thought forever lost, and impossible. Perhaps Brigham Young prayed for a martyr's death. He will have his immortality one way or the other as America's homespun Moses. But he called out for no help. Did he wish for the true martyrdom that is assassination? Was that what ruptured his bowels? My presence? Hers? God's?

I can report that to this day Olivia remains unrepentant. She lives now in Pittsburgh, having remarried some five years afterward to a Catholic steel magnate whom I have never met. We were on our way toward Fort Douglas within an hour of our leaving the Prophet writhing in agony upon the floor. The city was in a panic as word spread of the stricken Prophet. Already mourners and well-wishers had begun to throng the roads toward Temple Square by the time we left for the Fort. I didn't think I'd ever seen James, or the light of the sun, again. On our breathless flight toward Fort Douglas, thinking we may still be arrested.

The thunderstorm moved off to the east. Finally I asked Olivia, "Did you mean to kill the Prophet all along?" She looked at the sky going violet as her eyes.

"I don't know," she finally said. "I never dreamed he would turn me down. I know a long time ago I decided that if he would not grant me my divorce, he deserved to die. I knew that much. And then he insulted both of us. Such power!"

"You carried that pistol all this way," I reminded her.

"I'm never without it, as you are never without your little Derringer," she sniffed. "Had I been you, I should have long ago availed myself of the opportunity," she added, looking at me as if expecting a reply. We contemplated the dusty backs of the rented horses. "You were going to kill him yourself, weren't you Emeline?"

"What does it matter what we intend?" I replied. "The road to hell is paved with intentions, good or bad, don't we say? But intentions remain things undone, so do they matter so much? If God reads our minds, then we are all damned, the saintly and the wicked. And if he does not read our minds, then what does it matter, after all? Your question shall remain unanswered, dear one. You would think less of me if you knew the truth. It's best that way."

"God's hand," she said.

"You don't intend to go to Cedar City to shoot Bishop Coates, do you?" I asked, suddenly alarmed.

"Not worth the bullet," she snorted, her nostrils flared. And we left the matter like that between us. A silence ensued, and over the years we write, but it is of family and friends, and never of the past.

If there was any question or suspicion of Olivia and I and our . . . intentions, it was not apparent. Last year I had a letter from Richards inquiring of me if I would relate to him the details of Brigham Young's last words. I did not reply to the man. It was none of his business. But now the world does know the truth of John D. Lee, and from this day forward I am as free a creature as was ever breathed to life from dust.

When we arrived at Fort Douglas, James Dellenbaugh wasn't sure I was the same woman who had left a few days ago. And indeed I wasn't. I was a women who had been relieved of an enormous burden by the hand of God.

We met again in the officer's mess, and I was so glad to see him it was I who gave him a body-molding, back-cracking hug. I threw myself at him, and cared not who saw.

"What has happened to you?" he asked, looking at my dancing eyes. "You look as if the weight of the world has been taken off your shoulders."

"The word may be redemption," I said lightly.

"Or perhaps reprieve," Olivia said with a sly, conspiratorial glace.

"Did Brigham see you before he died?" he asked Olivia. "Was your petition successful?"

"Moot," she said mysteriously, and disappeared.

James gaped at Olivia who edged towards her crowd of soldier-suitors on the porch. Not having a divorce signed by Brigham Young didn't seem to give her a moment's pause after we'd left the Beehive House. It was as if she wanted an audience with the Prophet just for the opportunity to shoot out his liver. In later days

I reflected that the lady protested too much about Brigham's power to free her. Perhaps she had played a cunning theater for my consumption. Perhaps she didn't care a fig if the man signed some papers. What are papers? All the time had she meant to slay Brigham Young for my sake as well as her own? Or did she want her name etched in history? I remember when she offered to be my Mrs. Cooke. Of this we never spoke, but I knew the moment I saw her on the porch playing the young men like puppets on a string, that Bishop Coates would be lucky if he never saw her again.

"She doesn't seem overly distressed," James said doubtfully. "What have you two been up to in the city? I was worried. And I've got news."

"What news?" I asked.

"My Captaincy has been approved by Congress, and I'm being transferred to Washington to work in the new office of the Geographic Survey. Major Powell's doing, I suspect."

"That's wonderful, James," I said. "In that case, sir, I expect we'd better marry before you change your mind," I said, and he swept me up with a shout, and I heard a giggle from the grizzled steward with the soiled suit as he eavesdropped while polishing the silver. The light, the joy on his face and mine made the steward drop a plate.

Thus I was married to Capt. James Cameron Dellenbaugh by an Episcopal Priest in Washington ten weeks later. Elizabeth and Porter came east with me, while David stayed in Utah and eventually developed a large ranch out of the small start we'd made in Zion Canyon. I was happy to leave the west, and the Church. The train east passed places where I'd walked with the hand carters. I stopped off in Wyoming to visit the graves of my mother and father. As the west receded, I reflected upon the faith it took to build in such a wilderness.

Despite Brigham's passing, the work goes on, but without this Christian woman. As we crossed the Green River, one of the headwaters of the Colorado, I thought of the ferry. Indeed we all disappear, like the wake of the ferry. There is nothing but a ripple of our passing. On quiet evenings James and I sit in the parlor and speak not of the past, but of the future. But I often think of John resting on the star of Kolob—whether on His right hand or left hand, I know not. I do know that God's mercy is nearby, there on that star nearest the throne of God.

Washington, The District of Columbia, 1895

About the Author:

Gerald Grimmett is a poet, novelist and fourth generation Idaho native. He's the author of three collections of poetry including *Last Entries: Poems from the Ice* from Limberlost Press, and he has published numerous poems, articles, and stories over a thirty-year writing career. He's made his living as a freelance writer, long-distance endurance rider, award-winning newspaper journalist, sailor and occasional adventure guide. Widely traveled, he has lived or worked on most of the world's continents including Antarctica. He currently lives with his wife Cynthia near St. George, Utah. *The Ferry Woman* is his first published novel.